JACK DANIELS STORIES VOL. 4

Lt. Jacqueline "Jack" Daniels is known by thriller readers worldwide, with millions of novels sold. But did you know Jack has also appeared in dozens of ridiculously fun shorter works?

This collection contains a fistful of Jack stories, written by best-selling author J.A. Konrath. Many are co-written by some of the best authors in the biz.

Join Jack as she fights crime, slings justice, and dishes out some cool servings of mystery enjoyment. Along for the ride are some of Jack's craziest and most memorable cohorts.

It's a wild trip, available as a collection for the very first time.

JACK DANIELS STORIES by J.A. Konrath

Same Jack. Faster pace.

JACK DANIELS STORIES VOL. 4

J.A. KONRATH

CONTENTS

FOREWORD

In a previous collection, JACK DANIELS STORIES VOL 1, I included all of the Jack short stories that had been published in anthologies and magazines throughout the years.

This book is something different.

In 2016, Amazon tried an experiment called Kindle Worlds, which allowed other authors to write stories using my characters.

Because I enjoy collaboration, I co-wrote stories with a select few of these authors. I had a lot of fun, and got to work with many talented people, some of them old pros, some of them rising stars.

This resulted in over 1000 pages of good stuff featuring Jack Daniels, Phineas Troutt, Harry McGlade, Chandler, Hammett, and Tequila.

For the first time, these stories have been compiled into three new collections. Including my previous shorts, I now have four volumes of Jack Daniels Stories, which I have integrated into the "Jack Daniels and Accociates Mysteries" series.

I hope you enjoy reading these as much as I enjoyed writing them.

Joe Konrath, October 2019

STRAIGHT UP
(WITH IAIN ROB WRIGHT)

Before Iain and I wrote the horror novel HOLES IN THE GROUND *(a sequel to* ORIGIN*) we collaborated on this, bringing Jack Daniels together with with series character Sarah Stone on an airplane. What could possibly go wrong?*

Ding!

"The seatbelt sign is now deactivated and all passengers are free to move about the cabin. We are slightly ahead of schedule and should touch down in Jacksonville in a little under three hours. We thank you for flying Domestic Airways, and hope you have a pleasant flight."

Lt. Jacqueline Daniels frowned. Was there such a thing as a pleasant flight? Did anyone like waiting in lines, being crammed into seats with strangers, confined for hours at a stretch? The only difference between travel and prison was you paid to travel.

And the food is probably better in prison.

She eased back in the creaking chair of 8b and tried in vain to find some space for her feet—a near impossible task with her oversized purse jammed under the seat in front of her. Jack wasn't claustrophobic, but the cramped A320 airbus was testing her limits. She felt more like a sardine than a passenger.

Although I bet sardines have room to move their elbows.

Jack didn't often leave Chicago, and she preferred that. While her home and work in Illinois wasn't always pleasant, it was familiar, and there was comfort in that. But it was her mother's birthday tomorrow and, like the rest of the nation over the age of sixty-five, she lived in Florida. Mom was the only family Jack had left, and it would be worth the aggravation of travel to spend some time with her, even if it was only a weekend.

A skinny blonde flight attendant, pretty enough to be a model, attempted to rush past with the refreshment cart, but Jack put an arm out and stopped her. The woman jerked to a stop and looked down at Jack, a forced smile beneath several layers of expertly-applied makeup.

"Yes, ma'am?"

"Whiskey."

"We're just starting beverage service now. I'll be with you in just a moment."

"And when you come by again in a moment, I'll be ready for another. But I'll also have one now." Jack added, "Please."

The woman's forced smile remained in place, but there was a slight twitch at the corner of her left eye that suggested disapproval. Her name badge read: *Brandy.* "Of course. It's five dollars a miniature. We only accept cash."

"I'll take two."

Jack fished through her purse for a loose ten, and traded it for two small bottles of Canadian Club.

"Any sour mix?" Jack asked.

"Sorry, no."

Too bad. Jack preferred mixed drinks to straight alcohol, be it a bloody mary, a rusty nail, or even a fuzzy navel. A whiskey sour would have really hit the spot.

"I'll take a couple of vodkas," said the woman next to Jack. She had what sounded like an English accent, but not the plummy tones of Hugh Grant or the Queen–it was more working class.

Jack acted as the middle-man in the exchange and passed along the beverages and cash. Glancing at the other woman, she saw that the entire left side of her face was covered by a spider web of deep scar tissue. The wound was mostly healed, but the pinkish hue around the edges suggested that it had happened in the recent past.

Jack unscrewed the cap on one of her whiskey miniatures and nodded to the other woman. "Cheers."

The woman didn't respond with anything more than a grunt. She unscrewed both her vodkas and splashed them both into the plastic cup they'd come with. Then she downed the entire drink in a single sip.

Perhaps she hated travelling as much as Jack did.

Jack poured her liquor and fell into the cop habit of sizing the woman up. She was dressed in a crisp white shirt and denim jeans, toned and wide in the shoulders. From the way she sat, the way her rigid posture held itself, something was pretty obvious.

"You're military."

The woman turned and looked at Jack. The scar across her face seemed even wider from the front. It went all the way from the bridge of her nose to the edge of her left ear. There was even a scrap of hair missing from her temple where the damaged tissue intersected.

"Why do you think I'm military?"

Jack shrugged her shoulders. "Because of the way you sit to attention, even when you're relaxed. That's a military thing. A constant state of readiness."

The woman's expression was unflinching. It was like looking at a still life painting with a bad attitude.

"War can do that to a person."

"So, you *are* military, then?"

"No. I'm not military. You must be a cop, I take it?"

Jack nodded. "How'd you know?"

"Because only cops stick their noses in where they're not wanted."

Jack rolled her eyes, then took a sip of whiskey. "Okay, fine. I get it. Was just being friendly. Next time I'll know better."

The woman turned away and glanced out the window at the clouds passing by.

Jack eased back into her seat again and closed her eyes. Sleep was something that eluded her even in her own comfy bed, so the chance of catching a few winks in an uncomfortable airline chair was next to impossible. Still, it would at least help her to ignore the scar-faced sourpuss sitting next to her.

And here I was always thinking that the English were always polite and proper.

The plane jolted, hitting a patch of turbulence. Jack opened her eyes and saw the worried looks on the faces of some of the more nervous fliers, but then noticed the absolute indifference on the stewardess's faces. There was nothing to be concerned about.

To Jack's right, the grumpy English woman was now scowling.

Lighten up, lady. Life is too short. We could all be dead tomorrow.

That turned out to be an eerily prescient thought.

The cabin's intercom abruptly switched on, the channel opening up with static. There was a moment of silence, followed by what sounded like scuffling, accompanied by two men grunting.

The stewardesses had stopped what they were doing and were looking at one another with questions in their eyes.

Then there was a loud *BANG!* Followed by another.

Having worked Chicago homicide for decades, Jack knew instantly what the sound was.

Someone had discharged a weapon.

"Those were gunshots," the English woman said.

"Yeah, they were."

There was a dead silence in the cabin. Nobody moved, nobody reacted. Jack knew that the passengers, and the crew, were panicking inside, while secretly praying that there was nothing to worry about. People didn't accept the worst until it was staring them in the face, and right now there was only the suggestion of danger. No real proof.

The flight attendants' expressions of confusion were a far cry from their stoicism during the turbulence. The blonde woman who had sold Jack the whiskey hurried off towards the front of the plane.

"What's going on?" the Brit asked. "Can you see anything?"

Jack glanced down the aisle and tried to make out what was happening. A privacy curtain blocked her view of the crew compartment at the end, and the cockpit beyond it. The blonde stewardess slipped past the partition, then drew it closed behind her.

"No," Jack said. "Maybe, they weren't shots. Maybe something blew in the cockpit."

"Wow, that sounds so much better. Thank you for the reassurance, *officer.*"

Jack glanced at her. "Were you always this cuddly, or did you take a class?"

Without waiting for an answer, Jack got up from her seat and side-stepped into the aisle. Now that several seconds had passed since the noise, she began to wonder if maybe she had jumped to a conclusion. After spending your whole life as a cop, you tended to hear gunshots even when there were none. Every time a car backfired in the street, Jack would automatically flinch.

The Brit got up out of her seat and stepped out into the aisle behind Jack. "I'm coming with you."

Jack shook her head. "You should stay seated."

"Unless you're an Air Marshall, you should explain why I have to follow your orders." Her eyes crinkled at the corners. "I learned that in cuddly class."

Jack studied the woman, looking for any sign of nervousness. If this were some sort of crime in progress, or terrorist act, this woman could be a part of it. But all Jack saw was steadfast calm. Not the reaction she'd expect from someone nervous or guilty.

If some shit was going down, it wouldn't hurt to have backup. Or if this woman was involved somehow, it wouldn't hurt to keep an eye on her. Either way it was win-win to have her come along.

Or lose-lose, depending on your point of view.

A flight attendant walked over, spreading her hands. "Ladies, please take your seats. There's nothing to be concerned about."

"You don't know that," Jack said. "You've been standing right there the whole time. You don't know anything more than we do."

The stewardess gave her a stern look, like that of a schoolteacher staring down an unruly child. "Ma'am…"

Jack pulled her shield out of her inside pocket and held it aloft so that everyone could see. "I'm a police officer. I just want to make sure that the captain doesn't need assistance."

She looked around, seeing relief in people's faces. It was familiar to Jack. Individuals moved much faster, and acted much smarter, than groups did. When there were more than three people in an unusual situation, they tended to look to each other for cues on how to act. Now that Jack had taken control, shown authority, they could all relax a little. Someone was going to get the answers they sought.

Hopefully that someone wouldn't get shot doing so.

The plane shook again as it hit more turbulence. Jack stumbled in her Jimmy Choo boots but her backup caught her shoulders and kept her up straight.

"Thanks."

"It doesn't make us friends."

Jack turned and looked at her. "Too bad. I love making friends with cranky bitches."

The woman didn't respond, but Jack saw the tiniest hint of a smile.

The rough air got worse. Jack had to place a hand on the back of the nearest seat and row herself forward down the aisle. There was no movement up ahead. The privacy curtain remained in place, blocking any view of the cockpit door. The intercom was no longer open and the only sound was the worried nattering of the passengers behind her.

"You're not armed," said the Brit. She'd been trying to spot Jack's weapon. But there was nothing to spot.

"Only TSA, and maybe the feebies, are allowed to carry on planes. And there aren't any aboard. If there were, they would have acted already. What's your name?"

"It's… Sarah."

"I'm Jack."

"If there's trouble, Jack, how do you expect to deal with the situation if he has a gun and you don't?"

"Smart question, Sarah. I plan on using you as a human shield and, when the shooter runs out of ammo, beating him with your dead body."

Sarah blew out a long breath. "Thank goodness. For a minute there I was worried you didn't have a plan."

Jack made her way through business class and approached the separation curtain tentatively. She couldn't see around it, but there was a gap of several inches between the fabric and the floor. As she was bending down to look for feet, she realized Sarah was doing the same thing.

Jack noticed a pair of feet standing behind the curtain just as it was yanked open. Those feet belonged to one of the pilots, dressed in the traditional white and black cap and an airline branded tie.

What wasn't so traditional was the gun he was gripping. A Glock. And before Jack could react it was pointed at her head.

"What are you doing?" he demanded.

Jack wanted to ask him the same thing. She'd heard that since 9/11 some airlines had guns in the cockpit, the pilots authorized and trained to use them. But far outweighing Jack's curiosity was fear. Even if the pilot had a reason to be holding the weapon, looking up the barrel of a gun was a terrifying experience, and there weren't many things she hated more. Jack forced composure, standing up slowly.

"We heard a gunshot. Is everything okay?"

The pilot's face bunched up, and Jack noticed the sweat on his forehead. "Okay? Yes, everything is fine. Never better. It is a joyous day for everyone on board. A day of atonement. A day of repentance."

"Put the gun down and tell me what happened."

"No. No no no. I don't think I'll do that."

The pilot looked even more nervous than Jack felt, and she had a bad hunch he wasn't reacting to something that had happened. Instead, she postulated he was the cause of it.

"Is someone hurt?" Jack asked. She wanted to take a look behind him, but didn't want to take her eyes off the gun, even for a second.

"Just go back to your seats. I'll… I'll make an announcement soon."

If this had been on the ground, where she had authority, she would have identified herself as a police officer. She also would have taken a chance at disarming him. But it didn't seem wise at that moment to proclaim she was a cop, and the scene at the end of the James Bond movie, Goldfinger, was playing in her head; where a gun went off in a plane and blew out the window, depressurizing the cabin and sucking the bad guy out through the hole.

Jack spoke calmly, as if the gun in her face meant nothing. "If you've got the situation under control, Captain, I can explain that to the passengers. We don't want them to panic."

She didn't know if he was the captain or not, but addressing him as such couldn't hurt. Neither could giving him a moment to calm down. His gun hand was shaking, his finger tight on the trigger.

"I've got it all under control, lady. I'm in complete control. The Lord is my shepherd."

The pilot didn't look like he was in control. He looked like the poster boy for mental illness. Red faced, sweating, trembling, on the verge of screaming.

"Fine, we'll return to our seats." Sarah put her hand on Jack's shoulder and was firmly pulling her away. It caused the pilot to switch targets, swinging the gun to Sarah.

Jack could have made a move, but Sarah's grip restricted her, and any attempt at getting the gun would have put Sarah at risk. You didn't rush a person who had a finger on the trigger unless all other alternatives were exhausted.

But being out of the line of fire for a moment gave Jack a different opportunity. She'd been wondering what happened to the blonde stewardess and the others in the cockpit. Clenching her jaw, she chanced a look behind the armed pilot, but saw nothing.

Realizing there was nothing to be done but get out of the bad situation, she and Sarah backed slowly away, one foot carefully behind the other. The armed man yanked the privacy curtain closed with a violent tug.

When he did, half of business class turned to Jack, some of them getting out of their seats.

"Everyone keep calm," she ordered. "I'm a police officer. Remain in your seats."

"What's going on?" someone asked.

"Why did the pilot have a gun?" asked another.

"I'm ordering all of you to remain seated. I'm returning to my seat right now. Everything is under control."

Jack had no authority to order them to do anything, and things certainly weren't under control. But panic could kill just as many, if not more, than a wacko with a handgun.

The first class passengers still looked panicked, but they listened for the time being.

Jack spoke to Sarah out of the side of her mouth as they made their way back to their seats. "What do you think?"

"He's unhinged. You hear the religious references?"

"Yeah. There are at least two people in the cabin, the captain and the first officer. Some planes also have a flight engineer."

"Two shots. He could have taken both of them out."

"Or he could have stopped an attempted terrorist, and is just freaked out."

"Do pilots normally freak out? Serious question. I've met a few. They're pretty cool-headed."

Jack agreed. She'd been privy to black box recordings right before planes went down. Right up until the crash, the pilots were amazingly calm and collected. The man with the gun was anything but.

Then another thought struck her. "If he killed them both, who is flying the plane?"

"We're flying on autopilot," said Sarah. "We should be okay for the time being."

They took their seats. Jack unscrewed the cap of her unopened whiskey miniature and necked it in one. She gasped and wiped her mouth. "Remember the announcement about having a pleasant flight? I'm not having one."

Sarah frowned, her scars turning whiter. "Me, neither. Know what else I'm not enjoying?"

"What?"

"Arseholes shoving guns in my face."

Ding!

"Attention. This is your new captain. If you look to the left, you may see the sinner sitting next to you. If you look to the right, more sinners. But today you'll be looking in the mirror. Today is judgement day. You'll be given a chance to confess your sins and beg forgiveness. I will be administering penance to business class shortly."

Jack didn't say anything for a moment. She processed.

She knew mania, up close and personal. She'd chased and caught those who were obsessed, fanatical, on insane missions that only made sense to them. Years ago, she's had a case where a murderer insisted his electric toothbrush had ordered him to kill his boss. She'd also had the unfortunate distinction of arresting a mother who had killed her infant son by beating him to death with a bible. One of the worst was a school shooting; it still gave her nightmares.

People, even crazy, evil people, tended to believe they have a good reason for doing what they do. Though some consider religion the opiate of the masses, others use it to further their obsessions, or rationalize their crimes.

A ranting pilot with a gun, seeking to make passengers atone for their sins, sounded like a textbook fanatic.

Or, as Sarah put it, "The sodding nutcase has gone barmy."

Those Brits had a way with words. As they should. They did invent the language.

Jack yelled for a flight attendant and motioned the nearest to come over. Nametag said 'Summer'.

"I'm a cop. Who was that, who just spoke?"

"It's Clive Harlington. First officer."

"He has a gun. A Glock 19. Did you know if there was one in the cockpit?"

Summer hesitated, then nodded.

"Do they keep extra rounds?" Sarah asked, beating Jack to the question.

"I… I think so."

Jack frowned. The situation was getting worse and worse. A Glock 19 held at least fifteen bullets per magazine. If he had extras, Captain Clive could kill a lot of people before he ran out of bullets. And if he started killing, the stampede to get away from him would almost certainly kill others. There was also the *Goldfinger* scenario to worry about.

Jack felt her heart rate kick up.

"We get all the carryon bags in the overhead compartments," Sarah said. "Make a barrier between the cockpit and the passengers."

It was a smart idea, except for one thing. "What happens when the plane runs out of fuel? Or he deliberately crashes us into the ground?"

"Did you pack any Kevlar?" Sarah asked.

"I packed Versace."

"Maybe someone carried on something bulletproof. We rush him, absorb a few shots, hit him hard."

"So we're back to my human shield idea?"

Sarah shook her head slowly. "All this preparation to make sure no one attacks the pilot, but no safeguard if the pilot goes bonkers."

Jack was sure they had performance checks, ways to monitor the mental health of pilots, but that didn't really matter right now. She stood up.

"So you've made a decision?" Sarah asked. "You'll be the human shield?"

She was pretty cool-headed, considering the fix they were in. Or maybe Sarah, like Jack, used humor to deal with stressful situations.

"I'm going to talk to him, see if I can get through."

Sarah also got up. "I'm coming with you."

"That's not a good idea."

"I'm supposed to wait for him to work his way back to me? No way."

They met two people in the aisle—first class passengers eager to give up their preferred seating. Jack and Sarah took their places in the third row. When Sarah sat down, Jack noticed the tiniest of grins appear on her face.

"What?"

"It's just that I've never been in first class before. It's a lot more comfortable up here."

"Sure it is," Jack whispered. "Until we get shot."

Jack looked around at her fellow passengers, but no one spoke; they only traded anxious glances. These people really didn't understand they were in danger. It was common. Just as crowds looked to each other for guidance, they also refused to believe the situation had gotten bad. No one runs out of a burning building unless they see others running, or can't breathe. Everyone assumes someone else knows better.

Captain Clive appeared again, and he was pushing the blonde stewardess, Brandy, in front of him. Her hair was matted with blood and her eyes were swollen.

Jack knew a coldcocking when she saw one. Clive must have given the woman a whack with the pistol butt when she'd gone to investigate. At least she was still alive.

"Find somewhere to sit and stay there," he ordered. "I'm almost ready."

"Why are you doing this, Clive?"

"Just sit down, Brandy. I don't want to have to hurt you again."

The woman sniffled and hurried down the aisle. Jack reached out an arm and grabbed her. They made eye-contact.

"Sit down, sweetheart. Everything will be okay."

The stewardess sat down in the aisle next to Jack's seat and hugged her knees up against her chest. Captain Clive was pacing back and forth by the plane door, his lips moving, his brow furrowed. He looked like he was rehearsing a speech.

"You okay?" Jack asked the frightened woman.

"I'm still kind of dizzy. My head hurts."

Jack gave her head a quick inspection. A big bump was present, but the bleeding had stopped.

"Are you nauseous? Seeing double?"

"I think I'm okay. Is it bad?"

"I'm not a doctor, but I don't think it's a concussion."

"How does it look?"

"Like a big bump with a gash in it."

"I'm an actor," Brandy said. "I've got an audition when I get back."

If any of us get back, we'll be lucky. But instead of saying that, Jack asked, "What's the deal with this guy?"

She looked up at Jack and shrugged. "I… I've worked with him for years. Clive has always been very nice. I don't know what has gotten into him. He…*oh God*…he shot the co-pilot. Poor Andrew."

"Is he dead?"

"I… I don't know…"

The tears began. Jack squeezed her shoulder.

"Take it easy. We need to keep our heads clear and deal with this situation, and we don't want others to panic." Jack said that as every passenger in first class stared wide-eyed at the stewardess. "Can you do that for me, Brandy?"

The woman nodded. Behind the tears in her eyes was a steely determination.

"I can cry on cue," she said. "I guess I can try stopping on cue."

A moment later, Brandy seemed to gain control over her emotions. *Good girl.*

Sarah leaned over Jack's lap. "What happens with nobody steering this thing? How long will the autopilot keep us safe?"

"Until we run out of fuel. Air traffic control will be trying to contact us, and when they get no reply they'll re-route all other traffic out of our way."

"And how long will that be?"

"We have some reserve fuel. But I guess, if we miss landing in Jacksonville, we'll run out somewhere over the Caribbean."

Sarah sighed. "I've always wanted to go there."

Jack didn't relish the idea, considering how they would get there – nose-down in the sea.

Sarah eyeballed the pilot. "Any idea why Clive is doing this? He seems to be in some kind of religious mania."

"Like I said, this is nothing like him. He's always been a devout Christian, but never like this. That's what makes what he's doing so insane. He doesn't believe in violence."

"He seems to have gotten pretty onboard with it recently," Sarah said.

No shit, Jack thought.

"We need to get that gun away from him," Jack said. "The question is, how do we get close enough?"

Brandy took a deep breath and held it. Then she let it out in a burst. "I think I can get close to him," she said. "I've known him a few years. He'll trust me."

Jack appraised Brandy. Though her make-up was running, and her hair matted, she was an attractive woman.

"Is Clive married?" she asked.

"No. I don't think so."

"He's not wearing a ring," Sarah said.

Jack hesitated before continuing. She didn't want the woman to risk her life.

"You look like you want to say something." Brandy reached out and gripped Jack's wrist. "Tell me."

"If you could distract him for a few seconds, I could go for his gun."

"How?"

"Kiss him," Sarah said.

Jack had been thinking the same thing, but hadn't wanted to suggest it. Instead, she said, "He hit her, Sarah."

"Hit her. But didn't shoot her. Has he ever come onto you, Brandy?"

"What? No."

"Asked you out? Flirted?"

"No, I... wait. A few months ago, he did invite me to go to church with him during a stopover."

Jack looked at Sarah. "If he's a religious nut, kissing him could freak him out."

Sarah frowned. "If he starts shooting everyone, it'll freak *me* out."

Jack considered telling Sarah that she should do it since it was her idea, but she wasn't sure that Sarah, with her horribly-scarred face, would be able to distract Clive.

That just leaves me.

Clive appeared, banging his fist against one of the overhead bins to get everybody's attention.

"I'm ready," he said. "It's time."

"Time for what?" someone asked.

"Time to seek forgiveness. The world is dead and this is your final chance to unburden your souls; your only chance to get into God's magnificent kingdom. Fail to repent and your soul is destined for Hell."

"What the hell are you talking about?" another passenger asked.

The pilot shook his head and suddenly seemed very weary. "Hell indeed! You are guilty of a thousand sins. All of you are. Greed, lust, gluttony, envy, pride. All committed with big smiles and no shame. Just check a random page on Facebook to see what this world has degenerated into. We 'tweet' our arrogance into the world and allow it to fester. God has frowned upon us all, and if we do not change our ways immediately, it will be too late."

"Oh, bloody hell," Sarah whispered. "He's lost it."

Clive pointed the gun at a woman in the front row of the section. "You! Confess your sins or die."

The woman spluttered, her face stark with shock. "I-I don't know what you're talking about."

Clive put the barrel of the Glock to the woman's head. Jack tensed, ready to spring. She wasn't sure what to do, but she couldn't sit there idly and watch someone get executed.

"Confess or die," Clive ordered.

"What? I…"

He's going to shoot this woman.

Jack waved her hand. "Captain! I'm a sinner! I want to confess."

"We'll get to you soon enough," he barked at Jack. Then he turned back to the woman. "Three seconds. Confess your secrets, your sins. Now!"

"I cheated on my husband!" the woman blurted out. The man who was holding her suddenly let go and pushed her away. He seemed surprised—obviously the husband in question.

"With who?" The man asked.

"It was… it was your cousin, Mark."

The man's face twisted in disgust. "How could you do that? You bitch…"

Clive pointed the gun at the husband. "Your turn to confess. What have you done?"

The man's confession seemed to come more easily than his wife's. "I cheated on her, with a woman I work with."

The young wife started sobbing.

Clive grinned and opened both arms in a gesture of victory. "You see? This man chastises his wife for being a whore, then confesses to the very same sins just a moment later. The world is full of screwing hypocrites, sodomites and catamites, thieves and abusers."

Jack was only partly paying attention to his crazy rants. Her focus was primarily on the gun and reading his movements. Jack had a black belt in tae-kwon-do, and she knew there were always signals and signs before an attack. A change of posture. A shift in weight. A subtle variance in expression. It was the same with shooters. Unless a person had a lot of training, firing a gun was an emotional experience. Jack scrutinized Clive, waiting for him to telegraph his move. He'd come close to shooting the woman, but now he'd seemed to ease up a bit.

Clive pointed the gun at someone else—a teenaged girl. "So young," he said, "yet so full of sin, I have no doubt. Confess, young lady. Take the opportunity while you still can."

The girl's eyes went wide like saucers. She put her hands up and pled. "I have nothing to confess. Please. I'm just going to meet my grandmother in Lake City."

Clive clutched at his head again, shoving a palm into his left eyeball. It was as if a rhythm was thumping in his head and got louder every few minutes. "No...nobody here is innocent, whore!"

"No," she cried out. "I'm not a whore. I'm a...I'm a virgin."

Clive lowered the handgun and smiled. "Then you shall be welcomed in heaven." Then he raised the gun back at her face and looked ready to pull the trigger. "May God bless you on your way."

Jack stood up in a stoop, encumbered by the overhead compartment. Sarah did the same. But it was Brandy who shouted, "Stop!"

The stewardess sprang to her feet and headed down the aisle toward the pilot.

He waved the gun at her. "Get back, Brandy. This isn't your business."

"You're my friend," she said. "Let me help you."

Clive's eyes narrowed. "Help me how?"

"I can help you get what you need from these people. You want them to confess. Let me help you. I believe in what you're doing."

Clive let out a long breath through his nose and seemed to consider it.

"There's a lot of bad in the world," Brandy said. "I know that. Maybe we can change some of it here. Together."

She's good, Jack thought.

Clive seemed to think so, too. "Don't make me regret this, Brandy. I don't want to have to shoot you."

Brandy moved up to within three feet of the pilot. "And I don't wish to give you any reason to."

"Go on, then. Make them confess."

Brandy nodded and smiled at him. "Of course. But perhaps I should begin. It… it would only be right to confess my own sins before demanding those of others."

Clive nodded enthusiastically. "Yes, yes. Cleanse your soul so that it may transition with purity."

Brandy let her expression slip for a moment and Jack wondered if this wannabe-actress had taken on a role she couldn't handle. But she recovered quickly and managed to wear a smile again. This time it was sultry, almost flirtatious.

Jack shifted her weight, easing into the aisle. Beside her, she could see Sarah doing the same.

Brandy pouted and took a step closer to Clive. He seemed uncomfortable by her proximity, yet also curious.

"My biggest secret is that I am in love with a man but have been afraid to tell him. I've been lusting after him for years. But I've never been able to find the courage to tell him.

Clive shook his head and seemed disappointed. A tiny sliver of blood had made an appearance beneath his nostrils. Jack started to wonder if the man was ill.

Wouldn't be the first time someone's tried to blame murder on a brain tumour.

Brandy lowered her voice so that it was almost a purr. Clive's eyes were glued to hers. His expression was still one of disappointment, but also expressed a great deal of interest in what the woman had to say.

Typical guy. A woman hints that she's interested in him and all other thoughts are forgotten.

Jack stepped into the aisle and dropped into a crouch, taking advantage of the distraction. She remained low, creeping past passengers who stared at her with mouths agape, but so far she hadn't aroused the attention of Captain Clive. If she was lucky, she could get herself within a few feet of the gunman before he even noticed.

But then what? If he takes a wild shot, that could be it for all of us.

Brandy continued with the greatest role of her career. "I've wanted to be with you for so long, Clive. Ever since my first flight with you, to Panama. Do you remember? We were both working for another airline back then, but when you moved, I followed. I'm in love with you, Clive. And if this is indeed the end, and our last moments on this earth, all I want, more than anything in the world, is to feel your arms around me before I die."

From on the floor, peeking through the gaps, Jack saw Clive go bright red. His nose was bleeding worse now, but he didn't seem to notice.

If we get through this I'm going to go on eBay and buy Brandy an Academy Award.

"B-Brandy, what are you saying. What are you doing?"

Brandy took the final step so that she was right up against Clive. "Please, just hold me tight. I want to feel you close to me."

Clive looked utterly lost. He reached forward with both arms, but then pulled them back. Then forwards again, then back. His face had taken on the expression of a zombie attempting algebra.

Brandy snatched at the gun. Her fingers closed around the muzzle.

Jack leapt to her feet, already knowing that the stewardess had made a grave mistake.

You don't pull the gun towards you, you push it away!

The gun went off.

Brandy staggered back, clutching her midsection where her crisp white blouse quickly became a sodden wet rag.

First class erupted in screams, and people scrambled out of their seats to run away.

Jack shouldered past the oncoming stampede and launched herself over the final row of chairs, barrelling into Clive while he gaped at Brandy and what he had done to her. She struck Clive in the chest with her shoulder and sent him rocking back into the cabin's partition wall. She'd been hoping to knock the gun loose from his hand, but he held onto it firmly.

Jack hit the floor and rolled onto her back. Clive recovered himself and stood over her. "Bitch!" he shouted at her and raised the gun.

"Some coffee, Captain?"

Jack and Clive both looked up at Sarah, who swung the stainless steel coffee pot like she was throwing a haymaker. It hit Clive on the chin, and his eyes rolled up into his head and he crumpled into a small pile. Textbook prizefighter knockout.

Jack looked up at Sarah, and the woman's deeply scarred face had the faintest glimmer of a smirk.

"He seemed stressed out. Thought he could do with a hot beverage." She released her grip on the heavy object and let it hit the ground, where it promptly rolled down the aisle.

Jack reached for the gun, ejected the magazine, and shoved it into her blazer pocket. Then she pulled the slide to clear the chamber. When she looked back at Sarah, the Brit was attending to Brandy.

"How bad?" Jack asked.

"Gut shot. But not much blood, and it doesn't look like it hit anything vital. Pulse is strong."

Jack was going to tell Sarah to keep pressure on the wound, but Sarah was already applying a field dressing with her belt and the stewardess's neck scarf. So Jack went into the overhead compartment and found the length of seatbelt used for pre-flight demonstrations. She tied Clive's hands behind him, tight. Then she stood up and grabbed the flight attendant microphone.

"Attention, ladies and gentleman. My name is Lt. Daniels. I'm a police officer. There was a situation in first class, but the threat has been dealt with. I repeat, we're all okay."

Jack had to pause as the yelling and questioning became a wave of thunderous applause.

"I need two men to help me up front. Young and strong. If you ever wanted to put *hero* on your resume, now is the time."

As Sarah helped Brandy into a seat, two guys came up to first class, one a young football type, the other older and thick like a pro wrestler.

"The Captain went crazy," she told them. "I need him buckled into his seat, tight, and you both to watch him."

They followed orders, and Jack went back to check on Brandy.

"Nice work," she told the brave stewardess. "You've got a future at this acting thing."

"Hurts like hell," Brandy moaned.

"Don't think about the pain," Jack told her. "Think about the media attention you're going to get. *Actor saves whole planeload of passengers.* You'll get on Oprah."

Brandy managed to smile. "You think so?"

"Your summer stock days are over, girl."

Then Jack motioned for Sarah to come with.

"What is it?"

"I'm going to check the cockpit, may need some back up."

"You mean you'll need me to save your life again?"

Jack smirked. "Thanks for that. I didn't think they made coffee that strong."

They made their way up through the first class cabin. Jack's two volunteers were hovering over an unconscious Clive like he was a sandwich they were about to fight over. She opened the cockpit and saw—

"Oh, shit."

The co-pilot was slumped in his chair, his chest matted with blood. Sarah immediately went to him. Jack made the mistake of looking out the windshield, at the clouds rushing past, and felt her stomach roll over and her bladder shrink three sizes.

Sarah said, "Can't feel a pulse."

"Please tell me that you were a pilot in the army."

Sarah shrugged her wide shoulders. "No such luck. You were right, I am military. Just plain old infantry, I'm afraid. There has to be some sort of contingency that airlines have in place for emergencies. It's not inconceivable that a plane's pilots would become incapacitated."

"Okay, do you want to land us, then?"

"Bloody hell no." Sarah took the headset off the co-pilot and put it on. "Mayday, mayday, this is flight..."

She shot Jack a look. Jack dug out her ticket. "One one nine four."

"Flight one one nine four heading into Jacksonville. We have lost both pilots. Repeat, we are flying without pilots."

Jack watched Sarah listen to the reply from ground control.

Sarah turned to Jack and said, "We need to ask if there is anyone on-board with flight experience."

Jack frowned. That wouldn't go over well with the passengers.

"Okay, I'll check. Give me a minute."

Jack went back to the mic. She cleared her throat, and then spoke. "This is Lt. Daniels again. There is no reason to panic, but…" Jack couldn't believe she was about to say it, "if anyone on board has had any flight experience, please see me up at the cockpit."

As expected, the murmuring crowd increased in volume and people began to shout angry, frightened questions.

"Everyone calm down, right now. The pilot simply needs a bit of assistance. That's all. Everything is fine. Now has anyone flown before?"

There was no reply from anyone.

We're so screwed.

"Go on, tell her…"

Jack scanned the passengers and tried to locate the person who had just spoken. It was a young girl raising her hand, perhaps ten rows down. Jack went to her. The girl was perhaps fourteen, sitting next to a boy about five years older, prodding him frantically. He had his eyes turned downwards and looked like he was trying to be invisible.

Jack smiled at the girl. "What is it, sweetheart?"

"My brother. He can fly."

"Lieutenant," Sarah's voice boomed over the intercom. "Have you found a pilot yet? This plane isn't going to land itself."

Jack shook her head. *Nice.*

The boy's sister spoke. "He's training to be a pilot."

Jack smiled at the terrified boy and tried to show him that no one was out to get him. "Is it true? Can you fly, son?"

He shook his head, but then nodded. "I-I only have thirty hours flight time. It's not enough. I'm just a student."

"It's thirty hours more than anybody else here. We need you."

The young lad seemed absolutely mortified. His eyes were wide and white like a rabid dog and it looked like he might faint at any moment. "I don't feel so good."

Jack placed her hands on the boy's shoulders and looked into his eyes. Her voice was a whisper. "You do this, you'll be a hero. They'll probably make a film about you. I even have a friend who could make it happen. If you don't help us, then we all die. That's the choice you have here. Seems like an easy one to me: be a hero or be dead."

The boy's lips pursed so hard they lost color, but then he nodded. "Okay. Okay, I'll try."

"That's all anybody is asking for, son. What's your name?"

"Tom. Tom Collins."

"Pleased to meet you, Tom. Come with me."

When he stood up, Jack almost did a double-take. Tom couldn't have been taller than five-two. She wondered if, like a car, a plane had pedals, and if he was tall enough to reach them.

Pushing the thought aside, Jack led the youth up through the first class cabin, into the cockpit. It felt like being inside an electrical womb, hot and cramped. A million blinking lights made concentration impossible.

Tom looked at the pilot and made a gagging sound.

"Sarah, this is Tom Collins," Jack said.

"Seriously? I'm on this plane with Tom Collins, Jack Daniels, and a stewardess named Brandy?"

"You should have met the guy I turned down. His name was Strawberry Margarita."

"And here I am not even the least bit pissed. What I would give to be rat-arsed right about now."

Jack laughed. Again with the language. "Rat-arsed? You mean drunk, right?"

"Yes. And if this child you brought is going to crash us into the ground, then getting pie-eyed wouldn't be such a bad plan."

"I'm not a child," Tom said. "I'm nineteen."

"No offense, kid, but I've played with Barbies bigger than you."

"You're not helping," Jack said to Sarah. "And how could that possibly not offend?"

Sarah made that face again where her scar turned white.

"Look," Jack said, "I know we're all scared…"

"You think you know what scared is, Lt. Designer Heels?"

Jack moved her nose within an inch of Sarah's. "Yeah. I do. Right now, I don't need bravado, soldier. I need Zen. Can you do that, or are we going to have a problem?"

Sarah's anger seemed to fade, and her eyes crinkled. "No problem, ma'am. Anything I can do to help. But if we get through this, the jars are on you."

"If you mean drinks, then it's a deal," Jack said.

The women shook hands.

"This is… I… I can't…" Tom backed away, wrapping his arms across his own shoulders.

"Sure you can," Jack said, putting a hand on his back. It was the wrong move, because Tom freaked out, instantly trying to leave the cockpit. He pushed past Jack, but Sarah stopped him. She whispered something in Tom's ear and his eyes went wide. Then, without another word, he climbed back into the pilot's seat and put on the headphones.

"Can you fly this thing?" Jack asked. "Does it all make sense?"

The boy was pale as a spectre, but he nodded. "I-I think so."

"Okay, Tom. Thank you for helping us. Do your thing."

Tom got to work, checking in with ground control and relaying the situation. As he spoke he flipped switches and prodded buttons. As nervous as the boy was, he seemed to know what he was doing. A typical member of the PlayStation generation, more at home with a computer and flashing LEDs than with people. They watched him for a few moments, and Jack felt herself relax a notch.

Maybe we're going to get through this after all.

Jack moved close to Sarah and whispered. "What did you say to him to get him to come back?"

"He's a young male. I appealed to his base instincts and promised him something if we landed safely. Something to do with his obvious virginity."

"You said you'd sleep with him?" Jack asked, incredulous.

"Of course not. I said *you'd* sleep with him."

"Great," Jack said.

Tom looked back at Jack, giving her a thumbs up and smiling widely.

Jack tried offering him an encouraging smile back—

—and Tom promptly fainted.

Jack put both hands to her forehead. "I hate air travel."

Sarah rushed over to Tom, giving him a shake. "Hey, Tom. Wake up, kid. If you want Lt. Daniels to blow you, you have to wake your arse up."

"I'm blowing him too?"

Sarah looked at Jack. "I didn't specifically state that, but isn't it inferred?"

"Sex always infers a blowjob?"

"Have you ever been with a bloke? It's all about their knob and bollocks."

Sarah had a point.

"It's really hard understanding you at times. The words you use." Jack said.

"I'm just speaking English. Stop being such a wanker."

Jack knew that one.

Outside the cockpit's panoramic front window, they continued to cut through the clouds.

"We need to wake this kid up," Jack said.

"Look for a first aid kit. It should have smelling salts or ammonia."

Jack nodded, then began to search the cockpit as Sarah commenced shaking and slapping Tom.

I've been in worse spots than this, but please oh please don't let me die on this plane.

"You okay?" Sarah asked her. "You look a bit wound up."

"Yeah, don't worry about me. Believe it or not, I'm kind of used to this sort of thing."

Sarah huffed. "Me, too. Sucks, don't it?"

"I don't believe in karma, but if it's real I was a bad, bad girl in a previous life."

Sarah snorted. "I'm a bad, bad girl in this life." Her eyes looked far away.

"Is that how you got the scar?" Jack asked.

Sarah looked up at her and suddenly seemed very frail and small. She'd lost her Amazonian qualities and was just a young woman in need of comfort.

"IED in Afghanistan," she said. "Helmand province. Offshoot of the Taliban."

"I'm sorry."

"I can't even remember why the hell I signed up in the first place. Just a kid, I guess."

Jack searched under the seats. No first aid kit.

"I was pregnant, too," Sarah blurted out. "Lost the baby. It would have been a girl."

Jack wasn't sure how to respond. She went with honesty. "That's terrible. I didn't even realise that you were allowed to get pregnant in the Army."

Sarah shrugged. "My discharge was due in less than three months. I was on my final duty. My husband had less than six months left on his. We were both leaving the forces to settle down and start a family."

Jack frowned. She sometimes forgot that tragedy didn't always have to include murder. There were a million other ways that life could bite a person in the ass so hard that they might never recover.

"Where is your husband now?"

"Dead."

This wasn't the right time for this conversation, but Jack sensed that Sarah had never talked about this before with a stranger and needed to unburden herself.

"How did he die?" Jack asked, checking the compartments in the rear of the cockpit. Spare blankets, tea and coffee, charts, and bags and bags of mints. Nothing else. Maybe she needed to go and ask Brandy or that other flight attendant where the first aid kit was. *Summer*? Was that her name?

"Friendly fire."

"Shit, I'm sorry. Was it us? Did we shoot your husband?"

Sarah shook her head solemnly. "No. It was our side. British forces fired on his convoy, thinking it was a group of insurgents. My husband was trying to gain deep Intel on the enemy. His unit was completely un-marked, dressed as civilians. No insignia."

"Wait, what? Wouldn't British intelligence know that the unit belonged to them? Are you saying that the British Armed Forces fired on its own men?"

Sarah shook her head again. "My husband was an American. We met at camp Bastion while his unit were sharing Intel and resupplying. That's why I'm here."

Jack sighed. "To bury him?"

"Yes. His body is already here, with his family. I've come for the funeral and to deal with his estate. He died almost six months ago, but there was an investigation. I haven't been able to see him this whole time. I…miss him."

Jack knew what it was like to lose people. She often felt unlucky due to her own failed marriage, but hearing Sarah's story made her realize that she was in fact the lucky one.

She checked another compartment, and there was the first aid kit.

"Got it." She brought a vial of ammonium to Sarah, who broke the capsule and wafted it under Tom's nose.

Tom stirred—

—and immediately vomited all over the controls.

"Aw, God," he said, looking at Jack with tears in his eyes. "I'm so not gonna get laid, am I?"

"You need to focus, Tom," Sarah said. "We're depending on you. All of these people are depending on you. Do you understand?"

Tom nodded. "I understand."

Then he passed out again.

"Is there more ammonia?"

Jack searched the kit. "One more."

Sarah snapped it under Tom's nose.

Tom woke up, barfed again, and passed right back out.

"What the hell is wrong with this kid?" Sarah asked. "Narcolepsy?"

"Pukolepsy." Jack found herself squinting at the disaster on the controls. Were those bits of a… chulupa? How the hell could such a small kid eat that much Taco Bell?

"What did that youth eat?" Sarah asked. "A Jackson Pollock painting?"

"I think it's Taco Bell."

"What the hell is wrong with you Yanks? That's not food. Food shouldn't look like that. It's practically neon."

Jack looked out the window again, mostly to take her eyes away from the vomit, despite the smell being unavoidable. Jacksonville blinked a million lights in the near distance.

Tom had obviously begun his descent.

"We're going down," Jack said.

"What?"

Jack squinted at the control panel, and found an altimeter.

"We're at five thousand feet and descending."

"Bugger it."

"Can you do me a favor and swear in American?"

"Holy shit."

"Thank you."

"So what do we do?"

That's when Jack heard something.

"Do you hear that?" asked Sarah.

"Yeah, it's like a hissing sound. You think something got damaged with all the vomiting?"

Sarah shook her head. "No… it's breathing." She spun around to face the co-pilot and placed her ear against his mouth, then stared at Jack with another one of those slight-smirks on her scarred face. "He's alive."

"You said he didn't have a pulse."

"I was obviously wrong. Or his name is Lazarus von Jesus."

Jack huffed and let her shoulders sag. "We need to get him awake. How bad is he wounded?"

Sarah examined the man, checked his head and neck but found nothing; ripped open his shirt and found blood, but no bullet hole.

"Take off his shirt," Jack suggested.

Sarah did so and revealed the man's torso in full, slick with blood.

Jack raised an eyebrow. *Wow, this guy is ripped.*

"That's why I couldn't feel his pulse. Look at all the muscles in his neck," Sarah said.

"I am, I am."

The two women marvelled for a moment.

"Lotta hours in the gym," Jack said.

"I finally understand."

"What?"

"Why men gawk at and objectify women. Would you hoot and holler if you saw him walking across the street?"

Jack found herself nodding, then said, "We need to find where he was hit."

Sarah began to run her hands over his bloody chest. "It's like someone sculpted him out of marble."

"Check his back."

Sarah managed to locate the bullet wound. It had gone in just under his collar bone at an angle. The bullet was probably lodged in his thick deltoid muscle. The fact that the guy worked out so much had provided him with a natural set of body armor.

"He must have passed out from the shock, or the pain. We need to get him awake."

Sarah slapped the guy, but he remained out.

Jack frowned. "We wasted all the smelling salts on Pukey, the eighth dwarf."

"Check the first aid kit for eppy."

"Good thinking."

Jack rummaged through the kit, pulling out the various small items. Bandages, aspirin, air sickness pills, tourniquets, syringes... After half a minute's searching, she found a vial of epinephrine. Also known as adrenaline.

Shot of this would wake anybody up from anything. And it needed to be quick. A glance out the panoramic window showed the ground was getting closer.

"How much?" Jack asked, handing Sarah the bottle and syringe.

Sarah studied the bottle. "One to one thousand solution. A milliliter should do it."

"So you just stick it in his heart? Like in Pulp Fiction?"

"That scene was bollocks. Uma Thurman needed something to block heroin receptors, like Narcan. And there was no reason to jab it into her heart."

"Great dialog, though."

"The best dialog. I loved the *royale with cheese* bit."

"So where do you inject it?"

"Help me take off his pants. We need to inject it into his penis."

"Huh?"

"Kidding," Sarah said, sticking the needle into the co-pilot's arm. "Got you excited, though, didn't it?"

Jack didn't respond.

But she couldn't help but smirk.

A moment later, the co-pilot shot forward, gasping. Then he slumped back in his chair, panting and glancing around nervously.

Jack put a hand on his cheek and looked him in the eyes. "Hey, hey. Everything is going to be okay. The pilot has been injured and you've been shot. We need you to land the plane. We can explain everything to you on the ground."

The co-pilot took some deep breaths, then said, "Clive, that son of a bitch. He shot me. He's lost his frickin' mind"

"I know. He's been dealt with."

"Dealt with?"

Jack nodded. "We've got him restrained."

The co-pilot shook his head at the news, but didn't express anything verbally. He glanced at Tom, covered with vomit.

"And who's that guy, and what has he got against Taco Bell?"

"Long story," Sarah handed him the headset. "Can you land us?"

The pilot nodded and got to work.

Jack stepped away from the man to let him concentrate. She let out a long, weary sigh.

Sarah smiled, her eyes once again hard and emotionless. "Looks like you're going to be able to get the jars in after all."

Jack laughed. "I'll happily get them in all night."

"You need to get yourself sat down and strapped in," said the co-pilot. Then he got on the mic.

"Passengers, this is acting Captain Andrew McKendry. I've put on the fasten seatbelt sign. Please return to your seats, stow away all personal items, and prepare for landing at Jacksonville International Airport."

Jack and Sarah walked out of the cockpit to a round of tremendous applause. Clive had awoken, his face contorted and his eyes daggers.

"You'll both burn in hell," he said.

"Probably," Sarah said. "But not today."

They passed Brandy in First Class. She was pale and clutching her stomach in obvious pain, but still able to smile.

"How do I look?" she asked.

"Like a hero," Jack said. "When we land, the cameras are going to love you."

Sarah found her empty business class seat, and Jack ducked into the space between cabins and grabbed several small bottles of alcohol from the abandoned drinks cart.

This goddamn airline owes us a drink.

Heck, it owes us a ton of them.

Jack sat down and passed a few miniatures to Sarah. They toasted and Jack unscrewed the lid from the bottle. As she knocked back the whiskey, she couldn't help thinking, *I wish I had some sour mix...*

WATCHED TOO LONG
(WITH ANN VOSS PETERSON)

Ann's Val Ryker thriller series is one of the best of all time, and I'm not just sayign that because they feature constant cameos by Jack Daniels and Harry McGlade. A few years ago I wrote two thrillers that happened during the same few days, RUM RUNNER *and* WEBCAM, *with some crossover characters. To make it even more complicated, I made this novella take place during the same time, bringing Jack Daniels into Val's world. It's very funny, and very tense.*

JET ROW

His full name, courtesy of parents who had done too many drugs, was Sylvester Tweety Bird Hoffman.

He thought that name sucked, so he called himself Jethro Muhammad Ali Ice Cube Lotsa Dollas King Shaquille Hussein Kanye Williams.

That was a mouthful, so on the street he was known as Jet Row.

When Jet Row was sixteen, he set fire to the bed where his mom and dad were passed out from too many drugs. He did it partly because they'd spent his whole life neglecting and abusing him, but mostly because the dumb ass crackheads had named him Sylvester Tweety Bird. How was a young brother supposed to get ahead in the hood with a name like that? Especially since, technically, he wasn't a brother.

Jet Row, like his parents, was white. He grew up in a mostly black neighborhood, with mostly black peers, and, like his parents, tried to fit in best he could. For the most part, he fit in fine.

Except for that starting fires thing. That was a peculiarity that transcended race. Which was why Jet Row, entirely independent of the color of his skin, was pretty much thought of as an asshole by everyone who knew him. Including his parents. Whom he set on fire.

His parents hadn't died. But they weren't very forgiving, either, and kicked Jet Row out of their apartment on Chicago's south side.

Living on the streets, no longer held back by anything family-related, Jet Row hooked up with the Folk Nation, in a set known as the C-Notes, and quickly worked his way up the gang hierarchy with mostly arson-related jobs, even when arson wasn't called for, or even a wise idea. When a fellow C-Note opined that Jet Row was perhaps having some difficulties controlling his growing reliance on pyromania, Jet Row torched his car.

He was made a lieutenant in the gang shortly after his nineteenth birthday. And it was on his watch, while he was in an alley setting fire to a dumpster that was filled with pieces of a smaller dumpster, that he got the call from the C-Note General, a serious cat named Del Ray, about kidnapping some cop's kid.

"You want I should torch the shorty?"

"Naw."

"Maybe light the place up, scare the kid?"

"Naw, man. It's a two year old. Just grab it, bring it back to Chi-town."

"Who the kid with?"

"I dunno. Some peeps. Grab the kid and jet."

"What?"

"What do you mean *what*?"

"You said my name. Jet."

"Naw, I mean *jet*. Skate. Bounce. Get out of there. Grab the kid and leave."

"And then burn them all?"

"Brother, I don't care what you do to them. We just want the kid."

"I hear you. Burn those muthas to the ground. Check. Leave nothing but ash. Shake 'n bake, homey."

"You got some psychological shit to work out, you feel me?"

"What?"

Jet Row had been squirting lighter fluid on the burning dumpster and hadn't been paying attention.

"I said you need to deal with your shit. Now take three boppers and some wheels. Address is Lake Loyal. Up in Wisconsin."

"I got these Molotovs, man. Made with detergent. Homemade napalm. Sticks to you as it burns. Peeps be like, 'Ah! I can't brush it off! It's burning!'"

"Whatever, man. Just get it done."

And so it began.

VAL

It's only a closet.

So why do I feel like I'm giving up all of my earthly possessions?

Val stared at the dent she made in her bedroom storage. She'd promised Lund that she would clean out half her stuff to make room for his. There was a bureau, a dresser, and a small closet, and each was filled with mostly outdated clothing and shoes that Val rarely, if ever, wore.

But they were *hers*. Having to get rid of any of it triggered some dormant, selfish gene she'd thought she'd buried long ago. The same gene that didn't want to share the four-square ball at second grade recess. Even at seven years old, Val had known it was difficult to get that ball and holding onto it was more important than actually playing with it. So she'd stand there, without playing four-square, clutching the ball and whining if any other child got too close.

Not her proudest childhood memories.

"How about these?" Grace said. Her niece was holding up a pair of metallic silver boots with chunky heels.

"Those are my clubbing boots," Val said.

"Clubbing? In Lake Loyal, Wisconsin?"

"I used to go."

"When? Back when you lived in Chicago?"

Grace was right. She hadn't worn them since her rookie cop days in the Windy City. But Val didn't want to admit it. "There are clubs in Madison."

"And you've gone to those... when?"

"There's always the potential to go clubbing."

"It's not even called clubbing anymore. It's called raving. And these aren't rave-worthy. They look like something you'd wear to a Kiss show."

"There's also the potential for that. See all the possibility in these boots?"

Grace made a *come-on* face, a dead ringer for Val's sister. "Can you name a single Kiss song?"

"The one where they aren't going to take it anymore."

"That's Twisted Sister."

"I wasn't a big fan of hair bands."

"Then you shouldn't be a fan of these boots."

"Freakfest on State Street. I can wear them on Halloween."

Grace was unmoved. "Goodwill pile."

She tossed the boots on top of a pair of hemp sandals, green Crocs with a broken strap, and some high-waisted, acid-wash jeans Val was still reluctant to part with.

Val picked the pants up for the fourth time. "I bet they still fit."

"When was the last time you wore them?"

"High school." Val shifted onto her butt, hiked up her skirt, and began to scootch her legs into denim.

"They're not in style anymore, Aunt Val."

Val sucked in a deep breath and managed to zip the fly. "See? They fit."

"You're turning bright red. Can you feel your feet?"

"A little."

"Those are too tight."

"Tight is the style."

"Is camel toe the style?"

Val looked down. The jeans were so tight Val could see she needed a bikini wax.

"Goodwill," Val said, trying to tug them off. "Can you grab the legs?"

The women spent the hard part of thirty seconds peeling the jeans off of Val. When they went back into the Goodwill pile, Val picked up the broken Croc.

"This can be fixed."

Grace snatched the plastic shoe from her. "Is this about your crappy old wardrobe, or is this about David?"

"What are you saying?"

"I'm saying if he was moving in with me, I'd throw away everything to make room."

Val narrowed her eyes. "Do you have a crush on my fiancé?"

Grace laughed and gave her aunt a shove. "How about you be serious and actually try to own your feelings? Do you want him to move in or not?"

"Yes."

"That's going to require some changes. Making concessions. Possibly even sacrifices. How are you supposed to live with a guy when you can't even give up a pair of ugly, broken Crocs to make room for him?"

"You should switch your major to psychology."

"My major is psychology. Well, one of them, anyway. And I gotta run. Early class tomorrow. Give David a kiss for me, and tell him I'm sorry."

"For what?"

"For how you're going to act all evening."

Val walked her niece to the front door, gave her a hug, and watched her pull on her coat, duck into the barn to say goodbye to the horses, and finally climb into her car. Val also found herself scanning the treeline for anyone who might be watching. Old habit.

Grace left to go back to UW-Madison, and Val watched until her car was swallowed by the road.

The kitchen phone rang, and Val picked it up. Like most of her wardrobe, her phone was old school, a Princess model with a curly cord. Grace had loved it when she'd come to live with Val at twelve years old. Now she mocked it endlessly.

"Ryker."

"Val, it's Jack."

It was always sad when Grace left, but Val perked up at her old friend's voice. "Jack! How long has it been?"

"Too long. I'm sorry I don't call more often."

"Blame is on me, too."

"You're busy with cop stuff. I'm retired. I have no excuse."

It wasn't exactly full-time cop stuff, not anything like it used to be when she was chief, but that wasn't the point. Val had just never been good at friendship maintenance. The fact that Jack forgave her that fault was a big reason they had remained friends so long. "A baby is a perfect excuse. How's Samantha?"

"That's why I'm calling. I need a favor. Would you mind watching her for a few days?"

Val's automatic reaction was to say yes. She owed Jack a few big favors. The huge type of big. But even though Val could run a police station, she hadn't babysat a toddler in…

Well. Ever.

"She's really well behaved," Jack filled in the silence, "and she's potty trained. It would just be for a few days. Phin and I are… well…"

"You okay, Jack?"

"We haven't had sex in six months."

Wow. Yuck. Val had gone six months without sex, even longer, but never while in a relationship. Jack was married, and she was married to a younger guy.

"So you need me to watch Sam so you can make a booty call?" Val asked, trying to make light of the bombshell.

"It'll be that, or I kick him out."

"Jesus, Jack."

"Relationships are hard, Val. Hey, how are you and Lund doing? Set a date yet?"

"No, but he's, uh, moving in today."

"That's great! I… ah, shit. It's a bad time, then. I'm sorry I bothered you."

"No! It's okay, Jack. We can watch Sam for you."

"Are you sure?"

"Not a problem. We've both taken a couple of days off for the move. And Lund will love a chance to be domestic. He adores kids."

"Thanks, Val. This means a lot. Can we drop her off in three hours?"

That soon? "Yeah. Sure."

"She's a really good kid. She practically watches herself. I'll see you soon. Thanks!"

Jack hung up. Val stared at the receiver. She knew Lund had planned a romantic dinner tonight after moving his stuff in. But if they were watching Sam, that would have to be postponed. Would he be annoyed?

Well, if he was, then he shouldn't be moving in. Things came up. Life happened. As Lake Loyal Fire Chief, Lund was used to having to roll with the punches. He'd have to learn that the same thing happened in his personal life. Sometimes the best laid plans went astray. Better he learn to accept that now.

Val went back into her bedroom, threw the Goodwill pile back into her closet to deal with at a more appropriate time, and walked over to her DVD collection to search for something kid-friendly.

.   .   .

After ten minutes of searching, the only moderately kid-friendly movies Val found were *Legally Blonde*, *The Devil Wears Prada*, and *Aliens*. Sam was probably too young to understand post-feminist comedies, and Val wasn't sure if giant, acid-blooded aliens devouring an entire planet and stalking a little girl would be appropriate for a little girl. Best put it in the *maybe* pile.

Her cell rang—the ringtone was *It's Raining Men*. Lund's number. He'd programmed it in after they'd shared a second bottle of wine, thinking he was funny. Which he was. Every time Val heard it, she had to suppress a smile.

"You ready to join our lives?" he said when she picked up. "And by that I mean; join my crap with your crap."

"Bad news," Val said. "I've got to babysit Jack's daughter, Sam, for a few days."

"Why is that bad news?"

"Well, I know we were both excited about you moving in."

"No problem. How old is Sam? Two? Two-year-olds are fun. I'll pick up some kid food before I come over."

Kid food? Val hadn't thought of that.

"You got any Disney movies?" she asked.

"All of Pixar. Already packed it."

"Lund, I know you're disappointed..."

"Not one bit. Sam can help us unpack. Did you make room in the closet?"

"I haven't really had time. Been childproofing the house."

Val frowned. She actually had no idea how to childproof a house, beyond the safety pamphlets her officers used to hand out at local community festivals. By the time Grace had come to live with her, she had already turned twelve. Val eyed her living room, trying to mentally check off all the ways a two year old could die. Electrocution via outlet? Smothering behind the sofa? Pulling a TV on top of herself? Choking on a Hummel figurine?

Maybe it was a good thing all her mother's Hummel figurines were broken a few years back.

"No problem," Lund said. "I can help."

"Help childproof the house?"

"Yes. And help clean out your closet. What time is Sam coming over?"

Val checked the clock. "About two and a half hours."

"I should be there around then. Love you."

"Uh, love you, too."

HACKQUEEM

Hackqueem, spelled with a C, a K, and a Q, stared at the flaming car and shook his head.

"Jet Row, man, why you have to torch our ride?"

Jet Row shrugged. "It's life, homey. Shit burns."

Hackqueem spat on the side of the road. "Del Ray is gonna be pissed, man. No reason to light up a perfectly good Prius."

"That car was bullshit," Jet Row said.

"It got fifty miles per gallon, homeboy."

"Sixty on the highway," Sha Nay Nay said. "Prius was solid."

"I'm calling Del Ray." Bön Dawg—no *e* but with an umlaut over the *o*—had his cell phone out, and Hackqueem slapped it away.

"Don't be stupid. You gonna buy Del Ray a new Prius?"

"Wasn't new," Sha Nay Nay said. "It was an '11."

"Are you gonna buy Del Ray an '11 Prius?"

"Naw. I'm busted. Just bought an Xbox. That *Lego Batman 3* shit is dope."

"Dawg, you get to the Braniac boss fight yet?"

"I'm stuck on a level. I can't put out that fire."

"Gotta use Superman to blow it out. Or Batman's arctic suit."

"Why you want to put it out?" Jet Row said. "Let it burn, baby."

"We need new wheels," Hackqueem said. Then he stomped out the small fire Jet Row had started on the side of the road. "What are you, five damn years old? Do I have to take your matches away from you?"

"Got a Zippo."

"Do I have to take your Zippo?"

"I'm straight."

Hackqueem thought about the 9mm in his pocket, wondered if he could kill them all and blame it on another gang.

"How about we jack a ride?" Bön Dawg said.

"Good idea," said Jet Row. "We jack a car, then burn that mo-fo."

"We're not burning anything," Hackqueem said. "Lemme think."

That's when a van pulled up to them. Four old people, two men and two women.

"We saw a burning car down the road," said the old geezer who was driving. "Are you kids okay?"

And so it was on, like Donkey Kong.

VAL

Val spent an hour tending to her deathtrap of a kitchen, moving poisonous cleaners to higher shelves, putting duct tape on sharp corners, taping over outlets, making sure cords were tucked away, hiding the mop bucket (she'd read a warning about children drowning in mop buckets in one of those safety pamphlets). Crawling around at toddler-level was an eye-opener. Almost everything in sight had the potential to maim or kill. It was a wonder any child reached the age of four.

The living room was equally fraught with danger. What if Sam got caught in the recliner? What if she slipped on the loose rug? What if she managed to climb on top of the bookshelf and topple it over, getting crushed by a very outdated and very heavy 1998 set of the Encyclopedia Britannica (minus volume 8—Menago through Ottowa—which Val had thrown away after smoke damage.)

Val made sure the gun safe was locked, then made sure again, even though she always kept it locked. She went into the bedroom and put her vibrator on a top shelf in the closet—not that it was lethal, but it would be weird if Sam found it. She got online and bookmarked *CPR for toddlers*. That led to learning that choking was one of the most common causes of child death, so Val broke out the vacuum cleaner to ensure there wasn't anything on the floor that could clog a small person's throat.

When she shut it off, she heard knocking. Val checked her watch. Had it been three hours already? She still hadn't made sure all the matches and lighters were put away; Val had lived through one bad fire, she didn't want to try to survive one with a toddler.

"Val!"

She and Jack exchanged a brief hug. Jack's husband, Phin, held Sam on his hip. He offered Val a handshake, and Val couldn't help but notice that he was in very good shape. A sign that he and Jack weren't having sex because he was cheating? Val couldn't possibly know, but her opinion of him sank all the same.

"Sam, do you remember Val?" Jack asked.

Sam buried her face in her father's chest.

"Stranger danger!" Sam yelled. "Stranger danger!"

"It's okay, Sam," Phin said, setting his daughter on the ground. "She's not a stranger. She's a friend."

Sam cautiously turned from Phin, but one tiny hand clutched the leg of his jeans. Val crouched down to Sam's level, another online bit of advice, and stretched out her hand. "Last time I saw you, you were only one."

"I'm two," Sam said.

"Your name is two?" Val smiled. "I thought it was Sam."

Sam stared at her. Her face was almost a perfect circle, and her blue eyes were wide. "I'm Sam. And I'm two."

"I see. I'm Val, and I'm more than two. Nice to see you, Sam."

Sam let go of her father and shook Val's hand, then tugged it a little, looking toward the barn. "Can I ride your horsey?"

Val shot a panicked look at Jack. She hadn't thought about the horses. Talk about dangerous. The barn alone was filled with sharp edges and hard surfaces and…

"Maybe when Mommy and Daddy get back," Phin said. "You can ask Val if you can pet the horse, but no riding until we're around."

"Can I pet the horsey?" Sam asked.

"Do all two year olds talk like this?" While Sam had some pronunciation issues, she was pretty easy to understand.

Jack shook her head. "Naw. She's early."

Behind Jack's car, a moving truck pulled onto the front lawn. A large, much larger than expected, moving truck.

David Lund, wearing a worn leather jacket and Lake Loyal Fire Department ball cap, bounded out of the cab, a big grin on his face. He turned it on Jack. "Great to see you again, Jack."

"You too, Lund. This is my husband, Phin."

Lund extended his hand and Phin shook it. A year or two older than Phin, Lund was equally fit, and Val watched their arms flex as they sized each other up.

"A pleasure," Lund said.

"Thanks for watching my little girl."

"She's in good hands."

Phin nodded.

Good, they aren't trying to play alpha, Val thought, exchanging glances with Jack.

Lund knelt down to Sam's level, like it was the most natural thing in the world. "Hey, Sam, my name is David. Did you know there are bears out here?"

Sam's eyes got wide and she shook her head.

"Just a second. I'll show you." He trotted back to the truck, reached into the cab, and pulled out the largest teddy bear Val had ever seen. It was practically Sam's size and wore a red checked bow around its neck. "This bear is for you. What should its name be?"

"Harry."

"Because he has so much hair?"

"Because he looks like Dickhead."

Lund let out a guffaw. "Did she say *Dickhead*?"

Jack shrugged. "That's her name for Harry." Harry McGlade was Jack's partner in the detective agency where they both worked. "I may have used it a few times around the house, and it stuck. You know, the bear does sort of look like McGlade."

Val squinted. There was a certain resemblance. The bear immediately went from cute to slightly annoying.

"So, do you have all the rules written down?" Val asked, having discovered on a babysitting blog that good parents made such lists.

"Rules?"

"You know. Food. Bedtime. Baths. Allergies. All the stuff I need to know."

Jack shrugged. "She's highly flammable, so keep her away from open flames."

"Huh?"

"And don't give her any helium," Phin said. "She might float away."

"No helium," Lund was pretending to jot it down. "Check."

Val made a face. Ha ha. Everyone was in on the joke. It must be obvious she didn't know a thing about little kids.

Jack patted her shoulder. "Seriously, Val. Just ask Sam what she needs. It's not like children are so fragile they'll break from the smallest thing."

"I knew that," Val said, thinking of her mother's shattered Hummel collection.

"Do you guys want to come in for coffee?" Lund asked.

"Sure. Come in," Val said, eyeing the moving van and experiencing a sudden urge to avoid the inevitable. "I'll throw on a pot. Shouldn't take long."

"We've got to get going. Got a lot of hours ahead of us."

"Whereabouts you going?" Lund asked.

"Spoonward. Near the Minnesota border."

"Way up in the woods. Beautiful country. But be careful. Hunting season just started. A lot of jackasses out there shooting anything that looks like a deer. And after a few beers, everything looks like a deer." Lund paused. "You hear that?"

There was indeed rifle fire, less than a few miles away.

"That means no antler hat, young lady," Phin said, giving Sam a tickle. "Promise me."

"I promise, Daddy. No taddle hat."

Phin gave her a hug and told her he loved her. "Bye, sweetie. Be good for Val and David."

"I will. Love you, daddy."

"Val," Phin nodded at her. "Lund." They shook hands again. Then he walked back to the car.

Val looked at Jack, saw some anxiety there.

"She'll be fine," Val said.

"I know. That's not who I'm worried about." Jack glanced back at Phin.

"That'll work out," Val said.

Lund apparently picked up on their need for private time, and he scooped up Sam and Sam's little suitcase. "How about we go inside and I show you our house?"

Val winced at the *our house* comment.

"You having doubts, too?" Jack asked when they were alone.

"Maybe there are always doubts."

"Maybe. That would kinda suck."

Val laughed. "Yeah, it would. Go work your stuff out, Jack. You'll do the right thing."

"So will you. And thanks for the favor."

"My pleasure. God knows you've always been there for me."

"I don't know what cell reception will be like up there, but I'll get into town and call every day. Either we'll pick her up on Wednesday," Jack exhaled. "Or I'll pick her up on Wednesday."

The women embraced, Jack yelled *I love you* and waved goodbye to Sam in the kitchen, , then Val watched her friend walk off, disappearing behind Lund's enormous truck.

Seriously, Val didn't even know he owned that much stuff.

Was some of it his wife's? Val didn't know how she felt about that. Lund was a widower and had issues where his wife was concerned. Many issues. Most arising from feelings of guilt that he'd failed to save her. Had he filled the truck with things that had belonged to her?

Val pushed those thoughts away. At one time, she'd talked to Lund ad nauseam about his wife, Kelly Ann, Back when she and Lund had first met. Back when he was a suspect in Kelly's murder. The last thing Val wanted was to revisit those days.

If the truck was filled with Kelly's things, Val could deal with it. Couldn't she?

Maybe Lund could store them in the barn. Val was pretty sure he'd be okay with that.

Pushing those thoughts from her mind and plastering a smile on her face, Val found Lund and Sam in Grace's room, putting a little purple sweatshirt on the bear.

"Look at that," Lund said. "It fits perfectly."

"Fits perlecky," Sam repeated. "He wants a hat."

Lund set his on the bear's head. It sloped to the side, covering one eye.

"No," Sam said. "Your head's too big."

Lund chuckled. "I've heard that before."

As luck would have it, Grace hadn't taken her winter clothes to school yet. Val located two stocking caps that fit the bear perfectly. Since the Packer colors clashed with the bear's bow, Sam opted for the red and white of the Badgers.

"He's a handsome bear," Lund said. "Now let's get at that truck."

Val checked her watch. "Are you hungry, Sam? I bet you're hungry."

Lund started for the door. "How about we bring in a few boxes then take a break to eat?"

"It's important that kids eat on a schedule."

"Jack and Phin didn't say anything about a schedule."

"Just because they didn't say anything to you about a schedule doesn't mean there's no schedule." Didn't the babysitting blog she'd read mention a strict schedule? Val was sure it had.

"Val…"

"You said you were going to pick up some kid food, right?"

"I did."

"And you have movies?"

"Yes."

"Then it's settled. We'll eat and then watch a movie. How does that sound, Sam?"

"I want to see horsey."

"And we have to see horsies," Val said. Jack had said kids weren't fragile. Surely she wouldn't get hurt petting Grace's mare. Banshee was as quiet as horses got. "We'd better get going. We have so much to do, and it will be bedtime before you know it."

They went downstairs, Val helped Sam back into her little coat, and they went outside.

Lund followed them out. "I'll get the food and movies from the truck."

"Yeah, good."

When Val opened the barn door, all hell broke loose. All hell in the form of nickers and whinnies and hooves clacking against stall walls.

"They mad," Sam said, her eyes impossibly wide.

"Nope. They're just hungry."

"Can I feed horsies?"

Visions of tiny fingers being chomped off by sharp teeth careened through Val's mind. She glanced behind her, wishing Lund had come with them. "Ahh, I'm not sure if that's—"

"Please?"

"We'll see."

Val smiled. *We'll see* was something she remembered from her own youth. When Mom hadn't wanted to say no, she'd say *we'll see*. It had always worked with Val and her little sister, Melissa.

"We'll see when?" Sam asked.

Damn. Smart kid.

"Um..."

"Now?"

Those big eyes. That bright smile. Why not? What could possibly go wrong? "Okay."

"Goody." The little girl gave a few short hops.

Val eyed the stalls. Max could get a little demanding and bitey until he'd had his grain. Bo was already busy alternating pawing and begging, throwing in the occasional thump of hoof against the wall. But Grace's mare Banshee was a sweetheart. There was nothing to fear with her.

Val cut the twine off a bale and peeled off a couple of flakes. Taking a handful of alfalfa from one, she gave it to Sam. "Hold onto it at the end, and when the horsey puts her head out, let go. Okay?"

The girl nodded.

Val picked Sam up and carried her to Banshee's stall. Sam held out the hay. Banshee opened her mouth and reached for it with grasping lips.

Sam squealed, her whole body shuddering.

"Oh my God! Oh my God!" Val jolted away from the stall and clamped the child to her shoulder. "What happened, honey? Are you hurt?"

The little girl's entire body quaked.

What had Val done? She never should have let Sam feed a horse. Not even Banshee. And now…

She set the little girl on the floor. Kneeling down, she looked for damage.

And found none.

Sam wasn't hurt. Not even a little. In fact, she wasn't even upset.

She was laughing. "Again! Again!"

And so she did. Val filled the three grain buckets to quiet the horses, then Sam tossed hay into each stall, handful by handful.

By the time they locked up the barn and headed back to the house, darkness had fallen, and Val was starving. She eyed the truck, still sitting in front of the house, and felt embarrassingly relieved. They really wouldn't have time to unload it tonight. By the time they ate, they would be lucky to squeeze in a kids' movie before Sam's bedtime.

The moving in would have to wait until tomorrow. And even then, with a little girl to keep them busy, who knew how they'd find the time?

Holding Sam's hand, Val led her up the steps and opened the kitchen door. The warm, comfort-food scent of macaroni and cheese wafted out into the night. And when Val stepped inside, she let out a strangled yelp.

Boxes.

Piles of boxes. Filling her living room, cluttering her dinette, even jamming the corners of her kitchen. And Lund stood in the middle of it all, an apron around his waist, holding two glasses of milk. "Just in time! Dinner's ready. And the truck is empty, too. How about that?"

"How about that?" Val said, her teeth clenched behind her smile.

They'd jacked the bag of ice from outside a gas station, in one of those honor system coolers where you were supposed to pay when you took it.

They didn't pay. That's how you roll when you're a gangsta.

Sha Nay Nay held some cubes to his shiner. Bön Dawg was pinching closed his bloody nose. Jet Row was trying, unsuccessfully, to light a small pile of ice on fire.

"Man, that old lady kicked yo ass," Sha Nay Nay said to Hackqueem.

"Shut up, fool."

Hackqueem's face had puffed up to the size of a parade float, thanks to half a can of pepper spray.

"And you be begging, 'I'm sorry, old lady! Didn't mean nothing! Please stop spraying me!'"

Hackqueem pulled out his 9mm and pointed it. He was nowhere near Sha Nay Nay because he couldn't see shit out of his swollen-ass eyes. "I said shut up! Y'all didn't do no better. Old guy messed you up."

"He knew some wu tang kung fu or some shit," Bön Dawg said. "Maybe he was a Shaolin monk."

"They were crackers," Hackqueem said.

"Crackers can go to China, study Shaolin."

"Hey, why we gotta get all racist and shit?" Jet Row said.

"Cracker ain't racist. It's just the color of your skin. Like a Saltine. No offense, homey."

"So what if I call you hamburger, cuz you're the color of a quarter pounder? Or what if I called Sha Nay Nay a beaner cuz he's Mexican and has skin the color of refried beans?"

"I'm Bolvian," Sha Nay Nay said. "My real name is Walter."

"Why your parents call you Sha Nay Nay?"

"I dunno. Some Martin Lawrence shit."

"I still say those crackers—I mean whities—trained in kung fu."

"Whities don't know kung fu."

"Van Damme does."

"He's not a whitey. He's one of those Frenchies."

"My moms is half French," Bön Dawg said. "I thought we were cooling it with the racist BS. We all the same color. We C-Notes. We fight proud an' bleed red. That's what matters."

"You're right. Sorry, my man."

"Plus," Bön Dawg said, "everyone knows whitey don't know kung fu."

"Chuck Norris is a whitey who knows kung fu. And Chuck be like eighty years old."

"Maybe that old guy was Chuck Norris," said Bön Dawg.

"Man, Chuck Norris hit you so hard, yo mama feel it."

"Well, yo mama so skinny she got to wear snow shoes or she'll fall in the sidewalk cracks."

"Yo mama so stupid she thought the civil war was won by Col. Sanders."

"Yo mama so fat she got to grease her hips to fit in the horizon."

"Not cool," Sha Nay Nay said. "You know my mama got the diabetes."

"Yo, sorry man. Forgot."

"Man, you need to check yourself. Diabetes is the silent killer."

"I thought hypertension was the silent killer. Saw that shit on TV."

"She got that, too. Stop ragging on my fat sick mama."

"Yo, man, heard your mama so sick the doctor came over," Bön Dawg said. "And the bitch ate him."

"Everyone shut it!" Hackqueem said. "No more yo mama jokes. Sha Nay Nay, how far to Lake Loyal?"

"Do I look like a map?"

"Dumb ass, look at your map."

"Oh." Sha Nay Nay tapped his cell phone. "Forty miles."

"We could hitchhike," Bön Dawg said. "But ain't nobody gonna pick up Puff Daddy here."

Everyone except for Hackqueem gave each other high fives.

"So what do we do?" Jet Row asked.

"Got to be a motel around here someplace."

"Right on," Jet Row said. "We find a motel and burn it to the ground."

"We find a motel and sleep," Hackqueem said. "We'll get to the kid in the morning. Where's the nearest motel, Sha Nay Nay?"

"Motel 6. Two miles north. And yo, they got a free continental breakfast!"

Continental breakfast? Hells yeah! They'd been in some cheese shop earlier, but some dumb ass pigs chased them out before they could order any food. A free breakfast would really hit home.

And so they headed north.

VAL

How Val got through the night without running screaming into the darkness while ripping out her hair, she wasn't sure. He was a fireman, for God's sake. Didn't they have rules about blocking every escape route with gigantic stacks of guy stuff?

And worse, as freaked out as she felt about the boxes invading every nook of her home, she knew she'd brought it on herself. And she didn't have any earthly idea what to do about it.

She loved Lund, didn't she? Years ago, she'd agreed to marry him, someday. And last summer, when he'd suggested selling his house and moving in, she'd agreed to that, too. And yet…

What was wrong with her?

She climbed over a box of who-knew-what and set a glass of apple juice in front of Sam and a cup of coffee on the table in front of Lund.

He smiled up at her. "Thanks. I'll get these bad boys unpacked and out of the way this morning. After I help you make space in your closet. Okay?"

Val stared at him, not sure what to say.

"You feeling alright, Val?"

"Sure, uh, fine."

"Nothing wrong, is there?"

"Uh, no."

"I don't want to put pressure on you. If you're not feeling well, let me know, okay?"

"Lund…"

"Yeah, yeah, you don't want to be coddled, but—"

"I'm fine. I'm taking my medication. I haven't had any issues in over a year. I don't want to talk about MS. Okay?"

"Okay. Sorry."

Val felt like she was deceiving him. It was only natural he'd assumed her less than enthusiastic response to his moving in was caused by her condition. She should be upfront and tell him what was really bothering her. But truth was, she didn't quite know. *I love you, but not enough to get rid of my old 80s jeans and tacky silver boots?*

How weak was that? How petty? How self-destructive?

"Okay then, we'll get on it." Lund set down his cup. "Sam? Can you and Harry the Bear help out?"

"I can."

"Not Harry?"

"No. He's lazy."

"Okay then, maybe he'll change his mind later."

"No," she sing-songed. "He's a Dickhead."

Lund plopped a box onto Val's counter. It was labeled Kitchen Stuff.

"It might seem like a lot," Lund said, "but most of this stuff will just meld with yours. See?"

He took out a pint glass with the Hooters logo on it. "This can go right into the cupboard, next to your tea cups."

"That's bone China I got from my grandmother."

"I was wondering why you'd keep something that ugly. Family heirloom."

"It's not ugly. It's pretty." Val reached for one of the saucers. "Sam, do you think this is pretty?"

"I like the boobies," she said, reaching for Lund's glass.

"None of my silverware matches," Lund said, "does that bug you?"

It went on like that for four hours.

"Val, I moved your itchy, knitted blankets upstairs, and put my flannel ones in the hall closet."

"Val, is it okay if I put this antler lamp in the living room?"

"Val, where should I hang Bigmouth Billy Bass? He sings *Take Me To The River*."

"Val, you got that bedroom closet cleaned out yet?"

"Val, you've got a lot of space on your bookshelf, but all the books are alphabetized. Do you want me to alphabetize mine, too? I kinda like to shelve by size."

"Val, where can I put my collection of German pewter beer steins? Some of these are almost thirty years old."

"Val, this is cast iron cookware. It's quality stuff. Can we move your pots and pans to the attic?"

"Val, how's that bedroom closet?"

"Val, can I staple my eight hundred back issues of Hustler to the ceiling?"

Okay, Val made up that last one. But it was pretty rough just the same.

The lackluster lunch of microwaved chicken nuggets gave Val a stomach ache. It was amplified by how well Lund and Sam seemed to be getting along. Sam delighted in every new box he opened, and seemed to soak up all the stories he told. When Val tried to engage Sam's interest in an antique Singer sewing machine from the last turn of the century, Sam declared it to be farty and then sat Harry the Bear on top and made fart noises until she cried with laughter.

Val popped some Tums, and brewed her fourth cup of coffee. Caffeine. That made everything better. A few cups of strong black coffee to settle her nerves and—

The banging on the door was so abrupt, Val automatically reached for the sidearm she wasn't currently carrying.

"Expecting anyone?" Lund asked.

Val shook her head.

Another hard knock.

"Seems urgent." Picking his way through boxes, Lund sidled up to the door, opened it a crack.

No one could have been more shocked than Val when she saw who it was.

SHA NAY NAY

Apparently, *continental breakfast* meant *some stale-ass donuts and an apple.*

They ate it anyway.

It hadn't been a good night sleep. Hackqueem had booked them all into one room, so it was two to a bed. Bön Dawg had some weed, but there were huge signs saying tampering with the smoke detectors resulted in a fine, and the goddamn windows only opened an inch. At least it stopped Jet Row from burning them all in their sleep. Sha Nay Nay heard he did that with his parents. That was some cold shit, even for a cracker.

Er… for a *white guy*.

Hackqueem's swelling had gone down enough that he didn't look like a Cabbage Patch Kid no more, but they were still about forty miles from their destination, and still didn't have a car.

"Open to suggestions," Hackqueem said, "that don't involve setting fire to nothing."

Jet Row put his hand down.

"Jack a car," Bön Dawg said. He had the TV on.

"Any of you know how to hotwire a vehicle?"

"Naw, man. We jack it. Stick a gat in their face, take that shit from them."

"You know we gonna kidnap a baby, right?"

Everyone nodded.

"You know that's some federal shit, right? Serious FBI federal penitentiary time. So before we commit some interstate felony that's going to have every TV station in the world looking for our asses, you want to draw attention to ourselves by jacking a car?"

"When you say it like that, it makes me sound stupid."

"It is stupid, Dawg! What you watching?"

"Nuthin'."

"You watching pay-per-view?"

"Naw."

"That shit is like $19.99 a movie! They took my credit card number, yo! You paying for that!"

"I'm just watching the preview! Don't freak out, man!"

"How long the preview been on?"

"Like ten minutes."

"You baby-daddy ditch weed stupid ass fool! You watch the preview longer than five minutes, it charges the room!"

"How was I supposed to know that?"

"It says it on the screen when you order the damn movie!"

"So what are we supposed to do?" Bön Dawg said.

"We need a plan," Hackqueem said.

"I meant with the movie. If we gotta pay for it anyway, shouldn't we watch 'till the end?"

"You don't turn off that goddamn TV right now, I'm shooting you."

Bön Dawg turned off the TV.

"We could call a taxi," Jet Row said.

Everyone looked at him. Hackqueem nodded. "Now you're thinking."

"And burn that shit up," Jet Row said.

"No burning," Hackqueem said. "But a taxi is a solid idea."

They tried to look up taxis on their phones.

"No taxi service out here?" Hackqueem frowned. "What kind of podunk backward-ass town don't have taxis?"

"Is that a rhetorical question?" Sha Nay Nay asked. "Because we already know the answer."

"So what do we do?" Hackqueem pointed at Bön Dawg, who was reaching for the TV remote. "Other than watch television?"

Bön Dawg left the remote alone.

"Yo, yo, yo, I got it," Sha Nay Nay said. "Uber."

"What's Uber?' Jet Row asked.

"Regular folks who get paid like cab drivers, but it's all freelance."

"We can call them?" Hackqueem asked.

"Naw. It's all app-based. Just gotta download it."

And so they downloaded Uber.

LUND

Harry McGlade stood at the front door, looking like he always did; wrinkled and sleazy. Plus he had an odor that for some reason reminded Lund of exotic birds.

"You lost?" Lund asked.

"Hey, the fire guy. Lump, right? Val here?"

"It's Lund. David Lund."

"Right, Lund. You live here now? You guys couldn't make it alone on your public service salaries so you pooled resources?"

"Something like that." Lund looked past Harry, focusing on the screaming red Winnebago parked in the driveway. "Nice RV, Harry."

"It's the Crimebago Deux. Like a Winnebago, but built for fighting crime."

"Of course, it is," Lund deadpanned. "And the tank? Don't tell me. You're still collecting weird vehicles to have sex on."

Harry beamed. "Remember the duck?"

"How could I forget?"

"Right?"

"Really, I tried." And tried. And tried. "What do you want, McGlade?"

"Val owes me a favor. I'm calling it in."

Val sighed so loudly, Lund could hear her from the other side of the kitchen. "Let him in," she said.

Lund fully opened the door, surprised to see that McGlade had a child on his hip. "You have a kid?"

"This is Harry Junior. I need you to watch him for a few days."

"Uh…" Val said.

"Listen Val, it's Jack. Someone she put away, he broke out of prison. He's the War Chief of the Folk Nation. And he's got a big grudge. Me and some friends are going up to warn Jack. She's not answering our calls."

"Do you think…"

"I dunno what to think. But I figure you're already watching Sam, and I don't want to take Junior into any firefight." He looked at Lund. "The shooting kind, not the wimpy firefighting kind that you do." Back to Val. "Junior and Sam are already buds. It would only be for a few days. And you owe me one. Actually, you owe me two."

Val sighed. "At least two."

"Hi, Dickhead!" Sam had waddled up. "Hi, Dickhead junior!"

"She calls me *dig it*," Harry said. "Like, *can you dig it*?"

"I don't think that's it," Lund offered.

"Blababaglab ba baaa!" Harry Jr. said.

"He's still working on the talking thing. No worries. I didn't talk until I was nine years old. Also, he's still not potty trained, and I've only got the one cloth diaper. But you can use anything. Old shirts, table cloths, wrap him in paper towels. I once set him down in a silk plant. He was fine. Got a list of instructions and allergies in his diaper bag. This cool?"

Lund deferred to Val on that one.

"Oh shit, Harry. Go find Jack. I'm not going to tell you no."

"Yeah, we know you have a hard time saying no. Right, Lump?" Harry waggled his eyebrows.

"Who exactly is after Jack?" Lund asked as Harry handed him his child.

"A street gang."

"A big one?"

"Mid-sized. No more than two or three thousand members."

"Are we in danger?"

Harry laughed. "I'd know if I was followed, Lump. I'm a private detective. You'll be fine. Just don't open the door to strangers, like you just did with me. That was stupid, by the way."

"No shit," Lund muttered.

"I'll call you when I hear something. High five, Junior!"

McGlade held up a palm. Harry Jr. didn't return his father's high five. Instead, he peed right through his cloth diaper, dripping onto the floor and forming a large puddle, some of which started soaking into the cardboard of the nearest box.

"Gotta run, talk soon!"

"Bye, Dickhead!" Sam waved.

And McGlade was gone.

Lund brought Junior to the sink, and Val broke out the mop. "Have you seen the mop bucket around here?"

"Dickhead went pee-pee," Sam said.

"Yes, he did, sweetheart." Val picked up McGlade's diaper bag. "Maybe there are wipes in here."

Lund eyed the bag, then instead of waiting for a miracle, he reached for a paper towel and turned the tap on warm.

Val opened the bag, releasing a distinct, pickled egg odor. While Val dug through it, Lund unpinned and removed the wet diaper, washed the little boy up, grabbed a nicely absorbent dish towel from a drawer, folded it into a triangle, put it under Junior, threaded it between the toddler's legs, spread it out just right, and pinned it into place.

Not so bad, even if he did say so himself.

Lund checked back to see how Val was doing. "Find anything?"

"Six cans of energy drink. Four of them empty." She stacked them on a box then went back inside. "This." She pulled out a crumpled sock, possibly the source of the pickled egg smell.

"Anything else?"

She held up a six-month-old copy of Entertainment Weekly.

"Perhaps *diaper bag* is a misnomer."

"And the real treasure." She pulled out a plastic cutting board with some words printed on it in black Sharpie.

Lund picked up Harry Junior and moved close to Val to read the writing over her shoulder.

JR'S ALLERGY LIST

—PENISILAN

—SOME KIND OF BERRY

—PEANUTS

—BEES

—OTHER BUGS THAT STING LIKE BEES

—COBRAS

—THE AMISH

—JACK'S EXPANDING BUTT

—YOU READING THIS JACK? TIME TO LOSE THAT BABY WEIGHT! PHIN IS GONNA CHEAT ON YOU!

—NAH, HE PROBABLY WON'T. HE'S A GOOD DUDE. PROBABLY.

Man, that Harry McGlade was a piece of work. "I don't see any instructions."

Val searched the bag's outer pockets, pulling out some dried up baby wipes, a used Chipotle napkin, and a DVD titled *Anal Blasters 7*.

"I didn't know they made any past part 5," Lund said.

"Huh?"

"That DVD. You never told me you were into that kind of thing, Val."

"It's from Harry's bag."

"Sure it is." Lund set Junior on the floor, on his butt, fencing him in with a cluster of boxes.

"DVD!" Sam yelled, reaching for the disk.

"No, honey. That's not—"

"DVD!"

She and Val played tug of war, while Lund struggled to keep a straight face.

"You don't really think that DVD belongs to me. Do you?"

"Of course not. Why on earth would I think that?"

"You don't."

"Moving in with someone means accepting all of their eccentricities."

"Lund, come on."

Unable to hold it in, he smiled.

"Smart ass," Val said.

"Smart ass. Smart ass." Sam giggled, pointing at Lund.

"How about this one, Sam?" Lund grabbed a DVD from one of his boxes, the movie *Cars*.

"Okay, smart ass!"

Val groaned. "Jack will never forgive me."

"Hey, she already knows *Dickhead*, so how bad could this be?"

Val offered him a relieved half-smile.

Now that was more like it. Lund ran his fingers down her arm. "Children aren't fragile, you know. I heard that somewhere."

"Hmm, sounds familiar."

"I'll tell you what, I'll take care of these two, okay? You just relax."

The half-smile turned into the full, beautiful thing. "That sounds terrific."

Lund started up the movie, and Sam settled on his lap. Harry Junior also crawled up onto Lund, along with Sam's bear. Val couldn't help but notice how adorable the scene looked.

"So, you don't think we're in any danger from that gang Harry mentioned, do you?" Val asked.

"You know McGlade better than I do. He's irresponsible. But he dropped his kid off here to keep him out of danger. Go relax. We'll be fine."

"Thanks, Lund," Val said from behind him.

He shot her a grin. "Not a problem. This will give you a chance to clean out your closet in peace."

BÖN DAWG

When he was a kid, Tyrell Jean-Phillipe Ginsberg, now known by his street name Bön Dawg, thought the key to cracking lots of dollars was joining a gang.

Then he and his homies spent over two hundred bucks on Uber fare to get to Lake Loyal, and Bön Dawg realized that gangbanging was bullshit. If you really wanted to get paid, drive for Uber.

"That wiped out the rest of my PayPal account," he whined. "All that cheddar I made selling my old *Star Wars* toys on eBay."

"You sold those, Dawg? Man, that Princess Leia figurine was def."

Bön Dawg shook his head in regret. "Mint in the box. Never even took it out the package to touch her titties. You guys gotta pay me back."

"I got nothing," Sha Nay Nay said, pockets turned inside out like a broke ass hobo.

"Did he jack us?" Hackqueem said. "Couldn't see the meter."

"Because your eyes are all swole shut."

"Did he jack us?"

"Naw. Uber is expensive, homeboy. That's why Jay-Z takes a limousine. Limo is cheaper."

"Shoulda burned his Uber ass," Jet Row said.

"You guys payin' your part or not?"

"Dawg Del Ray will pay you when we get back with the shorty."

"He gonna be too pissed off about his Prius to pay me. Man, I got that Leia figurine for my Bar Mitzvah." He sighed. "Rabbi Schlomo is gonna lecture me for like five hours, man."

"Do we even know where this place is?" Sha Nay Nay asked.

"You got the map."

"Oh, yeah." Sha Nay Nay consulted his phone. "Less than a mile away. We have to go southeast."

"Which direction is southeast?" Bön Dawg asked. "Anyone got a compass app?"

No one did.

"Well, which direction are we facing?"

Sha Nay Nay pointed forward. "This direction."

"You kidding, right?" said Bön Dawg. "Because you are the stereotype for uneducated inner city youth."

"Well, you're the stereotype for assholes."

"See? That was an uneducated thing to say."

"And that was an asshole thing to say. Asshole."

"You the asshole."

"Naw, you the asshole."

"Both y'all are assholes, now shut it," Hackqueem said. "Gonna be dark in a few hours."

"Grab some branches," Jet Row said. "We can make torches."

"No one is making torches. Sun goes down in the west, so southeast is this way. We'll keep it on the down low 'till we get there. "

"And then?" Bön Dawg asked.

"And then it's on, brother."

VAL

Val made progress. Not very much progress, but progress just the same. She stared at the Goodwill pile and the pair of culottes she'd last worn in junior high, the only item she managed to add.

She'd worked so hard to get the smoke smell out of them after the fire Dixon Hess had started in the middle of her living room. Those were dark times. Horrible times. Tragic times. But in the end, she, Grace, and Lund had survived. Most of the police and fire departments had survived. The town had survived.

Maybe she should keep the culottes as a testament to all they'd overcome.

Maybe she couldn't do this.

Maybe she should be honest with Lund.

Plucking the culottes from the pile, she made for the door. In the hallway, she could hear the video from downstairs. The music sounded lame enough to be in a cartoon, only instead of the voices of animated autos, Val heard groaning, moaning, and the occasional *harder!*

Had Lund lost his mind?

She raced down the stairs. "Lund!"

He jolted upright on the loveseat, nearly dumping Harry Jr. onto the floor. "What? What is it? Fire?"

Always a fire with him. Go fig.

"Were you sleeping?"

"What? No. Of course not."

"What are you watching?"

Lund blinked and squinted at the TV. "Aw, what the hell?"

"DVD," Sam said, waving the remote in the air.

He snatched it away and switched the television off. "Sam, did you put that movie in?"

"They were naked."

Val pressed eject on the player, plucked out Harry's DVD, and walked into the kitchen to toss it in the garbage. "Let's not tell Jack about this one."

"Are you throwing that out?" Lund asked. "It didn't look too bad."

And that's when a brick crashed through the kitchen window.

HACKQUEEM

That's it?" Sha Nay Nay said. "That's your plan? You cut the phone line and then chuck a rock through the window?"

"We coulda at least set the rock on fire," said Jet Row.

"Shh. Stay down. Now we wait for them to come outside and see who threw it."

"Then what?"

"Then we go inside and snatch the kid."

"Which kid?"

"What?"

Bön Dawg was staring at the house with some plastic night vision goggles he got at his Bar Mitzvah but hadn't sold on eBay yet.

"They got two shorties in there."

"Two?"

"And they were watching porn. Some freaky shit."

Hackqueem took the goggles, yanking Bön Dawg's head to the side because the strap was around his neck.

"Easy, man!"

"Lemme see."

There were, indeed, two children in the living room. Some cute little girl, and some ugly boy that looked a lot like a teddy bear.

And the porn was off the hook. Hackqueem didn't know the human body could do shit like that.

"Are we grabbing the boy or the girl?" Hackqueem asked Jet Row.

"Hell if I know." Jet Row had gathered up a pile of pine needles.

Hackqueem kicked the pile over. "Okay. We take them both. Jet Row, Sha Nay Nay, go around to the other side of the house. You grab the girl. Me and Bön Dawg are gonna snatch that Teddy Ruxpin-looking bastard."

"Teddy who?" Bön Dawg asked.

"Didn't you have a Teddy Ruxpin when you was a kid? Talking bear? Read you stories and shit?"

"I had a Tickle Me Elmo. Used to scare the crap outta me. Little red dude be laughing like Satan got inside him, all shaking and giggling and going mental. Had nightmares 'till I was fifteen, homes. Then my moms got the diabetes. Bad times. Why you gotta bring up bad times?"

"Shh! Dude is coming outside. Damn. Big dude."

"He doesn't look so big."

"Look at his arms, man. He'd break yo ass in two equal pieces."

"I could take him," Hackqueem said. "Ain't no thing."

"Who's there?" said the big dude, shining a flashlight their way.

"Dude is huge! Run!" Hackqueem ordered.

And so they ran.

VAL

Val had strapped on her Serpa holster with the Glock 17 inside. She kept it there; the children wouldn't be able to pull it out, and neither could anyone else except her. That was the point of a Serpa holster.

"Anything?" she said to Lund as he scanned the treeline with a Maglite.

"I don't see anything. Might have heard some talking. Hard to tell."

"Someone threw the brick, right?"

"That would be my guess. Wind isn't quite strong enough to lift a brick."

Sometimes Lund had a weird sense of humor.

"I'm going to call it in," Val said.

She backtracked to the kitchen and found the children standing in the middle of the cardboard box jungle, holding hands.

"It's okay," Val told them.

"Dickhead went poo-poo," Sam said.

Harry Junior said, "Blabooga!"

"He's stupid and he smells," Sam said.

"I'm going to use the phone," Val told them. "You guys stay right here."

She picked up the princess model in the kitchen, dialed the station. No sound came out of the receiver.

Val tapped the hang up button, like they do in the movies whenever the phone doesn't work. But it stayed dead.

"Phone doesn't work," Val called to Lund.

"Try your cell."

Val tugged it out.

"No bars," she told Lund as he came back into the house.

She watched Lund dig into his own pocket and check.

"Me, neither," he said. "We'd better make sure the doors are locked."

HACKQUEEM

He tripped on some sticks, and the cell phone jammer went flying. It should still work; the jammer blocked radio signals for about fifty yards. But if he lost it, he'd be in deep shit. Hackqueem squinted, trying to spot it in the dark. He didn't want to turn on his flashlight because he didn't want that big white dude to see him and break him into two equal pieces.

Del Ray was gonna be pissed. First the car, then the jammer. According to Del Ray, those things were damn expensive.

Hackqueem wondered what punishment he'd have to face when they got back. Del Ray was pure psycho when it came to disciplining his men. And rumor was T-Nail—the general they'd busted out of prison—was even worse.

Back when he was a new jack, Hackqueem had to brave the gauntlet. They called it a rum runner. Ten guys beating on you, and if you fell down you got kicked to death. He ended up in the ER and still had scars. It was used for gang initiation and for punishment. Hackqueem didn't want to go through that shit again.

But maybe he wouldn't have to. This wasn't his fault. He wasn't the one who set the Prius on fire. Jet Row could take the heat for that screw-up.

The thing to do, the thing that would salvage this mess, was to make sure they got the kid. Del Ray and T-Nail could forgive all the other stuff. But if they messed up grabbing the kid, all four of them would be dead. Nailed to the floor, or scalped, or minus some vital and much loved appendage.

It made a brother contemplate the consequences of his life choices. Hackqueem hadn't ever thought much about going legit, but at least with those white collar jobs you could leave without dismemberment, and maybe even get some kind of severance package. Stocks and pension and health benefits. If Hackqueem left the C-Notes, all he'd get is his ass beat. And he'd lose body parts. Try to crip walk with toes cut off. B-ball ain't easy without all ten toes. He didn't want to try a fadeaway jumper with both little piggies gone.

He stayed low, moving fast, grateful for his toes, circling the house and coming around the other side. That's when he saw a flickering orange light.

"Ah, hells no."

He ran around to the front, saw the moving truck parked there, all lit up like a Christmas tree.

A burning Christmas tree.

And so he slapped himself in the forehead in disbelief.

JET ROW

"Take that, truck! I warned you not to play me!"
    And so the truck burned.

HACKQUEEM

He came up from behind the truck, and saw some kind of crazy-ass giant pry bar on the ground next to it. Made of silver metal, with a spike on the end. He picked it up, and it was heavy.

Ahead of him, oblivious, was Jet Row, lighting matches. Hackqueem came up from behind and smacked him in the back of his head.

"What the hell you doing, fool?"

"Burnin' it down, homey."

"Why you setting fire to a truck? How is that part of the plan?"

Jet Row scowled. "Damn truck tried to play me, man."

"Tried to play you?"

"Truck is all parked there, like, *look at me, I'm a truck. What you gonna do, set me on fire?* So I did."

"Now what you think gonna happen when the fire department comes, Einstein?"

Jet Row's eyes got wide, like he just saw Jesus. "Firemen come, we burn them up, dog."

He took out his lighter fluid and started to soak a brick.

And so Hackqueem took off, putting distance between him and that crazy cracker fool.

VAL

Val liked living in the country. She could keep the horses on her property. She had privacy, a rare thing for a public official in a small town. And ever since Old Man Meinholz had passed away and Lund had inherited the dairy farm next door, she hadn't had any annoying neighbors to deal with.

Unfortunately that last plus had just turned into a minus.

"No one is going to see this fire," Val said, stating the obvious. She, Lund, and the kids were peering out the living room windows that faced the road, light from the flames flickering across their faces.

"Kasdorf might," Lund said. "Not that he'd call for help or anything."

Val's only remaining neighbor lived on the other side of a forested bluff, yet he seemed to notice everything around him. Unfortunately he also hated police and wouldn't call 911 if his life depended on it.

When they'd ducked back in the house, she and Lund had immediately doused all the lights and double checked the locks. As a cop, Val had always been mindful about security. And as a cop who'd been through all she had, she was downright paranoid. She was reasonably sure no one could get in the house without her knowledge, but she'd still rather have the cavalry on its way. Instead, they were on their own.

But what were they facing?

So far, a rock through the window and a flaming truck. This didn't seem like the work of some criminal mastermind. Or even someone with a plan of any kind. This seemed like kids. Or maybe someone Val had arrested, who held a grudge.

"You assessing the threat level?" Lund asked, as if reading her mind.

"I'm pissed off, but not fearing for my life yet. No firearms. No attempt to do grievous bodily harm. So far, vandalism, and destruction of property. They could be here to taunt me. Could be random. Or it could be that gang McGlade told us about."

"What's our move?"

Val chewed her lower lip. "The truck isn't going to blow up." She was pretty sure things like that only happened in the movies.

"Boom!" said Samantha.

"Fibbababaa fritos!" said Junior.

"Of course not. Gas vapors burn. If it gets hot enough, the tank will melt, the gas will ignite. But no explosion. And it was down to only a few gallons anyway. Not much wind, it's far enough away from the house and barn. It should just burn itself out."

"Did you pay for the extra insurance?"

"Of course. I wouldn't risk anything happening to my stein collection."

Yeah. That would have been a tragedy.

"Anything else left inside?" Val asked. At least the destruction of some of Lund's endless stuff might be an upside.

"A few boxes of tools I was going to drop off at the station."

"Marshmawows?" Sam flashed a coercive little smile Lund's way. "Mmm, marshmawows."

"Mabopppaa!" Junior agreed.

"That's a good idea, Sam. I love toasting marshmallows. Maybe later."

"When?"

"We'll see."

"We'll see, when?"

"After we go upstairs," Val said. "You three can watch a little television in my bedroom."

Lund crooked a brow. "Our bedroom?"

"Uh, sure."

"And what are you going to do?"

"Figure out what's going on."

"Alone? Not a chance. I'll take care of it."

"This is not the time to be macho, Lund."

"Seems like a pretty good time to me."

"And the kids? Who is going to take care of them?"

"You."

Val let out an exasperated breath and turned to Sam. "Would you rather watch TV with me or David?"

"David! David!" said Sam.

"Mar-boro!" said Junior.

"Did Harry Junior just say *Marlboro*?" Lund asked.

"If he did, he's talking about you, and your affection for flannel shirts and Stetsons. So it's unanimous."

"I don't have a Stetson." He pointed at Junior. "But you and I are going to have a talk about the dangers of smoking."

"Upstairs," she said.

Lund took Sam, leaving Val to deal with Harry Junior, Samantha was right about the little boy's scent. His hand towel diaper sagged heavy under his belly. Holding him away from her body, she managed to get him upstairs without incident and settled the kids in front of the old tube television. While Lund tried to find a channel suitable for children out of the nine million available, Val unstrapped her Glock and Serpa holster and gave it to him.

"You remember how to draw the weapon?" she asked.

Lund looked at her, eyes crinkling. "Are you mansplaining something to me?"

"What?"

"I read the term in *Cosmo*."

"Why the hell are you reading *Cosmo*?"

"I picked up an issue about moving in with your boyfriend. Thanks to their handy tips, I made it painless for you. Don't you think?"

Val struggled to keep from rolling her eyes. "Just remember to press the button on the holster when drawing the weapon, And if you start telling me stories about the Kardashians, we're done."

"Roger. But did you hear Kim and Kanye might be splittsville?"

"Lund…"

"Gotcha. No *Cosmo*."

Val ducked into her office and made for her gun safe. She punched in the combination—028469—and turned the wheel, reminding herself to tell Lund the number, so he could open it as needed. Inside, she kept two long guns, Grace's Glock, and various ammunition.

Val pulled out a Remington 870 tactical shotgun for herself and considered the shells. She put a bandolier of buckshot around her shoulder, but loaded the gun with non-lethal rounds Kasdorf made for her, something he called *seasoners*. They wouldn't kill, or even maim, but they were a damn powerful deterrent. Val had used them to good effect with some visiting black bears who were more interested in the horses than she was comfortable with. The bears removed themselves from her property, in search of easier pickings. Hopefully, the shells would do the same for her current pests.

She loaded the shotgun with seven shells, and put on a belt of ten more. Then she crept back downstairs, going into a state of hyper-alertness. Val moved easily through the darkness, weapon ready, knowing the layout of the rooms without thinking. This was her comfort zone. Not toddlers. Not relationships.

Police work, she understood.

Eight feet into the living room, Val took an angle on the sliding glass door. Knees bent, she stepped to the side, opening her field of vision bit by bit to the yard. Eventually, she could take in the entire yard, spotting whoever was outside before they spotted her. The sky was cloudy, cloaking the moon, but with the glow from the burning truck in the front yard and the darkness indoors, it seemed as bright as twilight.

She took a step.

Saw nothing.

Took another step.

A shadow separated from the old oak and surged forward. No, not a shadow. A stupid, gangly kid. A flash ignited in his hand.

Then a flaming brick crashed into the glass door.

JET ROW

Hells yeah!

Never lit no brick on fire before!

Take that, brick! Who's the man now? Enough lighter fluid and anything will—

BANG!

Jet Row felt it across his legs, tearing through his jeans, his skin, his muscles and bones.

Shot!

I just got shot!

"Why?!?" he yelled to the universe, cursing the unfairness of it all. He was still a young man. Cut down in his prime, just for being born in the ghetto. He thought about all the stuff he'd never get to do in life. Like start more fires. Or burn things. But now he was snuffed, like a poor little match caught in a strong breeze, all because gun laws weren't harsh enough.

The pain was crazy. Like a million bees stinging him, he imagined, because he never got stung by a bee before. He was afraid to look. From the agony he felt, his legs had to be shredded. Hamburger meat. He knew he'd see tendons and arteries and all kinds of crazy anatomical shit. Dude just minding his own business, and the Man gotta break out a shotgun. That shit ain't right.

Jet Row reached down, touching his thighs, expecting to touch bone.

Instead, there were just a few small dots of blood. And some white flakes.

What the hell crazy shit was this?

He pinched a white crystal, squinted at it, and put it to his lips.

Salt.

They shot me with salt.

And it hurt like nobody's business.

Jet Row sneezed. Then his mouth and eyes began to burn.

What was that?

Pepper?

He rubbed his face, but all that did was get more pepper in his eyes. It wasn't fair. What kind of crazy crackers shot people with spices? Weren't there laws? No one ever gives inner city kids a chance. Soon as they try to do something with their lives, *BAM!*; salt and pepper all up in your face.

It was enough to make a kid join a street gang.

"Yo, Jet Row, you hit?"

Jet Row couldn't see who said it. Sounded like Bön Dawg.

"They shot me, man!"

"You look okay."

"They shot me with condiments, man!"

"Condiments?"

"Like I'm some kinda side dish! Without enough flava!"

"What you saying, fool?"

"Salt and pepper! Crazy bitch got spices in her shotgun!"

"What the hell is wrong with you white people?"

"Man, I don't shoot that shit! You being racist again!"

"Sorry."

"It hurts, dog."

"Aw, shit! There's pepper in the air!"

"I'm telling you, she's goin' all Iron Chef on a coupla bangers."

"Shit, it's in my eyes!"

"It's in my eyes, too, man."

"What do we do?"

"Only one thing we can do, Bön Dawg."

And so Jet Row started to cry.

VAL

The glass door didn't break. It was reinforced. Val waited until the brick flickered out. Then she shut the adjacent window, racked another round, and watched the kid who chucked the brick thrash around and paw at his eyes. Another young man joined him, reached the pepper cloud, and had a similar reaction.

Served them right.

Dumb kids or not, these guys were really starting to get on Val's nerves. One stupid stunt after another. What they lacked in brains, she was beginning to think they made up for in tenacity.

Another kid ran up, and obviously didn't see her through the glass, because he tried to pry the door open.

Seriously? Who wouldn't look through the glass door before trying to open it?

He had a fireman's Halligan bar. Lund's, from the look of it, probably taken from the moving truck before they'd set it on fire. The youth strained against the pry bar—what Val jokingly referred to as a hooligan bar—totally oblivious to the long, plain old steel bar that blocked the door's track. That steel wasn't going to bend, no matter how hard he pried.

Unfortunately, he was succeeding in chewing up the edges of her expensive glass door, and that was starting to piss Val off.

Big time.

She took a step toward the door, sighting down the barrel at the kid's head.

He went on prying.

Idiot.

She took another step forward, then another. When she was only a foot from the door, he finally glanced up.

His eyes went round.

His mouth formed an O.

He bolted, letting the Halligan bar clatter to the patio. Tripping, falling, climbing back to his feet, and taking off into the pine trees. If he and his buddies were smart, that would be it. In the face of stinging consequences, they would give up their pranks and go the hell back to wherever they came from.

She checked her cell again. Still no signal.

Val frowned, tucked the phone away, and found herself looking at Lund's German mug collection, which had taken up residence in her curio cabinet. Big, ugly, pewter, and just about the last thing she would ever want to display in her home. Yet there they were. And she'd be stuck looking at them. Possibly forever.

It made no sense, but Val wanted to blame Lund for their current situation. They were stuck watching two babies, surrounded by a lead contender for the World's Dumbest Gang, and somehow it was Lund's fault. He moves in, and everything goes bananas. What was supposed to be the romantic joining of two lives in peaceful cohabitation had devolved into chaos.

Chaos and ugly pewter beer steins.

In the years she'd known Lund, he'd never mentioned the stein collection. And why would he? If Val had a stein collection, she'd hide it from the public, like a wart. No good could come from anyone knowing about it. If anything, it was like a big neon sign that said, "I'm Not Normal."

Come to think of it, Val had been to Lund's place many times and had never seen the steins. Did he have them stored up in the attic? If so, why hadn't he left them there? What about moving in with Val made him want to display them?

She wondered if *Cosmo* was to blame, and made a mental note to read that stupid article Lund mentioned and write a scathing letter to the editor.

Then gunfire, the real bullet kind, shattered the reinforced glass door.

HACKQUEEM

Guns? Bitch wants to start waving around guns?

No prob. Hackqueem had a piece.

She wants to play, we can play.

He stood up from the weeds he'd been squatting in, then reached around and took out his 9mm.

Hackqueem had never killed no one before.

But there was a first time for everything.

He ran at the patio door and held out his nine sideways, gangsta style, punching the glass with bullets. Then he kicked it in like a boss and pointed the gat at the woman.

"Time to die, bitch."

And so he smoked her ass.

LUND

L und didn't like this. Not at all.

He paced across Val's bedroom floor, alternately glancing out the window at the branches of the old oak and watching Sam put the Badger stocking cap on Harry Junior, then the teddy bear. Back and forth. Back and forth. Totally ignoring the blue cartoon penguin singing songs on TV.

Normally Lund enjoyed that show right up until his brain was hijacked by the earworm tunes. He enjoyed hanging out with toddlers and playing house with Val. But the one thing he couldn't stand was feeling useless. And that's how he felt right now.

"See?" Sam said, arranging the hat on Junior for the eight millionth time. "Now he's a pretty bear."

"Ptferoooga!" screamed Harry.

Sam yanked the stocking cap off. "Now he's a dickhead!"

"Goob!"

While she was jamming the hat back on Harry the bear, Lund glanced out into the hall. Val had fired her seasoning shells at the idiot kids outside, but it had been quiet for a while. What was going on down there?

He listened, heard nothing, then turned back to the kids.

That's when the gunfire started, and Lund dashed for the stairs.

SHA NAY NAY

Was that gunfire?

Oh, hells no.

Sha Nay Nay just turned eighteen. If he got caught pulling a 187, he wouldn't be sent to no rudy poo juvee hall. They'd lock him up for real. And Sha Nay Nay knew how pretty he was. Didn't want no skinhead punks running no train on his sweet cheeks. That street was exit only. Being passed around for squares at the crowbar hotel was not how he wanted to spend the next thirty-to-life.

So he stayed low in the weeds, away from the house and those fools trying to break in. Del Ray would be furious, but he could blame it all on Hackqueem and that pyro, Jet Row. He reached into his pocket and pulled out the old ass apple he snatched from their continental breakfast, which was the last time he'd eaten.

The apple was squished.

Sha Nay Nay tossed it away, disgusted. There was nothing grosser than squishy, slimy food. Once, when he was a shorty, he was running with a big ol' bologna sandwich with extra mustard and his stupid ass brother, Sha Ray Ray, tripped him. Sha Nay Nay fell right on the sandwich, and it squished all over him, totally ruining his pimp ass Garanimals jumpsuit. To this day, Sha Nay Nay had never eaten another bologna sandwich, or worn any Garanimals, but that last thing was because his Mom never bought him no more.

He winced, scooping apple guts out of his pocket, and then started thinking about going to jail again. Sha Nay Nay looked into the darkness, where he'd thrown that busted ass apple. Could 5-0 get his prints off that? His DNA?

Shit. This trip just kept getting better.

He crawled around, feeling for the apple.

Put his weight right on it.

SQUISH.

"Oh, hells no."

A new pair of D&G jeans, dogged. Proof that there was no God. Because God wouldn't put a brother through so much fashion hardship in one lifetime. First Garanimals, now Dolce & Gabbana.

Then Sha Nay Nay started thinking about God, and he silently told God he was sorry.

And that's when God guided him on the righteous path.

Something, probably God, or maybe one of the saints like Jesus or Moses or Mary, made Sha Nay Nay look back at the house he'd run from. He was on a slight hill, and from this distance he could see straight into the second floor window. There, sitting on the bed, were two babies.

All alone, no one to protect them.

Better yet, God or John the Baptist or whoever, put a tree right next to the house.

Sha Nay Nay just had to climb the tree, snatch the kid, and they could get the hell out of there. Go back to Chi-Town as heroes. Maybe Del Ray would be so grateful he'd even buy him some new D&Gs. Or some Ralph Lauren. Ralph Lauren had some dope jeans.

Sha Nay Nay jogged up to the house, one hand on his D&Gs because he was wearing them baggy, and stood beneath the tree that God grew for him. Looked solid. Good branches. He didn't climb a lot of trees in the hood, but he could scale a fence like a cat, and this looked easy-peasy.

Time to get this shit done.

And so he began to climb.

VAL

For some fraction of a second, Val stared at the pewter beer stein, the largest in Lund's collection. More specifically, she stared at the way the faint outside light highlighted the large dimple where the bullet had struck.

She was going to die.

She'd weathered the debilitating symptoms of Multiple Sclerosis and survived the horror of Dixon Hess only to be shot in her home by the most inept criminals she'd ever encountered.

How sad was that?

How wrong?

How maddening?

Grace would have no family left.

If Lund survived this idiotic onslaught, he'd have to arrange a funeral instead of a wedding. He'd bury her in her dress uniform, the cut of which made her resemble a pear. He'd spend a mint on flowers, music, a luncheon for the whole town. He'd have to choose her coffin. She could picture it now. Based on his secret, peculiar tastes, it would be ornately carved with lions and dragons, eagles and fleur de lis, and made of pewter. A coffin that could stop bullets.

A coffin that could stop bullets.

Like hell she was going to die.

She grabbed a corner of the curio cabinet, yanked it away from the wall, and dove behind.

The endless series of pops outside blended with the drum of her pulse, shattering of glass, and bullets hitting pewter in crazy syncopation.

And when the barrage ceased, she was still there.

Val rose just enough to see over the top of the cabinet, the shotgun in front of her, peering down the barrel. She could see the kid fumbling with his pistol, trying to slap another magazine home.

She slipped her finger onto the trigger. Squeezed.

BOOM!

"Ahhhhhh! Shit!"

He backpedaled away from the window, dropping the mag. A second later and he had run away into the night.

A movement came from Val's left. She swung the shotgun around, took a breath, and stared at Lund's rounded brown eyes.

Val lowered her weapon.

"Val? What happened?"

Val could read Lund's lips, although her ears failed to pick up the sound of his voice.

"What happened? Are you okay?"

She held up a hand, signaling for a moment to catch her breath, to let her eardrums recover, to allow the adrenaline in her bloodstream to ebb. "The kids?"

"They're okay. They're sitting upstairs."

"Lund, these assholes outside, they aren't playing around anymore. They haven't burned my car or anything, have they?"

"Not that I saw."

"We need to get out of here."

"I'll get Sam and Junior."

Val nodded. "I'll get my car keys."

BÖN DAWG

Pepper in the face was the *worst*. Hurt like hell, and wouldn't stop. It was so effective. Bön Dawg wondered why nobody ever thought to weaponize it somehow.

"There's a building over there," he said to Jet Row. "Maybe we can wash off."

They staggered, half blind, over to a metal house that smelled like a barn. Bön Dawg found a barrel next to it, filled with water. He splashed his face and eyes, and Jet Row muscled in and did the same.

"My legs hurt so bad, B-Dawg."

"Better than dying, man."

"Hurts so bad. You ever get a cut on your lip, then eat salty French fries, and it makes it hurt ten times as bad?"

"Yeah."

"It's like that. Except it's my legs. And I don't got French fries. And it was from a shotgun. But it's like that. You know what I'm sayin'?"

"Sayin' it hurts."

"Yeah."

"But it's better than dying, man."

"Hurts so bad. It's like, you ever get a paper cut, and then you're eating tabasco—"

"Shh. You hear that?"

"I don't hear anything."

"It's cuz you're talking."

"No, I'm not."

"Yes, you are."

"I ain't talking. I'm just thinking out loud."

"Shh. Listen."

They listened. Bön Dawg heard shuffling, like some kind of animal. Then some weird sort of sound. *Errerrerrerrerr...*

"What the hell was that shit? Some kind of demon or bigfoot or freaky ass cannibal ghost? First they shoot me, then they gonna eat me."

"Shh, fool. It's a horse," Bön Dawg said. "C'mon."

He led Jet Row into the building, metal on the outside, wood on the inside. The place had a long concrete strip down the middle. On one side, there was hay or straw or whatever that shit was called, and some other junk. On the other, there were saddles and a place that looked like a big shower. And there at the end, caged in pens, were three horses.

Bön Dawg wasn't impressed by much. But these animals were cool. He'd seen horses before in the city, pulling rich people in carriages on Michigan Avenue, but had never gone up to one. Up close they were bigger than he expected. And they looked at you. They were aware he and Jet Row were there. Following some inner impulse, Bön Dawg took a handful of hay and stretched it out to the nearest horse, a brown one.

The horse ate the hay.

Bön Dawg grinned. He turned to look at Jet Row.

Jet Row had his Zippo lit, and was holding up his bottle of lighter fluid.

"What are you doing, fool?"

"Gonna light this place up."

"Why would you do that crazy shit, man? A horse is a majestic animal."

"Everything is more majestic when it's on fire."

"What is wrong with you?"

"People always be asking me that."

"Then maybe you need to quit lighting every goddamn thing you see on fire."

"Maybe I'll light you on fire."

"Maybe I'll kick your ass."

Jet Row gave Bön Dawg a shove. Bön Dawg shoved back, which caused Jet Row to squirt lighter fluid all over himself.

"Aw, come on, Dawg! My shirt is all soaked. This is a proprietary mixture. It's got petroleum solvents in it and shit. Are my colors streaking?"

Jet Row brought the lighter closer to his shirt, squinting to see it in the light of the fire.

Not his best idea.

Jet Row burst into flames like Johnny The Human Torch.

"Oh, shit! I'm on fire!" Jet Row began to flail around. "How can this be happening!?"

Bön Dawg was actually surprised it didn't happen more often.

"It hurts! It hurts bad! Fire burns!" He took two steps toward Bön Dawg.

Bön Dawg backed away. "Don't touch me, man!"

"Help me! It won't come off! This ain't fair!"

"Stop, drop, and roll, or some shit."

Jet Row dropped down, and began to roll around.

He rolled into the big pile of hay.

Which ignited.

And so, the barn began to burn.

SHA NAY NAY

At the top of the tree, Sha Nay Nay eased open the window and crawled into the room. The two toddlers were still sitting on the bed.

"Stranger danger!" yelled the little girl.

"Plapp!" yelled the little boy.

He wasn't sure which one to grab. No one told him. And he wouldn't be able to get back down the tree with one in each arm. His Mom, she could carry four kids, five bags of groceries, the dog, and a TV, all at the same time. The woman had skills. Sha Nay Nay did not.

He whipped out his cell phone, tried to call Hackqueem. No signal.

Oh, yeah. The cell jammer.

Well, maybe he could make two trips. He reached for the closest kid—

—and tripped over the lamp cord.

The floor lamp fell, hit the carpet, and winked out.

Sha Nay Nay couldn't see shit. But he could hear. He heard someone from downstairs say, "There's someone upstairs!"

He reached around blindly in the darkness, touched a kid in a knit hat. Wasn't the boy wearing a hat like that? Good enough. Sha Nay Nay scooped up the kid, adrenaline giving him a burst of strength, and then pushed through the window—

—flailing at the tree—

—missing a branch—

—falling—

—falling—

SMACK!

It didn't hurt as much as he expected. Because the baby broke his fall.

"Ah, shit! I squished him!"

Sha Nay Nay rolled over, pawing at his chest.

"Baby guts! I got baby guts all over me!"

Man, baby guts was way worse than a bologna sandwich with mustard, or an old apple. Baby guts might have been the worst squishy thing in the whole world.

But nothing felt squishy.

And the baby felt strangely boneless.

Sha Nay Nay held the toddler up in the moonlight and stared hard.

It wasn't a baby.

It was a teddy bear.

And so he screwed up, big time.

VAL

Val found her keys hanging in their spot next to the door. She'd just re-loaded the shotgun, buckshot this time, when Lund came downstairs with a child in each arm.

"Dickhead went bye-bye," Sam said.

Lund shook his head. "Junior is right here."

"Dickhead bear."

"The bear?" Val asked. There wasn't a chance they were going to waste time looking for a stuffed bear. "He's going to stay and guard the house until we get back. We have to go." She turned to Lund. "Ready?"

He nodded. Grabbing a kid in each arm, he stayed behind her while she pulled open the door. A few feet back in the kitchen, she brought the shotgun to her shoulder and stepped to the side, scanning the driveway outside. Between the truck in front and the farm's yard light in back, the night glowed as if there was a full moon.

No shadows.

No punks.

"It's clear," she told Lund. "Now." Then she led the way out onto the stoop.

But the truck wasn't burning that brightly anymore, and the yard light wasn't on. The glow was coming from somewhere totally different.

Oh no. The barn.

"They set fire to the barn!"

"Oh shit." Lund backpedaled, returning to the house. By the time Val joined him and locked the door, he had set down the children and was busy digging through his boxes. He pulled out a turnout coat and a helmet.

Val dug into another box, trying to help. "You have bunker pants? Boots? A mask and oxygen tank?"

"Not here. No."

Val kept digging.

He grabbed her arm and pulled her to face him. "I can handle it."

"But there's a lot of smoke and…"

"Val, I can handle it," he repeated. "Seems like this might be a good time to be macho."

"Marlboro!" Junior squealed.

"There you go." Lund grinned. "Gotta get out there and save some horses."

Not sure her voice would work, Val nodded.

Lund threw on the coat and helmet, then pulled her close and kissed her. "Keep the kids safe."

And then he was gone.

"Is he going to die?" Sam asked.

Val pulled in a sharp breath and paced across the floor, still holding the shotgun. "Of course not," she told Sam.

"Don't play with fire."

"Daehdehbahbah."

"Fire burns."

"Flagahaabeh."

"That's right, honey," Val said absently. She couldn't handle this. Standing here, doing nothing, while Lund was out risking his life. He could be shot by one of the punks outside. He could be trampled by one of the horses. He could be burned…

Val dodged an open box, and hit something hard with her toe. "Ouch."

"Owowowtchch."

"Don't play with fire," Sam said.

Bending down, Val checked to make sure her toe wasn't broken, then picked up the offending item, one of Lund's pewter beer steins.

Garishly ornate, the tacky thing featured famous Bavarian landmarks. A bullet hole threaded one of the towers of Neuschwanstein.

"Broken," Sam said.

Val nodded.

"Gimme," Sam reached for it.

Val hated not being in charge, hated sharing her space, and most of all, she hated these damn steins. And yet, if Lund died out in that barn trying to save the horses, or if he was shot by one of those punks, this pewter monstrosity would be all she had left of him.

Just like her grandmother's china cups and her mother's curio cabinet.

Val hugged it to her chest, unwilling to let it go.

LUND

Lund crossed the driveway, circled Val's car, and headed for the barn, scanning the shadows along the tree line. He hadn't taken the kids seriously at first. Who would have? They'd been so inept, their efforts seemed like mischief left over from Halloween, albeit more destructive.

The moment Lund had heard gunfire shattering the glass patio door, things had changed. He was done goofing around. Whoever these idiots were, they were dangerous.

The barn door stood open, the unmistakable glow of flame inside, smoke billowing out. Hooves slammed against wood walls inside. A panicked whinny pierced the night.

He slipped inside. Smoke stung his eyes. Heat hit him like a wall. The fire was located in the feed stall, a three-walled area right inside the door. Bales of alfalfa and bags of wood shavings were extremely flammable and burned quickly, the fire growing fast. It was already raging, flame climbing up the corners and threatening to spill into the adjacent vacant stall. After that, it would reach the horses. He had no time to lose.

For a barn, most guidelines suggested one extinguisher every twenty to thirty feet. Even though Val's barn was only forty feet long, Lund had insisted she buy three large Class A extinguishers; one on each end and one in the middle. He found the first immediately, plucked it from its bracket, and pulled the pin. Moving as close to the inferno as he could stand, he laid down the retardant, focusing on the base of the flame. By the time the extinguisher was empty, much of the hay pile was a smoldering pile of white, but Lund wasn't fooled.

A fire needed four elements to burn; heat, fuel, oxygen, and a chemical reaction to link the other three. It also needed a rigid, porous structure so the fire could be self-sustaining. To put out a fire, at least initially, it was only necessary to take away one part of the fire tetrahedron.

But bales of hay and bags of cedar shavings provided a textbook rigid, porous structure, as good at sustaining smolder as the tobacco in a cigarette. The fire might look dead, but it was anything but. With so much fuel, much of it still not smothered by retardant, and fresh air readily available, any smolder would eventually spark back into flame, like a cigarette did when the smoker took a drag. It was only a matter of time, and judging from the smoke still issuing from the bales, not very much time at that.

Lund needed another extinguisher. But first, he had to get the horses clear of this smoke before it hurt their lungs.

He continued down the aisle to the far end door, unlocked it, and slid it open. This end of the barn led directly into a large pasture where the horses spent most of their days. All he had to do was let them out of their stalls, and direct them out of the barn, and they would be safely corralled by the pasture fences.

Already the front end of the barn glowed, turning the smoke a lighter shade of black. Not long and the fire would be back to where it was. Lund had to move quickly.

The first stall he came to was Max's. The palomino nearly glowed in the smoky dark, dancing and tossing his head. Spotting Lund, he emitted a loud whinny.

"Hold on, big guy." Lund grasped the stall latch, wrenched it up and slid the door—

Max surged forward, trying to squeeze through before Lund had it open. The horse's shoulder plowed into him, sending him backward, smacking him into the wall. Steel shoes clattered on concrete, legs flying everywhere. Max slid, almost fell, then regained his balance, and raced out the paddock door.

Lund righted himself and moved for Bo's stall. He sure hoped the mares were more polite than Max.

Bo peered through the bars in the top half of her stall door. She waited patiently for him to unlock the stall and slide the door wide.

Then she leaped into the aisle, turned in the opposite direction, and ran toward the fire.

No, no, no…

Lund held his breath as Val's mare ran right past the fire as if it was of little concern, and flew out the front.

No paddock to fence her in out there. And no time to chase her down until he'd evacuated Grace's mare and controlled the fire.

The fire was growing. Smoke blocked the skylights, filling the barn from the ceiling down. Each breath seared Lund's throat, making him wish he'd unloaded all his gear from the truck, instead of leaving it to burn and be ransacked by idiots.

A whinny rose from Banshee's stall, high and shrill as a scream.

Lund felt his way to the mare's stall, keeping as low as he could to take advantage of the more breathable air. He found the latch, slipped it free, and glided the door open, bracing himself for the thundering rush of horseflesh.

Nothing.

Lund stepped into the stall, the shavings soft under his boots. A thousand pounds of horseflesh stood cowering against the far wall. Grace's show horse might be bomb proof, as horse people were fond of saying, but apparently fire was another matter.

"It's okay, girl." Lund entered the stall. "I'm going to get you out of here, you little scaredy horse."

The mare shifted, snorting and whinnying.

Lund touched the mare's shoulder, her skin trembling under his palm. He moved his hands firmly along her neck and up to her head.

Shit.

He'd forgotten the horses didn't wear halters inside their stalls. How in the hell was he going to get Banshee out without anything to grab?

Wait. Lund had seen Grace ride the mare without a bridle, using just her legs to cue the animal and a hold on her mane.

He wasn't going to try to climb on sans saddle and bridle, but the mane thing was worth a try.

Lund took a handful of mane in his left hand, then circled his right arm under the mare's throatlatch, and pulled her sideways.

She didn't move.

"Come on, Banshee. Work with me here."

He tried again, rocking her to the side. Once. Twice.

Off balance, the mare took a step, then another, moving away from the wall.

So far, so good.

Lund could hear the flames crackle, gaining strength. Fire doubled itself every seventeen to thirty seconds. Soon the remaining extinguishers wouldn't be enough to do the job. He had to clear the barn and knock the flame down soon, or the whole barn would be gone.

Sweat soaked the back of his neck and trickled down his back. He pulled the horse to the side again, gained another step.

"Come on, Banshee. Grace would be so disappointed if we both died. You've never disappointed her in your life, don't start now."

Another pull, another step.

They were close to the door now. Lund couldn't see the stall wall, but he could sense it. He turned toward it, peering into the gloom and flickers of light from the flame.

Banshee snorted. She lurched backward, yanking Lund off his feet, and scurried back to her spot, hugging the wall.

Shit, shit, shit.

Obviously Banshee felt safe in her stall, far safer than she did with him. How in the hell was he going to get the horse out of here? It wasn't as if he could just pick her up and throw her over his shoulder.

Wait.

Lund might not be much of a horse person, despite the efforts of Grace and Val to teach him. But he had read horse stories to kids as part of his role as fire chief of a small-town district. He remembered an illustration in Black Beauty, a drawing of the horses being saved from a barn fire, cloths tied over their eyes.

He pulled off the turnout coat, struggled out of his flannel shirt, and then put the coat back on. Shirt in hand, he felt his way back to Banshee's head. "What you don't see might hurt you, girl, but it will be better than staying here and dying."

He draped the flannel over the mare's eyes, tying the arms under her throatlatch. The mare's face covered, Lund gripped her mane again and resumed pulling her from side to side. With each shift of the horse's weight, she took a step forward, and soon Lund felt the rubber matt under his shoes change to hard concrete.

He led her to the paddock door before removing her blindfold. For a second, the mare stood there, unmoving, as if trying to decide between real safety and the perceived safety of her stall. Then Max let out a whinny, and Banshee ran out to meet him.

Horses evacuated. Now to see about that fire.

He grabbed the second extinguisher and headed back down the dark aisle. Reaching the fire, he once again attacked the base of the flame, laying another smothering coat over everything until he'd emptied the second unit as well.

Next he went for the hose in the wash stall. Turning the water on full, he soaked the bales and what remained of the shavings, taking out another element in the fire tetrahedron. Where the fire extinguisher had deprived the fire of oxygen, the water deprived it of heat.

Lund left the water running, thoroughly swamping the feed stall and running in rivers down the concrete aisle. Confident the fire was truly dead this time, he grabbed a halter and lead rope from a hook on the outside of the tack room and went off in search of Bo.

Lund had just stepped outside of the barn when he heard a noise. Not the movements of a horse. Not the voice of a human. Something else.

What the hell?

He reached for the pistol Val had given him, pulled it…

The gun didn't move.

Shit. He pressed the button on the holster and freed the weapon, swearing to never tell Val that even after her lecture, he'd forgotten. Glock in hand and pulse pounding in his ears, he tried to pick up the sound.

A soft mew.

A faint snuffling.

Someone crying?

Lund spotted him. One of the dumb ass kids sitting on the ground, back against a tree trunk, sobbing his eyes out.

"Don't move. I have a gun."

"Ohshitohshitohshit. Man. Don't kill me."

Lund sized the kid up. Ripped shirt and jeans. Puffy eyes and runny nose. He cradled his right arm, his hand and forearm a blazing red, as obvious as neon.

"You burned yourself?"

"It hurts!"

Not willing to mess around with these kids a moment longer, Lund took the rope he'd intended for Bo and trussed up the kid. Like any firefighter, Lund was an expert in tying knots, training on them constantly, in the dark, behind his back, timed to the second. When he was done, the kid was going nowhere.

"What the hell you tying me for? I look like I'm running away? I'm burned, dog!"

Lund fished a Zippo out of his pocket.

The kid cringed. "You gonna light me up?"

Ignoring his wails, Lund used the light of the flame to study his injuries. "You're a mess. Probably from setting that fire in the barn, right?"

The punk nodded.

"And the truck out front?"

Another nod.

"But it's not too bad. Only first degree. Maybe a bit of second degree."

"The pain is unreal! It has to be eighth degree! No lie! I'm starting to rethink some of the shit I done in life!"

Lund decided not to mention that second degree was as painful as burns got. By the time you crossed to third degree, there was nothing left to convey the pain to your brain. And of course, eighth degree was just silly. "This is what happens when you play with matches."

"Why didn't nobody tell me fire hurts so bad? Moms! Pops! I'm sorry!"

As a fireman, Lund had seen his share of grief. But he'd never seen anyone cry like this kid did. And his injuries weren't that bad.

A whinny sounded from somewhere near the house.

Shit, Bo was still out there. At least she was still around and hadn't beelined for the road.

Leaving the wailing kid, he went to find another rope.

VAL

What was taking Lund so long?

Shoving aside the worries bombarding her, Val scanned her wreck of a living room. With the patio door shattered, the house was far from secure. Even a gang as inept as this one could probably negotiate a little broken glass on the floor.

Come on, Lund.

"Broke," Sam repeated, sticking her finger in the stein's bullet wound.

"Deeeb," agreed Junior.

Val moved to the kitchen. Peering through the window, she tried to get a glimpse at the barn. The smoke that had been pouring out of the structure earlier was dissipating. A good sign. Lund must have been successful or the whole building would be up in flames by now. So where was he? They needed to get out of here before the firebugs decided to torch her car.

And—

Something streaked past the window. Something far too large to be a human.

Val set her rifle on the countertop and leaned forward to get a better look. It couldn't be—

Oh, no.

Val raced to the door, checked to make sure no one was lurking outside, and then pulled it open just in time to see Bo trot around to the back of the house.

Sam squealed and bolted through the door. "Horsey!"

"Sam, stop!" Val went after her and found Sam standing still on a step outside, staring at one of the gang members running toward them.

Val plucked the beer stein from Sam's hands and fired it at the teen's head.

Clang!

The kid folded to the pavement.

Val was on top of him before he could move, leveraging his right arm to pin him face down on the ground. "Don't move."

"Man this day has been the *worst.*"

Reaching into her pocket, Val found the zip ties she'd been intending to use to close garbage bags full of clothing from her closet. She connected several together and fastened the kid's wrists and ankles. When she finished, she turned back to the house, surprised to see Harry Junior balanced precariously on the porch steps.

"Harry—" She caught him just as he was about to topple forward. Plopping him on her hip, she turned back to the house and…

No Sam.

Val's whole body stuttered. Her pulse accelerated to double time. "Sam?" she yelled, racing up the steps and into the kitchen. The *empty* kitchen. "Sam? Where are you?"

"A man took her," Junior said.

"You talk?" She stared at the little boy, not entirely sure she hadn't imagined it. "Do you know which way they went?"

Junior pointed into the house and through the shattered patio door. He glanced back to her and smiled.

"Nice work, Harry."

"Poogababbaaa! Blopp!"

Val glanced back toward the open kitchen door. She was already seconds behind the kid who'd taken Sam. She'd never be able to run fast enough to catch up with someone half her age.

But she had an idea that just might work. "Come on, Harry. There's no time to lose."

HACKQUEEM

Carrying a kid wasn't easy, and Hackqueem gave his moms big props for carrying him around until he was five because he didn't have good balance. She also had a little Bears helmet for him that he wore because he kept falling and banging his head on things.

Moms was the best.

But lugging that squirming kid was tough. And she wasn't quiet, neither. Shorty kept yelling "Stranger danger!" which freaked Hackqueem out because this kid was too small to be talking in big words like that. Like some kinda Exorcist demon baby.

"Shh. Quiet."

"Stranger danger!"

"Girl, I ain't no stranger. Name is Hackqueem. Can you say Hackqueem?"

"Horsey!"

"Nah, not Horsey. Hackqueem."

That's when Hackqueem heard the galloping sound, coming up fast from behind.

And so Hackqueem ran faster.

VAL

Val squeezed Bo's sides with her calves, urging the mare to go faster. She could see Sam now, the little girl's hands flailing, her screams audible even over hoofbeats and the drumming of Val's pulse.

"Stranger danger! Stranger danger!"

Val had run into Lund near the barn. After trading Harry Jr. for the rope and halter Lund was carrying, she'd whistled for her mare, slung herself up on Bo's back, and was off. She'd caught up to the punk in seconds.

The kid was slowing down, probably getting tired, and Val recognized his shirt. It was the one who had shot at her, shattered her glass door, scarred Lund's pewter stein collection, and almost killed Val in her own living room.

Val wasn't in a charitable mood.

Coming close, she shifted her weight back and pulled up a little on the lead rope. Riding bareback with only a halter and lead wasn't easy, but it had been quick. Just halter, mount, and go. This part would be trickier.

Val switched the rope to her left hand and took a firm hold on Bo's mane, legging the horse over until she was coming up directly in line behind the punk.

Slow down , Bo. Steady.

"Stop immediately!" Val yelled.

The kid swung toward her, his shoulders moving to the side, still running. His eyes rounded and he let out a strangled shout.

"Sam!"

Already pulling away from the kid's shoulder, Sam looked straight at Val and reached for her with both hands.

Val's right arm threaded the space between Sam and her captor, pulling her up onto—

For a moment the boy didn't let go. Bo kept moving, and Val felt herself shifting off balance, slipping to the side… teetering… teetering…

"Stranger danger!" Sam screamed, right into the kid's ear.

He released Sam. A stride later, Bo's hip plowed into him. He flew about a meter, hit the ground, and rolled. But instead of popping to his feet, as so often happened in the movies, he lay still.

Regaining her balance on Bo's back, Val positioned Sam astride in front of her. "Hold on to the horsey's mane, Sam. Okay?"

The little girl did as she was told, smiling as she did.

Val circled the mare, heading back to the teen on the ground, and that's when she spotted a second punk racing toward them. "Hold on tight, Sam."

"Giddyup!"

"Giddyup? Where did you learn that?"

"Giddyup! Giddyup! Giddyup!" Sam sang. "Little horsey saw it all!"

Sounded like an Internet meme. Val decided she didn't want to know.

She squeezed Bo, and the mare set off in a rocking canter, straight at the second kid.

He dodged to the side.

Bo dodged with him.

He tried to double back.

Val cued the mare to circle him.

"Giddyup!" Sam said and cackled with glee.

Another fake from the kid, picked up perfectly by the mare, barely a touch from Val this time. Bo was obviously enjoying this, her quarter horse genes expressing themselves. Maybe Val would have to take up cutting cattle in the future. But first…

"Down on the ground!" Val shouted. "Down on the ground now!"

The teen dropped to his belly and assumed the position; hands clapped to the back of his head, ankles crossed.

Someone who obviously knew the drill. Sad, but no surprise.

LUND

"Val."

Lund ran to catch up, Harry bouncing on his hip. When Val jumped on Bo and took off, he thought she was nuts. Even now, every cell in his body was shaking. "I've seen you do some crazy things, but that was insane."

"It got the job done."

Val tossed him some zip ties from her pocket. Setting Harry a safe distance away, Lund secured both teens.

Val stopped her mare in front of one of the gangbangers. "How many of you are there?"

The kid stared up at the horse, a look of terror on his face. "Four."

"Just four?"

"I swear."

Two here, one next to the house, and one in front of the barn. "All accounted for," he said to Val.

"And why are you here?"

He spit out the whole story. They'd been sent to kidnap one of the kids. They didn't know which one. They decided to take both, but somehow everything around them seemed to burst into flame.

Lund had the feeling he knew who was responsible for the last bit.

"There's a kid back by the barn, name is Jet Row. He's burned. Really bad," Lund lied. "He's in a lot of pain. Might even die. I'd love to call for some help, but I have no cell signal."

"Cell jammer," muttered the kid who Val had run down on the horse. He was still groggy but awake. And looked embarrassed as hell.

"What's that?" Lund asked.

"Cell jammer. I dropped it that way," he pointed.

Turning on the outdoor spotlight, Lund found the device while Val returned Bo to the barn. Then Val called the police station, reported the punks, and asked if officers could come and pick them up.

"Tell them to throw in some diapers and wipes," Lund said, giving Harry Jr. a wink. The little boy winked back, then toddled toward Lund, his dish towel diaper sagging.

Lund glanced back at Val. "Better go for the value packs."

Val finally gave up trying to reach Jack on her tenth try. No doubt, the cell coverage up north was to blame. Just as well. As soon as either Jack or Harry could get a signal, Val was certain they'd call. Especially once they heard all the voicemail messages she'd left.

The night was reasonably warm, so Val elected to leave the horses out. Tomorrow, she and Lund could clean up the mess in the barn and get things back to normal. Tonight, they had the house to worry about.

The temperature might not be cold for the horses, but humans were a different story. A Wisconsin night in November with no sliding glass door was an ugly thing, but dozens of moving boxes and a roll of duct tape improved the coziness factor quite a lot.

After a dinner of Chef Boyardee that Junior discovered in the bottom of his diaper bag, Val and Lund sat the kids in front of the television with a G-rated DVD while they turned their attention to the destroyed curio cabinet.

"What a mess." Lund picked up one of the pewter beer steins and examined the damage.

"Broke," Sam said, turning away from the television, her voice steeped in sadness.

"Brrurpftkk," Harry Jr. added in a matching tone.

"Yeah, it sure did." Lund let out a heavy sigh, walked into the kitchen, and dumped it in the kitchen wastebasket.

Val couldn't believe what she was seeing. "What are you doing?"

"Cleaning up."

"But that… that beer stein. It's part of your collection."

"Yeah."

"I thought it was important to you."

"It was." A slow smile crept over his lips, his eyes looking off over Val's shoulder, as if he was watching a scene playing out miles away. "Backpacking through Germany. Summer before I graduated from college. I had hardly any money, you know? Just a rail pass, a map, and a list of cheap youth hostels. Probably the only time in my life I felt totally free."

Val could understand why he'd want a souvenir of that time. It sounded wonderful. Strong. Independent. Like a distant dream. "So why are you tossing it?"

"For one, it's got a bullet hole in it. For two, I might be clueless most of the time, but even I can tell you don't like the steins."

"But I would never ask you to give them up."

"I know. But that doesn't mean you should have to put up with them. And I'm sorry I asked you to give up your closet, Val."

Val's face flushed hot. She had been acting so petty, so self-centered and selfish. It embarrassed her to think Lund had seen her like that.

Maybe that was the problem.

She wasn't reacting to the annoying things Lund did. She was afraid he'd find her annoying, too. Or worse.

Living apart gave Val space to stuff her closet with silver boots and horrible 80's jeans and culottes that reeked of smoke. To leave her dishes in the sink or eat a quart of ice cream for dinner just because she was feeling fat anyway. To be at her worst without worrying that Lund would see, that he would judge her and recognize she came up short.

"How can you stand me?" Val could feel the kids staring up at her, eyes wide, and she felt like crying.

"Val?" Lund's voice was soft.

"Moving in together, I thought it would be great. I wanted to do it. Really…"

"But?"

"But I'm afraid I'm going to disappoint you."

Lund's eyes went wide. A chuckle escaped from his lips. "Disappoint *me*? You're kidding, right?"

"Don't make fun of me."

"I'm not making fun. You? Disappoint me? The other way around, I could see, but you could never disappoint me."

Val didn't believe that. Not for a second. She shook her head.

"Try me. What's the worst I could see?"

Val braced herself. If they were going to have this conversation, she might as well be as honest as she could manage. He'd see her in all her imperfect glory soon enough. And if he couldn't take it, she'd rather know now. "I squeeze the toothpaste tube from the center."

"But don't you waste a lot of—" He shook his head and took a deep breath. "Never mind. We'll just buy more. Not a problem."

"Sometimes I wear granny panties."

Sam exploded in giggles. "Granny panties! Granny panties!"

"Blab!"

"Okay, I don't like granny panties," Lund said. He lowered one lid in a wink. "So if you do that, I guess I'll just have to take them off."

Val couldn't hide her smile. "Sometimes I want to clear out all the old stuff in this house, my mother's grandfather clock, the china cups, this stupid old princess phone... just throw it all in the trash. And then the next moment, I'm sure I can't live without it."

Instead of saying anything, Lund just took her in his arms. They stood like that for a long time, then Val felt little arms encircle her legs, one set then another.

"It's just stuff, Val," he finally said.

"I know."

"And yet, it's something that connects us to the past. To people we loved."

Val nodded. "And to memories of who we were."

"Yes. But the memories aren't really attached to stuff. They're all up here." He tapped his temple. "And now that we're living together, we have the chance to make a whole bunch more."

"Keep the steins, Lund. Really."

"You, too. Keep all of it, as long as you want."

"Even the granny panties?"

Lund kissed her. "When it comes to those, we'll negotiate."

They picked up the steins, Lund electing to put them in a box in the basement instead of the trash. But before Lund closed the flaps and taped them shut, Val fished out the one featuring Neuschwanstein.

Lund raised a brow. "You want to display it?"

"I want to remember."

"To remember almost getting shot?"

"To remember the day you gave up your steins for me."

"Are you sure you want me to put them in the basement? They did save your life…"

"Compromise, Lund. You hide away your pewter fetish, I give up half my closet."

"Really?"

"Really. There's enough room. I was just…"

"Making sure?"

"You'd think I'd be sure by now."

"It doesn't matter. I love you, Val, and I plan to make my case for why we should be together every day for the rest of our lives."

"Did you get that gooey sentiment from Cosmo?"

He winked. "That gooey sentiment is 100% Marlboro Man."

The movie ended and they put the kids to bed in Grace's room. Standing at the doorway, watching the two kids sleep, Val finally felt at peace.

When Val's sister had died and twelve-year-old Grace had come to live with Val, Val's life had changed drastically. And yet she never felt as if she'd given up anything, at least not anything that mattered. Standing here with Lund, she was beginning to feel the same way. Maybe that was normal. Maybe that was the way love worked.

Lund set Dickhead the Bear in the space between the bed where Sam slept and the box they'd fashioned into a makeshift crib for Harry.

Val gave him a smile. "If they were always like this, I'd consider adopting."

"Would you?"

The eagerness on his face made her take a step back. "Uh, maybe we should get used to living together first."

"And setting a wedding date? Soon?" Lund wiggled his brows.

Maybe, Val thought. Maybe. But instead of answering, she just smiled. That was a subject for another day.

JET ROW

It was inhumane treatment. Someone needed to call one of those activist groups that protected human rights. Amity International, or the ASCPALU. The hospital had lied to Jet Row and told him his burns were only minor, when he was sure he needed skin grafts on 90% of his body. Plus, he got no sympathy at all for being shot. Just one more gangbanger getting plugged. Treating him like a statistic rather than a human being. All they did was slap some cream and gauze on him, then send him to jail.

That was some Guantanamo shit right there.

And the amenities in the Lake Loyal holding cell were downright terrible. The cop in charge, Officer Ginny Jones, was some kind of sadist. Jet Row and his crew pleaded to be fed because they hadn't eaten since that continental breakfast the day before, and all she gave them was a box of powdered donuts.

Powdered! She had to know that no one liked the powdered ones. And she was a sister, too. Just another Uncle Tom working for the Man, sucking up to whitey.

"Cop bitch is just another Uncle Tom working for the Man, sucking up to whitey," Jet Row said, taking a bite of his third donut.

"First of all," Hackqueem said, "look in the damn mirror. You're white. You're so white, you look like someone spilled bleach on Casper."

"That's racist," Jet Row said.

"Second, you talk about how much you hate racism, and then you call her a bitch. Sexism is just as bad."

"I'm not saying I wouldn't have sex with her. She's fine. I'm saying the bitch is a bitch because of these punk ass donuts. Don't they have chocolate in Wisconsin?"

Hackqueem rubbed his face, obviously embarrassed because he couldn't respond to Jet Row dropping the hard truths.

"How long you think we're going to jail for?" Bön Dawg asked.

"Depends on what the district attorney charges us with," Sha Nay Nay said. "B&E, assault with intent, kidnapping…" he threw a pointed look at Jet Row. "Arson."

"That's BS. I'm the one who got burned. I'm the victim here."

Sha Nay Nay sighed. "It's actually a good thing we got pinched. If we went back to Del Ray empty handed, we'd be dead. At least now we got a good excuse. We do a little easy time, come out heroes. I been inside. It ain't too bad."

"You got arrested for playin' your music too loud in public," Hackqueem said. "You were in jail for ten minutes before your moms bailed your cryin' ass out."

"I seen things," Sha Nay Nay said, his gaze far away. "Terrible things."

Bön Dawg shook his head "Wisconsin prison can't be that hardcore. The crackers up here, they don't shoot people, they season 'em. Right Jet Row?"

Jet Row remembered what that seasoning shit felt like. It was bad. Not as bad as burning. But rough just the same.

"What you think, Jet Row?" Sha Nay Nay said. "You scared of Wisconsin prisons?"

"Naw. It's Wisconsin, man. It ain't Stateville. Ain't no really bad dudes in Wisconsin."

"You gentlemen know about Jeffery Dahmer?" It was Officer Jones, the good-looking cop bitch who gave them the shitty donuts.

"Who's that?" Jet Row asked.

"Dahmer killed seventeen young men. He injected them in their brains with boiling water to make them sex slaves. When they died, he cooked them and ate them."

"For real?" Hackqueem asked.

She nodded. "For real."

"But he was a white dude, right?" asked Sha Nay Nay. "Didn't pay people of color no mind."

"Jeffrey Dahmer was an equal opportunity serial killer. He murdered white boys, black boys, and Hispanic boys," Officer Jones said, looking at each kid in turn. "You fellas think Wisconsin jail time is gonna be like a vacation in the Dells, think again."

The gang all exchanged alarmed looks.

"What the hell?" Jet Row moaned. "It's like we're being punished for doin' bad things!"

And so it began,

OCTOBER DARK
(WITH JOSHUA SIMCOX)

Phineas Troutt is one of my favorite characters. When Joshua approached me with a Phin story, I jumped at the chance. It's lean, mean, and a perfect remedy for all of those 'feel good' mysteries saturating the market. Proceed with caution...

In a filthy, hot alley cloaked in October dark, the man with two broken hands writhed on the ground in front of Phineas Troutt, biting his tongue in a useless attempt to dampen the pain.

Phin held the claw-hammer perpendicular to his leg and paused for a few beats. He would use it again if he needed to, but that possibility seemed remote.

"His name is Mackie. Macklin Dailey," the man said after pulling his tongue from the grip of his teeth. "He's in North Carolina somewhere. The mountains, I think."

At least a ten hour drive from this Tampa shithole, maybe farther.

That wasn't a problem. Phin had flown here from Chicago, and he didn't mind adding a little road trip to his itinerary. He had the time.

Phin checked the mouth of the alley for passerby, but no one was out at four in the morning. He flicked on his tactical flashlight and pointed the beam at his unhappy informant.

"What's Mackie doing up there?"

The asshole on the ground took a few seconds to catch his breath. "He's got a girl up there. She's in college in some small town. I don't think they're together now, but he goes up there, checks up on her when Krider gives him some free time."

Phin ran the beam over the man's hands, which had turned the color of eggplant.

"You're telling me the truth?"

"That's what I hear! I swear! I don't talk to Mackie myself."

"So he, what, stalks this girl?" The beads of sweat that had pooled on Phin's naked scalp ran down his face in rivulets.

It was autumn and hours before sunrise, but shit, the Florida heat was miserable.

"I don't think it's like that," the man said. "Mackie's not like that."

Phin raised an eyebrow. *So you're telling me he's harmless?* This kid performed hits for a Dixie Mafia lieutenant legendary for his sadism. You can't put a guy like that in the same zip code as *harmless.*

Eggplant Hands noticed Phin's look of surprise and picked up on the unasked question. "No, no, I mean… I mean, yeah, he works for Krider, but not by choice. He does what Krider wants, but he doesn't have a taste for it."

A reluctant hit man? There was a story there, but Phin wasn't interested.

"I need an address."

The guy on the ground didn't have one to offer, but that changed after making a quick cell phone call. Phin had to dial for him. He did a competent job of disguising the agony from his shattered hands while speaking to the person on the other end.

Phin jotted down the address on his palm. Evans-Lawson, a small liberal arts college in western North Carolina.

Mackie obviously had skills, but if he was hanging around campus waiting to catch glimpses of his girl, he wouldn't be hard to find.

Phin tossed the hammer into a nearby Dumpster and pulled a handful of hydrocodone tablets from his jeans pocket. He dropped them onto the man's legs.

"These'll help. Ask your boss for something stronger when you see him. But I'd prefer if you wouldn't tell him I was here."

The man nodded weakly, and Phin stepped out into the blanket-thick humidity, pulling the keys to his rental car from one pocket and his cell phone from the other. Once back in the car, he tucked his suppressed Sig-Saur—an expensive throw-away piece he'd bought an hour earlier from a shady contact of one equally shady PI named Harrison Harold McGlade—in between the seats. Then he started up and hit the road.

Phin dialed a number and waited for the voicemail to pick up, but wasn't surprised when a person did.

"It's late," was how Lt. Jacqueline Daniels answered. "You in trouble?"

"Working." Phin heard a TV on in the background. "You?"

"Can't sleep. I just spent three hundred dollars on a pair of Ferragamo heels that are half a size too small."

"Why'd you buy them small?"

"The Home Shopping Network ran out of my size. What do you need, Phin?"

"I could use all you can find on a Macklin Dailey from Tampa, Florida. And send me a photo, too."

"I'll add this to the list of things you owe me. Morning okay?"

"That's fine. Text to my cell phone."

"Do I want to know what this is about?"

"It's better if you don't. Thanks."

"If a cop can't help out a criminal every now and then," Jack said, "where's the fun in life?"

MACKIE

Allie chatted robotically with her friends inside the student union, fresh from the end of Professor Tannen's 4:30 class, seemingly distracted. Her classmates probably wouldn't pick up on that, but Mackie could read her in a way few others could.

He kept a safe distance at a table near the front entrance, his windbreaker's hood up and the brim of his baseball cap pulled low. The student union was—fortunately, at this time in the evening—too crowded for any one person to stand out. And he was close enough to the entrance to make a hasty retreat if he needed to.

Mackie knew he wasn't exercising a professional level of caution (the hooded windbreaker and baseball cap were hardly effective disguises), but he wasn't too concerned about Allie spotting him. The crowds of students sipping coffee and smoothies and eating deli sandwiches from the snack bar served as effective camouflage.

Allie kept her head low while talking, barely took even a moment to observe her surroundings. Her posture was poor, and she didn't seem to be paying attention to the conversation.

It was victim behavior. Behavior that blinded people to dangers around them.

Behavior that made her a perfect target for what was coming.

A representative from the local police department had discussed that very thing during a safety assembly held earlier that week. If any of it stuck with Allie, she showed no signs.

In contrast, Mackie was hyper-aware of everything going on around him. The people in front of him. Behind him. On either side. The cars pulling into the parking lot, outside the east windows. The sun casting shadows through the west windows. Conversation babble and traffic noise and someone in the union wearing headphones and playing Nirvana loud enough to cause hearing loss.

Mackie was particularly paranoid that someone would recognize him from his time here as a student. If that happened, word could get back to Allie.

Would she get the cops involved if she knew he was on campus?

If he was found and taken in, Mackie might seem just suspicious enough to warrant some questioning about the disappearances in the community.

If the cops took him in, it would get back to Krider.

And Krider would assume the worst.

Mackie saw the bald guy in his peripheral vision, watched how he was doing his best to blend in just like Mackie was. He was good at it, seeming like he was waiting for someone, not ever staring directly at Mackie.

But Mackie knew he was the bald man's target. A fact that was confirmed when they locked eyes, and the bald guy dropped pretense and walked over, pulling out the chair at the other end of the table and sitting down, facing Mackie.

He wore a simple green t-shirt beneath a denim jacket and his eyes had the hollow, sunken look of a cancer patient or a drug addict. Possibly both.

He pulled three white tablets from his jacket pocket and fed them from his palm into his mouth. He chewed, and then washed down the gritty mixture with a sip from a cup of coffee.

Mackie felt his mouth go dry and his pulse accelerate. Whoever this guy was, maybe he was willing to share.

Or sell.

"So, which one is she?" the man asked.

Mackie kept his eyes locked with the stranger's. "I know you?"

"We know some of the same people."

The stranger aimed his gaze into the crowd of students where Mackie had been looking earlier. This man obviously didn't know Allie, but he knew *of* Allie.

"What do you want?"

The man took another sip of coffee. "I hear you got a girl up here that you keep tabs on. Since you're sitting here, I'm betting she's somewhere in this room." He locked eyes with Mackie again. "Does she even know you're here?"

Mackie felt sure the man wasn't a cop. A private investigator, maybe? He was here to, what, pinch Mackie for stalking? Try to scare him off?

Allie had nothing to do with this, but maybe her parents did.

"Look, asshole—" Mackie kept his voice low but his hand instinctively flew to the Glock tucked in his waistband and hidden by the length of his windbreaker.

He had planned on using only one bullet this evening. A firefight with a P.I. or whatever the hell Mr. Clean billed himself as… that wasn't something he was prepared for.

The stranger held up a palm. "This has nothing to do with her. And whatever you're reaching for, don't bother."

Mackie understood. His gaze moved from the stranger's face to the hand he held beneath the table. The hand that, a moment ago, had held a Styrofoam coffee cup.

Mackie couldn't see from this angle, but he was sure that hand now held a pistol.

"I'm here for the same reason that you've shown up somewhere unannounced many times yourself," the man said. "I'm here because somebody paid me to be."

So that was it. He wasn't a private eye. This guy was a hitter, same as Mackie.

Did he have any idea who he was dealing with? Krider would never let something like this stand.

Unless Krider ordered the hit himself.

This guy wasn't anyone Mackie knew, but Krider occasionally brought in outside talent.

And he wouldn't stop with Mackie. That was Krider's way.

Allie…

"Why me?" Mackie asked.

"Your boss asked you to fly to Chicago a few months back, put a beating on some punk college kid that wasn't honoring his financial agreement with the almighty Lucas Krider."

The name of the college kid escaped him, but Mackie remembered the face. Some scared student from Tampa that took a loan from Krider he couldn't repay. He moved to Chicago to attend college and stay with family in the city.

He thought the distance might keep him safe. Or at least buy him a little time.

Krider had ordered entire families executed for less. Many times. Inexplicably, he was content to let the kid off—for the time being—with some broken bones, and leave his family untouched.

Mackie never knew the reason why, but occasionally Krider showed younger marks a little mercy.

He had done the same for Mackie once.

It was one of Mackie's easier jobs, and one he felt less guilt over.

But he had a feeling he knew what the stranger's next words would be.

"The beating was a little too effective, Mackie. He died from a brain hemorrhage a few days later. Naturally, his parents weren't thrilled."

Shit.

Mackie closed his eyes. He had killed a number of people on Krider's orders. Afterward, even with all the Vicodin he routinely ingested, he never felt sufficiently numb.

Most of his marks were junkies or associates that were stupid enough to get caught and were a little too close to having conversations about Krider's operations with law enforcement. Conversations that would've been inconvenient for Lucas Krider. Occasionally, the job called for Mackie to pay visits to broke idiots foolish enough to accept loans they couldn't hope to repay. But those jobs weren't as common.

Bottom line being that these people usually weren't among society's great contributors. Sometimes, that helped Mackie's guilt.

He spent most of his days wishing he could walk away, fade like vapor. From Krider's employ. From his own existence.

But he knew what either option would bring.

A college kid was something new for Mackie, and he had been relieved that the assignment wasn't a kill order.

"I don't understand… I went easy…"

Mackie remembered pulling his punches, aiming for areas that would cause pain but not necessarily damage. He'd offered some comforting words between hits and even tossed the kid a few Vicodin after it was over.

"Yeah, well," the stranger said. "If that's your idea of going 'easy' on a mark, Krider's getting his money's worth from your services."

Krider never tolerated any form of failure from his associates. Failure was the same as a freshly dug grave for you and any members of your family Krider's men could track down. Mackie's job had been to bruise and batter, not murder. It was overkill, maybe, and certainly unintentional, but would it qualify as failure to Krider? The man did have a tendency to be less than pleased if his orders weren't followed to the letter.

Mackie knew if he was careful he might have a small chance of evading this asshole, maybe even take him out before he had a chance to do the same to Mackie. But if Krider was behind this, it wouldn't stop with one hitter. If Mackie escaped, Krider's men would never stop looking for him.

And his parents, his sister, even Allie, were all as good as dead.

"Krider sent you?"

Mackie felt sand in his throat as he voiced the question. The answer would determine his next move.

The bald man laughed. "I'm a piece of shit, but even I wouldn't take money from Lucas Krider. No, the kid's parents wanted to find the guy responsible for their little scholar's untimely passing and have him dealt with without the benefit of law enforcement. I've been known to do that sort of thing from time to time for a paycheck. The kid's family in Chicago got wind of me and what I do, they sent word back to the parents in

Florida, and well…" He grinned and turned his open palm upward in a *Here-I-am-and-ain't-that-just-your-shitty-luck* gesture.

So Krider wasn't involved. That changed things.

Keep him talking. Wait for an opportunity.

The hitter wouldn't open fire in the middle of a crowded student union. If anything, approaching Mackie here seemed like a careless move.

"I may have put a beating on that kid, but I did it on Lucas Krider's orders," Mackie said. "Why not go after him instead of me?"

The man nodded and took another sip of coffee with his free hand. "Normally, I'd agree with that logic. But first of all, getting to Krider would be extremely difficult, and more money than the kid's parents could afford. And second, Krider didn't order you to kill that kid. That was *your* screw-up. You were given a job, you did it poorly, and for the purposes of this assignment, I'm choosing to hold *you* responsible for what came after."

"But none of this makes any sense. If the kid's parents had the money to hire you, I'm sure they could've paid off his debt to Krider before any of this had to happen."

The man shrugged. "File it under: Shitty Things that Happened but Didn't Have to Happen. Who knows what the kid was thinking? He was scared and young and obviously lacking in smarts and maybe he wanted that money for something he didn't want his parents to know about. But it doesn't matter now and it doesn't change what has to happen here."

The bastard was confident. He spoke as if finishing this job was a foregone conclusion. In the world of murder for hire, hitters with that level of confidence usually had the skills to back it up.

"So how did you track me down?"

"It didn't take any substantial detective work. Everything about the assault screamed organized crime. What little the kid said afterward before he died made it obvious he was hiding something. And since he's from Tampa, it wasn't a stretch to assume Krider might be involved. His name has a long reach. Once I landed in Tampa, it wasn't hard to track down one of his low-level asshats. He told me what I needed to know."

Mackie said nothing. Bald Guy had another sip of coffee.

"And honestly, you didn't make it that difficult for me. Hanging around here stalking your girl like this, it made you pretty easy to find. What's the story with that anyway? She an ex of yours?"

Again, Mackie said nothing.

Bald Guy studied him for a moment. "You don't seem like the type that would work for a man like Lucas Krider by choice. That poor bastard in Tampa told me as much. Let me take a guess: you do something stupid that puts you in over your head with Krider, and he gives you the option of either allowing yourself to be recruited or he executes you and your entire family. Your girl finds out about the people you're working for and wants nothing else to do with you. Close?"

There was more to it than that. But yeah, the guy was close.

"Something like that."

"You wanna tell me about it?"

In Mackie's experience, marks sometimes wanted to open up about things before the hit. It was easy to think of your hitter as almost like a priest performing last rites. It was probably the same for Bald Guy.

"Not particularly."

The man nodded and his gaze found the table where Allie was seated with her friends. "I saw you stealing a lot of glances at that table over there before I sat down. Your girl's sitting over there, isn't she?"

No point in denying it, but Mackie didn't want to say anything that might give Bald Guy a clue as to which girl Allie was. Again, he said nothing.

"Ok, then," Bald Guy said. "I told you this has nothing to do with your girl, and it doesn't. And she doesn't have to get involved if you're willing to quietly get up and take a walk out to my car with me. We'll take a ride, find a quiet place to get this done, and it won't hurt. You've got my word on that."

Mackie hung his head, gave it a slight, weary shake, and finally looked up again, his eyes meeting Bald Guy's.

"It's not that simple," Mackie said. "I'm here because I have to stop something bad from happening. To her." He nodded toward the table where Allie sat.

"And what would that be?"

Mackie sighed, closed his eyes. "Girls have been disappearing here lately. Two since early September."

Bald Guy shook his head. He didn't know. It's not as if he stopped to pick up a newspaper when he came into town to perform a hit.

"I'm pretty sure I know who's behind it. And I think he's going after Allie next. Tonight."

Bald Guy let out a sigh of his own. *The shit marks would come up with to buy time…*

"And how could you possibly know that?"

Mackie nodded at Bald Guy's denim jacket. "Those pills I saw you take, you have any more of those?"

The man across the table lifted an eyebrow. "You have some aches and pains?"

"Nope."

The man smiled. "Damn. A hitman with a heart of gold and a taste for narcotics. I'm starting to feel bad about taking this job. You seem like a kindred spirit." He reached into his jacket pocket, pulled out three hydrocodone tablets and passed them across the table to Mackie. "This isn't the first time I've shared my stash with a mark. It makes what comes next a little easier to take."

Mackie couldn't hide the gratitude on his face as he popped the tablets into his mouth and chewed. He picked up Bald Guy's coffee cup and poured enough of the lukewarm liquid into his mouth to swallow the powdered remains of the crushed pills. Bald Guy didn't object.

"Thanks. What's your name?"

"Phineas Troutt."

Mackie snorted. "Bullshit."

"People call me Phin."

"Okay, Phin. I'm going to be above the board with you."

Mackie leaned his head back and closed his eyes. Waited for the numbing warmth of the hydrocodone to wash through his system.

"I was still in Florida when I heard about the disappearences," he continued, "I used Krider's resources to do a little digging. Since the victims were both students, I started right here on campus, beginning with faculty. New faculty in particular. I was a student here not long ago, and most of my old professors still teach here. Most of them I knew couldn't be capable of this."

Phin waited.

"There's a new English professor here, a Morris Tannen. He came here from another small liberal arts college in Iowa. Turns out three female students disappeared during his stint there. Their remains were found in a shallow grave a forty-five minute drive from campus. Somehow, Tannen avoided suspicion."

"Covered his tracks."

"I dig into his background a little further, and I see that the same thing happened while he was a grad student in Vermont. Again, no evidence, no connection to the victims, no reason to suspect Tannen. This guy has a sickness that he tries to control, but he can only hold it off for so long. He moves from place to place because he wants to start fresh, but his urges always catch up with him. He won't stop with those first two girls, and I think Allie's next."

Phin held up a hand. "If what you say is true, then sure, Tannen is your perp. But that last part you told me about how he tries to control his impulses, how can you know that? How can you be sure he's targeted your girl specifically?"

"I had one of Krider's tech guys give me access to Tannen's computer by sending him an email with a virus attached. I read his emails. He's been corresponding with a Rev. Douglas Harrell, and he all but confessed to the two disappearances in September. He also made references to the previous murders in Iowa and Vermont. And he also talked about one of his students, a girl matching Allie's description and personality. She's an English major, so of course she'd have classes with this guy. Seems they've gotten close and he told the Rev about his feelings for her, and how he was convinced his sickness would take over again."

Phin nodded. "So, he uses this Reverend for the benefit of a little free therapy. He confesses his sins, unburdens himself. But you have nothing to go to the cops with because those emails were illegally obtained and his conversations with a minister probably wouldn't stick as admissible evidence in court anyway."

"Exactly. And he was careful about how he worded things. But anyone familiar with these disappearances and deaths would know what he was referring to."

"But you said you're sure he's going after your girl *tonight*."

Mackie nodded. "His last email exchange with the Rev was last night. He spouted off some bullshit about how the 'dark' was consuming him again, all these clichéd metaphors. He didn't refer to Allie by name, but I know she's the one he told Harell about. He made a lot of cryptic references to something that would happen tonight. The Rev begged him to sit tight, get help, not take any action that would bring harm to someone else. But I think Tannen's at his breaking point."

Phin leaned back, rubbed his face with his free hand. "So that's why you're here now. What, did you think you could keep eyes on her all night long?"

"Only when she isn't in her dorm. But she's not exactly a night owl. She's usually in bed by ten, ten-thirty. I figure if I can make sure she makes it back safely to her dorm tonight, I can think of the best way to deal with Tannen tomorrow. Lean on him, get a confession out of him, whatever. And if he makes a move tonight, I'll be here to keep Allie safe, and the cops will have all they need. I won't kill this piece of shit if I don't have to. I want him to rot in a cell for what he's done, experience a little of the classic sodomy prisons are so famous for."

"You think Tannen would try to take her by force? On a small campus like this, with her friends and campus security close by?"

"No. They know each other. They have a relationship. He'll find a way to lure her to his car and they'll drive somewhere, maybe to the place he rents just outside of town. She doesn't know she has a reason to be afraid of him. She'd never consider the possibility."

"What does any of this have to do with our situation?"

Mackie continued. "You can do what you need to do, Phin. But I need to make sure she's safe first."

Phin said nothing for a moment. And then: "I'm here to do a job, Macklin. I took a lot of money from that kid's parents. Even if this isn't some bullshit you made up to buy yourself some time, I can't exactly give you a free pass just so you can protect your girl from a psycho."

Mackie closed his eyes again, wished he could will the hydrocodone to rush through his bloodstream, bring on the soothing effects faster. He opened his eyes and glanced over at the table where Allie sat. Two of her friends had left, so she sat with only one other girl; a thick, curvy red-head in black sweats.

"I need time to catch Tannen when he makes his move and take him down before he hurts Allie. I have nothing to go to the cops with."

"Why not just make an anonymous call to the police, at least cast enough suspicion on Tannen to screw up whatever plans he has for to-night. They could keep an eye on Allie."

"But there's no guarantee that the cops would find anything that'll stick. A phone call might, *might* keep Allie safe for the time being. But if the cops close in, Tannen might get desperate. And I think he's too fix-ated on Allie to let her go."

Phin said nothing for a few beats. When he spoke again, he said, "I can't just take your word for this, Mackie. I can't put this job on hold based on this story you've told me. But I'll do this: you come take a ride with me, let me make this quick, and I'll come back here when we're done and make sure Allie's safe. I'll put a bullet in Tannen or anyone else that tries to make a move on your girl tonight, and tomorrow I'll make an anonymous call to the cops and tell them what you told me."

"Not good enough."

"Well, kid, it kind of has to be."

Mackie looked over at Allie's table again. She had a small chunk of sandwich left uneaten on her plate and was sucking down with a straw what looked to be a small puddle of smoothie from the bottom of a plas-tic cup. She would probably leave soon, head back to her dorm or maybe the library.

It would give Tannen an opportunity to put his plan in action, if he had one.

"What are you gonna do, Phin? You're not gonna shoot me right here in the student union."

"I've got a suppressor on my pistol. It's noisy in here. I cough and shoot at the same time, and you fall over. Then I get up and leave."

"There are security cameras."

"And I don't care. Getting arrested isn't among my primary concerns."

"So why haven't you done it already?"

"Because it would be easier, and cleaner, to do this elsewhere. But if you don't give me any choice, I can end you here, in front of your girl-friend. And I promise you that if you try something, I'll do her as well. This guy Tannen, if he exists, might be a sick piece of shit, but what makes you think I'm *that* much better? I've killed lots of people. I'm good at it. And unlike you, I'm not reluctant about it."

"You're bluffing."

"Bluffing is for people who have something to gain, or something to lose. I have neither."

If Mackie played along and followed Phin out of the union, he could possibly incapacitate him, or escape. It was a slim chance, but it beat being shot there in the student union.

Mackie sighed. "If I go along with this, you promise you'll come back later and make sure she's safe?"

"I can't stick around and play bodyguard, but she'll be safe tonight, and I'll make a call to the authorities and tell them about Tannen. You've got my word on it."

"And if you can't find her when you get back, what then? What if Tannen takes her while you're dealing with me?"

Phin shrugged. "There's only so much I can control here. It's a chance you'll have to take. No disrespect to Allie, but this job comes be-fore your girl. And if you don't make this easy for me, Tannen won't be the only person she needs to worry about."

Mackie took one last look at Allie's table. She was tapping away on her smart phone while the redhead guffawed and munched from a bag of Frito's.

"Let's get this done."

"Sure, kid." He slid a newspaper over to Mackie. "If you wouldn't mind, place your gun in there, slowly, butt first. If you move any faster than a turtle on Valium, I'll gut shoot you so you'll live just long enough to see me kill your girlfriend."

Mackie felt his heart harden. "You're really going to be that cold about this?"

"It's a cold world, Mackie. People die every day. And today it's your turn. If you care about Allie, you'll follow my orders."

Mackie did as he was told, and then Phin made him stand up and march out of the union. Mackie gave Allie one last, sidelong glance, and then they left the building.

Mackie's hope was that Phin would take them to a car. The easiest way to control a target before dispatch and disposal was putting them into a trunk. Phin probably had a rental, so he wouldn't have cut the trunk release cable, or reinforced the latch, back seat, or brake lights, as Mackie had done with his car. If Phin put him in a trunk, Mackie would be able to get out.

Assuming he went into the trunk alive.

They followed a paved walkway from the student union to a co-ed residence hall where Mackie had spent a couple of his semesters during his student days, and took a right that led them to the highway that ran parallel to the Evans-Lawson campus. The visitor's lot was across the street, deserted except for three vehicles, one of them Mackie's, and dimly lit by softly burning sodium vapor lights.

Phin followed Mackie at a close distance to his right, his gun pointed discreetly and mostly obscured by his denim jacket. He also had Mackie's Glock tucked in the waist of his jeans.

The October air was clean and bracing with its distinctive autumnal bite. The atmosphere was colored with the scent of smoke from wood fires burning in homes near campus. Mackie had always loved the fall season on the Evans-Lawson campus. You just didn't get the same kind of autumn in Tampa, Florida.

The walk from the student union to the visitor's parking lot would take no more than 5-7 minutes. Evans-Lawson was such a small campus, traversing in any direction from Point A to Point B was never a long walk. That was part of the Evans-Lawson charm.

"So, you're not worried at all about blowback from Krider over this?" Mackie asked. "You don't think he'll be displeased that someone took out one of his hitters?"

"If he wants to come to Chicago and have a conversation with me about it, he's welcome to," Phin said. "The way I see it, considering how sloppy your work obviously is, he probably won't miss you all that much. I'm just doing what one of his men would have eventually done anyway."

"You're hurting my feelings."

"You're a big boy. Get over it."

In the visitor's lot, Phin directed Mackie to a dark sedan parked at the rear. In the low light, it was difficult to make out the car's color; green or dark blue, maybe, or black. Phin used a key fob to unlock the doors.

Mackie could feel the hydrocodone tighten its grip, the warm euphoria working its way through his bloodstream. It would soften his focus, possibly slow his reaction time. But he had taken enough of it over the last few years to learn how to function effectively with a moderate dose in his system. And Phin had consumed a dose himself earlier, so he would be at the same disadvantage.

The key here was quick, focused strikes. Even with a slight buzz, Mackie could handle that.

And the hydrocodone would dampen the pain of any hits he might take from Phin.

Not that it would do much for a gunshot.

Phin gave him a pat down, but missed the loose bullets in Mackie's front pocket, nestled alongside his key ring.

"In the trunk," he ordered. "Quicker you hop in, the quicker I can get back here and look after Allie," Phin said.

Mackie opened the trunk—

—and saw the severed cable. Phin had rigged it so Mackie couldn't escape.

That was bad news. But also a ray of hope. If he'd gone through this trouble, it meant he wasn't planning on shooting Mackie the moment he climbed in. Phin wanted to take Mackie someplace else to do it.

Mackie couldn't let that happen.

He turned slightly to get a better look at Phin. No point in waiting for a better moment. Mackie just didn't have that kind of time.

Mackie moved as if to climb inside, and in one fluid movement, Mackie shot his left leg out to the side and brought his right leg in to join it in a motion that looked similar to a closing pair of scissors. It was a martial arts technique he had picked up while training under Krider's men and it took him out of Phin's immediate firing range.

It was also one Phin apparently had never experienced before, because he immediately fired where Mackie had been, the suppressed shot making a sound no louder than a hand clap, missing Mackie by inches and burying itself into the trunk.

Mackie pivoted around, fully facing Phin now, and with his left hand grabbed the wrist holding the pistol—a Sig Sauer semi-auto from what Mackie could see in the dim light. He held Phin's gun-hand wrist low and drove the knuckles of his right hand into Phin's windpipe.

Mackie followed the strike with an open-hand blow to Phin's solar plexus, and with a hard tug on Phin's wrist he freed the Sig Sauer. He backed up a couple of steps and started lifting the pistol to aim it at Phin.

But before he could fully do so, Phin was on him, driving his head into Mackie's abdomen like a battering ram and wrapping his arms around Mackie's waist. He drove Mackie backward into the open trunk.

Mackie felt certain the impact couldn't have been more painful if he'd fallen from the Sears Tower. The force from the hit punched the breath out of him, and a wave of pain cut through the hydrocodone his head was swimming in.

He struck Phin's ears with the knuckles of the hand holding the Sig and the open palm of his other. Phin barked, and as his hold loosened on Mackie's mid-section, Mackie brought the barrel of the Sig down on the back of Phin's head, and slipped out of Phin's grip.

Mackie aimed the Sig at Phin and fired, but Phin sidestepped him and began to slam the trunk closed on Mackie's outstretched legs. Again and again and again. It wasn't doing permanent damage, but it hurt like hell.

Mackie pulled his legs inside, and the trunk slammed shut. He immediately began to fire the Sig, first at where Phin was, then at the lock mechanism until the magazine ran out. It popped open just as Mackie heard the *BANG!* of an unsuppressed gunshot.

His Glock. The round punched through the roof and missed Mackie's head by a few inches.

Too bad, Phin. That was your one chance.

Just as drug dealers knew not to get high on their own supply, Mackie wasn't going to let himself get killed with his own gun. He kept one round in the chamber, but otherwise the gun was empty.

While Phin was no doubt wondering what was up with Mackie's Glock, Mackie got his sore legs under him and leapt out of the trunk, hurling himself at the bald man. He caught Phin off guard, tackling him, and they both hit the ground, both the Sig and the Glock skittering off onto the pavement.

Phin made a bridge of his back, heaving Mackie off of him, and Mackie went with the motion, scrambling on his hands and knees for the Glock. He snatched it, fished a bullet out of his pocket, and loaded it with the speed of someone who had practiced the move ten thousand times, which he had. The gun was pointed at Phin just as he was raising a tire iron—how'd he get *that* so fast?—over Mackie's head.

"Drop it."

Phin hesitated.

"Now."

Mackie took a quick look around. Still no sign of campus security. A few students ambled about near a couple of the residence halls on campus, but none seemed to be looking his way. From this distance, in such low light, there wasn't much they could see even if they did.

"What kind of hitter only keeps one bullet in his pistol?" Phin asked.

"The kind who is going to shoot you if you don't drop the damn tire iron."

Phin lowered his hands and set it gently onto the pavement. Apparently he was just as worried about making noise and drawing attention as Mackie was. Mackie continued to cover Phin, and bent to pick up the dropped Sig. He stuffed it into his pants and pulled his shirt over it.

"Someone heard the gunshot," Phin said. "Your Glock isn't suppressed."

"Someone heard a firecracker. Or a car backfire. But even if it was reported, we'll be finished before anyone comes by. My car's the Subaru parked over there. Start walking toward it."

Phin did as instructed while Mackie kept a safe distance behind. He pulled his keys from his jeans pocket and pressed the button to open the trunk. "In."

Phin looked first where Mackie knew he would: to the trunk release cable. His face gave away nothing when he saw that it had been disabled. Like recognized like.

"You think I'm gonna stay in there and wait for you to come back?" Phin asked

"Just long enough for me to do what I need to. We can finish this later."

"My advice to you would be to kill me now. Letting me live is only gonna make things worse for you."

"Just get in."

Phin climbed inside the trunk, took a moment to situate himself comfortably. "Last chance to not be stupid about this."

Mackie said nothing as he closed the lid. He holstered his Glock and took off at a run through the lot, across the street, and back toward the student union.

If Allie wasn't there still, he wouldn't panic. He would have to find a way to make sure she wasn't in her dorm, a friend's dorm, or in the library before he assumed that Tannen was involved.

But while he checked to see if Allie was still on campus, that would cost him precious time if Tannen had taken her.

Your timing couldn't have been worse, Phineas Troutt.

He barreled through the student union's front entrance, unconcerned with the attention he was drawing. The students inside turned in Mackie's direction at the sound of his noisy entrance. Allie wasn't among them. In fact, she was nowhere inside.

Shit. The incident with Phin in the parking lot had taken, what, a few minutes at most?

The table where Allie had sat was empty, but Mackie saw the curvy redhead in sweats sitting on a sofa, her finger scrolling downward on a tablet screen. Mackie made his way to her quickly.

"Allie. Where is she?"

The girl looked up from her tablet, her expression blank. She was no one Mackie recognized, so she probably hadn't been a student here at the same time he was. Under normal circumstances, he never would've approached a friend of Allie's, even one that wouldn't recognize him. But right now, that level of caution would do more harm than good.

"Umm, she, I think she left earlier."

"Did she leave with anyone?"

"Don't think so. Why?"

Mackie knew his impatience was showing, but he wasn't concerned with trying to disguise it. "Listen. Professor Tannen, have you seen him here in the last few minutes?"

The redhead wrinkled her face. "Tannen? Not in here. But I went out for a smoke a few minutes ago and I think I saw him hanging around."

It didn't necessarily mean anything. Maybe Tannen got a grip on himself and left before he approached Allie. But entertaining that possibility was a waste of time. Tannen was obviously beyond hope at this point.

And it wasn't as if he hadn't already demonstrated a remarkable lack of self-control.

By the time Mackie had determined whether or not Allie was still on campus, it could be too late if Tannen already had her.

Finding him first was the best option by far. Fortunately, Mackie had an address.

In the few blurred moments it took to run from the student union to the parking lot, he made a decision. He pressed the button on his key fob and the trunk lid disengaged. He approached slowly with the Glock and lifted the lid.

Phin's knees were slightly bent and pointed to his right. His hands were folded across his chest like a corpse in a casket. His gaze fell to the pistol in Mackie's hand and then lifted to his face. He said nothing.

"So here's the deal," Mackie said. "Allie's gone. Someone spotted Tannen hanging around outside the student union, so I'm sure he has her. This isn't your problem, but I'm thinking you're good at this sort of thing. Help me get her back, and you can put a bullet in me. No arguments, no tricks."

Phin seemed to consider. When he finally spoke, he asked, "You know where to find Tannen?"

.   .   .

Unlike most other professors, and for reasons that were now obvious, Morris Tannen had elected not to live in faculty housing. His rental house sat on a secluded stretch of densely wooded property bisected by unpaved road. There were neighbors, but few of them, and their homes were scattered at lengthy intervals from Tannen's rental.

It was just private enough for a man with Tannen's proclivities, but not so isolated as to draw attention.

Plenty of undisturbed land for body disposal, as well.

Phin sat in the passenger seat, his expression blank. "Why take me along?" he asked. "You don't think you could handle Tannen on your own?"

"I'm walking into a house I've never set foot in before. It's night. I don't know what precautions Tannen may have taken. He may have partners. Too many variables here, too many unknowns. Better to have an extra person along. One that's capable of what you're capable of."

"There's something else you're not telling me. That cute little evasion move you did by the car to get out of firing range. Keeping loose bullets so I wouldn't feel a clip when I frisked you. You're just as capable as I am. And you're the one holding the gun, not me. So what's the real reason I'm here?"

Mackie took a deep breath. "I'm tired. Tired of what I do, tired of living under Krider's thumb. I can't tell you how many times I've wanted to eat a bullet myself after putting one in a mark. But Krider made it clear that if I ever took myself out like that, he'd go after my family. But if I'm murdered, that's different. If you kill me, it's over. Allie and my family are safe. And like you said, it would happen sooner or later anyway."

Phin didn't reply. Mackie voiced a question that had been weighing on his mind. "What you said about hurting Allie if I didn't cooperate, that true?"

Phin stared straight ahead through the windshield as he spoke. "No. That's not what I do. But family, loved ones, they do make for useful leverage. You knew I was bluffing, didn't you?"

"Had a feeling."

"How could you tell?"

Mackie's tone suggested that the answer should've been obvious. "Because I've done the same thing."

"So why go along with me?"

"Figured I had a better chance outside than in the union."

Phin chuckled. "All this up close bullshit, all the things that can and do go wrong. Next time I'm just buying a sniper rifle."

"I've got a nice one you can have, after you kill me."

Phin glanced at him. "As a guy who has been facing his own mortality for a while, I can tell you you're firmly in the denial stage."

"I'm in the distracted stage. When we save Allie, I'll grieve for my shitty life."

"Fair enough."

Mackie kept the speedometer at seven miles over the speed limit and fought to keep his impatience in check. He couldn't waste even one minute, but getting pulled for speeding was the last thing he needed. And these roads were hardly designed for fast travel, with their sharp curves and reputation for deer crossings that had led to more than a few accidents.

"You do realize he may not even be there," Phin said.

"Maybe not. But it's likely. His place is just secluded enough to give him the privacy he wants. Makes sense that he'd want to spend time with Allie and do what he has planned in the comfort of his own home."

"And what does he have planned?"

The words stuck in Mackie's throat like fish hooks. "He... skins them alive. Among other things."

"My detective friend in Chicago, she's dealt with people like that more than a few times," Phin said. "I'll never understand what's wrong with some people."

Mackie noticed Phin was staring at his own reflection in the window when he said that last part.

Mackie parked his car beside the road. Tannen's rental, a ranch style with peeling paint the color of lead in the dull light, sat in the distance ahead. A car was in the driveway, a Toyota beater that had probably rolled off the assembly line during the Reagan administration.

Phin: "You got a plan in mind?"

"We'll cut through the woods, approach from behind. You go around front, knock on the door. If someone answers, make up some bullshit about car trouble and keep them talking. Get them on the porch if you can. I'll get in the backdoor and go inside from there."

Mackie opened the glove compartment and took out a tension wrench and a specially made lock picking tool. It was a skill he had some experience with.

"Do I get my gun back?"

This was the tricky part. If he handed Phin a weapon, Phin may be more concerned with finishing his assignment than protecting Allie. Still, Mackie couldn't expect Phin to enter the house unarmed.

"Give it to you when we get there."

"Fine."

They both exited the car, closing their doors quietly. They hopped over the ditch to the left of the car and entered the woods, their shoes crunching dead fallen leaves with a sound like eggshells.

Mackie and Phin wound their way among trees with naked, skeletal branches, and cut a trail to the right that led to the rear of Tannen's rental house.

Once the back of the house was visible, they crouched in heavy brush. Through a window, a soft light burned. No sounds they could hear as of yet. No screams.

Mackie pulled out Phin's empty Sig and passed it to him. Earlier, Phin had gone to his rental car and pocketed a spare magazine from his luggage.

"I'd feel better if you waited until I was out of sight before you reloaded."

Phin took the pistol and rose from the brush. He tucked the gun in the back of his jeans and jogged into the backyard. Mackie watched as he made his way to the front.

His Glock in one hand, the tension wrench and pick in the other, Mackie darted across the yard to the backdoor.

His hydrocodone buzz lingered, but was mostly forgotten.

The lock on Tannen's backdoor was a garden-variety deadbolt, easily pickable. Mackie could hear Phin's fist rapping on the front door. He stayed out of view of the backdoor's glass insets as he listened for footsteps inside the house.

He heard nothing. From the front porch, there was the sound of Phin pounding the door again. Harder this time.

Still, no sounds from inside.

With the right amount of torque and pressure from his tools, it was the work of less than a minute to pick the backdoor's lock.

Mackie turned the knob slowly and entered, his Glock held out in front of him. He was in a kitchen; tidy and freshly cleaned, if the Pine-Sol odor was any indication.

Phin knocked on the front door once more. Mackie held his position, waited to hear sounds inside the house, any indication of human presence.

After a few moments, he walked from the kitchen into the living room and opened the front door for Phin.

Phin stepped inside without saying anything and drew his Sig Sauer.

The living room was dimly lit by a lamp and tastefully, albeit modestly, furnished. A small stack of books sat beside a recliner; an entertainment center held a mid-sized flat screen television and an inexpensive DVD player. A stack of DVDs was positioned tidily beside the television.

Mackie took a look through the stack. Rom-coms, musicals. The first season of Mad Men. No bondage films, porn, or snuff. It was hardly the viewing material one would expect a serial murderer to enjoy.

"You sure our boy lives here?" Phin asked quietly.

"Positive."

When Mackie turned to explore the rest of the house, he saw the man with the revolver standing in the hallway.

Stocky, middle-aged. Glasses and a few wisps of hair floating on the surface of a mostly bald pate.

Mackie had seen photos. This wasn't Morris Tannen.

"Why are you here?" His voice was soft, the tone more bemused than startled or upset.

Mackie and Phin raised their pistols. "Where's Tannen?" Mackie asked.

Phin looked at Mackie. "You mean this isn't the guy?"

Mackie shook his head.

"Morris told me someone was coming," the man said. "His friend told him that someone was asking about him on campus. He was quite upset."

His friend…

Curvy redhead in the student union?

"What friend?" Mackie asked.

"A student of his. Lovely girl. Her job was to bring Morris his prize this evening."

So Tannen and the redhead were working together. She'd called to warn him after Mackie approached her asking about Tannen.

But if her job had been to deliver Allie to Tannen…

"Allie's not here." Mackie said.

The man nodded. "That was her name, yes. Allie. Morris was infatuated with her. I believe their friendship helped keep him sane. For a little while, at least."

"You're Rev. Harrell, aren't you?" Phin asked.

"I am. But I still don't know who you two are. How do you know Morris?"

Mackie ignored him. "Where's Morris now?"

The man turned and walked down the hall. "Follow me."

He entered a bedroom at the end of the hall. Mackie and Phin followed him inside.

Morris Tannen was on the floor, his shoulder length dark hair pooled behind his head. He wore green slacks and a demin button-down.

His throat had a dark red bloom where a bullet had pierced it.

"He would've killed her, like the others," Harrell said. "I came here to stop him. Convince him to get help. Pray with him. I was getting through. He called his friend, told her not to bring Allie. He was fighting it. And then he got that phone call warning him that someone was looking for him. He became agitated. And then desperate. Oh God, he would've killed her…"

"Her?" Phin asked.

Harrell shook his head sadly and opened a closet door. A girl tumbled out, her feet and wrists bound with several layers of duct tape. A ball gag was wedged in her mouth. Her clothes were filthy and damp from what was obviously urine. Her eyes were lit with a wild, tortured desperation.

Mackie recognized her from a photo. Lacey Bittner. The second of the two missing girls from September.

Mackie's mouth felt like sandpaper. "There… there were two…"

Another mournful look from Harrell. "Yes, there was. The first, he killed her several days ago. Buried her not far from here." He held his revolver as if he wasn't quite sure what it was. "I brought this because I knew if I couldn't convince him to keep his demons bottled, I'd have to put him down like an animal. When I knew he intended to kill the young lady here, I… I knew I didn't have a choice."

"You knew all along what Tannen was doing," Phin said. "You could've stopped him, turned him in."

Harrell kept his eyes on the revolver in his hand. "It's not that simple. Morris and I… years ago, we… we shared those demons."

Mackie understood. "The murders in Iowa, in Vermont… the two of you were partners."

Harrell's voice shook as he spoke. "I learned to control it… keep it locked inside. God has forgiven me for my sins."

"We'll see if he does," Phin said. "You can ask him when you see him." He raised his Sig Sauer and fired a round through Reverend Harrell's left eye.

Lacey moaned through the ball gag. Mackie sucked in a hard breath, felt a wave of dizziness wash over him. He bent forward and gripped his knees as Phin knelt down and began to peel off the tape binding Lacey's hands and feet.

·　　　　·　　　　·

Phin drove.

After getting Lacey loose and giving her water, Phin placed a call to 911 from Tannen's landline. He strongly urged Lacey to be extremely vague when describing her rescuers to authorities.

If she heard anything he said, she gave no indication.

"Your girl's safe, we rescued another, and two sick pieces of shit are dead," Phin said. "I think we did ok."

Mackie nodded. They rode in silence for several minutes. Then Mackie said, "So where do you want to do this?"

This. Mackie's end of the bargain. It seemed surreal. But at the same time, liberating. Mackie searched himself for the grief Phin said he'd feel, but couldn't find it. Instead, he was feeling something much more like relief.

No more killing. No more worry. No more pain. No more regret.

Mackie had a mark, one of his first, who seemed fearless in the face of death. Before he shot the guy in the head, Mackie asked what made him so brave. Was it religion? Belief in an afterlife? How could a person die so stoically?

"I had no feelings before I was born," the man said. *"I've lived a life with feelings, many of them bad. I don't fear returning to that void. I welcome it."*

Mackie understood. He believed in an afterlife, but even if he was wrong…well, to not feel anymore would still be a gift.

Phin was silent for a few moments. And then he said: "I'll return the money to the kid's parents. Minus a small fee for my trouble, of course. Can't promise they won't send someone else after you at some point, though."

Mackie felt anger well up inside him. "Why would you let me go? I'm giving you an opportunity to finish your job. Didn't you hear what I said? I'm tired. I'm done. I want out."

Phin smiled. "No, kid, you don't. You want to be around to protect that girl. Me killing you might keep her safe from Krider, but it may not. Somehow I get the feeling she's better off with you around."

Mackie closed his eyes, leaned his head against his seat's headrest. "I'm so tired, Phin."

"But miles to go before you sleep."

Phin was right. There was a redheaded bitch on campus that needed to be dealt with, and as soon as Mackie and Phin made it back, her life would change in a substantial and vastly unpleasant way.

"Here's how I see it," Phin said. "We come into this world without any choice in the matter. But once we're here, we can choose how we live our lives. Maybe we do some good in the world. Maybe we do some bad. But we always have a choice."

"Not always," Mackie said. "Sometimes people get trapped."

"Only if you allow yourself to be trapped, kid. We decide how to spend the time we have. We decide who has power over us. And we can also decide how we leave this world. You can leave with a whimper. Or you can leave with one hell of a bang."

It began to rain, the water beating all the dust and dirt off the windshield until Phin put the wipers on, making it clear again.

Macklin Dailey stared out into the chilled, rainy, October dark, thinking hard about Phin's words. And for one brief, clear moment, he dared to feel hope.

BEAT DOWN
(WITH GARTH PERRY)

My second (so far) collaboration with Garth and his psychic character, Ava Jane Rakowski. We really should do a third story and make it a trilogy. If you want to see that, shoot me an email.

"So how the hell did he get out?" Lieutenant Jacqueline 'Jack' Daniels frowned at her partner, Homicide Detective First Class Herb Benedict, as if he were the one who unlocked Ortega's cell and personally freed the criminal.

Rafael Ortega had abducted a young teen named Maria Cantu and had held her captive in his basement for six months. He'd been preparing to abduct another girl, Alanza De Luisa, when luck intervened a few weeks ago and police knocked on his door and found a terrified Maria tied to a bed, half-starved, naked, and abused.

He'd been released from Cook County Jail the day before.

"Presumably, he walked," Benedict said. "Or he might have pranced. Maybe hopped on one foot."

Jack shot him a withering look. The two were sitting at her desk, reviewing the morning blotter. They each had their customary coffee, and Herb had his customary chocolate éclair. He'd been limiting himself to only one a day at the request of his wife, a lovely woman who was slowly being inched out of their queen size bed by his increasing bulk. But Jack knew Herb had side-stepped the issue by convincing the bakery owner to supersize his daily éclair. It looked like a chocolate-frosted loaf of French bread.

Well, half a loaf. Herb had been powering through it with the conviction of a beaver gnawing a redwood.

"Herb, I can't handle you trying to be funny *and* chewing loudly. Pick one or the other."

"Can I chew loudly in a funny way?"

"How about answering my question."

He shrugged. "I thought it was rhetorical. But if I made a guess, it was a clerical error. Accidentally placed on the early release list."

With over 12,000 inmates, it wasn't unheard of. Cook County was the largest jail in America, and hundreds of prisoners' files were updated every day. When scads of low-priority criminals were sent home each month in an effort to ease overcrowding, mix-ups were bound to happen.

"Ortega is dangerous. He shouldn't have been on any clerk's list for anything, especially early release." Daniels snorted and got up from her desk to pace her small office. "I want to see an internal audit. Someone's head should roll."

"You know how backlogged they are at County. An audit will take weeks. No one's head will roll. They protect their own, just like us. Circle the wagons, cover their asses."

"We could always take care of it," Jack said. "Track down Ortega."

"Not our jurisdiction."

"It could be. We don't know where he went. He could be right down the street."

"It's also not a homicide."

"Yet," Jack countered, "Alanza did end up dead. Just happened that her brother killed her before Ortega could. It's only a matter of time before Ortega kills someone."

"We've got a full caseload already."

"Are you playing devil's advocate, or are you in?"

"I'm in. This guy can't be allowed out in a free society. He's nuts. He shouldn't have wound up in County at all. Why he wasn't tossed in the loony bin pre-trial is beyond me. But our job is just to catch them. Beyond that, the system does what it does."

Jack sat in silence for a moment, dwelling on the idiocy of it, as Herb worked on éclairzilla. It was the shape of a city bus, and damn near the size.

"Seriously, Herb. That's got to be ten thousand calories."

"What? A single éclair? My nutritional book says it's only three hundred."

"Per serving. You have twenty servings there."

"It can't be twenty servings. There's only one pastry."

Jack had been having similar conversations with Herb for years, but she still wasn't able to stop herself. If he lacked self-control in the eating department, she lacked it in reminding him.

"There's enough sugar there to power a small village."

"You're exaggerating."

"You need both hands to hold it and you're shaking."

"I'm quivering with pastry joy. Next you'll ask if it comes with a defibrillator for when my heart seizes."

It was, indeed, what Jack was about to ask.

"Want a bite?" Herb offered.

"I'd take a piece for later, but it won't fit in my mini-fridge."

"You made your point, Jack. The éclair is large. Let's move on."

"Also, how many calories in the giant pop you're drinking?"

Jack indicated Herb's Big Gulp cup on her desk.

"It's Mountain Dew. The high caffeine boosts the metabolism, off-setting the sugar."

"Yeah. The Mountain Dew Diet. I've heard of it. People dropping thirty pounds a week."

"I sense sarcasm."

"You think? You're a cop, Herb. Cops are supposed to drink coffee. It's one of the rules."

"I drink coffee, too. Yesterday I had a choco-mocha-vanil-latte, with hazelnut syrup. Remember? With the ice cream in it?"

"You've become a parody of yourself."

More silence. Herb continued to munch, but the éclair didn't seem to get any smaller.

"We need to get people on Maria," Jack said, knowing they didn't have the manpower for it but she could pull some strings. "He could make another play for her."

"AJ, too," Herb said, mouth full.

Jack's frown deepened. AJ Rakowski was one of a handful of psychic consultants hired by the Chicago Police Department. She had a part-time contract to assist with the caseload of crimes against minorities, predominantly homicides and kidnappings of people of color. It was a PR move that their precinct captain had signed on to and then handed over to his leading lieutenant.

Jack didn't like it. She didn't believe in that stuff, even if the newspapers did.

"The guy was obsessing on her during that interview a few weeks back," Herb went on.

"I told you she shouldn't have been there."

"She also helped catch the guy."

"I chalk that up to luck."

"Luck or not, she could be in danger, Jack. She needs to be told. And maybe put a team on her."

"Why bother? If she's a real psychic, she knows already. Unless her 'aurasphere' is scrambled for whatever reason. Sunspots can do that, I understand."

Herb made a thoughtful face. "AJ's more mentalist than medium. Gave up her séances to pursue psychic investigation. And as she'll readily admit, she's not infallible. And I know you like her, at least a little."

Jack shrugged. "She has nice taste in clothes."

"Like recognizes like. What do you have on today, Armani?"

"Are you getting smarter, or is he the only designer you've heard of?"

"Yes."

Detective Tom Mankowski poked his head in her office. "Got some bad news, Lieut."

"Ortega? We heard already."

"Ortega?" Tom shook his head. "I'm talking about Roberto De Luisa. He's out on bail."

Now Herb frowned. "What? How'd he manage that? And don't say clerical error."

"His court-appointed attorney, guy by the name of Louis Forest, somehow convinced the judge he was eligible. His parents scraped together the bond money."

"That makes no sense," Jack said. "What idiot judge would allow that?"

"And why would his parents bail him out when he killed his sister?" Benedict added.

Tom furrowed his brows, making him look like Thomas Jefferson. "I agree, it doesn't make sense."

Jack turned to her partner. "That's two we're going after. And I'll buy my next suit at Sears if it's a coincidence."

"What's wrong with Sears?" Herb asked. "I get all my suits at Sears."

"They have a big and tall department?" Tom asked.

"I'm average height," Herb said, eating more pastry.

Tom raised an eyebrow at Jack. "Can we catch diabetes being in the same room as him?"

"It wouldn't hurt to take an insulin shot," she answered.

"I am immune to your obvious envy," Herb said.

"So what about Ortega?" Tom asked.

"You know the missing persons case we worked with AJ? Led us to Alanza's killer—the brother who just made bail. Well, the man planning to abduct Alanza was Raphael Ortega. And he was released yesterday."

Tom scratched his chin. "That's… odd. So what's the plan?"

"Not much of one. Get eyes on both men. See if they lead us anywhere important. Organize an off-the-record surveillance team. I'll do some digging into the clerical error at Cook County, and inquire about the judge who sprang De Luisa."

"If it's an inside job, you won't get far," Herb said. "Official channels won't work."

"I can be persuasive."

"The harder you push, they harder they'll defend themselves, Jack. We should get someone private to look into it."

Jack thought it over. "I can get McGlade. He owes me."

Herb groaned. "C'mon, Jack. The man's an idiot."

"You want to pay someone private out of your own pocket?"

"On my salary? I can barely afford the éclair."

"You can barely lift the éclair," Tom said. "Do the Guinness World Record people know about it?"

"They're calling me back later today."

Tom eyed the confection.

"So how much does a pastry like that cost?" he asked.

"I'm not sure. I made a down payment, put the rest on layaway."

"I'm curious, did it have two little plastic people on top of it, that looked like a bride and groom?"

"Plastic?" Herb asked. "They didn't taste like plastic."

Jack folded her arms. "Are you two done?"

"I don't think he'll ever be done," Tom said. "It's like a chocolate-frosted French bread. Or a bus."

Jack nodded. "I thought the same thing. We could slap four wheels on it, charge people for rides."

Herb wiped his mouth with his sleeve, leaving a streak on Sears's finest. "Let's all stop talking about my breakfast and get back to your ex-partner. Do you really want to seek out Harry McGlade? On purpose?"

"No. But what's the alternative?"

"How about anything else? Anything at all? There's that blind guy who stands on the corner of Wabash and Balbo. The one with the monkey."

"You think a blind guy could help us get answers from County?" Jack asked.

"I was thinking the monkey."

"I don't like McGlade any better than you do, Herb, but he has a lot of contacts, and will be working gratis."

"Can we at least give the monkey a try?"

Jack's phone vibrated. She looked down at the screen and pursed her lips.

"Text from AJ. You were right, Herb."

"Why? What's it say?"

Jack showed the phone to her partner.

Got a threating email. Confused. Is Ortega out of jail?

"I'll call her and explain," Herb said as he tried to pry himself from the chair. "You call the idiot."

"I'll put a team together." Mankowski left.

Herb finally pushed himself to his feet and held out the remainder of his éclair. "I'll need to borrow your mini-fridge."

He waddled over to it and tried to shove the pastry onto one of the small shelves.

It didn't fit.

ORTEGA

He shouldn't have touched her.

That's what Raphael Ortega was thinking. That Roberto shouldn't have touched his own sister, Alanza.

Alanza was *his* girlfriend, not Roberto's. He had no right.

As he watched the young man embrace his parents outside the jail, he frowned. He was close enough to hear snippets of their conversation, and he wasn't happy. Roberto was hugging them, falling on them. He was sobbing, weeping in sorrow at what he'd done. He was sorry for killing his sister. He'd panicked. Hadn't meant to harm her. It was an accident, a terrible tragedy. Could they forgive him, could they love him again? Could they only give him another chance? He was only a kid, he didn't know what he was doing.

Ortega sneered at the pathetic display. It was all bullshit. The teen knew what he was doing. He'd stolen Alanza away from the person she really loved. Alanza didn't love her brother; she loved *him*. And Roberto knew it. That's why Roberto had killed her. To keep his sister for himself. The tears were false. The pleas were contrived.

That would change. Soon. Roberto would indeed sob and plead and cry out. This time the tears would be real. Raphael would make sure of that. However, this time there would be no forgiveness, no sympathy. No patience with desperate explanations.

Roberto had to pay.

But first he had to come clean.

There was only one thing that Raphael wanted to hear from the young man: a confession.

He wanted Alanza's older brother to confess that she had wanted *him* only.

That Alanza had wanted to move in with *him*.

That she'd loved *him*.

The truth. Raphael wanted the son of a bitch to tell the truth.

A sense of calm came over Ortega. He knew it would happen. Very soon, in fact.

He knew Roberto would admit to the truth within the hour. He had no doubts.

Once they were alone, he'd get it out of him. No matter how long it took.

It was easy to follow them. They'd taken the bus to the jail, and Ortega simply boarded behind them. He followed them to the stop nearest their house, watched them go inside, and then continued walking past, on the way to his own house located in the same neighborhood. Ortega was a little surprised to see a police squad car parked on his street, but realized they couldn't be there for him. The cops knew his love for Maria and Alanza and AJ was true. That's why they released him.

Still, he cut through some neighbors' lawns and made a long loop around to the back of his house, to make sure the police didn't see him. He didn't have time to deal with them right now. Not with so much else to do.

He had to pull the yellow tape that read POLICE INVESTIGATION DO NOT CROSS from his back door in order to enter, and then made his way into the basement, to the fake wall paneling. The cops hadn't discovered it, and his love kit was still there, everything in a leather satchel. Rope. Handcuffs. Binoculars. Two thousand dollars in cash. A 9mm Beretta with a full magazine. A glass bottle of ether. A plastic bottle of ammonia. Cotton rags. Brass knuckles. A serrated folding knife. Condoms. Pepper spray. A full roll of paper towels.

Ortega called it a love kit because sometimes love was difficult and needed to be persuaded.

He removed the case from behind the paneling, let himself out the back door, and took a roundabout route back to Roberto's house. He saw another police car parked on their street, so Ortega made his way to

Roberto's back yard, where he removed the paper towels and semi-auto from his bag and then knocked on a bedroom window.

Roberto's mother drew back the curtains to look. Older, heavier, but she had Alanza's eyes. With a deep pang of loss, Ortega shoved the barrel of the Beretta into the center tube of the paper towels and fired, shooting Senora De Luisa in the head. The window broke, but the makeshift suppressor made the gun no louder than a hard slap; not something the police up the street were likely to notice.

As Ortega crawled in through the window, Senor De Luisa rushed into the bedroom, and it took three bullets to his chest before he fell.

Roberto was right behind him, and his eyes got wide when he saw his father fall, and wider when he saw Ortega with the gun.

Ortega ordered him into the kitchen and sat him down. Surprisingly, Roberto said nothing, seemingly resigned to his fate.

Or perhaps it wasn't surprising. Roberto knew who his sister had truly loved. Deep down, he knew it.

All that remained was for him to admit it.

Ortega poured the ether on a rag, holding it to the boy's face until he passed out. Then he used the rope and duct tape to bind him securely to the chair. Opening the bottle of ammonia, he held it under Roberto's nose until the boy awoke.

"Who did your sister love, me or you?" he asked.

"What?"

Ortega frowned, and then he slipped on the brass knuckles.

Then he got to work.

RAKOWSKI

Ava Jane Rakowski read the email for the nth time, trying to tune in to the sender. She was at her desk in her home office, a safe and soothing room she'd used for séances before becoming a psychic investigator.

You think you're all that, solving a homicide. But if you don't stop working on your current case, you and your boyfriend are dead.

Though it was anonymous, Ortega may very well have sent it. De Luisa could have, as well. That was one of the problems with trying to catch bad guys. They tended not to like it. And if they were out of jail, both AJ and Tomen were in danger.

"You're upset," Tomen said. He'd been sitting at the table in their shared living/dining room, working on his laptop, and had somehow ended up behind her. AJ had been so preoccupied with the email she hadn't noticed. She closed the window before he could read it.

"Someone sent me an email."

She felt Tomen's hands on her shoulders.

"Wow, you're tense. Your neck is like a tree trunk." He gave her a quick neck massage and pecked the top of her head with a kiss.

"Thanks, Tomen. That's sweet."

"What was the email? A case?"

AJ hesitated. Tomen knew she got a lot of email—a result of her website, which he'd designed for her, and her phonebook ad, which he'd also designed—but she wasn't sure if she should tell him the truth. Tomen tended to be the sensitive type, and she didn't want him overly worried.

That wasn't fair, though. He needed to be told. Even though he wasn't technically her boyfriend, just her housemate.

"It was a death threat," AJ said.

"Is it serious?"

"I can't tell. I'm getting ambiguous feelings from it."

Tomen started kneading the knot in her neck again. "It doesn't feel ambiguous. It feels like you're really agitated."

"Both Raphael Ortega and Roberto De Luisa are out of jail."

Tomen stopped rubbing. "Both of them? How?"

"Lt. Daniels isn't sure."

"You think the email is from one of them?"

"It could be. But…"

She couldn't get a fix on the sender. Her psychic capabilities usually allowed her to catch the vibes of those who contacted her. It was one way she determined which cases to take. She only worked part time with the CPD, so as a freelance psychic detective she was free to pursue her own cases. These usually involved requests for help in tracking down long lost relatives or some variation on the theme.

She received so many emails from people who visited her website that she now had the luxury of picking and choosing her clients. And the 'signals' that came along with the request played an important role in her decision to take them on. The fact that this anonymous email was 'dark' made it all the more troublesome.

Perhaps it wasn't Ortego or De Luisa. Perhaps it was someone new. Or someone from the past. This wasn't the first time AJ had been threatened.

"But it doesn't feel like Ortega or de Luisa," he finished for her.

"Right."

"So it could be nothing?"

"I don't know…" And Ava genuinely didn't.

"What is it?"

"I wasn't the only one threatened."

Tomen's hands dug deeper into her trapezius, so deep it almost hurt. "Can I see the email?"

She hesitated, then brought the screen back up.

"Boyfriend, huh?" he said, reading.

"It's obviously about you," AJ said.

"So is it that you're worried about me? Or that you don't want anyone thinking we're a couple?"

AJ pulled away from him. "We *aren't* a couple, Tomen. We're friends. We share an apartment. Split the bills."

"Shop together. Eat together. Talk on the phone several times a day. Share a bed."

"We have separate bedrooms."

"Except when we don't."

When they first moved in together AJ had promised not to read Tomen. They both valued their privacy, had separate careers, different friends, kept different hours. It was a great arrangement, especially since she didn't have any romantic feelings for him. And she avoided asking him what his feelings were for her. He knew she didn't want a serious relationship. And he never pushed it. Tomen seemed content with whatever it was they had, just like AJ was. No commitment. No pressure.

AJ didn't want to mess things up by finding out he was in love with her.

"Just be careful," she told him. "I wouldn't want to have to look for a new roommate."

"I'll be fine."

"You're not exactly the macho type, Tomen."

"Why? Because I'm a wannabe vegan and wear cardigan sweaters?"

She stared up at him. "Because I can beat you at arm wrestling, and you're such a metrosexual you spend more time at the hairdresser than I do."

"Having regular mani-pedis doesn't mean I can't hold my own in a fight. It just means I value cuticle care."

"Tomen, I once saw a ten-year-old boy knock you over in the hallway."

"I didn't see him coming. And that boy was very large for his age."

She raised a skeptical eyebrow. "He was average size."

"He had a mustache."

"He was eating a Snickers. That was chocolate on his lip."

Tomen frowned. "It was a mustache. I'm thinking it wasn't a boy after all, but a dwarf. He had that stocky, muscular look."

"A dwarf holding hands with his mother?"

"Could have been his girlfriend. Little people often date average-sized women. Love is blind, AJ."

Ava Jane didn't like the twinkle in his eye when he said that about love, and she stood up and walked away from the debate.

"I have to get to work," she said without looking back. "Just be careful."

As she dressed, AJ tried not to think about Tomen's possible feelings for her. If he was in love with her, she'd have no choice but to kick him out. Because she didn't love him.

At least, she thought she didn't. Or more to the point, she never thought about if she did or not, so she assumed she didn't.

Whatever the case, AJ didn't want a boyfriend, and she was willing to get rid of Tomen if his intent was to pursue a serious relationship. She was 100% sure of that.

Probably.

AJ walked to the train station at Linden and took the Purple Line downtown. She arrived at the twenty-sixth precinct at two o'clock as usual, though she wasn't her usual bubbly self. A few minutes after she settled herself into her broom closet workspace, her boss popped in to say hi.

"You doing okay?" Jack asked, standing, since there wasn't an extra chair in the makeshift office.

Herb wandered by and stopped at the door, too large to do anything except block the entrance.

"Need any crystals or mood rings or anything?" he suggested.

AJ laughed in spite of her fretful mood. "Maybe a Buddha's tummy to rub."

"I'm glad you said it," Herb said, "otherwise I'd be accused of being racially insensitive."

Ava Jane Rakowski was Korean, petite and spry with a sly sense of humor. She'd been adopted by a Polish family from the west suburbs.

The fact that Jack had originally assumed she was male and of a certain European ethnicity was still an inside joke they shared.

"Actually, I was raised Catholic. I know very little about my biological heritage. I just like the idea of patting fat tummies for luck."

She and Daniels both looked at Benedict's wide girth.

"Maybe we should try it sometime," Jack said.

"Don't even think about it. Might make something pop. Oh jeez, that wasn't what I meant. Buttons. I was thinking shirt buttons. I'm married. I love my wife. I'm not interested in either of you. Not that you both aren't, you know, attractive. Hell, I'm going back to my éclair."

Both women smirked as Herb left, red-faced.

Jack unfolded a printout of the email and laid it on AJ's desk. "IT's still trying to trace the originating IP address, but they tell me it's spoofed. Could've come from anywhere."

"What does that mean?"

"It means the person who sent it knows how to hide his tracks on the World Wide Web. As much as I want this email to lead us to Ortega's or De Luisa's doorstep, I'm beginning to have my doubts."

AJ thought about this and nodded slowly. "I think you're probably right. Raphael Ortega's aura bounces back skewed feelings of imagined love and passion. De Luisa's is self-loathing and rage, though I can't seem to tune into him now. But the email message? I'm getting nothing. Could be a hoax."

"Weird timing if it is."

Rakowski nodded. "Plus, I'm not actually working on a specific case right now, though I think I'm making some headway with a couple of cold cases that share a few similarities with what happened to Maria and Alanza. One named Guadalupe Silva, one named Fernanda de la Rosa."

"Abductions, you mean? How cold?"

"Two years. Two Latina girls went missing within a few weeks of each other. Attended the same high school, but their brothers were in rival gangs. Police suspected at the time that they were possible targets of gang-related take downs. Retaliation killings. Both are presumed dead."

"Latin Kings and Spanish Cobras. Know them well enough, unfortunately. Part of the larger rival organizations, People Nation and Folk

Nation." Jack grimaced. "They could be dead, or they might have been trafficked. Sad world we live in, AJ, when there's something worse than death out there that preys on young girls."

"Possibly." AJ knew human trafficking was a growing problem in the city of Chicago, especially among minorities—both young men and women—and that gangs kidnapped and sold their victims like cattle, but she wasn't convinced this was the case in this situation.

Jack saw her hesitate. "You think there's a connection to Ortega or De Luisa?"

"That's what I'm trying to discern. Nothing definite, yet. But there might be a connection. These girls... it doesn't feel like... well, let me just say I'm not convinced they're dead. Anyway, on a more positive note, I understand that Maria Cantu was released from the hospital today?"

"Yes. First night back with her family since the police found her in Ortega's basement."

"She'll have police protection tonight, right? Especially now that Ortega is out of jail."

"Officially, no. The CPD does not have enough resources for that sort of thing."

"What? But that's—"

Daniels held up her hand. "I'm with you, AJ. And ahead of you. Tom, Herb, and I have already set up a surveillance rotation. I'm heading over to the Cantu's for the first shift after I clock out here."

"I want to go with you."

"Absolutely not. You have no experience in the field. You're a desk jockey."

"Who can provide on-site consultation. It's in my contract."

"At the discretion of your supervisor. Which is me. That's also in your contract."

The two engaged in a power glare, though it wasn't an unfriendly one. Finally, AJ acquiesced, brushing it off with a shrug of the shoulder. "No problem. You can text me later if you need anything from me."

Jack continued to glare, her eyes narrow. "You just tried to read me, didn't you?"

AJ laughed. "Tried? No. I did read you. I just wish I could change your mind." Her face became serious. "By the way, is your boyfriend okay?"

"How did you know he was sick?"

"I didn't, until just now."

Jack's features softened. "He's getting better."

"Good."

Tom Mankowski stuck his head in. "Sorry to be the bearer of bad news twice in one day, Jack, but someone broke into Roberto De Luisa's parents' house. Three dead. The mother and father shot, Roberto tied up and beaten to death. Neighbor called it in, heard screaming."

"Didn't we have a car on them?"

"On them, and on Ortega. When they arrived, the perp was gone."

Tom handed his superior a file. She skimmed it over and murmured out, "Shit."

AJ asked, "What?"

"A note was found on Roberto's body. It says: 'For Alanza.'"

"It's Ortega," the psychic said. "Keep reading."

Jack frowned. "The rest of the note says, 'Maria and AJ, you'll be safe soon.'"

The silence between the three of them was palpable.

Then AJ and Jack said simultaneously: "*I'm coming with you/you're not coming with us.*"

ORTEGA

'm not going to let him touch you, Maria. I promise. He won't get the chance.

Ortega was across the street from Maria's apartment, peering at her through his binoculars. He had to stay away for the moment, because there were police around her as well. It was a hot summer evening, her windows were open. He could see her every now and then when she got up off her bed, catch a glimpse of her as she changed clothes.

He smiled. He'd get her back. Even though the police had taken her away, she'd return to him. Very soon.

But first he had to protect her from her old boyfriend.

Ortega knew all about him. His name was Montel. She'd spoken of him a few times, but Ortega knew that she still loved *him*. Not Montel. She'd spent six months at *his* house, after all.

Maria wanted Ortega to rescue her, he was sure of it.

And he would. He'd come back for her once he took care of the old boyfriend. He'd find a place where they could be together. Like before.

Poor Alanza. Such a shame that she hadn't moved in with him before Roberto killed her. Looking at Maria through the window, he vowed that he'd protect her against bastards like that. Montel wouldn't touch her. He wouldn't even get to see her. Ortega would make sure the teenager would stay away. In fact, he'd do to Montel what he'd done to Roberto. During their time together, Maria had given him Montel's address.

Once Montel was dealt with, he and Maria could be alone again.

Well, not quite alone. There was someone else who loved him. Someone else he knew wanted to be with him. She'd visited him in jail. He could tell she wanted to spend more time with him.

Ava Jane.

She also had a boyfriend. While Ortega was in jail, he didn't have much use for his lawyer, but he did pay the man to hire a private investigator to get information about Ava Jane Rakowski. He found out she was currently working for the police, where she lived, and who she lived with, a graphic artist named Tomen Mure.

It was to be expected. With exceptional women, there were always rivals for their affection. And though Ortega knew they loved and wanted him alone, other suitors could cause trouble. Like Roberto did.

Best to get them out of the picture as soon as possible.

Ortega checked his watch, then walked out of the alley and stopped at the florist on the street corner, buying a dozen roses in a box. Then hailed a cab. He gave the taxi driver the address, reading it off the yellow advertisement he'd ripped out of the phone book. It wasn't too far from Maria's house, and ten minutes later he was knocking on an apartment door.

"Yeah?" A male voice said from behind the threshold.

Ortega held the roses out in front of the peephole with one hand, digging his hand into his pocket with the other. "Delivery."

The door opened, revealing an average looking white guy in his twenties, wearing a sweater. Ortega handed the man the flowers, then simultaneously stuck his foot in the door and blocked it while raising his 9mm.

"Inside. Now."

He led the boyfriend inside, sat him in a suitable kitchen chair, and cuffed him. A dose of ether, and few minutes of duct tape attention, and he was immobilized. Then he woke him up with the ammonia.

"Take whatever you want, man."

"What I want," Ortega said, pulling a framed photo of a lady off the wall and holding it up, "is for you to admit she loves me, not you."

"Wait... oh, Jesus. I know who you are."

Ortega opened up his satchel and found the brass knuckles, sticky with blood from his conversation with Roberto. He noticed the laptop on the kitchen table, open to some web design page. He quickly closed the lid, because it could have a camera in it. Webcams were supposed to be for chatting, but Ortega knew they were on all the time, and recorded everything you did. His own computer didn't have a camera, but just to be absolutely sure he wore a mask every time he went on the Internet.

Then he turned back to the so-called-boyfriend and raised his fist.

The coward cringed. "I don't know what you want me to say!"

"I want you to say the truth."

When no answer came, Ortega hit him in the face. There was blood, and a clicking sound on the tile floor.

Teeth.

"Tell me the truth," Ortega said.

"I… we're… I love her…"

"Liar."

Ortega went to work.

He never did get the truth. But it didn't really matter. Because, like Roberto, the man died, and would no longer interfere.

DANIELS

"Are you getting anything?" Herb asked AJ as they stared at the bloody, misshapen, bound corpse of Roberto De Luisa.

She's getting something all right, Jack thought. *Getting sick.*

Daniels hadn't wanted to bring the psychic to a crime scene, but Herb said it was the best way to keep an eye on her. And with Roberto and his family murdered, AJ definitely needed keeping an eye on.

"Smell that?" Jack asked.

"I'm trying not to," Herb said.

Roberto had voided his bowels either before, or perhaps after, he expired.

"Not that. On his face."

Herb took a sniff. "Ether. Explains why Roberto didn't put up more of a fight."

"This is... awful," AJ said. She was looking a bit green.

"You wanted to be involved in police work," Jack reminded her. "And insisted on coming along."

"I know... it's... just..."

AJ began to heave, which was a perfectly acceptable response to the atrocity before her. Everyone vomited seeing their first violent homicide.

"Herb. Don't let her contaminate the crime scene."

Herb eyed Jack, and saw his partner staring at the Big Gulp cup of pop he was sipping. "What? Aw, there's still Mountain Dew left."

"Drink fast."

Herb gulped at the straw like he'd been in the desert for three days without liquid, then squeezed his eyes shut.

"Dammit! Brain freeze!"

With one hand he pinched the bridge of his nose, and with the other he held out the cup to the psychic, who managed to get the top off before she hurled inside.

Jack walked away from the spectacle. She wandered past the crime scene team and into the bedroom, where Ortega had entered the residence through the window—behind the house and out of view of where Tom's team had been parked.

They should have been covering the back of the house as well, and had been chewed out accordingly. But what Jack didn't understand was why they hadn't heard any gunshots. Unlike the cute canned *BANG!* from movies and TV, real gunfire was loud as hell, and anything larger than a .22 required ear protection to avoid damaging the eardrums. The techies found 9mm casings, and that should have been loud enough to hear from a block away. Why hadn't Tom's team responded?

It might have been a suppressor. Suppressors were illegal in Illinois, and incredibly hard to get. But Ortega had no FOID—a state firearm owner ID—so maybe he picked one up at the same place he got the gun.

It had been Ortega. After getting the call, Jack called the team outside his house. They'd also neglected to place a man around back, and been chewed out. Ortega had entered his house, breaking the police tape. No sign of forced entry, so it must have been him, using his keys. The clincher was finding a secret panel in Ortega's basement, which hadn't been noticed on the previous search of his residence. No doubt that's where he'd hidden his gun.

So many screw-ups on this one case. It was a goddamn comedy of errors.

"Jack?" Herb was calling.

She returned to the corpse, and found AJ to still be in distress. She'd finished vomiting, an unhappy Herb left holding the cup, but her expression was pained.

"Someone else is dead," the psychic said.

"Other than Roberto and his parents?"

Ava nodded. She seemed so sure of herself, so confident she spoke the truth.

"Who is it?" Herb asked. Jack hoped he wouldn't forget and accidentally take a sip from the Big Gulp.

"I can't get a fix on it. But I can sense Oretga. He's killed again. It's a guy. And..."

"And?" Jack asked, genuinely curious now.

"And I just tried calling my roommate, Tomen. Both the apartment, and his cell." AJ's eyes met Jack's. "He's not answering."

ORTEGA

"Get into the trunk," Ortega commanded, indicating the back of the brown beat-up Buick.

The man's eyes were wide and he appeared appropriately frightened.

"Do it, and you'll have a chance to live. Don't, and I'll shoot you right here in the street."

That's where Ortega had found him; down the street, heading back to his home. Ortega wanted to take him someplace private, where they could have a little chat.

The man got into Ortega's trunk.

Ortega kept the car in a storage unit. It had belonged to his mother, and he'd gotten it when Mama passed. He couldn't bear to part with it. Mama was the one who taught him what love was. Love meant never letting go. So even though Ortega had no practical use for a car, he kept it, and all of Mama's things, and dutifully paid the two hundred dollars a month rental fee.

When he went to get the car, the tires were flat, and it took him half an hour to fill them again using Mama's old bike pump. The battery was dead, but he pushed it out of the unit and had gotten a jump start from the clerk at the desk.

Now he was going to head back to the unit, with the man in his trunk.

There were some things the man needed to confess to.

DANIELS

"Can't you tune into your roommate, or whatever it is you do?" Jack asked AJ. They were in Herb's car, the psychic in the back seat.

Ava Jane didn't answer. Jack sensed something unresolved there.

"We could stop by your apartment," Herb said, for the third time.

"If he was able to, he'd pick up." AJ's voice was flat.

"But if he's hurt…"

"I didn't sense *hurt*. I sensed *dead*."

Jack thought she understood. If Tomen had been killed, AJ was in no hurry to know it, or see it. She kept referring to him as her roommate, but Jack didn't have to be psychic to know she and Tomen were sleeping together.

Which made AJ's apparent lack of concern all the more strange.

Then again, denial was the first stage of grief. Maybe AJ was feeling more than she revealed. She had insisted they visit Maria Cantu—the girl Ortega had held captive for six months. Jack acquiesced not out of pity, or out of belief in the supernatural, but because Maria needed to go and hide somewhere, and Jack felt she had to be the one to tell her. Most people didn't take the news very well that they were in danger and had to give up their lives to run away. Especially when Maria had just gotten her life back.

They pulled up in front of Maria Cantu's home, a row house that had never seen better days, having been built for low income occupants right from the start.

"I'm going to wait in the car, keep an eye out for Ortega," Herb said.

Jack knew that wasn't the case. There was a 7-11 on the corner, and she knew her partner was going to replace the Mountain Dew he lost to AJ's hurling.

The cracks in the cement steps that led to the splintered wooden door were wide enough to break a heel, should the two women misstep, so they carefully climbed their way to the entrance.

They knocked and waited. Daniels noted there was no peep hole, and that the door frame looked weak enough to give in with one kick.

Even with police outside, Maria wasn't safe here.

A young woman, thin and sallow, eventually opened the door a few inches and peered out, safe behind a rusty chain that stretched between them. As if *that* would protect her.

"Maria?" Jack asked as she held up her police badge. "I'm Lt. Daniels, Chicago Police. May we speak with you a moment?" Daniels heard a fuss of conversation in Spanglish behind the teenager.

The girl turned and shouted, "No, Mama, *es la policía*. It's no problem." She unlatched the chain and let her guests inside. Jack and AJ were greeted by the stares of an older woman and three young children sitting on a shabby couch, motionless as if Tasered into silence.

"I thought you were someone else," Maria said. She was pretty, and Jack's first impression was of determination, not fear. It was good that she was healing emotionally, but not good when there was a nut after you.

Maria opened the door wider, and Jack saw the girl was holding a knife at her side. Jack glanced at the older woman standing behind Maria, and saw her place something small and weighty into the pocket of her housedress. A gun, no doubt.

Maybe they were safer than Jack had thought.

"Were you expecting your boyfriend?" AJ asked.

Wide-eyed, Maria reached out and grabbed the psychic. "How...? Is Montel okay? He was supposed to be here by now."

Jack scowled. She'd already made it clear AJ was supposed to keep quiet. Daniels made the introduction. "This is Ms. Rakowski, my, er, associate." She tried to block AJ from making any further conversation, but the damn consultant wouldn't shut up.

"Maria," she said, edging her way into the small front room, "do you have anything of Montel's? A piece of clothing? A gift he gave you? If I could hold it, maybe I could tune into him."

"You're a psychic?" The young woman's eyes filled with hope.

AJ nodded. Maria immediately took a heart shaped locket off her neck. It was gold or gold plated, the kind department stores sold.

While AJ divined the sooth or whatever nonsense she thought she did, Daniels took control of the interview. "Maria, Roberto De Luisa and his parents were just killed. We believe it was Ortega."

"*Hijo de puta.*" Maria turned her head and made a spitting sound like *ptuey*. "If he comes here, we'll be ready."

The elder Cantu sat on the couch, patting the weapon in her pocket. Jack doubted she had a FOID, but didn't pursue it.

"Where does Montel live?" AJ asked Maria.

"He lives in Lincoln Park. Why?"

Jack knew why. She could tell by the expression on the psychic's face.

AJ believed Montel was dead.

"Can you call him?" Jack asked Maria.

She nodded, placing the knife on a table near the door and digging her cell from her pocket. She dialed. Waited. Dialed again. Waited.

"What's his address?" AJ asked.

"Doesn't matter," Jack said. "If he hasn't picked up the phone, it's unlikely he'll answer his door."

"You can kick it in."

"No, I can't. There are these legal documents cops need to enter a premises. They're called warrants."

"You can enter if you suspect there is a crime being committed."

"Suspect how? A psychic told me?"

Maria leaned closer to them, whispering. "I have a key."

"That's still an illegal search."

"Not if I go," Maria said.

Jack's lips formed a thin line. The girl was right.

But if AJ was also right, did Maria need to see her dead boyfriend?

And why am I even considering that AJ might be right?

"Okay," Jack said. "We'll go. But if he doesn't answer, I'll go in first. You both will wait outside until I tell you it's okay. Got it?" Her gaze was directed at AJ.

"You're the boss," AJ replied.

Jack sighed. She might have been AJ's boss, but more and more often Jack felt like she wasn't the one in charge.

RAKOWSKI

When the four of them reached Montel's apartment, Ava Jane tried not to think about Tomen. She texted him during the car ride, and he hadn't replied. That was unusual.

AJ considered breaking her rule and tune into her housemate, but decided to leave it alone. Her recent impressions had been about Montel, after all, not Tomen.

Montel, she was sure, was dead. Ortega had killed him. AJ felt it in every atom in her body.

Jack confirmed it thirty seconds after Maria let her into Montel's apartment.

Maria bullied past the Lieutenant, wanting to see for herself, and AJ followed.

Maria fell to her knees, sobbing.

AJ managed to get to the kitchen sink before throwing up again. She was relatively new to this psychic detective work, after all, and hadn't developed Lieutenant Daniels's crime-hardened iron stomach and matching disposition. Yet.

Jack called in the troops and stayed to work the crime scene. Squad cars took Maria and AJ home, and AJ was glad to have a patrolman sweep each room of her small apartment to make sure it was safe. She felt a bit odd and helpless, though, when he left, even though he was sitting right outside her door.

It was Tomen. He wasn't home, and AJ still hadn't heard from him.

This wasn't unprecedented. They were just roommates. Tomen had his male friends over sometimes, and AJ knew he visited them as well. In fact, yesterday he'd mentioned a project he was working on with his pal Zach up in Waukegan. Maybe he was there. Or maybe he was with that old girlfriend from college. What was her name again? Sara? Sierra? He'd never brought an old flame home, but AJ couldn't rule out the possibility that Tomen had met up with a former girlfriend. Or found a new one.

She lay awake in bed, staring at the ceiling, trying to imagine what kind of woman Tomen would date.

For some reason, thinking about it made her annoyed. Which annoyed her even more. If he found some nice girl, AJ would be happy for him. Of course she would. There would be no reason not to be.

Well, she'd miss the casual sex. They'd gotten pretty good at it. But AJ had made clear from the very first time that it was purely physical and meant nothing.

Because it meant nothing.

So why was she dwelling on Tomen, unable to sleep?

AJ considered trying to tune into him. Dismissed it. Considered it again. Dismissed it again.

It was three in the morning before she finally fell asleep.

Tomen still hadn't returned.

DANIELS

At the bakery, Jack texted.

CU in 2, was the reply.

They were standing in a ridiculous line, waiting for Herb's morning éclair. Incredibly, the refrigerated display was full of them, and a crowd had arrived to buy them. Jack wondered why so many Chicagoans, in this enlightened age of health and fitness, had opted for suicide by pastry, but her partner looked damn pleased despite the wait.

"Proof I was, once again, ahead of my time," Herb said. "They should name it 'The Benedict.' I should be getting a percentage of sales."

"You should be getting a treadmill. But I don't think they make them big enough for you." Harry McGlade had jammed himself into the store, slipping in behind Herb and Jack. Jack's former partner and her current partner didn't get along, and she wasn't looking forward to the next few minutes. But Harry had been on his way to her office, only a block away, to share what he'd learned about Cook County Jail coincidentally releasing both Roberto de Luisa and Raphael Ortega on the same day. Jack thought it better to meet in the bakery than at the station, because Herb was less likely to shoot the PI here. He might miss, and hit a pastry.

"McGlade." Herb frowned. "My least favorite scumbag private eye in the whole country."

"Country?" Harry asked. "Not the whole world?"

"Shouldn't you be hiding in a closet and taking pictures of some adulterous wife?"

"Just finished." Harry grinned. "And I wasn't in the closet, I was tapping that ass myself. Want to see the pictures? But then, you've probably seen your wife naked before."

"Bullshit," Herb said. "My wife likes men."

"Then why did she marry a hippopotamus?"

Jack's cell buzzed, and she checked her text. *Where are you?*

AJ. She was no doubt in Jack's office, waiting for her, but the bakery line had made Jack late. She glanced behind the counter, saw the sign that said NOW SERVING 68. Herb had ticket number 83.

Jack texted back that she was still at the corner bakery while the boys continued their pissing contest.

"You're funny, McGlade. Like syphilis is funny. And like syphilis, I could get rid of you with one shot."

"You're fat, Benedict. Like walruses are fat. I have an urge to tie two tusks to your head and drop you off at Brookfield Zoo. But they'd probably be worried you'd eat the other walruses."

"Enough," Jack said. "McGlade, what did you get?"

"From Herb's wife? A hummer, then we did the spinning noodle."

Herb snarled, sounding more than a little like a walrus. "I'm going to get some rookies to follow you around and give you parking tickets everywhere you go."

"Send them to your house. Your wife wants me to come back. She said sex with you is like being sat on by an elephant. Except the elephant smells better, and has smoother skin."

"The information, Harry," Jack said. "Or I will let him shoot you."

Harry made a wounded face. "Ouch, Jackie. That hurts. After all we've been through. You're like a sister to me. A sister I'd like to drill."

"Cook County Jail. What did you find?"

"Louis Forest, the attorney for Roberto de Luisa, took the case pro bono. And the judge De Luisa got—check this out—is Forest's second cousin. I'd guess that's how Roberto made bail. But it gets better. A clerk was greased to mix up Raphael Ortega's release papers. And guess who provided the bribe?" Harry grinned. "Mr. Louis Forest, Esquire."

"He got both of them out?" Herb said. "Why?"

"That's the $64,000 question, jumbo. Maybe you should pretend you're a cop and go ask him."

"What's Forest's history?"

McGlade flipped open an old school note pad.

"Male, Hispanic, forty-four years old. Defense attorney. Used to be with a big firm, Neiman and Leel, but now has his own little practice. Mostly DUIs and domestic battery cases. Lives in Edgewater, rents, drives a four year old Nissan. Divorced, two brothers and two sisters, one daughter. Family name was originally Silva, he legally changed it to the English translation, Forest. Now this is disturbing…"

"What?"

McGlade showed Daniels the pad. It was a crude drawing of a naked fat man with tusks, and HERB written beneath it.

Herb hadn't been paying attention. He'd pulled his badge and forced himself to the front of the line, where he we negotiating for his éclair.

"Want to see the one I did of you?" Harry asked.

"Not if you like your teeth."

"Lieutenant?" Jack looked over McGlade's shoulder and saw AJ had squeezed into the store.

"Well, look at this hot little number. I'm Harry McGlade, private investigator extraordinaire. Are you in need of someone investigating your privates?"

"Excuse me?" Ava Jean said.

"I said I'd like to strap you on like a feedbag," Harry said.

"You're rude and gross," AJ said, dismissing McGlade and facing Jack. "Lieutenant, Ortega grabbed someone else yesterday."

Jack hadn't heard anything, so she realized this must have been another one of the psychic's impressions. She was about to dismiss it but instead she said, "Tomen?"

"I still haven't heard from him. But… I don't know… something is different… And Ortega, his psychosis is growing. I can feel him, more than ever before."

"Wait a second," McGlade said. "You're a psychic?"

AJ nodded.

Here we go, Jack thought.

"That's incredible," Harry said, surprising Jack by not making some lame joke. "I have great respect for those who have a third eye. I had an uncle who was a psychic. He actually predicted the exact date and time of his death. Down to the minute."

"That's impressive," said AJ.

"Not really. He killed himself." McGlade leered at her. "So can you guess what I'm thinking now?"

AJ slapped him.

"My God," McGlade said, "she's the real thing."

Herb held his white bakery bag over his head, triumphant, and as Jack turned to leave she saw—

Ortega. In the store. Holding something white in his hands.

Paper towels.

Jack put it all together, immediately drawing her Colt Detective Special from her shoulder holster.

"Everyone! Down!"

McGlade spun around. "Look out!" he yelled. "He's got a roll of paper towels!"

Ortega's first shot somehow missed the throng of people and shattered the glass of a side cooler, exploding one of the giant éclairs. The glass breaking made more noise than the gun did.

Before she could shoot back, a stampede of people crashed the exit, sweeping Ortega out with them.

Jack and Harry tried to follow, but there were too many people ahead of them. When they finally got out to the street, the shooter had disappeared.

"Well," McGlade said, holstering his .44 and staring at AJ, "you should have seen that coming."

Herb came out of the store last, cradling his bag like a running back with a football. Except footballs were smaller than the éclair. "Everyone okay?"

Jack nodded. "It was Ortega."

AJ was ashen. "I… I sensed him so strongly. But I thought he was just getting more obsessed. I didn't think it was because…"

"Because he was following you?" McGlade said. "Girl, you need to fine tune your shit." He turned to Jack. "Are we done here, Jackie? I gave you everything you need on the former Senor Silva."

"Silva?" AJ asked, snapping out of her moment of shock.

Daniels saw the wheels turn in her friend's mind; and she started connecting some dots as well. Maybe this psychic intuition stuff wasn't totally off-the-wall as it first appeared. Maybe the whole thing was more like hunches on steroids. She had to admit, with over twenty-five years on the force, her hunches could seem paranormal to an outsider. Maybe this new kid just had a knack. To AJ she said, "Name ring a bell?"

Her friend nodded. "Guadalupe Silva is one of the cold cases I'm working on."

"Does Forest have a daughter named Guadalupe?" Jack said to McGlade.

He shrugged. "Hell if I know. I've always done things half-assed."

"Guadalupe's father was named Luis," AJ said.

Jack nodded. "Luis Silva. Louis Forest. Same guy."

"I missed something," Herb said.

"It wasn't a meal," Harry told him.

"AJ is working on some older missing person cases. Young Hispanic girls. Like Ortega abducted and Roberto killed. One was Guadalupe Silva. Her father is Roberto's defense attorney, and the man who got Ortega out of jail."

"So he got them both out why?" Herb said. "For vigilante justice?"

AJ shook her head. "No. He's still looking for his daughter. That's why he sent me the threatening email. He didn't want me getting in the way."

"I think we need to pay this guy a visit," Herb said.

"Too late." AJ's head fell. "I think Ortega has him."

"We just saw Ortega."

AJ closed her eyes. "Ortega is holding him somewhere. Somewhere dark… and dusty. And it smells. It smells terrible."

"Ortega killed Roberto and Montel in their homes," Jack reminded her.

"This feels different."

Jack tried to think. Ortega's house was being staked out, correctly this time. If he had abducted Forest, where would he take him?

"McGlade, got any contacts at multinational financial services?" she asked.

"Huh?"

"Visa and Mastercard, dummy," Herb said, taking out his phone. "She wants you to trace Ortega's credit cards, see where he might have gone."

Herb walked away, making his calls.

"And credit history," Jack continued. "See if he has any liens against him, or another mortgage."

McGlade nodded. "Yeah, I got contacts. What's in it for me?"

"How about saving someone's life?" AJ said, putting her hands on her hips.

"Saving a life is that important to you?" he asked.

"Of course."

"Important enough for you to have dinner with me?"

AJ's eyebrows furrowed. "What?"

"I'll help. But you have to have dinner with me."

"Is that how you get dates? Extortion?"

"If I can. Other times I just pay escorts. But the good ones are a hundred bucks an hour. And the bad ones, well, let's just say for fifty dollars a night you're getting what you pay for. I was with this one escort, she had so many warts that doing her was like reading a book in braille."

"Fine," AJ said. "But hurry."

McGlade got on his phone the same time Herb flipped his cell closed. "Forest isn't picking up at home, and hasn't come into the office today."

"Send teams to both places."

A squad car showed up, sirens blaring, and Jack spent ten minutes filling them in. There would be statements, and witness interviews. With a little luck, she told the uniforms, if they caught Ortega they could book him for attempted murder.

"Attempted murder?" Herb said, joining in the conversation. "Did you see what that bastard did to that beautiful éclair?"

"I'm not sure *drive-by pastry* is on the books."

"It should be. And you should feel lucky."

"That I'm not a pastry?"

"Remember what you said about the release of Raphael and Roberto not being a coincidence? You made a bet there was some connection."

"Yeah, great connection. Roberto's dead and our psycho's on the loose."

"True, but you won't have to shop at Sears for your next suit."

McGlade interrupted. "I'm still not done, but I may have something on Ortega's Mastercard. He's had a large rental unit at U-Store-It for the past ten years. Ground level, semi-private entrance."

Jack shivered. She'd recently had a run-in with a psycho who tortured his victims to death in storage lockers, and it hadn't been a pleasant experience.

"Which location?" Herb asked.

"Ten minutes from here."

"Let's make it in five," Jack said.

FOREST

Louis Forest, previously known as Luis Silva, was duct taped to a chair in some sort of garage. His mouth was wrapped up, but he could see. It didn't matter though, because there was nothing to see in the darkness. He could feel the concrete under his shoes, smell car exhaust and moth balls, and something else.

Something rotten.

His master plan had gone all wrong. Roberto de Luisa was supposed to be the one tied to a chair. Forest needed him out of jail so he could question him about his missing daughter, Guadalupe. He was sure Roberto had murdered her. Absolutely sure of it. When he read about the case in the paper, weeks ago, it had burrowed deep into his soul, and he immediately offered to be his attorney.

He'd tried to talk about Lupe during their many meetings, but Roberto remained evasive. He needed stronger persuasion.

The strain of Lupe's disappearance had ruined Forest. Ruined his marriage. Ruined his career. He grew up a poor Latino kid in the neighborhood of Pilsen, got good grades, a scholarship to a decent college, and into law school. He worked hard to remove all the traces of an accent out of his voice, and Americanized his name to have a chance with a big firm, figuring he'd be accepted as one of them, and he was, getting into one of Chicago's biggest firms once he passed the bar. He'd been an up and comer, one to watch. Met his wife, had a daughter, and was on track to make junior partner when Lupe disappeared.

At first, Neiman and Leel was sympathetic. But when his drinking became too much, they let him go. His wife left him soon after, leaving

Forest with a deep hole in his soul that he filled with fantasies of revenge against the man who took Lupe.

And he finally believed he'd found that man. It was de Luisa. Forest would get the truth from him, and then he'd be able to move on with his life. Get his wife back. Get his old job back.

The problem was, no matter how much Forest burned with rage, he'd never be able to torture somebody. Causing another person physical harm was something he didn't have the stomach for.

But Raphael Ortega had the stomach for it. Ortega was a psychopath, no doubt, but he *hated* de Luisa. Forest met with him twice, offering him freedom in exchange for getting de Luisa to talk.

Ortega agreed. But he'd beaten de Luisa to death without getting any sort of information about Lupe.

And now he was going to kill Louis. And Forest would die without ever knowing what happened to his daughter.

The door opened, and then the lights came on, blinding Forest. He squinted, staring at Ortega, hating him so much he felt like he could kill the man with his eyes.

"You are deluding yourself," Ortega said.

It was, perhaps, a strangely appropriate statement. Forest had been deluding himself that this plan could work, but he'd also been deluding himself his entire life. Instead of being proud of his heritage, he'd denied it. Instead of facing tragedy, he hid in a bottle of whiskey. Instead of getting on with life, he'd nurtured outrageous revenge fantasies.

"You told me you wanted Roberto to suffer. He did. I never asked him about your daughter, Guadalupe, because I didn't need to. He had nothing to do with Lupe."

Forest screamed through his duct tape gag. Had he been wrong about De Luisa?

Had the real monster, this entire time, been Ortega? How else could he have known her nickname was Lupe?

"Yes, I knew your daughter," Ortega said, as if reading Forest's mind. "And I know what happened to her. I could tell you. But I want to show you something." The madman stroked Forest's cheek with the barrel of his gun, then walked over to a tarpaulin spread over a lumpy collection of furniture stacked in the corner of the room.

"The love of a father for a daughter, it must be like the love of a mother for a son, yes? I would like you to meet my mother."

Ortega grabbed the corner of the tarp, and pulled it off with a flourish.

Revealing—

Oh sweet Jesus...

It wasn't quite a skeleton because it still had hair, and some brown, withered meat on the bones. It wore a pink sun dress, and was seated in a chair—part of a kitchen set that matched the one Forest was bound to. In her lap was a coffee mug, one of her hands on it.

"Mama still loves me, and I love her. Not even death can halt such a love. Is that the feeling you have for your daughter?"

Forest nodded. Then he watched, terrified, as Ortega kissed the mummy of his dead mother. It resulted in a small cloud of dust—dead skin cells—to puff up around her, adding to the foul odor. With his mouth bound, Forest had no choice but to breathe in through his nostrils.

"Would you love her this much?" Ortega asked when he finished, a rope of saliva trailing down his chin. "Even if she were dead?"

As grotesque of a display as it was, Forest felt his eyes well up. He nodded again.

"How about Alanza de Luisa?"

Huh?

"You wanted Roberto killed. Is that because you fell in love with his sister and wanted revenge?"

Forest emphatically shook his head.

"And Maria Cantu? Do you love her as well? Did you visit her when I was in jail?"

More head shaking. This man was clearly insane.

"Do you love Ava Jane Rakowski?"

The psychic? Of course not! Forest tried to threaten her in an email, to get her to back off. Through teary eyes he stared at Ortega, the maniac, the man who may or may not have known what happened to Lupe, the man who was clearly having a psychotic break with reality.

"Perhaps you believe these women loved you." Ortega slipped his hand into his satchel, replacing his gun with some brass knuckles. "But I'm going to convince you that they did not."

Forest tried to protest through the gag. He screamed in his throat, shaking his head, his eyes imploring Ortega to let him speak.

Oretga tilted his head to the side, apparently studying Forest. "You want to talk?"

Forest nodded.

"I will take off the tape to let you talk. But if you yell or scream, the tape goes back on. Okay?"

Another nod.

The tape came off painfully. Forest tried to talk, but his mouth was dry.

"Water," he rasped.

"I have no water. But perhaps Mama will give you some of her coffee. We like to drink coffee together. Let me see if she has any left."

Forest watched, horrified, as Ortega approached the mummy—*his mummy* quite literally—and removed the coffee mug from her lap.

"She has some left, and she's willing to share."

Forest felt himself tense up, and when he stared into the cup as it was raised to his lips he saw clumps of dead skin, and a curled up spider, floating on top. He began to protest, and Oretga dumped some liquid into his open mouth.

The taste was like the smell; a rotten, desiccated flavor that Forest immediately choked on and spit back out.

"You don't like Mama's coffee?" Ortega asked, raising the brass knuckles.

"I'm… allergic to caffeine," he said in a burst of inspiration.

Ortega smiled broadly. "It's okay. This is decaf."

More pouring, and after the second gulp Forest felt his gorge begin to rise and he realized he'd rather be hit with brass knuckles than take another sip. Thankfully, Ortega took the mug away.

"So what did you want to say to me?"

Fighting the urge to spit, Forest said, "I will tell you about Alanza and Maria and…" what the hell was the third girl's name? "…Ava Jane.

But I beg you to tell me about Lupe, my daughter. We'll trade information. Three girls for one girl. Okay?"

Ortega seemed to consider it, then said, "Fair enough. You go first."

"I spoke to Maria Cantu while you were in ja… while you were away. She missed you terribly, and cannot wait to be reunited with you."

Ortega's eyes narrowed. "Does she love you?"

"No! No, she only has room in her heart for you. She said the time with you was the best in her life."

"How about you? Do you love her?" Forest watched Ortega's jaw clench.

"She is pretty, *but!*" he added quickly, "I am not the kind of man who would take a woman who belonged to another. Clearly she loves you, so I kept my distance."

Ortega nodded slowly.

"And Lupe?" Forest asked, letting a bit of hope break through the terror.

"Your daughter loved me," Ortega said. Forest fought not to scream. "But it was not meant to be. It didn't work out between us. Very headstrong, Lupe was. I was her first, you know. Now your turn. Tell me about Alanza."

Forest closed his eyes, his whole body shaking. The words *I was her first* ricocheted around in his head like a pinball. Lupe? With this monster? It was too much to handle.

"Did… did you kill her?" Forest managed.

The fist came hard and fast, slamming into Forest's jaw. It was like getting hit with a brick.

"Your. Turn. Tell me about Alanza."

Forest blinked away stars, blood seeping from his split lip. "Roberto loved Alanza. But she loved you, and only you."

"Did you love her?"

"I never met her."

"Liar! You loved her!"

Another crushing punch. Forest felt something like gravel in his mouth. A broken tooth.

"I admit it," Forest groaned. "I loved her. But she ignored me. She told me that she was waiting for you to claim her. So I forgot her and loved someone else."

"Is it Ava Jane?"

"It's your turn," Forest mumbled. The pain in his face was reaching the point where he was close to blacking out. "Is my daughter dead?"

"No," said Ortega. "I would never harm a girl who loved me, even though I stopped loving her. I sold Lupe. Now tell me about Ava Jane."

"Sold her?" Was that even possible? "Who did you sell her to?"

"You next!" Ortega ordered, raising his fist.

"Okay okay okay! Ava Jane…"

Forest had no idea who Ava Jane was. But he'd bullshitted his way through the other two, so maybe he could do the same with this. And then…

And then?

Ortega would say who he sold Lupe to, and then let him go? What was the likelihood of that?

Zero.

When Forest was done talking, Ortega would kill him. Then he'd never see his daughter—his daughter who could still be alive—again.

"I'm a lawyer," Forest said. "Lawyers are part of the judicial system, like judges."

"So what?"

"So I could marry you."

Ortega grimaced. "I don't want to marry you."

"I meant I could marry you and Maria. Like a judge or a priest. If you were married, you'd have a legal marriage license. The police couldn't bother you anymore."

Ortega's forehead crinkled up. Was he actually that dim-witted? Could he actually believe it?

It was possible. The maniac believed his dead mother drank coffee, and that all women loved him.

"But how could I marry Maria and Ava Jane at the same time?"

"It's simple," Forest said. "You can become a Mormon. Mormons are allowed to have several wives. But it takes a special kind of lawyer to perform two marriages at once."

"Can you do that?"

"Yes. I can do that. But you have to tell me who you sold my daughter to."

Ortega opened his mouth, but no words came out. He seemed confused.

"I can do it!" Forest said. "I swear I can!"

"It's too late," Ortega said, the siren growing louder. He drew his gun and aimed it at Forest's chest. "The police are here."

RAKOWSKI

Ava Jane hadn't ever ridden in a squad car before, and with the sirens blaring and the fast driving through traffic signals and around other vehicles, she'd have been happy to never ride in one again.

When they made it to the storage facility and screeched to a halt, they had to wait for Herb and the uniformed officer who'd driven them to let the women in the backseat out, since police cars didn't have back door handles.

But Lt. Daniels jabbed a finger at AJ. "You're staying here."

"But I—"

Jack slammed the door, locking the psychic in the squad car. Then she, Detective Benedict, and the patrolman all headed into U-Store-It.

Perturbed, AJ folded her arms and slumped in the seat. She'd been right about Maria's boyfriend, Montel. She'd been right about a lot on this case. And Jack Daniels still insisted on treating her like a civilian. Worse, like AJ's abilities were based on luck and intuition rather than actual psychic abilities.

Didn't the lieutenant know that AJ could actually help them? She could tune into things that they couldn't, and...

A chill came over Ava Jane, as real as if she'd jumped into a freezing lake. She immediately swiveled her head around coming face-to-face with—

Ortega.

He was only a few feet away, standing next to the squad car, staring at her through the window.

AJ looked around for…

For what?

She couldn't blow the horn or turn on the siren or call out on the radio. The back seats of squad cars were tiny little prison cells. No way to get out, or to tell the others what was happening.

Wait! My cell phone!

AJ kept her expression neutral, keeping eye contact as she dug her cell from her purse. Ortega approached slowly, a smile splitting his face.

AJ glanced down and quickly texted Jack, "*O here w/me*" and hit send just as Ortega reached her window and crouched to face her.

"Hello, Ava Jane."

"Hello, Raphael." She swallowed her fear. "It's good to see you again."

His smile broadened. "I knew you'd feel that way."

Was he going to open the car and grab her? He was much bigger than she was, but she would fight and kick and scream before she let him take her. She knew Ortega had ether on him, probably in that bag he was holding, and he'd try to use it to knock AJ out. But she swore she wouldn't let that…

Keys!

AJ wasn't sure why the image of keys flashed through her mind, but it made her look into the front seat—

—where the keys dangled from the ignition.

The patrolman had left them in the car.

All Ortega needed to do was climb in the front seat, and he could take her anywhere.

Ava Jane's phone buzzed. She glanced down, hoping it was Lt. Daniels.

Spent night with friend, home now, what's up?

It was Tomen. She was glad he was okay, but it wasn't whom AJ was hoping to hear from. She hit redial for Lt. Daniels, hoping she'd pick up.

"Who are you calling?" Ortega asked.

AJ thought fast. "My mother. You want us to be together, right?"

That was the understatement of the century. The psychic could feel the man's delusional lust through the car door.

"Yes. Just like you want it."

"I need my mother's permission," AJ said. "That's the tradition in my family. Koreans need their parents to approve."

Ortega watched silently.

Jack's voicemail picked up, and AJ said, "Mom? It's Ava Jane." She flashed a fake smile at Ortega. "I'm here, right now, in the back of a police car, and a man named Raphael Ortega is with me. He and I want to be together, and I need your permission."

AJ paused, as if her mother was answering, and Ortega's attention flitted to the driver side door. He stepped away from AJ, his hand stretching for it.

AJ frantically knocked on the window, getting him to look at her. "She wants to talk to you."

Ortega paused.

"Now," AJ said. "If you want us to be together, you need to ask my mother."

Ortega reached into his bag, taking out a rag and soaking it with ether.

"Open the door," AJ said, trying to keep smiling even as her body shook with fear. She held out the phone, as if waiting for him to take it.

Ortega placed his hand on the door handle.

AJ prepared herself as best she could. *Knock the rag away, then start screaming.*

Ortega lifted the handle—

—then his eyes went wide and he ran off.

Five seconds later, Lt. Daniels and the uniform ran past, chasing after him.

Ten seconds after that, Detective Benedict ran past, wheezing.

A minute later, the Lieutenant and the patrolman returned. Jack let AJ out of the back.

"Ortega parked up the block, got away," Jack said. "But thanks for the text."

"The keys were in the car," AJ said, half-hysterical. "He could have driven off with me!"

The lieutenant shot the uniform a stern look, and he went sheepish.

AJ wasn't sure whether to laugh or cry. She'd been so scared, and now she was exhilarated, angry, and still trembling. "Don't leave me behind again," she told Jack.

"I won't."

AJ closed her eyes, getting her emotions under control. When she opened them she said, "Louis Forest is dead."

Lt. Daniels nodded. "Ortega shot him twice in the chest. But he was still alive when we got to him. Before he died he said Ortega had his daughter."

"Lupe," AJ said.

"Yeah." Lt. Daniels rubbed her chin.

"Ortega sold her, didn't he?"

Daniels seemed surprised. "Yeah. How...?"

"You already know how. This is what I do, Lieutenant. I can help find her."

Benedict finally made it back to the car, breathing like an asthmatic in a Pilates class. "You were left alone with a killer. Are you okay?" he asked.

"I'm fine," AJ said. And the truth was, she was feeling a lot better. The immediate danger had passed.

But Detective Benedict wasn't talking to AJ. He was talking to his éclair. He went to the front seat and picked up the bakery bag, cradling it in his arms.

Then AJ remembered Tomen's text.

He was okay, and that made her happy.

But he'd taken a long time to reply, and that pissed her off.

Plus he said he was with a friend, but didn't mention which friend.

Was it a woman?

That pissed her off even more.

"I'm sorry I left you in the car," Jack said. "If you're going to get pissy about it..."

"It's not you," AJ interrupted. "It's Tomen. I heard from him. He was with a friend."

"And you're angry about that?"

"I... yeah. I don't understand why, though."

Jack laughed. "For someone who supposedly can see things, you can't see anything about yourself."

"What are you talking about?"

"It's obvious, AJ. You love the guy."

"Tomen? No, I don't."

Daniels shrugged. "I have to call in a team, it'll take a few hours. You can go through Ortega's storage space, see if you sense anything. Then we can talk about Tomen over lunch."

"I don't need to talk about Tomen."

"Sure you don't." Jack gave her a clap on the shoulder, then pulled out her cell phone.

The Lieutenant was wrong, of course. She liked Tomen, as a friend, and was relieved he was okay. She was mad because he was inconsiderate for...

For what? Not telling his roommate he was sleeping at a friend's house?

A *girl* friend's house?

The thought of it made AJ angry. First at Tomen. Then at herself.

Oh... wow. I'm actually jealous.

Which meant...

Could Lt. Daniels be right?

That realization was almost as scary as when Ortega tried to get into the squad car.

She thought about tuning in to Tomen. To sense, for the first time, what his feelings for her were. AJ closed her eyes, trying to read Tomen, trying to get a feel for his mindset.

"You coming?" Jack said. "We're working a crime scene, remember? You can think about your boyfriend later."

AJ blinked, surprised. "How did you...?"

"Maybe you aren't the only one around here who is psychic. Come on."

AJ dutifully followed her boss into the storage area. But she was puzzled.

For a brief moment, she had sensed Tomen.

And he'd been afraid.

TOMEN MURE

After working late into the evening designing a website at Zach's place in Waukegan, Tomen ended up spending the rest of the night playing World of Warcraft with his best friend.

He considered the phrase, rolling it around in his head.

Best friend.

It wasn't quite true anymore. His *best* friend was actually AJ. He'd only realized it himself a few months before and had been trying to figure out how to explain his growing feelings to her.

He wasn't getting anywhere.

Maybe if he just acted 'as if' they were a couple, things would naturally evolve that way. So nearing their apartment in the north suburb Village of Wilmette, he decided to let his domestic side shine. He stopped at a nearby farmers market to do some shopping. He'd make a nice dinner salad for them both and act as if they were a normal couple. Then he wouldn't have to actually say anything about his feelings for her. They'd just…grow closer.

Wandering through the temporary stalls, he looked over the summer vegetables that the area farmers trucked in from their fields, some as far away as Wisconsin. Squash, tomatoes, corn. Perfect season for a pair of aspiring vegetarians.

"You'll be needing some cheese—sharp cheddar," called out a vendor as Tomen made his way through the stalls.

"I will, eh?" He chuckled. Why not? He wasn't a vegan, after all. Too much work. He ate cheese every now and then. He'd even indulge in the occasional omelet, as long as his vegan friends didn't find out. Though he suspected they all harbored similar hypocrisies. But why the pretense? If everyone would just come clean with their silly secrets, the world would be a better place.

That's it. Transparency. People should just be real with one another. It could start with confessing their inconsistencies; sharing their true selves. An image of Ava came to mind. Maybe he should come clean with her after all, confess his actual feelings. But what did he really think and feel? Did he love her?

Yes.

Was it true love?

If not, it was getting pretty damn close.

He shook his head, puzzled as to his next move. The vendor, mistaking the gesture, said, "Well, your loss. If you change your mind, you know where to find me. But next time, it might be too late. Could be sold out. Could have moved on to a different market."

Heh. Maybe AJ's talent is rubbing off on me, Tomen thought. *If that's not a sign from heaven, I don't know what is.*

"Okay, sold. Give me a wedge of your sharpest cheddar."

"Careful. It's so sharp, you may cut yourself." The dairy farmer handed it over in exchange for a ten and was already on to the next customer.

After a few more purchases and satisfied with his haul, Tomen made his way back to his car, loaded the passenger seat with his bag of groceries, and headed to their apartment. On days like this when he took on a bit of the domestic role, he could definitely picture them together as a couple. For the long term. In fact, he'd considered saving up for a ring just in case she gave off any signals about wanting to take their relationship to a deeper level…beyond the mutual stress-relieving roll in the sheets.

At least, that's what AJ called it.

Tomen considered it more than that. Something much more important.

Intimacy.

Surely Ava Jane felt it as well. She could sense extraordinary things. She must have been able to sense his feelings.

As he thought about his roommate's intuitive powers, something nagged at the back of Tomen's brain. He looked in the rear view mirror. There, a few cars back, idled a brown, dilapidated Buick. The car didn't belong in the neighborhood.

Raphael Ortega?

When the light changed, Tomen pulled forward then made a quick turn at the next intersection. He doubted he was being followed, but it didn't hurt to make sure.

The car followed.

Then flashing blue light appeared in his mirror. A patrol car, coming up fast.

Damn.

Tomen eased his nondescript silver Civic to the curb while the police car pulled up behind him. The brown Buick passed them both, slowly, making its way down the street.

The officer tapped on the trunk as he approached, but Tomen had already rolled the driver's side window down. "Can I help you officer?"

"Your turn signal broken, son?" the cop said without preamble.

"I don't think so, why?"

"Wasn't working at the intersection you blew through. I'll need to see your driver's license."

Tomen fumbled with his wallet and handed it over.

"Tomen Mure." The man scrunched his eyebrows behind his dark glasses. "Name sounds familiar. You been in trouble with the law, Mr. Mure?"

"No, sir." He watched the brown Buick turn onto a side street, without seeing the driver's face.

The officer snapped his finger. "Wait a minute, you're that psychic's boyfriend, aren't you? Our chief mentioned your name at roll call this past week."

"Oh? In what context?"

"Said to keep our eyes and ears open." He handed Tomen his license back. "Said you might be in danger. Have you noticed anything unusual?"

Could that have been Ortega in the Buick? Tomen wondered if he should tell the cop. But if he did, what would that involve? Making a statement? Would he have to go to the station to do so? That would really but the brakes on the domestic scene he'd planned for AJ.

That probably wasn't Ortega, he decided. *It's just paranoia. Besides, if I were in trouble, Ava Jane would know.*

"No, nothing unusual," Tomen answered.

"Seeing as we're on the same team, so to speak, I'm going to let you off with a warning. You get that blinker checked, though, you hear me?"

"Yes, officer."

"Oh, and young man?"

"Yes?"

"Best be careful out there."

ORTEGA

Ava Jane had lied to him.

She hadn't been on the phone with her mother.

She'd been on the phone with her boyfriend.

If he and Ava Jane were ever going to be together, Tomen Mure would have to admit that she loved Ortega, not him.

Raphael Ortega passed a police car that was stopped behind a silver Civic and headed north, toward the apartment Tomen and Ava Jane shared.

It had been a very busy day.

But he had time for one more beat down.

A LETTER TO JACK
(WITH HARRY MCGLADE)

I'm lucky to get a reasonable amount of fan mail, and I'm always happy to hear from readers. But few emails have touched me as much as one I received from a mother, who told me about her teenage kid's enthusiasm for my books.

Instead of writing back, I had Harry McGlade do the honors. Later, with their permission, I published the letter, and an addendum, on my blog.

A LETTER TO JACK

TO: JACK ON HIS 15th BIRTHDAY
FROM: HARRISON HAROLD MCGLADE

Hey Jack.

Cool name.

My name is Harry McGlade. I heard you've read about me.

The guy who writes about all the awesome shit I do, J.A. Konrath, also known as Joe, told me it's your birthday today.

Happy birthday!

I remember turning 15. Best year of my life. I was on top of the world, and so happy all the time that you couldn't smack the smile off my face with a hockey stick.

Joking. Being 15 sucked sweaty balls.

School was brutal. I was pudgy, short, had a high voice. Got picked on. Had to deal with bullies. My grades were shit, and my merry-go-round of foster parents were always riding my ass about that. I didn't have any close friends, and I had no love life at all. I'd never kissed anyone. Never even had a date. Every day was a living hell.

You couldn't pay me a billion dollars to go back in time and be a teenager again. You know why?

Because you don't have a billion dollars, Jack. And time travel is impossible. You should know that.

If time travel was possible, there would be time travelers every-where, walking around acting like "Look at me, I'm from the future, and I got an iPhone 37! I can use it to call Moses!"

But we don't see that. Because there are no time travelers. And be-cause Moses isn't real.

Neither is Santa. Hope I didn't spoil that for you.

Where were we? Oh yeah, you brought up time travel billionaires.

C'mon, Jack. You can't come at me like that, bro. Bragging about having all that money and a time machine. That's insane!

(But if you actually do have a billion dollars and a time machine, hit me up.)

WTF was I talking about?

Right. Being a teenager was tough. I bet it's even harder for you. Transgender? Dude, I don't even know you, but I can imagine all the shit you have to deal with.

Actually, I CAN'T imagine it. No one can imagine it, unless they've gone through the same thing.

You're super brave, bro.

When I was your age, I was confused a lot about a lot of things. There was no one who understood me. I liked boys, and girls, and pretty much everyone no matter how they identified, and I didn't understand why. And back then, there was no internet. I couldn't find other peo-ple like me. Bisexuals were called faggots and got spat on. There term 'pansexual' wasn't even invented yet. People actually thought gender was fixed. They really believed that who you were attracted to was a choice, like you could turn off what turned you on.

What a bunch of backwards-ass pinheads. And some folks still haven't caught up to modern reality. Sad.

So I got a lot of hate and a lot of weird stares when I was your age. Or people tried to fix me. Like there was something wrong with me. Like my feelings were wrong, because they were different.

Turns out, there was nothing wrong with me. I liked what I liked, and that was fine. I am what I am, and my feelings are just as valid as anyone else's. Problem isn't me. It's the world.

People fear and hate and laugh at and try to change the things they don't understand. It's an unfortunate aspect of human nature. They think we need to look and act a certain way, and if we don't fit that mold, we're freaks.

That's garbage.

I never had body dysmorphia, so I don't know what that feels like. No one does, unless they go through it. I bet it's hard. I lost my hand. And even though its gone, sometimes I can still feel it. Phantom Limb Syndrome, it's called. Weird, huh? But you can't really understand it unless it happens to you.

For the record, I DO NOT recommend losing a hand. Just clarifying that. Had to relearn how to wipe my ass. Took four months. Four dark, messy months.

Worst part? I bite my fingernails. You don't want to bite the brown nail, buddy. Yuck Factor One Billion.

But pretty funny. Gotta laugh at yourself sometimes.

Anyway, the world has gotten a little better since I was your age. There are still asshats everywhere, but there are some good people, too. I've got a BFF named Jack Daniels that you know about. She's pretty cool. Her husband Phin is cool, too, and the dude is smoking hot. They accept me for who I am, and don't judge.

It's hard to find people who don't judge. I bet it's really hard for you. When you were a kid, everyone treated you like a girl. You had a girl name. You still have girl parts and girl hormones, and you know that doesn't feel right, and people don't understand.

And now you're telling people that you're not that girl with that old name, you're someone else. You're really a man named Jack.

Cool name. My buddy, Jack Daniels, would be real proud of that.

Gotta be tough to feel one way when the world sees you another way. Kinda like Bruce Wayne, and when he grows up he realizes he's the Batman. Maybe he's always been the Batman, but the only one who understands him is Alfred. No one else does.

Is it me, or did Bruce and Alfred have a gay vibe? Maybe it's me.

Anyway, I bet people have a hard time trying to understand you. I bet you don't even understand you sometimes.

Or maybe I'm wrong, and you've figured it all out and you've got your shit together and Everything Is Awesome like in the Lego Movie (I couldn't get that effing song outta my head for weeks—I actually thought about suing those little plastic bastards).

If you have figured it all out, let me know your secret. Because I'm 54 years old and I'm still confused about a lot.

But some things I do know. I'll share a few of these things with you, as a birthday gift. Which is great for me, because it doesn't cost me any cash.

I know you didn't ask for advice, and I get that. I'm an old white guy, and most of the problems in the world are caused by old white guys. What the hell do I know about anything?

Well, I don't know much about what it's like to be you. But I know a little about what it's like being me. Maybe some of it applies.

So let the Harry McGlade Wisdom commence…

Life gets better as you get older. You have more control over things, and you can find where you fit in. Right now you have to put up with stuff. You're not an adult yet. You live at home. You have to go to school. You don't feel right in the body you have. But when you get older, things change. You aren't forced to do as much, you get to make all your own decisions, and life gets better. I promise.

There are people out there who like people like us. And there are people who love people like us.

Never trust a fart. I just shit myself the other day, in line at the theater to see the new Godzilla. I blamed the smell on the old lady behind me, and then flushed my underwear down the toilet in the movie theater bathroom, which clogged it up and caused a big shitwater flood. Some kid came in and slipped on it and got all soaked with shitwater—dude was wearing white too—and it was so funny I couldn't stop laughing. So, actually, that story has a good ending. Unless you were that kid. But, truth, kid looked like a real d-bag and probably deserved it. Also, Godzilla was fun.

Where was I? Oh yeah, life lessons.

Pets are the best.

There will always be people who don't understand. But there are always people who do understand. Find those people. Those are your people. And the ones that don't understand, forgive them. They don't get it.

Everyone is a consumer. But you also need to give back. Everyone takes. Not everyone gives. Be a giver.

At the same time, no good deed goes unpunished. Sounds funny, but it seems like every time I do something nice, it comes back to bite me in the ass. For that reason, never do anything and expect to be thanked. If you help someone, do it because you feel they need help. Don't expect anyone to be grateful. Haters gonna hate, no matter how nice you are.

Never buy a burrito from a food cart. You're just paying for diarrhea. Explosive, sudden diarrhea. The kind that fills up your socks. The burrito may smell good, but resist, dammit! It's a hot zone of tasty viruses waiting to turn your colon into a firehose.

Don't litter. People who litter suck.

My life philosophy is this: Learn what you can. Pass along what you've learned. Leave the world a better place because you lived. And have as much fun as possible.

So do lotsa fun stuff. Whatever your thing is, do your thing. I like to fish (Catch and release, and fish don't feel pain. Look it up.) I like some sports. I don't like camping, except the shitting in the woods part. I love media. Not news media. Pop media.

Movies (The Abyss is my fave), TV (Invader Zim, ATHF), music (Neil Diamond and Judas Priest, don't judge) videogames (Adventure for the Atari 2600 is still the greatest videogame ever made and don't fight me on this), and of course, books.

My fave fiction books are The Judas Goat by Robert B. Parker (read that and see how much Konrath stole from that guy), and Silence of the Lambs by Thomas Harris (Konrath stole a shitload from that guy, too). But a caveat; Silence of the Lambs probably has the WORST depiction of a transgender person ever written. The villain kills women to wear their skins. I'm pretty sure that isn't common in the LGBTIQ community. I've never seen it, and I've seen A LOT.

Best non-fiction books are Parasite Rex by Carl Zimmer (that will scare the hell out of you) and Far From The Tree by Andrew Solomon.

You should get your parent to read Far From The Tree. Konrath's father was gay (he's dead now) and Joe raised a kid with developmental and behavior disorders, and this book helped Joe understand both his Dad and his son much better.

What other wisdom can I impart on your 15th birthday? I'm full of wisdom. I'm also full of beer and pizza. Chicago has the best pizza. Anyone who tells you different is wrong.

Forgive people who are wrong. Sometimes you'll be wrong. When you are, admit it, and apologize.

What else?

Learn to forgive yourself. I'm still working on that. I've done a lot of stupid shit. Like, a whole lot. But torturing myself with regret is pointless. I've made mistakes, but I've learned from them, so I guess I had to make them, even though they hurt like hell.

Life hurts like hell sometimes.

When you feel bad, talk to someone about it. And if you're feeling really, really bad, talk to a professional. A doctor. I've popped so many Zoloft in my life that when I piss on a flower bed, the flowers starting singing like a Disney movie. But the correct, prescribed meds can help with depression. So can a good shrink. No shame in that. We all need help sometimes.

Wear sunscreen. If you don't get the reference, Google Baz Luhrmann.

Never give up. You know Konrath wrote ten books and got over 500 rejections before he got published? He spent a decade of his life feeling like a failure because he couldn't sell anything. But he kept at it, he never quit, and eventually Whiskey Sour sold to a big publisher in New York.

And now Konrath has sold more than 3 million books, and the ungrateful asshole doesn't pay me a single dime. Bullshit, right? I'm the best thing in those books! Everyone knows that!

What other gems can I bestow upon you on this happy day of your birth? Did I mention pets are awesome? Did I talk about poo enough times? Poo is funny when you're 2 years old, and it's still funny when you're 102 years old. Hell, I'm wearing a diaper right now. Not for any medical reason, but the bathroom is like fifteen steps away from my desk.

I think that's everything I know.

Konrath is going to send you a Dropbox link, which has all of his books. You know I'm in more than just those drink books, right? Shit, have you read Banana Hammock? That whole book is all me! Time-caster? The Chandler series? I'm in all of those, and more. If you want the whole list, check my website.

When you get the Dropbox invite, accept it, and you can download all the .mobi files of all the books for free, then sideload or upload them to your Kindle or preferred reading device. I'd give you instructions, but you're 15. Figure it out yourself, smart guy.

And that's it from me. Your parent emailed Konrath and said you read his books and your birthday was today. Pretty cool parent. But that cool parent probably didn't expect me to write you instead of Joe. Especially me swearing and talking about the Hershey squirts every four sentences.

But you've read my books, so nothing in this email should shock you. Might shock your parent, though. Tell them not to be pissed at me.

Lemme know you got the Dropbox link, and if you have anything to pass along to Konrath, I'll tell him.

I'm raising my beer right now and toasting your transition, if that's what you decide to do. I'm guessing it won't be easy. But it wasn't easy for the Batman either. It wasn't easy for me growing up pansexual, or losing my hand. It wasn't easy for Konrath, dealing with all those rejections. It wasn't easy for that d-bag kid at the movie theater who got soaked with shitwater.

If life were easy, nothing would have value. It's the hard stuff that makes us realize how strong we are.

And you're strong. You're stronger than I'll ever be.

Happy birthday, Jack.

Cool fucking name, brother.

Best,
Harrison Harold McGlade

.   .   .

Joe sez: I've posted this email with the permission and encouragement of Jack and his parental unit.

If you aren't familiar with my work, and couldn't grasp the context, it's written in the POV of one of my characters, Harry McGlade, who happens to be in a few dozen of my books.

Jack chose to call himself Jack because he likes another one of my characters, Jack Daniels. Which is the coolest thing one of my readers has ever done. I wept when I heard that. I'm teary-eyed right now.

When I began this blog in 2005, I decided it would be about writing and publishing. I didn't want it to ever get political or personal. Different people have different viewpoints, and everyone is entitled to their opinion, and whether I agree or disagree with your ideologies has nothing to do with the focus of this blog.

But, you see, this blog post IS actually about writing.

I'm a 49 year old white straight male. When I grew up, the media was full of white, straight males. I was represented in books, movies, music, on TV, in comics, and pretty much everywhere.

I have never known what it feels like to be discriminated against. And I don't know what it would be like to grow up without seeing anyone similar to me in the media.

When my father was 49, he was diagnosed with cancer. He died at 50. Dad was openly gay toward the end of his life, but for most of it he was closeted. He married a woman because that's what he thought he was supposed to do. His doctors, his church, his parents, treated homosexuality as a bad choice, as a sin, as a mental disorder.

Back in 1972, my father went to a university to get "help" for being queer. Aversion therapy, they called it. They showed him a slide show, and whenever a homosexual act was depicted on the screen, they literally shocked him with electricity.

Disgusting and barbaric? Yes. Did it really happen? Yes.

My father was told by EVERYONE that his sexual preferences were wrong, and he believed them. He went to this "treatment" in the hope he could get "better."

Many years later, we all know that homosexuality is not a choice, and it is not a disease, and there is nothing wrong with being queer. It's natural, healthy, and should be viewed positively. Dad eventually embraced being gay, married a great guy, and lived happily for years before cancer took him.

My father was born with those feelings, and they were normal, and I understood why he divorced my mother, and I had a great relationship with him. But society made him afraid, ashamed, and feeling like he needed to be fixed. No one ever told him he was normal. They treated him differently. They made him feel bad about himself. And when he was growing up, he had no positive representation in the media.

After my father died, the main character in my thriller series, Jack Daniels, discovered her father was gay. I did this to honor my dad.

There are some who say that a straight white guy shouldn't write about anything other than straight white guys. I can understand this viewpoint. As I mentioned, I truly don't know what it is like to be discriminated against. How can I truthfully and honestly represent what I can never understand?

That said, I also wrote a book about Satan imprisoned for a century in an underground government facility. I have never been imprisoned for a hundred years. And I have never met Satan. I write about serial killers, and cannibals, and active shooters, and cops, and veterans, and scientists, and clones, and I am none of these things. I make shit up for a living.

As my career has advanced, and I've become older and hopefully wiser, I've tried to show more diversity in my books. My readers are diverse, and they want to read about more than white cis guys. So I try to write positive characters from different of points of view and walks of life. I write about people of colors and races that don't match mine. I write about people with different gender identities. I write about people with disabilities. I write about people with a variety of sexual preferences.

In short; I write about people.

So, for National Pride Month, I'm giving everyone reading this blog a writing exercise.

See? I told you this was about writing.

Your homework is to look at your Work In Progress and ask yourself, "What am I showing my readers?" And, more specifically, "What am I showing my readers who aren't representative of me?"

Look for diversity. Look for stereotypes. Look at the positive role models, and the negative role models, in your words.

Consider who is reading it, and what they'll think.

Because guess what? The LGBTQ+ community reads books. People with disabilities read books. People of color read books.

If you white cis guys want them to read YOUR books, maybe you should think about your characters a bit more.

And for those who aren't white cis guys, for people everywhere on the gender spectrum, for people of all races, colors, cultures, and religions, for people with illnesses and disabilities, for women, and for the LGBTTQQIAAP community; we need to hear your voices. I think I'm a pretty good writer, but I'll never be good enough to really understand your struggles, your triumphs, your perspectives. You need to write books to enlighten people like me about what it's like to be you. Also, please feel free to write about white straight guys, even if you aren't a straight white guy.

And for all you bigots, for people who hate others because they are different, for all the bullies, for the haters, for the homophobes, for the misogynists, for everyone who nurses prejudice in public or secretly, for those who make fun of people who are different so they can feel better about themselves, I have a message for you, too. Hate speech is protected by the First Amendment. We need to hear your small-minded ideas. We need you to express your fears and insecurities by lashing out at those who don't agree with your ideologies.

Ha! Kidding! You bigots can fuck off. Keep your hateful little circle jerk to yourselves. You can come sit at the adult table again when you've opened up your small, petty minds to a concept called equality.

We've come a long way since 1972. But we have a long way to go.

Everyone deserves acceptance. Everyone deserves representation.

And most of all, every writer should have a fan as cool as Jack.

Happy birthday, bro. I agree with Harry McGlade. You're braver than I'll ever be.

BURNERS
(WITH HENRY PEREZ)

Perhaps my favorite short story collab, with Jack once again team-ing up/plotting against Chicago reporter Alex Chapa. Henry and I rented a suite in Lake Geneva and wrote this during a long weekend. Beer was involved. So much fun to write, and to read.

CHAPA

I went through the whole routine again.

First I looked up at the clock perched above the door that led to the rest of the building, then down to my watch—no clue why I felt compelled to check one against the other—then a quick glance at the door to the courtroom, followed by yet another survey of the other folks in the room.

Only thirteen of us were left, many more open seats now than people to fill them. It hadn't been that way when this process began more than four hours ago. I had managed to drop into the last chair available. I edged out some guy who looked like a college professor circa 1975, complete with tweed sports jacket and patches on the elbows. He'd frowned when I beat him to the seat, like I gave a damn what he thought. But when his name was part of the next group called, the professor gave me a self-satisfied smirk.

There were around seventy potential jurors at the beginning. The questionnaire that we each filled out was most likely the reason a group of more than two dozen had been immediately sent back to their lives without being called into the courtroom. I had felt certain that a couple of my written answers would have led to a quick dismissal. But no such luck.

We'd been told to turn off our cell phones, so the room was quiet, had been most of the morning except for the occasional yawn and the sound of magazine pages being turned. From time to time one stranger would try to strike up a conversation with another, but that, thankfully, never lasted very long.

I went through my mental checklist of responses, the ones I'd been working on for more than a week. Each was designed to anticipate a likely question. As a whole, they were intended to deliver only one possible conclusion to this unwelcome experience—I would be thanked for taking the time to do my civic duty, then shown the door.

The court officer reappeared. He was a squat, heavyset man who looked like he hadn't had an interesting moment in his entire life.

He called out the next name, not a group this time, from a clipboard he was holding.

"Martin Gustafson."

A man with narrow shoulders and a strong chin got up from his seat in the far corner. He took off the dark green cap he'd been wearing, the way he probably did when walking into church for a mid-week trip to the confessional, and held it against his chest. His shirt was old, collar frayed along the bottom edge, but it had been neatly pressed. Martin may not have had much luck in life, but on this day he was trying his best.

I watched him disappear through the door, hoping he'd be the last one called, then returned to prepping my responses.

I've been a journalist for fifteen years—That was true.

In my work, I've covered a great many trials, most of which have ended in a conviction—Also true.

I believe that the police get it right nearly all of the time, and that anyone charged with a major crime is always there for a reason—Umm, sort of, a little true. Sometimes.

My experiences as a journalist make it impossible for me to be objective where accused criminals are concerned—A complete lie. Objectivity is the core of good reporting, and I happen to be a damn good reporter.

I was hoping it would not get that far, but if I had to... I'd killed a lot of long hours sitting in courtrooms as part of my job. But there was no way I was going to sacrifice weeks, perhaps months, to jury duty.

What I was not willing to do, however, was go down the racist road. Could not do it. Besides, with a last name like Chapa, and a birth certificate from Havana, Cuba, claiming a deep-seeded hatred of Latinos would never wash. And I had a pretty good idea which trial this jury selection was for. If I was right, the accused was a young male named Tony Beniquez, who, if convicted, would be gone for a very long time.

"Have you ever done this before?"

She was an attractive blonde, mid-thirties. Her high-impact makeup job looked professional.

"You mean sit in a room with a bunch of strangers who don't want to be there anymore than I do? Probably. Give me a minute and I'll come up with an example."

That made her smile. It was a nice, expensive smile.

"I meant jury duty." She smiled again.

"No. I was summoned once before, but I managed to avoid it."

"How'd you do that?"

"By using my extraordinary guile and cunning."

Another smile.

Actually, it was eight years earlier, and I'd been lost for several days in the woods on an assignment with what I came to believe was the worst militia group in the northern Midwest. And while I did get a good story out of my experience with The Wisconsin Free Rangers—the ill-conceived name was, as far as I know, not meant as an homage to the popular breed of chickens—I also concluded that those guys couldn't intimidate a grade school PTA, let alone overthrow a government. During my time with the Free Rangers I did learn how to disarm a man, how to stalk imaginary targets, and the value of a good compass, or at least the dangers of forgetting to bring one into the deep forest.

We were roaming the wilds of Wisconsin trying to find our way back to the place where we'd parked the SUVs as my jury date came and went. I cashed in a favor with a friend at the county and my name vanished from their records. Unfortunately, in the time since, I'd pissed off more than a few of the connections that might've kept me out of this room today.

I wondered why they were having so much trouble seating twelve jurors. Wondered how many challenges each side had carried into the courtroom. What the hell was going on in room 4B of the Birch Grove courthouse?

"I'm Marcia." The lady next to me was determined to have a conversation.

I smiled. "Were your parents big fans of the Brady Bunch?"

"No. I've been asked that before. It's my mom's name. Though, when I was a kid, I definitely got teased about it, but I didn't care. I think it's a pretty name."

"It is a pretty name."

Marcia kept talking the way some people nervously do when they're in an uncomfortable situation or are trying to connect with a complete stranger. I let her talk. She was attractive and pleasant, and though I was certain I would never see or speak to Marcia after today, listening to her story beat checking the clock every five minutes.

"Alex Chapa?"

The voice bounced off the walls and landed in the middle of Marcia's story about her high school field trip to Washington, D.C.

"I'm Alex Chapa."

"Didn't you hear me the first time?"

Mr. Excitement was standing in the open doorway, clipboard in hand.

"I did. I just wanted to make sure you didn't mean some other Alex Chapa."

"You mean there's more than one of you," he said, craning his neck to see if anyone else in the room was responding.

"Let's hope not." I got up, said goodbye to Marcia, and walked toward the agitated man waiting for me by the door.

I was determined to walk out of that courtroom a free man, just as soon as I could convince one or both of the attorneys that I was as unfit as any potential juror they had ever met.

DANIELS

Die! Die! Come on! Die you son of a—"

The last Space Invader got me. I frowned at the screen of my cell phone, then shut it off and tucked it back into my purse, wondering why I bothered playing a game where you were always destined to lose, no matter how good you were.

Oh yeah. I remember now. Because Space Invaders came free with the phone.

I sighed. Hollywood glamorized the lives of cops. Shootouts and car chases and saving the victim at the last possible second before the bomb went off. Stuff like that.

In reality, the majority of my time was spent doing paperwork, talking to unhelpful people who didn't want to talk to me, following leads that went nowhere, and going to court.

Of all that, I hated going to court most. Especially since this wasn't even one of my cases.

I smoothed out my black Anne Klein slacks and noticed a smudge on my Jean-Michel Cazabat penny suede wedge heels. They were the only thing about my outfit that didn't qualify as 100% professionally conservative, but I secretly loved wedges in the 70s and was happy to see them make a comeback. Besides, the jurors wouldn't see my feet when I took the stand, so they couldn't judge my testimony by my shoes.

I licked my thumb, bent down in the uncomfortable wooden chair, and brushed the dust mark off my toe. I was alone in one of the conference rooms across from the court, waiting for the jury to get selected. The D.A. promised I'd be the first witness, and I'd hoped to get my testimony done today. Unfortunately, it was moving up on one o'clock, and they hadn't finished selecting the jury yet. Irritation crept up my back and made my shoulders bunch. I stood up, shaking out the knots, stretching my legs.

Earlier, I'd checked into the same bed and breakfast I'd stayed at during my last visit to Birch Grove. It had been a pleasant trip, an extended weekend with my boyfriend, with good food and great sex. If it hadn't also included my becoming an eyewitness in a murder trial, I might have come back on my own, rather than by subpoena.

The door opened, and I turned and watched Simon Lebanon, the District Attorney, enter. He was about ten years my junior, wearing scuffed penny loafers and a jacket that had marks on the shoulders courtesy of a wire coat hanger. The cowlick in his brown hair reminded me of Dagwood from the old comic strip. He had a look on his face like he realized he was always late for something.

"Ms. Daniels…"

"Lieutenant Daniels," I corrected. "Are we starting?"

"Huh? Oh, not yet. Need one more juror. Judge Malvo called a quick recess so he could go to the bathroom. He's trying to pass a kidney stone."

It was that down-home country charm that made me never want to visit rural Illinois again.

"I was really hoping to get this over with today."

"We're going as fast as we can. This is a front page murder trial. No one wants to make any mistakes."

I appreciated how important that was to him, and to this town, but I'd been involved with too many front page murder trials to even remember them all.

"Can't you just use my deposition from discovery?"

He smoothed his palm across his cowlick, and it popped right back out. "The deposition is what I wanted to talk to you about. How sure are you of what you saw?"

"Very sure. Which is why I gave you a deposition, and why I'm here with you right now rather than someplace I'd rather be, such as anywhere else."

"Your reputation precedes you, Ms., uh, Lieutenant. But I'm sure you know how unreliable eyewitness testimony can be. I wouldn't want you to get tripped up in the cross-examination."

I made a face. "You read my deposition, right?"

"Of course."

"It is, at most, five sentences long. How could I get tripped up?"

From what I understood about the case, it was a slam dunk. Dumb teenager with an extensive history of run-ins with law enforcement torches a print shop and when the fire department arrives they find a dead body inside. Smoke inhalation. Maybe he was a fire bug, or could be it was just a stupid prank gone wrong. Probably didn't know someone was still inside. An unintended victim, but tough break, kid. You shouldn't have set the fire in the first place.

The cops on the scene, and the owner of the establishment across the street, saw the suspect committing the arson. My two minutes' worth of testimony would be used to establish the accused was in the area moments prior to the crime. So I had no idea why Lebanon seemed so uptight.

Lebanon stared at me and began to drum his fingers across the tabletop. "Yeah. Well. Uh, hopefully, we'll be ready for you soon. Remember, the important thing is you saw the defendant, with his duffle bag, just prior to the incident."

"And just after. When two of Birch Grove's finest tackled him." I added, "With perhaps a bit more force than necessary."

Lebanon's eyes narrowed. "You didn't say that in the deposition."

"Because that is opinion, not fact."

"Yes, well, a man died in that fire the defendant started."

"Allegedly," I said.

"Excuse me?"

"He hasn't been convicted yet. So he *allegedly* started the fire."

Scowling, Lebanon put his hands on the table and leaned toward me, an intimidation move that I bet he practiced in the mirror. "I trust you'll just stick to the facts and keep your opinion out of your testimony, Lieutenant. That goes for the attitude as well."

Though I bridled at the insult, I still managed to smile. Until he turned and started to leave. I followed him across the hall and into the courtroom.

"I'll answer any question asked of me," I said, lowering my voice so as to not interrupt the proceedings. The last thing I wanted to do was slow things down ever more. "But it sure would be nice if we could start sooner rather than later."

"I said, we will do our best to accommodate you," Lebanon hissed, his cowlick standing at attention.

So much for finishing today.

CHAPA

The courtroom smelled of fresh paint and new wood. Eleven jurors had already been selected. That meant they needed just one more, plus a couple of alternates, probably. The seven men and four women sitting in the jury box were feigning various levels of interest. Three were African American, one was Hispanic. Three had gray hair, one looked like the sort who sported a tattoo on her backside.

I recognized Martin Gustafson from the waiting room, and another guy named Bob who had been one of the first to be called and was genuinely thrilled for the opportunity. I guess he got his wish.

But beyond that cursory accounting of the jury in progress, I refused to invest any serious thought in the surroundings or my circumstances.

I just wanted to get the hell out of there as quickly as possible

I had been ushered into the room, past the jury box, and over to the witness stand. The slender man who administered the oath was in his late thirties, with a hunch in his shoulders that would likely become a serious problem sometime in his sixties. It was the usual oath, not unlike the ones in the movies or on any of the two dozen different versions of *Law and Order*.

Then I climbed into the stand and waited. And waited.

The attorneys were also waiting. Two sets of them. For the defense, a middle-aged guy who was a bit too tall and much too broad in the shoulders for his brown sport coat, and another man, smaller, a little younger, who wore thick-rimmed glasses and the respectable hairstyle his father had always insisted on.

"He should only be another minute or so," the elderly bailiff said to Anna Lipscomb, whom I recognized as a lead prosecutor for the county.

Lipscomb nodded, then resumed a whispered conversation with Simon Lebanon, Oakton County's chronically disheveled D.A, who had entered the courtroom a minute earlier.

My mind wandered beyond the beige walls of that courtroom and into another. In ten days I was scheduled to appear at the latest of what was now a four-year series of custody hearings. Carla, my ex, would be trying to further limit my opportunity to see my daughter, Nikki. Her attorneys—she had more than one while I could barely afford a para-legal—would do everything in their considerable power to erode my already tattered ability to parent my eight-year-old.

It has been this way since Carla left home and took Nikki with her three years earlier. Got worse when she remarried some wealth. I had drained my savings—such as they were—missed work time, and months of sleep. I was just about at the end of it. I'd done all I could think of to ease the transition for Nikki, until that responsibility was ripped away from me. And now I wondered how much more I could do. For the first time since the split, I was thinking about conceding everything.

The honorable Ezra D. Malvo finally entered the courtroom—slowly, very slowly. He had his left hand pressed against his abdomen, the right one reaching around his back to complete the vise. His face was as white as the thin strands of hair clinging to his liver-spotted head.

"Let's get this thing rolling," the judge said in a voice thick as concrete. "We got ourselves a jury yet?"

The attorneys for both sides looked at one another before the D.A. brushed back his unruly hair, a gesture that made it worse, not better, and spoke.

"Um, no, no Your Honor. We're still two short."

"Well let's get on with it then," Judge Malvo carefully turned to face me. "This gentleman been sworn in yet?"

The bailiff responded with a slow nod.

"This guy looks like a viable juror," the judge said, then gave me the once over. "More or less."

"Your name is Alex Chapa?" Prosecutor Lipscomb asked as she stood, eyes locked on the notes in her hand.

I rifled through a mental list of possible wise-ass responses, determined that my favorite was, *That's what the much better looking guy in the waiting room paid me to say*, but figured that under the circumstances it was best to play it straight.

"Yes, it is."

"Is that short for Alexander?"

"No, Alejandro. I was born in Cuba, but when I became a U.S. citizen my mother decided it was a good idea to go with something less ethnic, so she changed it to Alex."

I heard a high-pitched creaking to my left. Judge Malvo was slowly leaning in my direction.

"That was a wise decision," he said, his voice trailing the stench of his breath—coffee, cigarettes, and decay, wrapped in stale indifference.

Because the thing I wanted most at that moment was to get out of there and get on with the rest of my life, I chose to ignore the judge's remark. In a different setting I would have told the old fart how my mother had apologized to me on more than one occasion for a decision she'd long regretted. Instead, I waited for the next question.

Lipscomb, too, had chosen to ignore Judge Malvo. She was probably accustomed to his idiotic side comments. "It says here you work for a newspaper."

"On my good days, yes."

She looked up from her clipboard.

"And what about on your bad ones?"

"You don't want to know."

Lipscomb lowered her brow without taking her eyes off me, like a parent on the verge of unloading on an unruly child. This was good.

"You're a reporter, then, Mr. Chapa?"

"I'm a columnist."

I heard Simon Lebanon snicker, then he said, "Isn't a columnist just a reporter who gets his photo in the paper?" He sat back, apparently pleased with himself, and ran a hand through his hair. I watched the brown tufts retreat for a moment before beginning their southbound journey back to the usual resting place.

Still focused on escaping the stand and getting out the door, I opted to ignore Lebanon just as I had the judge, and turned my attention back to Lipscomb.

"Have you ever written any stories about crimes or criminals?"

"Many." What cave had this woman been living in the past fifteen years? There was even a better than fair chance I'd mentioned her in one or two of my stories. Or could be this was just a formality on the road to dismissing me. I hoped that was it.

"And how do you feel about the police and our justice system, based on your work experience?"

Finally.

"I believe that the police get it right nearly all of the time, and that anyone charged with a major crime is usually there for a reason."

"And what about the justice system, the courts?"

"In my work, I've covered a great many trials. Most have ended in a conviction."

Apparently Lebanon had somewhere else he needed to be. After sneaking a glance at his watch, the D.A. abruptly got up, left the table, and walked out the same set of doors he'd entered through.

"And how have you felt about those convictions? Have you disagreed with any of the decisions?"

"My job is to report and analyze, not to agree or disagree."

That was good. It suggested an inability or at least unwillingness to judge, which should give the prosecution some doubts about my reliability on a jury. Then again, it could also suggest an innate impartiality. That would be bad.

A young man in a tan suit, who I figured was a clerk, got Lipscomb's attention. She leaned down to hear him whisper something. Then she whispered something back and I began to imagine myself being dismissed, walking out of the courthouse, sitting in my car, slipping Bob Seger's *Against the Wind* into the CD player, and cranking the volume.

Lipscomb was nodding as she turned her attention back to me.

"One more question, Mr. Chapa. Would you have any trouble voting to send a man to jail for the rest of his life for murder?"

This was my shot. A "yes" answer would likely bring my part of this to an abrupt end. So easy. Just say "yes."

But not really easy at all. In my years as a journalist I've written about some of the worst monsters the Chicago area has ever spit up. Hell yeah, I could send a man to jail for murder.

"Would you like me to repeat the question, Mr. Chapa?"

No, I heard it the first time. I was just calculating my options, and determined I have a much better play with the defense.

"I could send a man to prison for life. No problem." I didn't add what I actually thought—*If I was certain he was guilty.*

"We have no further questions, or any objections to this potential juror."

Not what I wanted to hear. But I sensed I had a good shot of getting bounced by the defense.

As the younger of the two defense attorneys stood, I saw Lebanon abruptly re-enter the courtroom through the back door, followed an instant later by a tall, shapely woman who appeared to be more than a little irritated. She had dark shoulder-length hair, a nice figure, and an outfit to match. She looked like she'd just stepped out of the front window of an exclusive Mag Mile clothing store.

"Good afternoon, Mr. Chapa." The slender attorney had taken off the poindexter glasses he'd been wearing earlier.

I nodded, said nothing, since verbally agreeing under these circumstances would most certainly constitute perjury.

"Mr. Chapa, have you ever covered a case or written a story about arson?"

The defense attorney's question diverted my attention away from the woman—

"No."

—but only briefly. There was something familiar about her, and I wondered if she might be a fellow reporter. Someone whose path had crossed mine once or twice.

"Do you have any sort of prejudiced feelings toward Hispanics?"

"What?"

I hadn't been paying attention, and for a moment I wondered whether I'd missed a question.

"Hispanics in general, Mexicans in particular. Any feelings or history of prejudice?"

"No, of course not. As I said before, I'm Cuban."

"Cuban, yes, but—"

"No, I have no prejudice against anyone." *Besides asshole attorneys in particular, morons in general, and folks who forget to turn off their blinkers on the tollway as a matter of principle, that is.*

Though I could not make out what was being said, the hushed conversation in the back of the courtroom was anything but friendly. Fingers were being pointed, hands perched on hips, and it was clear that Lebanon was no match for this woman.

I was intrigued.

"Based on one of your earlier responses, do you believe you have a predisposition toward finding a defendant guilty?"

I had just decided that she was wearing too much money to be a reporter, when the woman turned and looked my way for an instant. Just long enough for me to confirm this was no reporter.

"Mr. Chapa?"

Lieutenant Jacqueline Daniels? What was she doing so far out her comfort zone, which included Chicago's most treacherous streets, dive bars, and crack houses, but not its western suburbs?

"I'm sorry, could you repeat the question?"

Judge Malvo let out a loud, purposeful sigh.

"I asked if you would be predisposed to finding a defendant guilty simply because he's on trial, based on an earlier response."

Then I put it together.

Daniels was connected to *this* case. As a…what? Couldn't be an arresting officer. So an expert? Maybe there had been similar crimes in her jurisdiction, or she'd had an earlier run-in with the defendant.

That meant she could wind up on the stand.

Hmm…

"Mr. Chapa," the judge was gradually tilting toward me. "We've been here a long time." Then he cupped a heavy hand over his microphone and whispered, "Could you please answer the goddamned question?"

Jack Daniels' head had snapped in my direction at the mention of my name. Now she was staring at me with a look that was equal parts disdain and confusion.

"I apologize, Your Honor."

"Would you like the nice attorney to repeat the question again?"

"Thank you, but no, I'm good."

Daniels was still staring at me, but the confusion half of the equation was gone from her face.

I smiled at her, then turned my attention to the defense lawyer. This was simple, now. If I informed them that I knew Officer Daniels, that we'd once solved a case together, one that involved pogs no less, and that I'd saved her life along the way, I would immediately be excused.

But it wasn't simple. A journalist's curiosity has a way of complicating things. If a Chicago cop was involved it meant that his trial had the potential of being a much bigger story than I had imagined. And while I could ask to be assigned to cover it and spend my days sitting in the gallery, I now had the opportunity to track it from the inside, as an active member, as a juror.

As the attorneys grew more impatient waiting for my answer, I imagined the series I could write after it was all over. I knew what I had to do.

"I have absolutely no predisposition about a defendant's guilt or innocence, and I'm certain I can render a just verdict based on the evidence as presented. If I was unable to do that, I wouldn't be much of a journalist." I leaned forward for emphasis. "And I'm a very good journalist."

I didn't have to look in her direction to know Daniels was staring at me. And as the defense team conferred, I did my best to avoid thinking about what I had just done to the next several days, weeks, or maybe even months of my life.

DANIELS

The last time I saw Alex Chapa I'd almost arrested him for B&E. He talked his way out of it, and wound up playing a significant role in solving a string of homicides. While I wasn't fond of his profession—cops and reporters are like oil and water—he was okay by me.

Seeing him on the stand, participating in his state-mandated civic duty, I figured he wanted to be here as much as I did. Which is why I found it odd that his answers indicated a desire to be selected as a jury member, especially since that didn't seem to be the route he was taking up until he noticed me.

Either he had the hots for me, or he thought there was a story to be had—Chapa sniffed out stories like hounds tracked foxes. I might have butted in, told the court that we knew each other, which probably would have resulted in his dismissal, but I had two good reasons to keep my mouth shut. A quick view of the courtroom showed me the jury hadn't been fully selected yet, and if Chapa was bounced it could be hours before he was replaced. Also, I was here in Birch Grove alone. If my stay in this quaint little suburb lasted for more than a day, and he was after a story, he'd no doubt want to talk to me, which would result in a few free drinks, maybe even dinner after the trial was over.

Plus, I'd once saved Chapa's life, so he owed me a drink—at the very least.

My stomach growled, and I realized I needed something more substantial than the Snickers bar I'd eaten back when I thought I'd be out of here around lunchtime. I exited the courtroom, intent on grabbing something nearby. Though a tourist town, Birch Grove was still old-fashioned enough to have a proper main street, and no doubt I could find a café or deli within walking distance.

When I got into the lobby, I ran into two men. I identified one of them as Officer Nicholas James, the cop who took my statement after the print shop fire. On that day, he'd been in his Birch Grove uniform. Today he was dressed to the nines, an Armani suit with creases so sharp they could slice day-old bread, and polished loafers that could be seen from space. The man with him was no slouch in the clothing department, either. I knew a bit about fashion, and pegged his jacket as Valentino. Both were tailored, fitting so perfectly they couldn't have been wearing shoulder holsters.

Though I liked to dress well, the vast majority of my clothes were bought at discount stores or the Home Shopping Network. Maybe I needed to quit the CPD and get on the Birch Grove force.

James was deep in hushed conversation when he noticed me, and stopped mid-sentence. He was tall, young, and I guessed his military haircut was a holdover from a recent tour of duty. His expression went from surprised, to neutral.

"Welcome back to Birch Grove, Lieutenant. This is my partner, Emmanuel Lewis."

His partner was black, and upon hearing his name I immediately began to search for any resemblance to the child star who played *Webster* on that old 80s sitcom.

"I'm not that one," Lewis said, reading my mind.

There was a quick round of handshaking. I noticed James had a Submariner Rolex, and Lewis had a much less ostentatious Movado that was a larger version of the one I was wearing.

"You staying at the Weatherby House again?" James asked.

"I love the fireplace."

James nodded. "Well, hopefully you'll be able to testify soon, get back to chasing real criminals in Chi-town."

I couldn't tell if he was being respectful or sarcastic. James had the cool cop demeanor down to a tee.

"Seems like you've found some real criminals here in Birch Grove. A murder/arson is a pretty big deal anywhere you go. Enjoying your newfound celebrity?"

James had been the arresting officer.

"Just doing my job. The people here have been pretty worried about the fires, so it's good they've ended. Too bad someone had to die in the last one."

"Fires?" I said. "There have been more than one?"

James and Lewis exchanged a glance.

"Been real tough around here," Lewis said. "Shop owners have been terrified. But there hasn't been another fire since the arrest. More proof we got our perp."

"What was the motive?" I asked, knowing I was overstepping my bounds. "Pyro?"

"We really can't discuss that, Lieutenant," James said. "No talking about the case. You understand."

"Well, can you tell me where to get a decent sandwich nearby?"

"Knuth's, around the corner. He'll set you up. Turn left when you exit, then another left."

"Thanks."

I nodded my goodbye and walked away, feeling their eyes on me. So the accused, Tony Beniquez, was a serial arsonist? I'd met a few pyromaniacs in my day, and they shared many traits with serial killers. Vivid fantasies, compulsive behavior, no remorse. In fact, many budding sociopaths started fires when they were children, before graduating to murder. If Beniquez was that type, it was a damn good thing they got him off the streets when they did, before more people were killed.

I pushed through the revolving door, leaving behind the stale courthouse air and walking outside into a beautiful summer day. As I walked Main Street, I passed the print shop Beniquez allegedly burned, its storefront windows boarded over with plywood, black char marks still on the brick frames. I recalled the last time I'd seen it, fire belching through those windows, drawn to the scene while my boyfriend was in the bathroom of the bar across the street. James already had Beniquez face-down on the sidewalk and cuffed. While I hadn't seen the crime, I'd bumped into Beniquez a few minutes prior, running in that direction, carrying a duffle bag. My boyfriend hadn't remembered him, but I had. Something about the teenager's face. Something between frantic and excited. I distinctly recalled thinking that the kid was up to something.

I stopped for a moment, sniffing the air. Even three months later, there was still a faint odor of burnt wood. I looked on either side of the print shop, but the other businesses attached to it hadn't been touched. The fire department had responded extremely fast.

I strolled by, turning left where instructed, and spotted the Knuth's Deli sign, neon and ceramic and probably unchanged since the 1960s. The inside was cool, smelling of cold cuts and fresh baked bread. I had to wait in a short line, and during that time I read over the list of sandwiches handwritten on the dry erase board behind the register. When I made my selection, I checked out the meat through the cooler windows to make sure it looked good.

It looked good.

An older man in a white apron took my order. He had a paunch and the bushiest eyebrows I'd ever seen. If he ever shaved them, he'd have enough hair to knit a sweater. A large sweater, that no one would want to wear.

"Is the Rueben good?" I asked.

"Everything is good," he said with a trace of a German accent. "The Rueben is very good."

"I'll take it."

"Half or full?"

My stomach growled. "How big is half?"

"Big."

"Sold. And some kettle chips. Thanks."

He padded over to the refrigerator and removed a slab of corned beef with his gloved hands, taking it over to the slicer. I didn't bother telling him I wanted it thin, trusting him to his work. Instead, I asked something else.

"So, I hear there have been some arsons in town."

The proprietor stopped mid-slice. After two full seconds he started up again.

"Terrible thing," he said.

"How many, so far?"

"Four."

"All business owners?"

"Yes. A shame. This used to be such a nice town."

"Isn't it okay, now?"

"Hmm?"

"They caught the guy. No more fires."

He might have snorted, but it was so brief I couldn't be sure. "Sure. No more fires. That would be wonderful."

"So what were the other shops that—"

"Look, Miss, I really don't want to talk about this." He put the corned beef back in the cooler with more force than necessary, shaking the counter. "You want regular or Asian coleslaw?"

"Regular."

He finished making my sandwich in silence, leaving me to puzzle over what had upset him. When it was time to pay for it, he didn't even try to upsell me on a drink.

"Eight-sixty-five," he said.

I placed my purse next to the register and hunted through it to find my wallet. As I tugged it out, the shopkeeper's eyes went wide. I followed his stare and saw he was staring into my purse, at my badge case. My gold shield was visible.

"I'm sorry, Officer. I didn't mean to be rude." He was smiling from ear to ear.

"Huh?"

"The Rueben is on the house."

"You really don't have to…"

"I don't know what we would do in this town without the good work of the police. Please. It's on me. I insist."

I thought about paying anyway, because I wasn't the type to trade on my authority. But it really is rude to refuse a gift.

"Thanks," I said, taking the sandwich and the chips. He replied with a broad smile.

I walked out of the deli, my free lunch tucked under my arm. Maybe I really should move to Birch Grove. The cops here seemed to have it a lot better than I did.

CHAPA

The first day—first afternoon, really—consisted entirely of opening statements from the two sides. The whole thing took about an hour-and-a-half. All the while, Judge Malvo fluctuated between appearing to be in agony, listing to one side, and nearly nodding off. A couple of times he moaned quietly and the proceedings came to a temporary stop as the attorneys waited to see if His Honor had something to add. He didn't.

I was certain the judge was a goner at one point when he spent the better part of fifteen minutes resting his chin on his fist, his only movement an occasional twitch that snapped him back to life. The guy was either heavily medicated or completely disinterested. Or maybe it was the heat, since apparently the county had forgotten to pay its electric bill and air conditioning wasn't an option. Or at least that's what I assumed, as another bead of sweat rolled down the side of my face.

Jack Daniels, on the other hand, looked far too icy to sweat as she passed the time fidgeting in a seat near the back of the courtroom. From time to time she would glare at the prosecutors, who never appeared to share as much as a glance with the Lieutenant.

My gaze drifted back to Jack often. It was odd to see her in this sort of situation, glued to a chair, anxious to do something, but unable to move or take charge of her surroundings. Like a caged bird of prey.

Several of my colleagues were seated in the gallery, there to cover the case for their papers. Right then I would've swapped places with any of them.

The kid seated at the defense table could not have been more than twenty, if that. At times, for a moment here and there, I sensed that he grasped the severity of his circumstances. But that clarity would slip away an instant later, and he'd look like a boy who'd been summoned to the principal's office on a charge of truancy.

He sure as hell didn't look capable of intentionally setting the fire that killed one Dennis Braun, who was trapped inside his print shop, Laserquick, when it went up. In my work I'd crossed paths with murderers, thieves, rapists, and blackmailers. Interviewed more than a few of each. But I'd never met a burner, and would not have imagined they looked anything like Tony Beniquez.

The man I assumed to be his father sat directly behind Tony in the first row of the gallery, wearing his Sunday best. As though he, rather than his son, was the one heading for Judgment Day. He was a small man with a large mustache and neatly cropped dark hair streaked with silver along the sides. Studying his face, and the look of concern he was doing nothing to hide, I was sure the man would trade places with his son if he could.

Sitting in the front row along the other side of the courtroom was what I assumed to be the family of the deceased, including a woman I pegged to be his mother, and next to her an elderly man who I guessed had suffered the horror of burying his son. There were no children that I could identify, young or grown, but the widow wasn't hard to spot. She wore a navy blue business suit, a simple silver necklace, and a face as impenetrable as hardened plaster.

When I wasn't watching the accused, scanning the courtroom, or trying to get a fix on my fellow jurors from my seat in the front row at the far end, the furthest away from the witness stand, I listened to the attorneys present overviews of their cases.

Five minutes into the prosecution's opening statement I learned the wife's name was Alice Braun. She and the deceased had been married for five years, no children yet, but they'd hope to change that as soon as the economy picked up.

I stared at a diagram of the Laserquick floor plan while the prosecution laid out its scenario. The shop wasn't very large. Just big enough to house a couples' dreams of a future that was now lost, along with Dennis Braun's life.

Led by Lipscomb, the prosecution was going to rely on eyewitness accounts from a fellow business owner whose store was located across the street from the print shop, and from a second witness, referred to as "a well-respected police officer from Chicago."

So that's why Jack Daniels was here. This was going to be good.

I imagined the headline for the story I'd write once all of this was over, *Chicago Police Lieutenant Daniels' Testimony Convicts Killer*.

Judging from her body language, which involved a lot of fidgeting and smoothing out various parts of her designer wardrobe, Jack wasn't planning to hang around for long. But any hope she had of making it to the stand on this day began to fade as what passed for a defense rambled through its opening statement.

The older of the two court-appointed attorneys representing Beniquez, a man who introduced himself as Scott Milledge, shook the discomfort out of his undersized sport coat just before he began his remarks. He touted the young man's good character, despite a few "youthful indiscretions," and emphasized his strong ties to his family and the community. His father Carlos had worked as a carpenter and handyman for more than twenty years, during which he'd done work for the city, and also the county.

"Much of the new woodwork in this courtroom was built by Carlos Beniquez," Milledge said, pointing to the witness stand, jury box, and the railings that separated the business half of the courtroom from the gallery.

Tony's mother had passed away several years earlier, but a couple of aunts and older cousins had stepped in to try and fill that void as best they could. According to Milledge, the Beniquez family went to church every Sunday, belonged to charitable organizations, and had done their best to assimilate into the community—no easy task in a town as white, protestant, and conservative as Birch Grove. And now Carlos' only son was on trial for murder.

But Milledge did little to address the motive the prosecutor had pinned on Beniquez, that of a troubled juvenile whose shady past inevitably gravitated toward arson and murder. Instead, the defense attorney promised to prove that his client did not do what he was accused of, and suggested he would challenge the prosecution's theory about the cause of death. That part I found interesting, but I didn't have much faith in the defense at the moment.

As soon as Milledge was finished, Judge Malvo, who had spent the past few minutes squirming like someone had slipped a randy weasel under his robe, summoned the attorneys to the bench. After a brief and mostly one-sided conversation, he adjourned until the following morning.

When Malvo was done telling the jurors what we could and could not do, I turned my attention to where Jack had been sitting, but she was already gone. Twenty minutes later I was in my car, driving home to Oakton, and calling Zack, my assistant at the *Chicago Record*, on my cell.

In his instructions to the jury, which the judge had delivered as though he was reading a script, he warned us against discussing the trial, told us to avoid any news coverage, and to resist doing any research on our own. I, of course, understood why this was part of the process, and that jurors were expected to render a verdict based solely on what was presented to them during the trial.

Despite the judge's orders, I had no desire to serve as little more than a referee in a contest between two teams of lawyers. Especially when one of those teams appeared to be so ill-equipped to meet the challenge.

No, if I was going to be part of the jury judging Tony Beniquez I was going to get it right. Whichever decision I made regarding the young man's guilt or innocence would be something I'd carry around with me long after the lawyers had moved on to other defendants.

I wanted to learn all that I could about Tony Beniquez and the crime he was supposed to have committed, and I needed to get started right away.

DANIELS

When it became apparent they weren't going to be calling me that day, I got out of there. I'd had my curiosity piqued and I wanted to see if I could find some answers.

To be a good cop meant possessing various traits that were needed on the job. Being able to command authority was a necessity. I could do that, along with shoot a gun, hold my own in a scuffle, and read people well enough to separate truth from bullshit. But one of the most important characteristics a good cop possessed was a burning need to figure things out.

I was a good cop. And even though this wasn't my case, I wanted to know more about the string of fires. The prosecutor didn't bring them up, perhaps in case the murder rap didn't stick so he could later charge Beniquez with arson. The defense didn't bring them up, which meant the attorney was either incompetent, or his client didn't have solid alibis for the earlier fires. If Beniquez could prove that he didn't commit any of the other arsons, that would introduce a big dose of reasonable doubt. So something was up.

Normally, the way I did research was on the Internet, but I hadn't brought my laptop with me. So I decided to go old school and visit the local library, which I located, ironically, using the Internet on my cell phone.

True to the original intent of having a Main Street, the library was situated on the east end of it, bookending the half mile stretch like the courthouse did on the west. My Nova was parked in the lot, and I opted to leave it there and make the journey on foot. I passed all the usual small town businesses: three antique shops, an ice cream parlor, a bookstore, three bars, two cafes, various restaurants, a music store, a shoe store, a locksmith, several clothing stores, a five and dime, a newsstand. Of those, one of the cafes, and the music store, had the same plywood windows and scorch marks as the print shop. That got me thinking, and I retraced my steps a block back and popped into Jay's Locksmithe Shoppe.

Jay's had seen better days. The tile floor was in bad need of a wax, the front counter had an ugly, dirty split in the Formica, and the glass showcase had a crack in it and only showcased a few dusty boxes of burglar alarm systems. There were three key trees boasting hundreds of metal blanks, and stacked along the wall were half a dozen large pieces of plywood.

There was a grinding sound coming from the rear of the shop, and I stood near the register and waited until the guy cutting keys noticed me. He was Caucasian, bearded, and even from the distance of five meters I could see the ink on his arms, dark blue against a deep tan.

When he noticed me, he put on a friendly smile and strolled over, letting his safety goggles fall across his chest on their elastic band.

"Can I help you, ma'am?"

I'd been meaning to get an extra front door key made, so I fished it out and pried it off the key ring as I spoke.

"I need two more copies of this. Can you do it while I wait?"

"There's an extra charge for rush service. Twenty-five percent."

"No problem."

He smiled again, then took my key and walked over to the racks of blanks. It took a few seconds of searching and jingling before he found the appropriate match. When he passed me up I pointed and said, "Those boards. Are they used to board up broken windows?"

"Yup. I'm the guy in town to call if a window gets broke. Come out anytime, even the middle of the night, but there's an extra charge for that."

"You the one who boarded up all the shops that were set on fire?"

The smile left his face and I got the look. The thousand-yard-stare, perfected by anyone who did time.

"What about those fires?" he asked.

"How many have there been?"

"You're not from around here. Haven't seen you before. You a cop?"

"Maybe I'm just curious. Or maybe I'm a reporter," I said, thinking of Chapa.

"I ain't done nothing wrong, and I don't got to talk to you."

"Are you Jay?"

"Ain't no Jay. Got the sign cheap from some store went out of business in Wisconsin."

"So who are you?"

"Who's asking?"

I thought about pulling out my badge, but I had no jurisdiction here. Besides, this man wouldn't talk to cops, just based on principal. The designs on his arms were obvious jailhouse tattoos, and we were the enemy. On one hand, it seemed odd that an ex-con got work in this quaint little town as a locksmith. But on the other hand, who is better suited to working with locks than someone who knows how to pick them?

"What are you being paranoid about?" I asked, trying to make my tone non-confrontational. "They caught the guy. There won't be any more fires."

"I do what I'm supposed to, and don't bother nobody. I ain't doin' nothing wrong."

"Nobody said you were."

"I'm just trying to make a living, Officer. Nothing more to say. Now please excuse me while I cut your keys."

He didn't wait for my reply, and returned to the grinder and went at it like he was punishing the metal for its many sins.

While he did that, I went over to the plywood, which still had an order receipt stapled to it. I checked the date. He'd bought the boards a month ago, a full two months after Beniquez's arrest.

That didn't jibe with someone who thought the fires were going to stop.

Zack wasn't technically *my* assistant. He was an intern and a gopher for the news department, a stand-up guy, and one of the people I trusted most at the *Record*. But none of that mattered now, since Zack had gone home for the day. I was due back at the courthouse by eight the next morning, so waiting until then was not an option.

I needed to get some background on this case. What I'd seen on this first day had not inspired confidence in the defense team. Sure, I knew I was supposed to go on the testimony and evidence alone. But if I was going to send a young man to jail for the rest of his life, I sure as hell was going to make sure he had it coming.

Though I could very easily go into the office myself and get on my computer, but that seemed a bit too brazen, even for me. I didn't know to what extent the court might go to find out whether a juror had violated the judge's orders, but I wasn't going to take any more chances than I had to.

The rotating construction—now in its third year—tied up traffic on Randall Road. Exhaust from idling cars and the occasional pointless honking of a horn invaded my thoughts and I responded in the only way that made sense at the moment. I cranked the Bob Seger CD that I'd had in my player for the better part of a week.

Michigan's native son was roaring through *You'll Accomp'ny Me* when I struck on another plan. I dialed up the paper's main number, and waited to hear Helen's voice.

"*Chicago Record.*"

"Helen?"

"*Chicago Record.*"

I turned the volume down on Bob, having long ago concluded that the couple in that song didn't make it in the end, anyhow.

"Helen, this is Alex Chapa."

"Okay."

The theory around the office was that Helen had been around since before the building got built, which was sometime during the Coolidge administration.

"I need you to tell me who might still be in the office right now."

"Okay, here you go."

Before I could stop her, Helen transferred my call. I was about to hang up and try calling back when someone picked up.

"Sports, this is Jerry."

"Rossiter?"

"That's right, can I help you?"

Jerry Rossiter was the senior sports reporter at the *Record*, a terrific writer, and an all-around decent guy who kept to himself more than most. But he didn't figure to be someone who could help me right then. Though, in his capacity as a high school sports reporter, Jerry had an encyclopedic knowledge of the Fox Valley area.

"Hey, Jerry, this is Alex Chapa."

"Alex, what's up?"

"I was actually trying to reach someone in news. I'm looking for info on an arson investigation in Birch Grove."

"Which one?"

Which one? There was more than one Birch Grove? As far as I was concerned one was plenty.

"What do you mean which one?"

"I mean that by my count there have been four unusual and suspicious fires in that town over the past two years."

Now I vaguely recalled one of the other fires, but Rossiter had the lowdown on all of them.

He explained that three other shops had been burned, and how the police had come up empty until they caught Beniquez while he was watching the Laserquick fire.

"How do you know all this, Jerry?"

"I spend my nights sitting in bleachers, and people talk about all sorts of things like I'm not even there. Why don't you remember these? You work in news, after all."

I didn't have a regular beat like most other reporters. At least not since I'd been given my own regular space in the paper several years ago. These days, any story I tagged typically involved a dead body, a crooked politician, or a dead crooked politician.

"You know how it is, Jerry, some stories just slip by. What have you got on the Laserquick fire, the one that killed—"

"Dennis Braun, the owner. His wife was a cheerleader at the high school way back when. Popular girl, if you know what I mean."

I thought I did.

"Yeah, I know Tony Beniquez is on trial for that, Alex, but I'm not buying it."

I nearly rear-ended a Mustang, a mistake that would've likely totaled my well-past-its-prime Toyota Celica, but Rossiter's words were reverberating in my head.

"You still there, Alex?"

"Why aren't you buying it?"

"Because I know the kid, interviewed him a few times when he was playing for the high school baseball team. A good player, too, third baseman, probably could've gone on to play Division III, but instead he went to work with his old man to help pay the bills."

That came a lot closer to matching the impression that had been forming in my mind than anything the prosecution had asserted during its opening statement.

"What about getting into trouble? I understand there was some of that, too."

I heard him cup the phone with his hand and spell out the name of some coach to another reporter in the room. I was starting to repeat myself when Rossiter turned his attention back my way and apologized for the interruption.

"When he was much younger, twelve, thirteen, he ran with some bangers on a couple of break-ins, got caught, finally. But I think he learned his lesson. As far as I understand, Tony changed a lot once he got into sports and when he started working with his dad."

So maybe this was just what the defense had suggested. A story of a young man, the son of immigrants, turning his life around and starting to make good. Until an arrest for a crime he did not commit landed him in court. Maybe.

"I just can't see him doing what they're saying he did, Alex. But between you and me, in that town, once they've turned against you, you're done. And they've certainly turned against Tony Beniquez."

I'd wondered about that. Birch Grove wasn't known for its diversity. As a Hispanic male with a history of problems with the law, Tony Beniquez would've made a perfect scapegoat.

Or could be Tony wasn't a scapegoat at all, just a young punk who had committed one stupid crime too many. I knew Rossiter wasn't the sort to put himself out for no reason, so the fact that he was coming to the kid's defense meant something. Or maybe he was just a bit too close to be objective.

"Could he still have been running with a bad crowd? Could he have hidden that part of his life from his family? From coaches? Reporters?"

I heard Rossiter let out a deep sigh.

"Sure, I guess that might be possible, though it's unlikely. Everyone has secrets, every place has them, too. And a town like Birch Grove has more than most. So yeah, he could've gotten mixed up with some bad characters. But like I said, I'm not buying it."

Rossiter sounded like he was growing tired of answering questions, and I knew what that meant. He was about to turn the tables on me.

Though I was determined to learn all that I could, I didn't know how much further I wanted to continue this discussion under false pretenses and risk putting a colleague, as well as myself, in a potentially difficult situation. Knowing that Rossiter was a very good reporter, sensing that as such he was about to start asking the questions instead of answering them, and not wanting to involve him in this in case it blew up on me, I thanked him, promised to buy him lunch sometime soon, and abruptly signed off.

DANIELS

At the library I discovered there had been four arsons in Birch Grove in the last twenty-two months. I also learned Beniquez played on the high school baseball team. I did a quick cross-reference between game dates and when the other arsons were committed, apparently trying to find an alibi for the kid, but didn't find anything conclusive.

As with the print shop, the arsonist had used an accelerant in the other three blazes, in each case gasoline. There were no witnesses, and apparently no leads. Besides the shops I already knew about, a toy store off the main drag was also burned down. I jotted down names of vics and then grabbed a local phone book to look up numbers. The first one I got an answering machine. Second one no answer at all. Third was disconnected, but had a forwarding number. Area code 212, which I knew to be New York. I tried that and a man picked up on the second ring.

"Mr. Steinblum?" I said, squinting at my notes. "My name is Lieutenant Jack Daniels. I'm in Birch Grove and I wanted to—"

"I want nothing to do with you people," he said, forcefully interrupting. "Leave me and my family alone!"

And he hung up.

Interesting.

I tried chatting up two librarians on the subject, and while they were open with their knowledge, they didn't teach me anything new, other than the name of the guy at Jay's Locksmithe Shoppe. Again I got on my cell.

"Benedict."

"Hey, Herb, it's me."

Detective First Class Herb Benedict was my partner in Homicide.

"Hi, Jack. I hope you're enjoying your time away while leaving me with a full workload."

I wasn't.

"I'll be back soon, no more than six or seven months. I need you to run a name for me. Vincent Corelli."

I spelled it for him, then listened to his keyboard clackety-clack.

"Got two of them."

"This one is in his mid-thirties, Caucasian, prison tats on his arms."

"Did a nickel at Joliet. Broke into a house, surprised the sleeping homeowner, beat him up pretty good."

"Parole?"

"No, he's one hundred percent free. He causing trouble?"

"I don't know." And I didn't.

"Speaking of non-sequiturs, any good food in town?"

"I had a Rueben that was pretty good."

"Can you fax me one? I'm starving."

I pictured my partner's ample gut. "I'm pretty sure you're not starving. And I believe Chicago has a good restaurant or two."

"I'm starving, and I'm unmotivated."

"Doesn't that greasy spoon up the street deliver? The one that serves the quadruple cheeseburger with a whole slab of bacon on it?"

"You mean the Fat Louie Burger?"

"Yeah."

"You didn't know? They closed. Fat Louie died last month. Massive heart attack."

"I'm shocked." I actually wasn't shocked.

"Needed twelve pallbearers to lift his coffin. Damn shame. I mourned for a week. That man was a genius with bacon. Only burger place nearby is a chain manned by apathetic teenagers. Teenagers should *not* be allowed to cook cheeseburgers."

"Much as this conversation is riveting me, I need to go."

"Keep safe, Jack."

"I do my best. Thanks, partner."

During the walk back to the car, I mulled over what I'd learned, but nothing gelled. Part of me wasn't sure why I cared. Not only was this not my case, but the case had been solved. Tony Beniquez was caught on the scene. This was pretty much open and shut.

Still, something nagged at me. Something that made me go off in search of a fast food place.

For the most part, I tried to eat healthy. But I wasn't looking for a burger and fries.

I was looking for who cooked them.

I pulled into a burger chain, walked into the half-full restaurant, waited in line behind an obese guy in a stained sweat suit, and struck pay dirt with a teenager, his face pitted with acne, working the register. His nametag read RANDY.

"Is the chicken sandwich good?"

He stared at me with a face completely devoid of expression. "I dunno. I guess."

"I'll take one, and a bottled water."

"Fries?"

"No thanks. But I do have a question. You know anything about the fires happening in town?"

His face lit up. "Yeah! It was a kid in my school. Tony Beniquez."

"Do you know Tony?"

"He was in my history class last year."

"Does he seem to be the type to start fires like that?"

"I guess so. I mean, they arrested him, right? He must have done it. He's been in trouble before. Ran with some gangbangers."

I knew about Tony's past juvee record. I'd pulled it before coming to Birch Grove. One prior arrest for being part of a group that committed a B&E. Though it was unclear in the report what role Tony had played in the actual crime.

"There anyone else working here who knows Tony?"

"Nah. But some of my buddies are sitting over there. They know him." He pointed to a group of teens at one of the rear tables.

"Uh, your bill is six-eighty-one."

I paid, but rather than wait for my food I walked toward the teenagers, trying hard to not look like a cop. It was two guys, two girls. The guys wore baggy jeans and T-shirts three sizes too large. The girls were in mini-skirts that my mother would have slapped the hell out of me for wearing, and enough make-up for a kabuki troop. When I approached they stopped talking and stared at me with apparent mistrust.

"Randy said you guys know Tony Beniquez."

"You a cop?" one of the guys said.

"No. I'm a reporter. My name is Alex Chapa. I work for the *Chicago Record*, and we're doing a story on the trial."

"Are we going to be in the paper?" one of the girls squealed. Then the other one squealed.

I don't think, in my entire life, I've ever squealed.

"I can't make any promises. What's Tony like?"

"Dawg was a banger, man. Fool got what was coming."

I wasn't sure why the boy was addressing me as *man*, but then I didn't understand why white kids from the burbs tried to dress and talk like black kids from the inner city.

"So you think he did it?"

I got general expressions of agreement. The other boy added, "Dude brought a knife to school back in junior high. Got suspended for two weeks. Bad shit, man."

"Thanks," I said. "If I need to speak to any of you again, I'll be in touch."

They nodded like that made sense, even though I hadn't written down anything or gotten any of their names.

I went back to the register to grab my sandwich, and on my way out the door one of the girls caught up to me. This close, her heavily made-up face couldn't mask her youth. She couldn't be more than sixteen.

"Hey, Alex, I used to date Tony."

"Really?" I said, letting my voice convey my skepticism.

"It didn't work out, but he was a sweet dude, you know what I'm saying? Always good to me. Helped his dad out a lot."

"So do you think he set fire to that print shop?"

"No way. Tony would never do that. Not in a billion years."

CHAPA

I picked up some General Tso's chicken and ham fried rice on the way home and treated myself to a fine two-course meal. Three, if you counted the fortune cookie. This one's message read: *You will attend an unusual event and meet some interesting people.* Fact is that could describe much of my professional life, assuming the word *interesting* was used in a liberal way.

After tossing the leftovers in the fridge and throwing out an old set of Chinese food boxes that had been in there long enough to claim squatter's rights, I sifted through a mental list of things I could do to keep my mind off the trial and avoid the urge to search for info online.

I knew I was probably being a little paranoid. But I'd recently read a story of a juror in the southwest who'd been charged with contempt of court after an investigation revealed that she had used her computer to research the background details of her case during the trial. Sure, there are ways to cover your tracks, but I'm only as computer literate as I need to be, and electronic forensics are way beyond my area of expertise.

A call to my daughter did nothing to smooth out the wrinkles in my night. I left a message after my ex-wife's recorded voice instructed me to do so, but knew there was zero chance Nikki would ever get to hear it. After debating whether to try again a few minutes later and deciding against it, I figured I'd better find some busy work.

I'd made it to Billy Squier's *Don't Say No* in the re-alphabetization of my CD collection, and was trying to remember when and why I bought that thing and realizing it probably belonged to Carla, when I heard my neighbor Kevin mowing the lawn. It seemed like Kevin spent a lot of his time cutting his grass, when he wasn't watering it. I wondered for a moment if he'd be willing to mow mine on one of the three or four days during the week that he didn't spend mowing his own.

Then I remembered something else about Kevin. He was a collector. No, not a collector, a *saver*. He wasn't one of those hoarders you see on TV, quite the opposite. Kevin's world was neat and orderly. From his perfectly even grass to his neatly pressed and color coordinated clothing.

He was also a loyal reader of the *Chicago Record*. So loyal that he'd once shown me his collection of back issues. Every one, in fact, going back at least three years.

"You never know when you're going to need to double-check something in an old story," he'd explained.

"But that's what the Internet is for, Kevin. All of the old stories are archived."

"True, but your paper charges a fee for any story that is more than a year old, and I'm not playing that game."

I couldn't argue with his logic. Though when I asked how long it had been since he'd last found a need to "double-check" anything in a three-year-old paper, all I got from Kevin was a cold glare.

But now I was the one walking over to his house, hoping I hadn't discouraged him from maintaining his collection. The smell of freshly cut grass invaded my senses as I crossed his yard. I found Kevin in the garage, wiping down his lawnmower.

"Hey, Kevin, how are things?"

"Alex, good to see you. You know that stack of logs you've had along your side of our fence, the one we share?"

"You mean the logs that Carla made me keep around for the fireplace we never bothered to light? Sure, I know what you're talking about."

"Well, I think they've attracted some nasty critters and I would appreciate it if you would move them, burn them, or just pitch the darn things."

"You know what, Kev, that's a great idea and I will get on it really soon. In the meantime, I need to ask you a favor."

I think Kevin got the wrong idea because his first response was to stand up and get into a defensive posture between me and his lawn-mower. Like a bear poised to protect its young.

"I don't need to borrow your lawnmower, Kevin, I just need to check out some old copies of the *Record*."

He flashed me exaggerated smirk. "Oh really? So you need to 'double-check' something?"

"In a sense, yes, so clearly you were on to something when you started stash—*preserving* every copy."

His smirk turned into a smile and he invited me into the house. I said hi to his quiet, gently attractive wife Rhonda as we walked past the kitchen, and followed Kevin to a den around the back of the house.

"Which one do you need?" he asked and opened a room-length walk-in closet revealing a dozen stacks of clear plastic containers, each labeled with the year and months.

"That's amazing, Kevin."

He nodded. "I also keep all of our *TV Guides*." He leaned toward me for added emphasis. "*All* of them."

"I don't have a need for those at the moment, but it's good just to know they're here."

I started with the week of the Laserquick fire, turning the still crisp pages while Kevin hovered. It had been a busy few days. The President had visited a high school in Wheaton, the Birch Grove police had rounded up a group of alleged gang members who were hanging out at a local ice cream shop, and there was also my story about an appliance plant in Larkin that closed down, leaving more than three hundred employees without a job.

That explained why I'd missed the story the first time around, and why it never made it above the fold on page three. There were two follow-up stories in the next four days. Much of what was there I already knew, but there were items in each that interested me. In the second story, there was a mention about this being the fourth such fire in Birch Grove in the past sixteen months, just as Jerry Rossiter had told me. In the third story, there was a reference by the police commissioner to the growing gang problem in the area. The commissioner also suggested that there may be a connection between the gang activity and the arsons.

All three of the stories were written by veteran reporter Jim Cha-kowski, a mentor and the closest thing I had to a friend at the paper. I thanked Kevin and returned home to call Jim.

DANIELS

The B&B where I was staying, known as the Weatherby House after the man who built it in 1905, was perfect in every way except for one—the owners were nuts.

So to get the beautifully decorated bedroom with the huge cast-iron bathtub and the ceiling-high stone fireplace, I had to put up with a few minutes of insane prattle every time I encountered one of them.

They were in their fifties, always smiling and offering pleasantries, and at first encounter you would take them to be charming.

But the more you talked to them, the more you realized their toolbox was missing most of its screws.

"Good evening, Miss Daniels." Greta Hauppdorf greeted me at the front door, opening it before I had a chance to use the key. Like she'd been standing there, waiting for me to show up. She wore a dress straight out of *Little House on the Prairie*, and her gray hair was done up in a bun. It was probably in a bun when she came out of the womb.

"Good evening, Mrs. Hauppdorf."

"Did you know there were 17,030 murders in the United States last year?"

"I did not know that," I said, having to step around her to get inside.

"I wonder how many of them were asking for it."

"Excuse me?"

"You know. Some folks deserve it. Don't you think so, Father?"

She looked to her left, where the tall figure of Arnold Hauppdorf had somehow materialized in the kitchen doorway.

"I do, Mother. Stupid people, especially. A lot of stupid people in the world."

Don't engage, I told myself. But my mouth was open before I could stop it.

"So you're saying that if people were smarter, they would have been able to outsmart their attacker?" I asked.

"Heavens, no," Greta said. "We mean they were murdered because they were stupid. Which is a good thing. There are too many stupid people, and they're having babies faster than the smart people are."

"The average IQ of the country is dropping," Arnold added. "At this rate, by the year 2030, our nation will be twenty-five percent stupider than it is now. Clearly the government needs to take action."

"By rounding up all the stupid people and killing them?" I asked.

Both the Hauppdorfs chuckled.

"Oh, my dear, nothing that drastic," said Greta. "We should just ship all the stupid people to some other country."

Arnold nodded. "Ship them to a smart country, like Japan or Germany. That will lower their national IQ, and help the U.S. better compete in a global market."

"What if they don't want to go?" I asked, wondering why I even bothered.

"They're stupid. They can be tricked. Like those stings where fugitives are told they won a free television, and they show up and get arrested."

"Exactly," added Greta. "The stupids could get free tickets to Germany, saying they won a free vacation, and when they arrive they can be denied re-entry into the U.S."

"A wonderful idea, Mother. I'm going to go write letters to our state senators right now."

"I'll join you, Father. Good night, Miss Daniels. Breakfast will be at eight a.m. I'm making blueberry pancakes."

I went into my gorgeous bedroom, with the gorgeous fireplace and bathtub, and locked the door behind me so the crazies couldn't get in.

After a bath and a phone call to my fiancée, I curled up in the enormous bed and buried myself in an Ed McBain novel until I was too tired to keep my eyes open.

CHAPA

Jim Chakowski answered on the second ring.

"So you managed to get out of jury duty."

"Not exactly."

Silence. Followed by more silence. Then, "Oh hell. Alex, please tell me you're calling to bullshit about the Cubs' lousy season."

"I need to ask you a couple of questions about the Birch Grove fires."

I heard him sigh. "You know you're not supposed to be doing this, right?"

"And now you've warned me, and we both know damned well you'd be doing the same thing if our roles were reversed."

He thought about it for a moment.

"True. So what do you need to know?"

I asked him what he knew about the other fires.

"Just some general background, those weren't my stories. If I re-member correctly, those were covered by a couple of new guys. Those stories weren't that big of a deal."

"Until the Laserquick fire."

"Right. Nobody died until the print shop went up. Maybe they're all linked, maybe not. I never found a connection. There are a lot of old buildings in Birch Grove, and I can tell you not all of them are up to code."

"But that's true about any of the old towns in the area."

"Yes, it is. I did a story on that once."

"I remember."

"A good one."

"They all are, Jim."

I heard his familiar laugh at the other end.

"Have there been any similar fires in Birch Grove since?"

"Not as far as I know."

"What about gangs? You mentioned that in one of your stories."

"In passing, if memory serves."

"That's right."

"You know why, don't you?"

I did. I'd been taught well. "Because you had a reliable quote, but not enough to hang much more on, and you sensed there was still something else to the story and wanted to get ahead of it."

"You might have a future in this business, Alex. Yeah, the gang thing. It's not kids from Birch Grove as much as from some of the neighboring towns. Larkin has an issue with gangs, Aurora, and Elgin, too."

"Even Oakton."

"Yes, Oakton, as well. And gangs that deal in drugs like to go where the money is, like Birch Grove. But those kids they rounded up a while back, that's a sign of the times in that town."

"What do you mean?"

I walked to the kitchen and poured myself a shot of Matusalem rum.

"With this new administration, a lot of things have changed there. The other guys were crooked as hell, the old mayor ran the place like his own personal country club. But the group that's in there now, one hand doesn't know what the other is up to, and you've got some rogue elements at every level of that government."

"What about the Beniquez kid?"

"He could've done it. Some sort of gang initiation thing, perhaps. But that will be up to a jury to decide, won't it, Alex?"

After that, the conversation turned to family and work, though not necessarily in that order. Before he signed off, Chakowski offered a final piece of advice.

"Remember, Alex, ninety percent of all crimes are committed for one of two reasons—money or love. If I were in your shoes, I'd be looking for one of those two motives."

"What about the other ten percent?"

"Fear, compulsion, or insanity. Maybe the defendant was driven by one those."

By the time I was done talking to Jim I didn't feel like I'd cleared up any of the questions I'd been asking about the trial. Which meant I'd likely have to rely entirely on the evidence that would be presented in court. The way it was supposed to be. The way every other juror would likely reach a verdict.

And if that was the case, based on what I'd heard so far, Tony Beniquez didn't have a prayer of walking out of there a free man.

And maybe he didn't deserve to.

DANIELS

I woke up in the middle of the night, positive there was someone in my room.

I wasn't sure how I knew it. The room was completely dark, curtains drawn and every light off. But I felt a presence. Someone standing there in the pitch black. Watching.

I didn't know what had awoken me, didn't recall any dreams, didn't remember hearing any sounds, but all the hair was standing up on my arms, and I had to force myself to breath naturally so whoever was there didn't know I knew.

My gun, a Colt Detective Special, was in the bathroom, in my overnight case. The intruder stood between me and it.

My mouth was dry. Hands were sweating. But I couldn't let the fear paralyze me, couldn't think about why the intruder was there, or what he wanted to do to me. I had to use the adrenalin and act. Get to my weapon. Fight. Escape.

I tensed my legs, picturing the move in my head; I'd roll off the side of the bed, land in a crouch, then follow the wall with my hand until I reached the—

"I can see you." The voice was male, a whisper. "I know you're awake."

I didn't recognize the voice, but it sounded forced, like the man was trying to disguise it. It was also unnaturally calm, which kicked my fear into overdrive. Anyone that relaxed breaking into someone's house was stone cold.

I needed to be stone cold as well to survive this. Now if I could just get my damn legs to move.

"Stop snooping around. Give your testimony, and then get the fuck out of town. This will be your only warning. If you don't do as you're told…"

The gunshot sounded like thunder, the bullet slamming into the headboard above me.

Raw terror fueled my actions, and I did the roll-and-crouch move, seeing a silhouette of a retreating figure, dressed in black and wearing a ski mask, open the bedroom door and slip through.

In four steps I was in the bathroom.

Six steps later I was in the hallway, gun in hand.

Movement, on the stairs. I swung around, saw a startled Greta clutching the V neck of her nightgown. Heard movement in the rear of the house, and tracked it, moving low and fast, seeing the back door yawing open. I sidled up to the doorway, back against it, squinting out into the darkness of the Hauppdorf's backyard. Quickly found the wall switch, but the porch light didn't come on.

"What's going on?" Greta moaned.

"Someone broke in. Stay back. Call the police."

I checked the doorknob, the frame, saw they were solid. I closed it, locked it, and tried to get my heart rate under control before the cops arrived.

# # #

No sign of forced entry.

The bulb to the outside porch light had been unscrewed. So had five other bulbs throughout the house.

The slug dug out of the wall behind the headboard was a .45.

Arnold Hauppdorf hadn't been home. He'd supposedly taken a walk, something he and his wife claimed he did every night. When Arnold arrived he looked more fascinated than shocked. He swore both doors were locked when he left.

The police on the scene were two uniforms I hadn't met before, a man and a woman. The woman took me aside and asked if I'd been molested. I told her I hadn't.

They sent a patrol car to Vincent Corelli's house, but the locksmith wasn't home.

Corelli made some sense for this. An ex-con, locksmith, and someone who clearly didn't want anyone stirring things up in Birch Grove. As long as buildings kept burning he'd keep boarding them up and making money. Extra, if it was in the middle of the night.

After they left, at close to three in the morning, Phin showed up.

Phineas Troutt was a friend of mine, ten years my junior, whom I met in a professional capacity some years ago. I'd arrested him. But even though he tended to operate in the gray areas of the law, we'd somehow managed to become friends. He was smart, and reliable, and I needed someone to watch my back. I could have called Herb, but my absence in Homicide was already putting a strain on the district, and I knew he couldn't have been spared. Phin was just as good, and in some ways even better.

By then, the fear had grown to the point where I was starting to freak out a little. I didn't like being threatened, and didn't like having someone break into my room and shoot at me. The more I dwelled on it, the creepier it became. Having Phin close by eased my mind a lot.

We talked over coffee at the kitchen table. I filled him in on everything that had gone on up to that point, not only to get his insight on the matter, but to set things straight in my own head.

"So you think it was the locksmith," Phin said. He didn't look too hot. He'd just done another round of chemo, and he was bald again. Like me, he wore a T-shirt and jeans, and like me, he had a gun tucked into the waistband.

"Could be. He said he could see me. Someone who deals with burglar equipment could also have some night vision goggles. And..." I closed my eyes and pictured the scene. "I think I saw a tiny green light when he was leaving."

Very tiny, more like a speck. It could have been the after-effects of the muzzle flash. But I knew starlight viewers showed images in luminous green, and maybe his goggles slipped when he was running off.

"So you think the locksmith is starting the fires just so he can get paid to board up the places afterward?"

Phin didn't sound convinced. Neither was I. But I'd seen stupider motives than that.

"Maybe. Or maybe the arsonist is just someone who likes to watch things burn."

"So it could be this Beniquez kid."

"Could be. Or it could be someone else entirely. Some weirdo I haven't met."

"What about the owner of this place? No alibi, and you said he's a nutjob."

"Possible, I suppose. Maybe this is how he and his wife get their kicks. But the intruder specifically mentioned my testimony. He knew about the trial."

"Sounds like everyone in town knows about the trial. You said Tony might be involved in gangs. Could it have been one of his crew?"

"Again, possible. But this sounded like an adult. Someone cool-headed."

"Who else is connected with the trial?"

"The District Attorney, Simon Lebanon, is an odd duck. He really wants to win this case. Maybe he knows something he doesn't want me to know."

"Can you see him as the intruder?"

"Not really. But again, it's possible."

"Was it a good arrest?"

"You're thinking the cops? Maybe a frame?"

Phin smiled. "Not all cops are good guys. Present company excepted."

"Nicholas James and Emmanuel Lewis."

He raised an eyebrow. "You were threatened by the kid who played Webster?"

"He's not Webster. But he and his partner both act like jarheads. They've got this metrosexual thing going that just doesn't seem to fit right, though their clothes certainly do. But other than that they seem okay."

"Lots of suspects," Phin said. "Hell, maybe it was me. I'm a known criminal."

I smiled for the first time all night. "If you crept into my bedroom at night, I hope you'd do something more interesting than threaten me."

I could swear he blushed a little. Phin was too young for me, and not stable at all, but I'd be lying if I said I didn't think he was attractive, and I was pretty sure he felt the same way.

Rather than flirt, he stood up. "Want me to stay in the house, or watch the perimeter?"

I wanted him to stay in the house. I was still scared, and the thought of being alone made my palms sweat.

Which is exactly why I needed to be alone. Fall off the horse, get right back on, or else you're afraid for the rest of your life.

"Outside. Thanks, buddy."

Phin winked at me. "For you, anytime. See you in the morning, Jack. Get some sleep."

He finished his coffee and slipped out the front door.

I made sure the door was locked behind him, then I went back to my room and crawled into bed, my gun on the nightstand next to me, the overhead light on.

I didn't sleep at all.

CHAPA

I hadn't slept well the night before, and when I got my first look at Jack Daniels seated in the courtroom on the second day, I knew I wasn't the only one.

I'd spent the evening resisting the urge to log on and start digging through every bit of material about the case I could find for fear that my records could be searched at a later date. I drank my shot of rum after I got off the phone with Jim, poured myself another, and eventually fell asleep on my couch. I was five minutes late to court, but no one seemed to notice or care.

The courtroom smelled a little less fresh than the day before. At least someone had managed to turn on the air conditioning, though nowhere near high enough.

Bob, the world's most enthusiastic juror seated next to me in the jury box, was much more into the morning than I could ever hope to be.

"This is a little like being at a boxing match, isn't it?" The guy was genuinely excited about being here. Something must've gone very wrong during his childhood.

"Sure, Bob, one with lots of talking, very little action, and no blood."

Bob furrowed his brow, then turned away. I had a feeling he'd keep to himself the rest of the day, and maybe even for the rest of the trial, though that was probably too much to hope for.

Marcia, the woman I'd met in the waiting room who wound up being the last juror chosen, turned to face me.

"My friends are so curious about all of this." She was wearing a beige business suit that blended too well with her light features, a flowery but subtle fragrance, and looked as though she'd been professionally made up for hours. "Though, of course, I didn't discuss any of the particulars with them," she added, clearly intent on amending her first remark and wanting to make certain we all heard her.

I had always assumed jurors sat in silence after they were brought into the courtroom, and judging from the scowl on the face of the tall, bald man to our right, that might've usually been the case. He'd been glaring at Marcia as she was talking. I found myself staring at his ears, or his *left* ear, to be exact, though I assumed there was a matching one on the other side to balance the weight. It was as though someone had attached a sandal to the side of the guy's head, and the way the outer ridge curved around I could easily imagine a trio of Cooper Minis racing in there—at least until they got stuck in the hair.

Its hypnotic effect was finally broken when Lipscomb got up from behind the prosecutor's table and called the next witness. His name was Joel Luzinsky, a former marine who owned a high end cigar store called Smoke Em' If You Have Em', that was located directly across the street from the crime scene.

Luzinsky looked like one of those men who were athletic and tightly built in their youth, but not anymore. He had neatly cut hair that he was still figuring out how best to color without tipping off anyone who'd notice or care.

He testified that he'd seen Beniquez around the print shop just minutes before smoke began flowing from its side windows. The kid had been carrying a duffle bag in his right hand, and cradling two gasoline cans in his left. He was very specific about this.

The prosecution produced the olive green duffle bag and a pair of beat up, rusty cans and entered them into evidence, placing them on a dark oak table in front of the jury box. Lipscomb then showed how the cans easily fit into the duffle bag. They clanged against one another inside like a pair of wind chimes as she lifted the bag for all to see.

On the stand, Luzinsky appeared uneasy, like he'd rather be anywhere else. Maybe it was natural to feel that way. I sure as hell would. It didn't help that he was a large man, bigger than the seat was made to accommodate. His meaty hands rested on the wood railing in front of him as he jostled in search of a comfortable position. I didn't like his chances of finding one.

Lipscomb took the cans out of the duffle bag. They clattered again as she set them on the table.

"Were those the cans that you saw the defendant carrying, Mr. Luzinsky?"

"Yes, ma'am."

"And is that the duffle bag?"

"That's right."

Luzinsky went on to repeat the time and date that he'd seen Beniquez skulking around the print shop, before Lipscomb turned him over to the defense.

"Are you certain that you specifically saw those two cans in the defendant's possession?" Milledge asked as he stood and straightened his jacket, the same one he'd been wearing the day before.

Luzinsky did not hesitate. "Absolutely."

"I mean, they're just a couple of old gas cans, nothing special about them, is there?"

"I'm sure those were the ones, I remember the rust on them." Luzinsky tightened his grip on the railing.

"And how far away were you from my client when you claim that you eagle-eyed those cans?"

"Objection, Your Honor, the defense—"

"I'll rephrase. How far away were you when you say you *saw* my client carrying two gas cans?"

"I don't know for sure, I was across the street. What is that? Maybe thirty, forty feet?"

"Well, you're about halfway there. Would you believe it's exactly seventy-two feet from the doorway of your store, where you've testified that you were standing, to Laserquick's front door?" Milledge approached the jury box and made eye-contact with each of us. "That's thirty-yards. You must have excellent vision."

Despite being a man of limited ability within his profession, Milledge was doing a better than a fair job of putting the heat on the ex-marine.

But what did it matter whether or not Luzinsky had actually made out the individual rust spots on the two cans that were resting on the table in front of us? The defense had conceded the duffle bag belonged to Beniquez, and if the kid was walking around with gas cans in the vicinity of a fire, then maybe Jerry Rossiter was wrong.

Milledge fired off a few more questions, and generated two more objections from Lipscomb, in a vain attempt to shake Luzinsky's certainty about what he'd seen. He took a few swipes at the man's credibility, and pressed him about his relationship with the deceased.

"We were cordial, not friends, you know, but we waved to each other now and then. We were good."

When Milledge finally dismissed Luzinsky, the man bolted to his feet, as quickly as someone his size could actually bolt, and hastily got off the stand. I watched him walk back toward the gallery, wondering whether he'd look over at the jury, or try to make eye-contact with Lipscomb.

But his gaze was locked on someone else. As Luzinsky made his way back to his seat in the third row he exchanged glances with Alice Braun. The two kept looking at one another, then turning away, only to reconnect like a magnet to steel.

I decided to keep an eye on Luzinsky and the widow, and was still watching them when Lipscomb called her next witness to the stand.

DANIELS

After an awkward breakfast where the Hauppdorf's stared at us without saying anything, Phin drove with me to the courthouse. At first, he was going to come in with me and watch from the gallery, but then he saw the cruisers and press trucks parked in front of the century old courthouse. Besides, there was a metal detector at the entrance, and he wouldn't have been able to get his gun in. I had to leave mine in the car. Instead, Phin watched from outside, looking for anything suspicious.

When I walked into the building I was struck by how empty it was except for the dozen or so people milling around the entrance to the courtroom where the Beniquez trial was being held. It was unlike any courthouse I'd ever been in during a major trial.

"We're a small community," Lebanon explained as he tried to tame his hair with one hand while flipping through a cell phone with the other. "With our resources being as limited as they are, I thought it best to shuffle the schedule around so that this was the only case of any significance being held in the courthouse this morning."

I nodded like I cared, which I didn't, and asked, "So you promised I'd be the first witness called, that's still the case, right?"

He was still poking at his phone.

"Reception in here is lousy. I'm one of the few people who are allowed to have a cell in the courtroom and it doesn't do me much good anyhow. You did check yours at the metal detectors, didn't you?"

Again, I nodded. "When will I be called?"

"Third, I believe. Maybe fourth."

"That's not what you told me—"

Lebanon snapped. "Look, Officer Daniels—"

"Lieutenant."

"Fine, *Lieutenant*, we've already shifted our witness list around to accommodate you, now I would appreciate it if you'd get with the program," Lebanon said and walked away.

I was poised to tear into him, but knew it wouldn't do me much good. Officers James and Lewis were huddled near the door to the courtroom. I walked by them and slipped inside. In the past, when I've testified in trials, I've waited outside of the courtroom until they called me to the stand. But I was tired from lack of sleep, and still a little edgy. So I sat down, and no one told me I couldn't.

The courtroom was nearly full, but I found a seat in the second row from back, next to a reporter and behind a tall Hispanic male who I made for a member of the defendant's family. Chapa was staring at me from the jury box while trying to pretend he was listening to something a female juror was saying to him.

Why the hell was he grinning at me? Was Chapa actually happy to be here?

I reviewed my deposition in my head as the first witness, a tall male named Luzinsky, gave testimony that he'd seen the accused around the print shop just before the fire. There was a discussion of some old gas cans, but that was of little interest to me. I was there to recite what little I knew about this case and then get on with my life.

As Luzinsky stepped down from the stand and took a seat near the front of the gallery, I took in a deep breath and tried to find comfort in the knowledge that there was only one more witness ahead of me. I failed, but then came the first piece of good news I'd gotten in the past two days.

"The prosecution calls Lieutenant Jacqueline Daniels to the stand."

The lead prosecutor, Anna Lipscomb, was tall and blonde, wearing a smart gray pantsuit and a no-nonsense expression. The bailiff, a hunched elderly man who looked old enough to have worked when Christ was tried, swore me in. I stepped around the railing, sat in the uncomfortable wooden chair and looked out over the courtroom.

I noticed Chapa, his demeanor relaxed but his eyes alert. A few seats away from him, a juror with exceptionally big ears stared at me with a leer that was off-putting. Officers James and Webster were near the back of the gallery, flanked by reporters. In the front row was a dour-faced Hispanic who I took to be Tony's father.

"State your name and profession."

"My name is Jacqueline Daniels, I'm a Homicide Lieutenant in Chicago's 26th District."

"How long have you been a police officer?"

"For over twenty years."

"Have you been involved with murder trials before?"

"Extensively."

"So you're no stranger to being on the stand?"

"Not at all."

"Could you take a guess at how many times your testimony has lead to convictions?"

The defense attorney leapt to his feet. "Objection, relevance."

Judge Malvo seemed to startle himself awake. He made a small groan, but before he could answer, Lipscomb cut in.

"We're establishing the integrity of the witness, your honor. Lieutenant Daniels is a professional, and her past performance is relevant."

"Sounds good. I'll overrule. You can answer the question, Lieutenant."

"Dozens of times," I said. "Possibly hundreds."

"So tell us where you were on the day of the fire at the Laserquick print shop on Main Street."

"My fiancée and I came to Birch Grove for a mini-vacation. We were walking east down Main Street at four-forty-six p.m., and we stopped into Dirty McCann's sports bar to have a drink."

"How can you be so sure of the time?"

"I rechecked. Right as we were entering the bar, I got a call from my partner. The phone call was time stamped."

"How long were you at the bar?"

"About twenty minutes. Long enough for us each to finish a beer. Then my boyfriend went to the washroom just as most of the bar patrons rushed outside. I followed them, wondering what was happening. Immediately I heard sirens, and saw what I learned was the Laserquick print shop, across the street, about forty meters away. It was on fire."

"When did you see the defendant?"

Now it was the defense's turn. "Objection, leading,"

Malvo responded with a little more urgency this time. "Sounds that way to me. Sustained," he groaned.

"Can you tell us what happened prior to you entering Dirty McCann's?"

"A minute before entering the bar, a teenage male ran by us on the sidewalk. He actually bumped me, and dropped his duffle bag. I made eye-contact with him as he picked it up."

"What was he wearing?"

"Blue jeans and a red top. His duffle bag was green."

"Is that teenage male in the courtroom today?"

"He is." I pointed without being asked. "It was Tony Beniquez."

Chatter from the gallery. I watched reporters furiously scribble in their notepads.

"What would you judge Mr. Beniquez's emotional state as at the time?"

"Objection, Your Honor. The witness is not a psychologist."

"Withdrawn. Can you describe Mr. Beniquez's actions and mannerisms?"

"He appeared to be in a hurry," I said. "And he looked a bit frantic." I made it a point to stare at the defense attorney before he could open his mouth. "And I've arrested enough perps to recognize frantic when I see it."

"Was that the only time you saw Mr. Beniquez that day?"

"No. He was among the group of people watching the fire."

"What happened next?"

"The fire department and the police arrived very quickly, within about a minute. I watched two firefighters break into the print shop, and very soon after they pulled out a body, who I later learned was the victim, Dennis Braun."

Lipscomb walked back to the prosecutor's table and flipped open a file.

"Let's talk about Tony Beniquez during the fire. Did he still have his duffle bag with him?"

"Yes."

"But the gas cans," she pointed to the evidence table, "you didn't see those, is that correct?"

"All I saw was the bag. He never opened it while I was watching."

"So you did not see them in his hands, as Mr. Luzinsky testified."

"No, I did not."

She turned to the jury. "Which meant they were already back inside the duffle bag where the officers found them."

I hesitated, staring at the defense attorney again. But he didn't cry speculation.

"I don't know whether they were in there or not, but the bag did appear to be containing something. I could tell by the way the strap hung on his shoulder."

"So the cans could very well have been in there?"

"The bag appeared to be full, but—"

"And you never saw Beniquez put anything else in the duffle bag."

"That's correct. But I already stated—"

"And you stated that there was something in the duffle bag that could have been gas cans."

"I stated," I said, louder than before, "that the bag appeared to be full. I didn't say—"

"Lieutenant Daniels, you were here earlier when it was shown that the cans do indeed fit inside the duffle bag."

I blew out a breath. "Yes."

"And they fit quite easily, yes?"

"They fit, yes."

"And that is the duffle bag you saw, yes?"

"Yes."

"Is it within the realm of possibility that the cans were in there both times when you saw the defendant?"

Again I waited for the speculation objection, but it didn't come. Was the defense attorney asleep? I looked at Malvo, and the judge certainly appeared to be.

"Yes," I reluctantly said.

"No further questions," Lipscomb said, turned her back to me and returned to her seat behind the prosecution table.

I understood what Lipscomb was doing with me. She wanted the jury to believe the cans were in the bag. But I never saw the cans in the bag, and didn't like words being put in my mouth. Even if Tony was guilty, and the cans were in the bag, I hadn't seen them and would never testify that I had. But I wasn't sure I'd conveyed that message.

I still had no idea if Tony Beniquez did it or didn't do it. But so far he was getting, in my learned opinion, and inadequate defense. Hopefully his team would step it up during the cross-examinations.

Milledge stood up. "No questions, your Honor."

"You're excused, Lieutenant Daniels," Malvo said.

As I walked down from the stand, I managed to meet eyes with Alex Chapa. He had a look of surprise on his face, and I saw him mouth the words *what the hell.*

No kidding. A few minutes ago, I was eager to get out of the courtroom. Not to run home—I didn't take kindly to threats. But I wanted to do a bit more investigating with Phin, maybe try to track down the locksmith.

But now I had no choice. I had to wait around to see what happened next.

A boy's life was at stake. And through no fault of my own, I might have just convicted him.

CHAPA

Jack shrugged when I looked at her. I was trying to process what had just happened, and wondering if they shouldn't just cart Tony Beniquez off to prison right now—*Go straight to jail, do not pass GO, do not collect anything other than an orange jumper, an inmate number, and a life sentence.*

That's exactly what was going to happen if the defense didn't get up to speed in a hurry. Maybe Tony was guilty. Maybe he wasn't. Didn't matter either way if his side wasn't ready to put up a fight.

I was also trying to figure out what it was that Jack had wanted to say on the stand, and why she was still sitting, fuming, in the back of the courtroom when she could have left. I wasn't the only one. The guy with the enormous ears—again, I assumed it was half of a pair, but as a reporter I could not verify that—was weirdly fixated on Jack. He'd been staring at her from the moment she was called to the stand and was still glaring at her now, while the attorneys for both sides held a whispered discussion with Judge Malvo.

As soon as the party broke up, Lipscomb called Officer Nicholas James to the stand. James looked like a thug in the sort of expensive suit that would wrinkle the instant I pulled it off the rack. Check that—no way the suit he was wearing had ever seen a rack.

He was thick all over, not fat, solid. Former military? Or maybe military wannabe. I'd met a few of those during my ill-fated trek with The Wisconsin Free Rangers. But those guys were comical, in a way. This guy I would not turn my back on.

James unbuttoned his suit and slid into the witness chair in one slick movement. He'd done this before. And enjoyed it.

Lipscomb stood and began.

"Please state your name and occupation."

"Nicholas James, Officer with the Birch Grove Police Department."

"Can you describe the events that occurred during the afternoon of the Laserquick fire?"

"My partner, Emmanuel Lewis, and I responded to a 206 called in by an anonymous tipster at the address in question. When we arrived on the scene in the alley behind it, at approximately five-ten p.m., we found the establishment to be on fire. As we pulled up I noticed a male in jeans and a red T-shirt, carrying a duffel bag, fleeing from the scene. We met Fire Chief Homer Davis on the scene, and he and another firefighter proceeded to break through the front door and enter the establishment. Two minutes later, the firefighters reappeared, dragging the corpse of the victim, Dennis Braun."

I was certain Officer James had said more stuff after revealing that his partner was named Emanuel Lewis. I knew this because I saw his lips moving. But I was fixated on the image of the little dude from *Webster* starting a new career as a suburban cop. How had Duane Wormley, the *Record*'s fluff piece maven, missed this human interest story? I scanned the courtroom for Emmanuel and settled on the only African American in the gallery.

Damn. Webster got big.

I semi-heard Lipscomb ask, "What happened next?"

"I was scanning the gathered crowd. It is often the case that an arsonist will stick around to watch the result of his efforts. So when I spotted a male in a red T-shirt, carrying a duffel bag, I alerted my partner. As I covered him, my partner rushed across the street, and proceeded to take down and arrest Mr. Beniquez on suspicion of arson and murder."

"You read him his rights?"

"Yes, ma'am."

"Did you then check the contents of his duffel bag?"

"We did."

"What did you find?"

"Two empty gasoline cans."

The gallery, and the jurors around me, began to murmur. Bob looked back at me and whispered, "This is getting good, isn't it?"

I didn't respond, but it was.

"Are the cans you found in the possession of Mr. Beniquez the ones entered as Exhibit A?" Lipscomb continued.

"Yes, they are."

More rumbles from the crowd. I looked over at Jack, who was sitting in the back of the courtroom, arms crossed. Then I turned my attention to the defendant's father, who had stood up from his seat. I wasn't sure whether the judge or prosecutor had noticed, because they didn't say anything as Carlos Beniquez walked forward, crouched when he reached the railing that separated the folks in the gallery from the main players, and removed a wooden panel about the size of a cutting board.

Now everyone was watching the self-made, hard-working carpenter as he stood and flashed a handgun he'd produced from the gaping hole where the panel used to be.

He was trembling just a little.

"Your gun," he said, pointing his weapon evenly at the surprised bailiff. "Take it out and put it on the floor, or I start shooting." He cleared his throat, and spoke again, louder this time. "If anyone tries to leave, I will shoot them."

The bailiff took his gun from its holster, his withered hands shaking, as he placed it on the floor.

Carlos walked over, picked up the gun, and shoved it into the waistband of his slacks.

I saw Jack instinctively reach for a weapon that wasn't under her armpit and come back with an empty hand.

No one tried to leave the courtroom.

Rather than fear, the first thing I felt was astonishment.

The defendant's father was pointing his gun at the jury, doing a slow, steady sweep.

But how did he get a weapon? How could he have stashed it in court?

I glanced first at Officer James on the stand, then at Officer Lewis in the gallery, both unarmed, probably because shoulder holsters would ruin the lines of their expensive, tailored suits.

Fail. But not as big a fail as me asking Phin to stay outside. While the arresting officers no doubt had military training, they likely had no idea how to react in a hostage situation. But Phin and I had plenty of experience in this area.

A moot point. I was unarmed, Phin wasn't here, and things had gotten very bad very fast.

That's when the fear came, like swallowing a large, cold stone.

People could die.

I could die.

Malvo was frantically pushing something under his desk. Then I remembered that most courtrooms are equipped with a panic button. The look on the judge's face, and the fact that no one had come rushing in to see what was going on, told me this one wasn't working.

The gunman signaled to the gallery. "Felipe, lock the doors."

The tall Hispanic man I'd sat behind earlier slowly stood. The expression on his face suggested that what was happening was as much a surprise to him as to the rest of us. He walked to the back of the courtroom and turned the heavy bolt on the large oak doors.

"Now the latch at the top," the gunman said, pointing to a brass slide lock that appeared to be brand new.

"Now look, you," Judge Malvo, raising his voice as he began working toward standing.

"Sit down, judge. Don't make me hurt anyone."

Malvo grimaced, muttered something under his breath and slowly eased himself back into his chair.

"No cell phones," the gunman said, then directed the bailiff, "Lock the door to the judge's chambers."

The old man did as instructed without protest or hesitation.

"Now the other door, on this side."

The bailiff exchanged looks with Malvo as he walked across the front of the bench and for a moment I hoped they had some sort of predetermined code, and maybe the bailiff would make a run for it, though running was probably a bit too much to expect, and go get help. But all he did was lock the door and shuffle back to his post.

"I don't want to shoot nobody, but I must protect my son and get the truth. Everyone take your hands out of your pockets, and put your purses on the floor. If you don't, I will shoot you."

Everyone listened. I don't know what the gunman actually hoped to accomplish with this stunt, but desperate men do desperate things. Was he really hoping to break Tony out of custody? Once he left the courthouse, how far did he think he'd get? And how was he going to get out now that he'd secured all of the doors?

Facing away from the bench, eyes continuously scanning the courtroom, the gunman took several deliberate steps back, until he was no more than a dozen feet from Judge Malvo.

Malvo looked like he was ready to throw up.

On the far right of the judge's bench, the court reporter, a woman in her mid-forties, her bottle-colored black hair cropped short in an indistinct style, had stopped typing. She started up again, however, when the defendant stood and said, "Papa, don't do this."

The defendant was standing behind the table, the assistant attorney clutching his arm.

"Sit down, Tony," his father ordered.

"You're going to get into trouble for this. I'll be okay. The jury will figure out I'm not guilty."

"No, no mijo, they won't. These people are trying to set you up. All they want is to send you to jail."

The gunman waved his weapon around the room, causing several onlookers to slump in their chairs. Then he pointed to the gas cans with his free hand. "My son did not do this!"

I rifled through my options, they weren't especially encouraging. No doubt someone in the room had discreetly dialed 911, or someone on the outside figured out what was happening, so the place would be surrounded soon. I could announce myself as a police officer, try to talk Mr. Beniquez down, but he didn't seem enamored with cops at that moment. The best course of action was to wait for the cavalry to arrive.

James and Emmanuel each looked fidgety, and I worried that one of them might do something stupid and endanger themselves, civilians, or me.

"No, your son did not do this."

The voice didn't come from the gallery or behind the bench, where Judge Malvo's face, slick with sweat, was turning different degrees of pale. It came from the jury box, and I didn't have to look to know whom it belonged to.

"Como se llama, usted?"

I'd never heard Chapa speak Spanish before, never gave it any thought, really. The gunman turned to face him, and I knew what James was thinking. If the guy let his guard down…

"Que?" the gunman asked, clearly surprised to see someone standing in the jury box, hands raised.

"Su nombre? Como se llama?"

"Me llamo Carlos, Carlos Beniquez."

Chapa nodded and began to make his way out of the jury box. What the hell was he doing?

"Yo se que su hijo es innocente. El no hizo por lo que esta acusado." Chapa seemed to be searching for the last word, which told me his Spanish might not be all that good. In which case, we might be one verbal misstep away from things turning even uglier.

Seeing the gunman's attention had been momentarily divided, Lewis stood from where he was seated near the back of the gallery. But he didn't get far with whatever he'd planned because Carlos Beniquez quickly turned and pointed the gun at him.

"You sit down."

"Just let me pull out my cell phone and call someone who can—"

"Sit down now!"

"—who can help resolve this situation in a peaceful—"

"Do I have to shoot you? Or shoot someone else?"

I saw Lewis glance over at James, who calmly nodded. Lewis slowly sat down, but Carlos kept the gun trained on him, until he seemed to remember Chapa.

"Are you a cop?" Carlos asked, without switching back to Spanish.

Chapa shook his head.

"No."

"A lawyer?"

"No, even better," Chapa said, and struck a pose that would've put John Wayne to shame. "My name is Alex Chapa, I'm a newspaper reporter. And I know your son is innocent."

I rolled my eyes and swore under my breath. Maybe Chapa had never been shot at, so perhaps his fear of loaded weapons and unstable gunmen wasn't as healthy as it needed to be. Whatever he had in mind—and I knew Chapa well enough to know there had to be something knocking around in there—was risky as hell.

But in the silence that followed, I didn't hear the sounds of rescue sirens. I didn't hear a hostage negotiator calling to us with a megaphone from the street. I didn't hear the court phone ring.

I remembered where we were. Not in the heart of Chicago, where help, in the form of backup, a SWAT team, or hostage specialist, was never too far away, but in a sleepy suburb, where news still traveled slowly.

Right then, we were on our own.

And Chapa was risking making things a whole lot worse.

CHAPA

I was glad Carlos had decided to switch back to English. Over the years, my Spanish, which wasn't that great to begin with, had slipped to the level of a high school sophomore. It was clear that Carlos had worked very hard to lose his accent. Much harder than I had at holding on to my native language.

Still, asking him his name, telling him that his son was innocent, and that he hadn't committed the crimes he was accused of in his native tongue had served to get Carlos' attention, kept him from shooting any-one, at least for the moment, and maybe earned a little of his confidence.

"You don't belong here on the floor." He pointed the gun at my chest. "You need to get back with the jury."

Well, perhaps not his confidence.

"I can help you and your son, Carlos."

"I am going to get to the truth."

It seems corny to say I could smell the fear in the room, but with the air conditioner still not turned up quite as high as it needed to be, and with the added stress a guy with a gun could trigger, the scent of perspi-ration was starting to drift through the stale air.

Out of the corner of my eye I saw Officer James slowly easing him-self out of the witness stand. He was planning to rush Carlos, and once that happened there would be a high probability that someone would get shot. Probably me, the way this week was going.

He was gradually lowering himself into a crouch, ready to cross the twenty feet of open courtroom that separated him from Carlos, when the defendant saw what was about to happen.

"Papa, lookout!"

Carlos spun around as James started to make his move. A gunshot echoed across the courtroom, sending James scrambling to the floor in retreat as the wall behind him coughed up a fistful of plaster.

"Do not make me shoot at anyone again." Carlos had intentionally missed, but I felt certain he would not be so generous the next time. "Go back up there," he ordered, pointing to the witness stand with his gun hand.

"No, you don't want him to do that." I took a chance and approached Carlos.

"I told you to get back."

"If you send him back to the witness stand he'll just try it again, and from up there he'll be able to communicate with his partner." I pointed to Emmanuel Lewis, whom I was starting to suspect was not the same one who played Webster.

Carlos looked toward the stand, then the gallery, then back at me.

"He's lying," Carlos said, pointing to James. "He needs to tell the truth."

This was an interesting development. My first assumption was that Carlos had planned his son's escape from the courtroom. That theory took a hit when he locked all the doors, and now it was dead altogether.

"You don't want to take your son and escape?"

"No. I want a fair trial. It is not fair so far. People are lying. I knew they would lie. Like this one." He turned his gun on James. "He lies like a snake."

So Carlos didn't want revenge. He didn't want to grab is son and run off. He wanted what he thought was justice.

"If he's lying," I said carefully, "there are other ways to figure it out. If you threaten him, he'll say whatever you want him to, just to keep you from shooting him."

Carlos seemed to be processing this, but I didn't kid myself into thinking I'd gotten through to him, and I had to find a way to do that or else lots of people were going to get hurt.

"This is not the way to do this, Carlos. You're a smart man, right? You're the one who did all of the new woodwork and built this railing here." I pointed to the hollowed out piece of oak where Carlos had hidden the gun.

"Si. Yes. When the job contract came up, I bid very low so I could build it and hide a gun inside. And I put that latch on the door, it's a strong one. I needed to help my son. They have been lying like I knew they would and—"

I risked cutting him off. "A smart man, in this situation, needs to play it cool. A smart man would tell Officer James to take off his coat, toss it aside, and just have a seat on the floor where you can keep an eye on him."

Then again, a smart man would've kept his ass in the jury box. Actually, a smart man would've gotten himself excused from jury duty when he had the chance. But here we were. So much for newspaper reporters being smart men.

From behind us, Malvo let out a groan.

"What about him?" Carlos asked, tilting his head toward the judge.

"I wouldn't worry about him, he looks like he's stoned." And he did. The judge was sweating like Texas livestock, but he had one of those goofy I-just-came-from-a-Grateful-Dead-concert-and-can't-remember-a-damn-thing looks in his eyes.

Carlos turned back toward James.

"Do what he said."

James gave me a look that could've split a lesser man in half, then slowly stepped out of the witness stand and walked to the front of the prosecution table.

"The coat, take off the coat."

For the first time since this showdown began, I saw a look of concern on the officer's face.

"I assure you there is nothing in the coat, and no reason why I should—"

"Take it off, now!"

His face painted with regret, James slipped off his coat, folded it with the care a priest takes when handling the Eucharist, slipped a handkerchief out of the breast pocket and draped the coat over the railing. James then used the handkerchief to wipe the floor before sitting down.

I turned to the court reporter, who I'd noticed typing a moment ago.

"Are you still getting all of this?"

She seemed surprised by the question.

"Of course," she said in a tinny voice, then continued, "Carlos Beniquez - *The coat, take off the coat.* Officer James – *I assure you there is nothing in the coat, and no reason why I should.* Carlos Beniquez - *Take it off now.* (Officer James removes coat, sits on floor). Alex Chapa - *Are you still getting all of this?*"

"You're good. What's your name?"

"It's a job, and it's Emily."

"Emily, I want you to continue recording everything that's said here. Okay?"

She shrugged.

"Sure. What else am I gonna do? Sail off on a cruise around the world with George Clooney? Not likely."

Apparently Emily had a lot on her mind.

"What do we do now?" Carlos asked, his eyes still locked on the gallery.

I had stepped out of the jury box and into the middle of this nightmare in the hope that I could keep Carlos Beniquez from shooting anyone or getting himself shot. I'd even entertained the crazy idea that maybe I could get Carlos to surrender his gun to me. And yeah, that would've made for one hell of a headline.

But now a different idea was driving my actions, and it extended well beyond something as basic as a newspaper story. I needed to learn the truth. Not just for myself, but for Carlos and Tony and Dennis Braun, and maybe his widow and family, too.

I looked at Jack in the back of the courtroom. She seemed to have a look of confusion on her face, and I knew I was about to make it worse.

"Now I call my first witness."

DANIELS

I stared at Chapa, wondering how the situation could get any more surreal.

That's when he called my name.

I shot him a look that said, *If I get shot and killed I swear I'll come back from the grave and haunt you forever.* But Chapa's expression remained unfazed. If anything, he looked like the proverbial cat with the canary in his mouth.

Frowning, I made my way back to the front of the courtroom. As I walked by Chapa on the way to the stand I whispered, "I hope you know what the hell you're doing, Alex."

He smiled and whispered back, "So do I," which did nothing to ease my concern.

I sat down, looked out at the terrified faces in the gallery and waited for Chapa to make his move. I didn't have to wait long.

"Lieutenant, you know you're still under oath."

Of course I knew that. But Chapa was reminding the jury.

"Yes."

"I sensed during your testimony that you had much more to tell us about what you saw on the day of the fire. Is that true?"

"Yes."

"Then this is your chance to tell everyone here the full story."

Lebanon sprung to his feet. "I object! This is most irregular."

Chapa turned to face him. "No shit, Sherlock. Did you just figure that out all by yourself?"

Lebanon started to say something, but Chapa interrupted.

"There's a guy over here holding a gun," Chapa said, then turned to the elder Beniquez. "No offense, Carlos."

"It's okay," Carlos responded with a half-smile.

"If you want to object, take it up with him. He's calling the shots."

"I overrule the objection." Carlos, again.

I glanced at Malvo. The judge looked like death warmed over. He groaned, then uttered something unintelligible as Chapa continued his dressing down of Lebanon.

"GQ cop down there on the floor may have just perjured himself. And I'm still trying to figure out whether or not that guy is the same Emmanuel Lewis who played Webster, or an impostor. Though I'm leaning toward the latter. So yes, Einstein, this is most irregular."

Having apparently said his peace, Chapa turned his attention back toward me.

"Jack, are you ready to tell us what you actually did and did not see?"

"Yes." I took a deep breath, let it out slow. "One of the tricks attorneys use is to only let witnesses say what suits their case. Good attorneys," I purposely glanced at Lipscomb, "will often phrase questions to make it seem like witnesses said something that they didn't."

Chapa nodded. "You seemed agitated about the duffel bag and the gasoline cans."

"I was. I did see Tony with the duffel bag. But I never saw the gas cans. I was there for the entire arrest. The bag was definitely not opened at that time."

"So Officer James is lying?"

"Emily," I turned to the court reporter. "Can you read back James' testimony in regard to the bag?"

Emily pressed a few buttons. "Lipscomb - *Did you then check the contents of his duffel bag?* James - *We did.* Lipscomb - *What did you find?* James - *Two empty gasoline cans.*"

I shrugged. "I can't say if Officer James is lying. He may have found those cans later. But I never saw them. And two full gas cans weigh a lot. We're talking six pounds a gallon."

Chapa raised an eyebrow. "You know how much gas weighs?"

"I drive a Nova with a broken gas gauge. I've done my share of hauling around gas cans. Can you check how big those cans are, Alex?"

Chapa nodded again. This seemed to be getting good to him. He strolled to the evidence table and picked one up.

"Two and a half gallons each," he said, reading the side.

"So that's thirty pounds. And when Tony rushed past me, it didn't look like he had thirty pounds of anything in his bag."

"So what if they weren't full?" This from Lebanon.

"Those cans do not belong to me, or my son," Carlos said, shaking his head.

Chapa turned to Tony. "Is that true?"

The old bailiff, who'd looked so forlorn since his gun was taken, cleared his throat loudly. "Uh, I should probably swear him in before he answers."

"Fine," Carlos said. "Do it."

"No!" Lebanon yelled, but no one paid attention.

The bailiff plodded to Tony with the court bible. "Put your left hand on the book and raise your right hand. Do you swear to tell the truth?"

"Yes." Tony looked back to Chapa. "I never saw those cans before. Papa says metal cans are dangerous. They can strike something, cause a spark. The only cans we have around his shop are the plastic kind."

Chapa, apparently curious, clanged the cans together.

Wait... clanged the cans?

Oh, hell, how did I miss that?

Chapa then gave me a look that told me we were both on the same page.

"Emily, can you read back my testimony about when I first saw Tony?"

She pressed more buttons. "Daniels - *A minute before entering the bar, a teenage male ran by us on the sidewalk. He actually bumped me, and dropped his duffel bag. I made eye-contact with him as he picked it up.*"

"He dropped his duffle bag," I said, triumphantly.

"Did you drop your duffel bag, Tony?" Chapa asked.

"Yes. I almost ran into the lady, uh, Officer Daniels, and my bag fell off and hit the sidewalk."

"What was in the bag, Tony?" I asked.

"My work clothes. My uniform and work boots. I was late."

"What does it matter if the bag was dropped or not?" Lebanon was close to whining.

Chapa smiled at me and I knew he understood what I was thinking. He lifted the bag until it was waist high, then let it go.

The cans hit the floor with an echoing CLANG!

"When the defendant dropped his bag in front of me," I said, addressing the jury. "It didn't make a sound."

'd noticed the noise the cans had made earlier, but had not put together what it meant until Jack laid it all out. It was obvious the kid never had those cans in his possession.

Now the question was who did.

I was almost certain I knew the answer, but time was running short. Carlos seemed to have calmed down some, but the two unarmed cops in the room were not going to wait forever to make their move. Especially now that they had skin in the game.

There were a few more questions I needed to ask Jack, and I was about to when Malvo suddenly stood, displaying more energy than I'd seen from him before.

"I need to go relieve myself," he said and started to leave the bench.

"You will sit down right now." Carlos wasn't calm anymore.

"I told you, I have to take a piss."

"And I have the gun and I told you to sit down."

Sensing that something very bad was about to happen, I walked to the bench and tried to reason with the man.

"Your Honor, if you could just hold on—"

"I have a goddamned kidney stone and I'm extremely uncomfortable. So I'm walking out of here and—"

Some people can't be reasoned with.

"Sit your tired ass down, Your Honor," I said, raising my voice. Then locked eyes with Malvo and whispered, "Before you wind up getting shot. Which is exactly what's going to happen if you try to leave."

He looked at Carlos, then back at me, grimaced, nodded, and sat down.

I turned my attention back to Jack, who gave me a *nicely done* look. At least that's what I think it was.

"Now, Lieutenant, you testified that you had been on the scene throughout the entire arrest."

"That's right."

"In fact, you were nearby during the entire event, from before the fire began until Tony was taken away."

"Yes. As I stated earlier, I noticed that everyone in the bar was rushing for the door, so I followed."

"And how much time would you say passed from when you became aware of the fire until it was put out?"

Jack appeared to consider it for a moment. "The fire department got there in a hurry and had it under control fairly quickly, but it took longer to get it out entirely."

Lebanon nearly jumped out of his chair to blurt out his latest idea. "He stashed the cans!"

Jack shook her head. "There wasn't anywhere for him to hide two gas cans. I know, I went by there yesterday to check the place out."

"You did some investigating on your own? Without jurisdiction?" Emmanuel Lewis said, sounding nothing like Webster.

"I walked around the block. The shops on either side of Laserquick are attached, so there are no alleys to stash anything. The storefront has no bushes, no benches, not even a fire hydrant—that's two doors to the east."

"What about around back?" Lebanon demanded.

"The only hiding place behind the shop is a Dumpster."

Lebanon put his hands on his hips. "And is the esteemed, big city lieutenant telling the court that she actually went Dumpster diving?"

"That would be tough, considering the Dumpster, along with all the others behind the shops, had a lock on it."

"Now that we've got that cleared up," I said, glaring at Lebanon who seemed to get the message and sat down. "Back to the scene of the crime. Lieutenant, how quickly did they get the body out of the building?"

"It didn't take them long at all. As soon as they had the fire under control, for the most part, three firefighters rushed in and pulled the deceased out a minute later."

"Did you see the body?"

"From across the street, yes."

"Was the deceased burned in any way?"

"Not that I could tell, but again, I was across the street."

I turned toward Officer James, who was still trying to find a comfortable way to sit on the floor. Or maybe he was worried about getting his pants dirty.

"Was the body burned?"

He just stared at me. No emotion. No response.

"Answer his question." Carlos was pointing the gun directly at James' head. It was clear he blamed this man, more than anyone else, for his son being on trial.

"He died of smoke inhalation," James mumbled.

"Could you repeat that," I said, just because the guy was starting to seriously rub me the wrong way.

"Smoke inhalation, that's what killed him."

I turned to Lipscomb, matched her look of indignation.

"Is that right, prosecutor?"

"That was determined to be the cause of death, yes. The coroner isn't supposed to testify until tomorrow, so he isn't here to corroborate, but that's what his report said."

"Lieutenant Daniels, in your experience, how long does it take for a person to die from smoke inhalation?"

Jack thought about it, and for a moment I worried that she might not know the answer. Then I realized she was trying to put some pieces together.

"It can take as long as twenty or thirty minutes, or as little as five if the fire is really thick and smoky."

"And would you say the Laserquick fire was thick and smoky?"

Jack shook her head. "No, not at all."

"So do you think it's possible that smoke inhalation was not the cause of the death?"

"Objection, calls for a conclusion."

I'd had enough of Lebanon. "Honestly, dude, you gotta stop doing that."

"I suppose it's possible, but I really can't speak to that since I only saw the deceased from a distance."

True to form, Milledge had not said a word during the time I'd been working harder than he had to save his client. But now I needed his input.

"You said in your opening statement something about challenging the established cause of death. What were you referring to?"

Milledge, apparently surprised to be included in the proceedings, squared his shoulders and fumbled with some notes on the table.

"Well, we were hoping to find a way to introduce evidence that the deceased was already dead before the fire began. Judge Malvo had denied our request to do so during the pre-trial."

"You didn't prove any of it was relevant," Malvo growled from behind the bench in a jagged, deathbed voice.

I ignored him, and so did Milledge.

"The victim had a huge gash across the back of his head. We have pictures."

"Which was caused by his falling when he passed out or was struck by part of the ceiling collapsing," James said while Milledge searched his files.

A few seconds later he produced the ghoulish photo of the back of Dennis Braun's head. Sure enough, it showed a hole big enough to kill anyone. I handed the picture to Jack.

"What do you think?"

"I'd want to know where the body was discovered." Jack said.

So did I. "Officer James?"

"The victim was found face down behind the counter."

"How far is the counter from the front door?" I asked, and watched James' head swivel back and forth from me to Lebanon and back again.

"Maybe thirty feet," James said, his eyes on Lebanon.

"I've been in a fire," Jack said. "Your one overwhelming urge is to get the hell out. That's what Braun would have done, had he been conscious and able. He wouldn't have waited around until he died of smoke inhalation. He would have run out the front door."

"Unless something prevented him from doing that. Something like a blow to the back of the head," I added.

"Which was caused by a ceiling beam that collapsed, like Officer James said," Lebanon, still trying to find a winning card in the losing hand he'd been dealt.

"Officer James, was the deceased found under that collapsed beam?"

"No, one room over. We believe he tried to make it the door, but couldn't. Then the smoke got him."

That seemed plausible, but I still wasn't buying. "So Braun stuck around until the fire was so out of control a beam collapsed? All the while choking on smoke?"

James didn't reply, but I could tell by his expression that he didn't like me much.

"I think I can settle all of this once I call my next witness," I said.

Jack seemed surprised. "Next witness?"

I turned to face the gallery. "I call Mr. Joel Luzinsky to the stand."

It wasn't hard to spot Luzinsky. Not only was he the biggest guy in the courtroom, but he was also one of the few people who didn't cower when Carlos pulled out the weapon. Must've been the marine training.

Even when Carlos fired the warning shot to stop Officer James, Luzinsky's first concern, his instinctive response, was to tell Alice Braun to get down.

"What do you want from me?" he said in a voice that matched his stature.

I walked toward the gallery, and decided to take a direct approach.

"I want to ask you about the affair you've been having with Alice Braun."

A collective gasp filled the courtroom. I looked back at Jack. She was shaking her head and rolling her eyes.

"I've seen the non-verbal exchanges between the two of you, and how she was your first concern when all hell broke loose in the courtroom. No offense, Carlos."

"It's okay."

Luzinsky slowly stood, and I started to turn toward Jack, anticipating the big man taking the stand. But that never happened.

"It's not an affair," Luzinsky said, then turned to look at Alice Braun, whose eyes were glassy with tears. A wave of not-so-quiet conversation filled the courtroom, prompting Luzinsky to raise his suddenly unsteady voice. "We're in love, we have been for more than a year, and I don't care who knows it. I'm proud of our love!"

Another gasp.

I considered asking him again to take the stand, then thought better of it. Figured Luzinsky would be more candid right where he was.

He looked away from the widow, down to his shoes, and when the crowd had quieted, he continued.

"I tried to talk to Dennis about it. Tried to reason with him, but he wouldn't listen. He came at me with a huge roll of paper. I hit him. Hit him hard and he fell back. He just laid there on the table, didn't move at all."

"He was dead?" I asked.

"I thought I'd killed him. Then his eyes snapped open, had a crazy look in them. That's when I slugged him again, even harder. His head slammed against the iron handle of that giant paper cutter he had in the shop."

I looked over at Alice Braun. She was sobbing, her head turned away from Luzinsky, who wasn't finished yet.

"He was dead that time."

"So, you killed him?"

"Yeah, I killed him."

"He did?" I heard Jack say behind me. Her eyes weren't rolling anymore.

"Yes, he did," I responded, nodding.

I was thinking about the best way to get Carlos to give me his gun so that I could turn this whole mess over to the authorities, when Luzinsky finished his statement.

"But I didn't start that fire. I had nothing to do with that."

"You didn't?"

"No, he didn't," it was Jack again, this time she was shaking her head.

From the direction of the jury box I heard someone say, "Wow." I turned and saw Bob mesmerized, his mouth open so wide that I thought he might be hyperventilating. He'd likely pass out if this got any more exciting.

And then it did.

A gunshot exploded in the courtroom and I saw Carlos Beniquez's body spew blood that splashed onto the defense table, the attorneys, and all over Tony's shirt.

For an instant, Carlos' eyes grew wide. Then his body went limp and he dropped the gun, an instant before collapsing to the floor.

That's when things really turned crazy.

DANIELS

Malvo.

The shot came from the judge's bench, and when I looked I saw the old guy standing there, one hand pressed to his kidney, the other extended toward Carlos and ending in a revolver.

Movement, on the floor to my right.

It was Officer James, scrambling on all fours, going for Carlos' dropped weapon. He was closer to it than I was.

Things had gone from bad, to worse.

"Give me the gun, Your Honor," I said, standing up and reaching out to him.

Malvo appeared to be somewhere between confused and shocked.

"I did what I had to do," the judge said in a monotone. "The man was holding us hostage."

"The gun."

By this time, James had secured Carlos' weapon, and the bailiff was approaching them, handcuffs in hand. Lewis had made his way over to Luzinsky, and they were in heated conversation.

"I didn't want anyone to get hurt," Malvo said to no one in particular. "So I waited until he was distracted, and—"

"Give me the gun!" I yelled.

Malvo startled, then handed it over. It was a .32 Smith and Wesson snubby, five still in the cylinder.

"Papa! Are you okay? Papa!"

In my peripheral vision, I saw Chapa wrestling with Tony, trying to keep him from rushing to his father. A smart move—James now had Carlos' gun, and his angry expression telegraphed his intent to use it on whoever gave him an excuse.

The courtroom had erupted into chaos. Screaming. Shouting. Movement everywhere. Many ran outside. Some—mostly press—stuck around, frantically scribbling on notepads or scrambling to get a quote.

"Someone call an ambulance!" I yelled over the din.

James stood up, the gun at his side, and stared at Luzinsky.

Luzinsky looked terrified, and he was frantically shaking his head *no.*

I left my vantage point on the stand and intercepted James as he made his way toward Luzinsky and Lewis.

"Get out of my way, Lieutenant."

He was bigger than me, and more important, his gun was bigger than mine. The .32 looked like a child's toy compared to Carlos' semi-auto .45.

"Shouldn't you be securing your prisoners, James?"

He looked to Luzinsky, and back to me. A frown creased his face.

"You're in no position to give orders, lady. This isn't your beat."

He tried to walk around me. If I wanted to do the smart thing, I should have let him pass. He had a gun. This was his jurisdiction. Any suspicions I had could wait until later, when things cooled down.

But instead, I stepped in front of him.

Sometimes the smart thing had to take a back seat to the right thing.

"It's over, James."

"What the hell are you talking about?"

"The fires. You've got this whole town scared. But Luzinsky has a murder wrap over him. He's going away for a long time. You don't think he'll spill everything to get a reduced charge? He wants to get out of jail while he's still young enough to be with his mistress. That means he'll sell out you, Lewis, and your whole bunch."

James actually snarled. "You little bitch. You don't know what the hell you're talking about."

"I've got a story for you, Alex," I said to Chapa without breaking eye-contact with James.

Chapa, had given up wrangling a hysterical teenager, and was two steps behind James, listening to our exchange. Bringing a reporter into this would make it less likely for James to do anything stupid.

At least, that was the hope.

"You know who is starting the fires," Chapa stated.

"Watch Officer James' face while I lay it all out. He and his partner didn't get those nice suits on their civil servants salaries. Instead, they're extorting money from the local shop keepers."

Chapa nodded slowly. "The old protection racket."

"Exactly. And if people don't pay up…"

"They get burned," Chapa finished. He appeared to be looking around for something. "May I quote you, Lieutenant?"

"Sure. And it gets better. Officer Nicholas James broke into my room early this morning and threatened me."

James' right eye twitched.

"He wore a mask and gloves, and he disguised his voice. But he made a big mistake. Want to know what your mistake was, Nick?"

He stayed silent, refusing to be baited. "Your Rolex. It's a Submariner, used for scuba diving. So it has luminous dials that glow green in the dark. I saw a flash of green when you were leaving my room. Had to be you, because your partner wears a Movado. Movados don't glow."

James had turned a bright shade of red, and his body hummed with obvious rage. I knew he was looking for an opening, any opportunity to raise his weapon. If he did that, I'd have to match his movements. Then things could turn really ugly really fast.

"Care to make a statement, Officer James?" Chapa asked, as he retreated a few steps.

"You can't prove any of that," he said through clenched teeth.

"I can prove enough to get a warrant. They'll look at your bank account, and all the nice things you have. They'll find the money, one way or another. And once Luzinsky talks, other merchants will follow."

James seemed ready to pounce.

"Throttle down, Officer," I ordered. "It's over. You try anything right now, it'll only be worse for you later on down the line."

I stared him down, and for a moment I thought he was ready to give himself up. Then—

"Jack!"

Chapa yelled just as I saw the movement.

CHAPA

Maybe it was my deep-seeded distrust of police officers, a prejudice I've carried with me since I was a very young boy in Castro's Cuba, when a man in uniform usually meant trouble.

Or maybe I read James' mind, knew the man was not ready to stand down. Never would be. His type simply isn't wired that way.

Could be I just got lucky.

I sensed James was about to make his move, so I reached back for the duffle bag on the evidence table. The cans shuffled around inside as I picked it up, made some noise, but not enough to get anyone's attention.

I meant to bring the bag down on his hand, hoping to knock his weapon to the floor. But then he sprang toward Jack, and I just reacted.

I swung, grazing his arm and continuing in an upward arc until I connected with his chin. I hadn't clocked James hard enough to knock him out, but with enough force to make him forget his plans of going after Daniels, loosen a filling or two, and spin him around—which it did. James involuntarily pirouetted one-hundred-eighty degrees, until he was facing the bench, his back turned toward Jack.

I was bringing the bag up, ready to whack him again, when his gun discharged. There was screaming and swearing, and everyone either ducked or froze.

Everyone except Malvo, who dropped like a bag of wet sand behind the bench, and Jack, who let go with a roundhouse to the side of James' head that knocked the man to the floor.

James lay on his back, his eyes open but unfocused. Jack squatted and took the gun from his hand. James offered no resistance.

"Give me those handcuffs," Jack ordered the bailiff.

The old guy hesitated for a moment. No doubt he'd worked with Officer James for a while, and this unusual turn of events had screwed with his bearings. Then he shrugged and handed the cuffs to Jack. She pounced on James, yanked his hands back and cuffed him.

"Go check out the judge," she said to me without taking her eyes off James, then yelled, "did anyone call an ambulance?"

I walked past Tony Beniquez on my way to look in on Malvo. The kid was cradling his father's head in his blood-soaked arms. Carlos' eyes were half-open, which was a good sign. He was in a bad way, but at least he was still alive. From the looks of it, Carlos had taken one in the right shoulder.

"Tony, take off your sport coat."

"No, I need to—"

"You need to take off your coat, bundle it up and use it to put pressure on your father's wound."

"Here, use mine." It was Milledge, stepping up to the plate. He was kneeling next to his client when I left them to go to Malvo.

I found the judge sprawled out on the steps leading down from the bench. Then I saw the large dark spot across the front of his robe. I didn't see and entry hole, but the blue cloth was shiny and wet with...

Blood?

No, wait. That's not blood. That's—

The judge held out a pale, wet fist. Then he opened it, revealing a tiny pebble resting on his palm. Like a clam showing off its pearl.

"I passed the stone," he said and smiled.

At that moment Malvo had to be the happiest person in the courtroom.

"Are you hurt?"

Malvo shook his head. "Not anymore. Here, help me up." He held out his free hand and signaled for me to take it.

Not a chance. Not in this lifetime.

I decided to track down the bailiff, figuring that this particular duty had to be part of his job description. But as I turned to look for ol' Rusty, or whatever the codger's name was, I heard Jack call out—

"Lewis is gone! I'm going after him!"

And she ran out of court just as uniformed cops began pouring in.

DANIELS

The cute suede wedges I was wearing turned out to be a bad choice for pursuing a perp. I managed to get outside without breaking an ankle, then kicked them off as I searched for Emmanuel Lewis. There was a crowd outside the building, not just the people who fled the courtroom, but a new group drawn by all the commotion. Lots of yelling, lots of crying.

I headed for the parking lot, figuring he was going for his car, and stopped abruptly when I realized someone was trailing me.

Chapa.

I took off again. He fell into pace beside me, and I said, "What the hell are you doing here?"

"I figure there's a story following you around twenty-four-seven, Lieutenant. In this case, it should end in the capture of Officer Emmanuel Lewis, who I'm now certain is not the same guy who played Webster."

We ran into the maze of several dozen vehicles, searching for Lewis.

"When he finds his car, he'll have a gun inside," I said. "If I tell you to get down, do it."

An engine started up, one aisle over. I swung the .32 in its direction, pointing at a Volkswagen Beetle. Definitely not Lewis' ride.

"There!" Chapa pointed in the other direction, at Lewis running toward a classic Corvette Stingray.

It was thirty yards away. A difficult shot with a snub-nosed .32. And risky, too; bullets liked to ricochet off of concrete and metal.

But I couldn't allow Lewis to get to his car. James had broken into my room and threatened my life. I didn't want to spend countless, sleepless nights waiting for his partner to make good on the threat.

I grabbed Chapa's arm and slowed both of us down, then fell into a Weaver stance, two hands on the revolver, aiming, exhaling as I squeezed the trigger.

There was a *BANG*, followed immediately by another one—the Corvette's fat rear tire popping.

"Freeze!" I yelled.

But Lewis didn't freeze. He veered away from the car, cutting behind an SUV.

Chapa and I pursued.

Lewis fled the parking lot, hauling ass down Main Street. He had a good head start, and seemed to be picking up speed. As expected on a beautiful summer day, there were a lot of people out. If we didn't catch up to Lewis, fast, we would lose him in the crowd and he'd get away.

Luckily, Birch Grove did a good job maintaining their sidewalks, so running wasn't as painful as it might have been. Chapa kept pace beside me, and I was grateful for the back-up.

But fast as we ran, Lewis was extending his lead. When he got a full block ahead of us, I lost him.

"You see him?" I said between huffs and puffs.

"He turned," Chapa pointed, "north on Lawndale."

We made it to Lawndale Avenue without either of us having a heart attack, and when we rounded the corner we both almost tripped over Lewis, who was sprawled out on the sidewalk, bleeding from his forehead.

I quickly patted him down, confirming he wasn't armed, then asked Chapa to help me roll him over.

"Check his pulse," I said, pulling the zip tie from my purse that I kept for occasions just like this one.

"He'll live," Chapa said, his fingers on Lewis' neck. "What the hell happened?"

I cuffed Lewis' hands behind him just as he began to groan.

"Looks like a Good Samaritan helped us out," I said, and indulged in a private smile.

I'd told Phin to keep an eye out for anything suspicious. This apparently qualified. I thought about looking around for him, but figured he'd be gone by now. Phin tended to shy away from authority.

"So," Chapa said, staring down at Lewis. "Alex Karras wasn't here to help him out this time."

"Who?"

"Former football player. Detroit Lions. He played Webster's dad on the show."

"You know that this isn't really—"

"Yes, Jack," Chapa said through a smirk. "Of course I know this guy isn't *that* Emmanuel Lewis."

"I was thinking about pointing at him and saying, *you've been cancelled.*"

"Or, as Alex Karras might have said," Chapa made his face stern and spoke in a baritone. "Webster, you're grounded."

I winced. "Don't use that one in your story," I said, tugging out my cell and calling for back-up.

EPILOGUE

I sat in my car waiting for Lieutenant Daniels to arrive for our lunch date. Engine running so I could get some heat to blow around inside my Celica, its hum just a bit quieter than the Clifford Brown CD in the player. It felt like a jazz day.

The parking lot at Jake's Bagels in Aurora was almost entirely empty. The lunch crowd had come and gone, which was fine by me.

It had been more than four months since that day when a couple of crooked cops, a well-meaning though somewhat misguided father, and a crackpot judge with a gun under his robe turned the Birch Grove courthouse into a shooting gallery. In that time, there had been arrests, indictments, and a series of front page stories.

Once it was all over and I'd gained some distance from the events, I realized I'd taken the risk of getting shot, or worse, by jumping into the middle of it all. I still wasn't sure why I had done something so dangerous, and got no comfort from the knowledge that given the opportunity I'd most likely do it the same way all over again.

I'd spent a lot of time thinking about Carlos Beniquez and the sacrifice he made for his son. He'd risked everything for Tony, like every parent should be willing to do for their own.

Any thoughts I'd had of giving in to my ex's demands, of going along to get along, vanished after that day in Birch Grove. I'd spent much of the past four months devoting my time, energy, and money to fighting Carla in court, and had no plans to back down any time soon.

Sometimes you've got to put it all on the line for the people you care about most.

Clifford Brown was winding through his lush version of *What's New?* when Daniels rapped her knuckles against my window. I hadn't seen her walk up. She smiled when I jumped just a little, and I wondered whether I'd ever seen a smile on her face before.

I climbed out of my car. "Lieutenant, you're late."

"Don't start on me with that, Chapa. This is my fourth trip out here to the suburbs over the past month."

The brisk wind off the Fox River greeted us as we began to walk toward the restaurant, her high heels clacking against the blacktop.

"Deposition?"

"Same damn questions each time, asked in different ways by different attorneys. Now the feds are involved."

"I heard they're investigating the police department." I held the door open for her. "Everyone from the commissioner to the coroner who got the cause of death wrong."

"They are, as well as the town's entire power structure. The crooked apple doesn't fall far from the crooked tree."

Except for an elderly couple sitting in the corner, and a mail carrier at one of the high tables, Jake's was ours. The place was usually quiet, with only the sound of conversation from behind the counter and the crackling of the fireplace interrupting the silence.

"What's good here?" Jack asked

"You can't go wrong with any of the food, though they do make a unique sandwich you may want to try."

We walked over to the counter where Millie was waiting. Like always.

"Chapa, you have a friend?"

I looked at Jack who was trying to suppress a laugh.

"Let's just say we're," I searched for the right word, wasn't sure I'd find one.

"Associates," Jack chimed in.

"Yeah, I figured it was something like that," Millie said with a smile. "Let me guess, the usual sandwich?"

"You mean The Alex Chapa? Of course."

Jack glanced at me, then scanned the large menu behind the counter.

"It's not up there, Jack, but it should be."

Millie closed her eyes and shook her head.

"So how many *Alex Chapas* do you sell in a typical month?" Jack asked through a smirk.

Millie thought about it, then looked at me and asked, "How often do you come in here, Alex?"

"Oh, I don't know. Once, sometimes twice a week."

"Then I'd say we sell about six Alex Chapas a month," Millie said, making air quotation marks around my sandwich's name.

I had my usual—Ham, Swiss, onion, light mayo on a garlic bagel, warmed not toasted. Jack ordered something else.

We sat at the much-coveted fireside table and waited for the food to arrive.

"That was some day we had in Birch Grove," she said, rubbing her hands together near the fire.

"A lot of people are going to jail."

"At least four, by my count."

Officer Nicholas James had been indicted for extortion, four counts of arson, assault with a deadly weapon, and breaking and entering. The last two indictments were the result of his attempt to intimidate Jack.

"Warrant uncovered night vision goggles in his house, and more than ten thousand dollars stuffed into his mattress. Also found a pair of combat boots, matched a print found in the backyard of the Weatherby House, where I was staying. I hear he's pleading not guilty. Bad call. He could have gotten off easier if he confessed, and I've heard they don't like cops in prison."

Millie brought our food over. "You need anything else?" she asked Jack.

"Thank you, but I'm good."

Mille nodded and walked away.

"Is it hard to testify against a fellow cop, even a scumbag like James?"

Jack took a bite of her sandwich and stared hard into my eyes.

"Can I assume all of this is off the record?"

"Absolutely." As usual, my sandwich was excellent.

"I hate seeing one of the good guys go down. But the fact that he went down means he was never a good guy in the first place."

Officer Emmanuel Lewis had been hit with four counts of arson and extortion. He and his partner were going away for a very long time.

The murder charge against Joel Luzinsky had been reduced to second degree. The big guy was cooperating with authorities and planned to testify against James and Lewis in exchange for a reduced sentence. Alice Braun would not be waiting for him, though. As far as anyone knew she'd been questioned by police, cleared of any role in her husband's murder, and moved out of town.

The poor sap had committed murder for the woman he loved and would have nothing to show for it but several lost years in a maximum security cell.

"How did you know about Luzinsky and the widow?"

I chewed slowly, mulling over the question. "Part observation, part hunch. I studied that layout the prosecution presented of the print shop, and thought almost anyone could have gotten out of there before the smoke took them down."

"Unless—"

"Unless they were already dead. I noticed the glances between Luzinsky and Alice, and the fact that he'd been coloring his hair. A big bad ex-marine isn't the sort to do that unless he's trying to impress someone."

I signaled to Millie that I was running low on coffee—she ignored me, like always.

"That's pretty good observation, Chapa."

"The best reporter I've ever known told me that ninety percent of all crimes are committed for love or money. I figured out the first of those two motives, you nailed the second."

Jack picked up the pickle, took a small bite. "The signs were all there. Nervous, frightened shop owners, young cops with too much money. I'd like to say I hadn't ever seen it before, but wherever there's power, there's corruption."

"James and Lewis must have been as shocked as hell when the firefighters pulled a body out of the fire."

"Tony was a target of opportunity. Figured they knew him from his gangbanger days, saw him in the crowd, and tried to pin it on him so they didn't have to deal with a murder rap if things ever came to light."

"It's a lot harder to sweep a murder under the rug than the latest in a series of arsons."

"They almost got away with it, too, if it wasn't for us meddling kids."

"For a minute there I thought Malvo might be involved somehow," I said, and heard the disappointment in my own voice.

"Really? I pegged him for an idiot, not a crook. I was ready to pin it on Vincent Corelli, the locksmith."

The name was new to me. I think Jack saw the confusion on my face.

"Believe me, he looked like prime suspect number one. Turns out the guy had an alibi. He drives nearly two hours every week to teach a pottery class to underprivileged youth."

"Doesn't sound like the homicidal type."

Jack shook her head. "So what's the deal with the D.A., Lebanon?"

"He's still being investigated, but it doesn't look like he was directly involved. He just wanted the glory of helping to put away an arsonist and murderer, whether they got the right person or not." I downed the rest of my coffee. "The guy wanted a political career, but that's over now."

Jack finished her sandwich, put her napkin on top of her plate, and pushed it away. "So I'm guessing you've hit a journalistic jackpot with all of this."

"You're right about that. I may not have to do any bullshit feel-good stories for a year. I'll be filing a daily journal once the trial starts. And then there's the ongoing effort to get the courts to go easy on Carlos Beniquez."

"I've been following that. I saw the website."

"You mean freecarlosnow.com? That was Tony's idea, he set it up. I've just written about it."

Jerry Rossiter walked in, we exchanged nods. He looked at Jack, made a wrong assumption, raised an eyebrow, and walked the other way.

"For an amateur, Carlos Beniquez planned his move like a professional," Jack said, not noticing Rossiter.

I nodded. "He even thought of disconnecting the judge's call button. That must've freaked out Malvo, big time."

"He did break the law, Alex, no matter his reasons," Jack said, though I sensed it was a bit half-hearted.

"And I, for one, am damn glad he did."

Tony Beniquez had taken over the running of his father's business with the help of a cousin, but was finding it hard to get work in Birch Grove. The man who'd followed Carlos' orders to lock the main door of the courtroom, an uncle named Felipe, had no clue when the day began that he'd be part of an armed standoff and was cleared of any involvement in the crime.

Jack looked at her watch, said, "Oh damn. It's already past two. I've got to hit the road before the Eisenhower turns into a parking lot. These trips out here have left me way behind on paperwork."

"Sounds like fun."

She stood up. "It's about as much fun as licking all the hair off a monkey."

"I'm gonna take your word for that, but it's too bad you have to run. There's a terrific brewpub across the street." I pointed to one of the windows that looked out onto Broadway Avenue.

Jack hesitated for a moment, seemed to be thinking about it.

"How 'bout a rain check? Maybe during the trial? I'll have a lot of reasons to want to drink then."

I nodded. "That'll work. But I'm the one who should be getting the rain check."

"What are you talking about, Alex? You just asked me to—"

"But *you* still owe *me* a beer."

"Are you kidding? I saved your life."

"You're joking, right? I mean, we were both in the same courtroom."

"Yes, the courtroom I took charge of after you nearly got everyone shot by trying to play Perry Mason."

"I saved lives by risking my own, and solved a crime," I raised my palms and smiled, "no need to thank me. A drink will be thanks enough."

"Thank you? You shouldn't have been on that jury in the first place!"

"Okay, that we can agree on, but if I hadn't whacked Officer James he probably would've shot you."

"And if I hadn't gotten my hands on Malvo's gun and subdued James he probably would've shot you, Tony, his father, Luzinsky, and who knows who else."

She had a point.

"But you never would've had the chance to get Malvo's gun if I hadn't called you to the stand and given you a chance to tell your story."

But so did I.

She grunted something unintelligible, stood, started to leave, and was almost at the door when she spun around to face me.

"Here's the deal, Chapa, from now on you stay on your side of the line, with other members of your dubious profession, and I'll continue doing a job that actually helps people, and hopefully we'll keep out of each other's way."

"So do I get that rain check or not?"

No answer, just the sound of the door clicking shut.

But as I watched Daniels striding across the parking lot to her car, I had a feeling our paths would eventually cross again.

JOE KONRATH'S
COMPLETE BIBLIOGRAPHY

JACQUELINE "JACK" DANIELS THRILLERS
WHISKEY SOUR (Book 1)

BLOODY MARY (Book 2)

RUSTY NAIL (Book 3)

DIRTY MARTINI (Book 4)

FUZZY NAVEL (Book 5)

CHERRY BOMB (Book 6)

SHAKEN (Book 7)

STIRRED with Blake Crouch (Book 8)

RUM RUNNER (Book 9)

LAST CALL (Book 10)

WHITE RUSSIAN (Book 11)

SHOT GIRL (Book 12)

CHASER (Book 13)

OLD FASHIONED (Book 14)

BITE FORCE (Book 15)

JACK ROSE (Book 16)

LADY 52 with Jude Hardin (Book 2.5)

JACK DANIELS AND ASSOCIATES MYSTERIES
DEAD ON MY FEET (Book 1)

JACK DANIELS STORIES VOL. 1 (Book 2)

SHOT OF TEQUILA (Book 3)

JACK DANIELS STORIES VOL. 2 (Book 4)

DYING BREATH (Book 5)

SERIAL KILLERS UNCUT with Blake Crouch (Book 6)

JACK DANIELS STORIES VOL. 3 (Book 7)

EVERYBODY DIES (Book 8)

JACK DANIELS STORIES VOL. 4 (Book 9)

BANANA HAMMOCK (Book 10)

KONRATH DARK THRILLER COLLECTIVE

THE LIST (Book 1)

ORIGIN (Book 2)

AFRAID (Book 3)

TRAPPED (Book 4)

ENDURANCE (Book 5)

HAUNTED HOUSE (Book 6)

WEBCAM (Book 7)

DISTURB (Book 8)

WHAT HAPPENED TO LORI (Book 9)

THE NINE (Book 10)

SECOND COMING (Book 11)

CLOSE YOUR EYES (Book 12)

HOLES IN THE GROUND with Iain Rob Wright (Book 4.5)

DRACULAS with Blake Crouch, Jeff Strand, F. Paul Wilson (Book 5.5)

GRANDMA? with Talon Konrath (Book 6.5)

STOP A MURDER PUZZLE BOOKS

STOP A MURDER – HOW: PUZZLES 1 – 12 (Book 1)

STOP A MURDER – WHERE: PUZZLES 13 – 24 (Book 2)

STOP A MURDER – WHY: PUZZLES 25 – 36 (Book 3)

STOP A MURDER – WHO: PUZZLES 37 – 48 (Book 4)

STOP A MURDER – WHEN: PUZZLES 49 – 60 (Book 5)

STOP A MURDER – ANSWERS (Book 6)

STOP A MURDER COMPLETE CASES (Books 1-5)

CODENAME: CHANDLER
(PETERSON & KONRATH)

FLEE (Book 1)

SPREE (Book 2)

THREE (Book 3)

HIT (Book 4)

EXPOSED (Book 5)

NAUGHTY (Book 6)

FIX with F. Paul Wilson (Book 7)

RESCUE (Book 8)

OLD FASHIONED

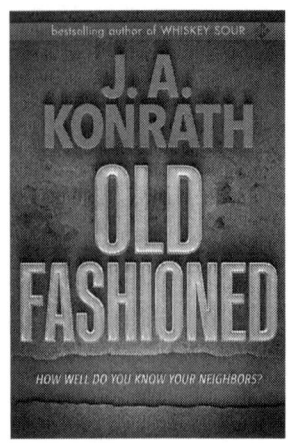

Former Chicago Homicide Lieutenant Jacqueline "Jack" Daniels has finally left her violent past behind, and she's moved into a new house with her family.

But her elderly next door neighbor is a bit… off.

Is he really as he appears, a kind old gentlemen with a few eccentricities?

Or are Jack's instincts correct, and he's something much, much darker?

And what is it he'd got in his basement?

Jack Daniels is about to learn that evil doesn't mellow with age.

OLD FASHIONED by JA Konrath
How well do you know your neighbors?

CHASER

Retired cop Jacqueline "Jack" Daniels and her ex-criminal husband Phineas Troutt have made a lot of enemies over the years. But none worse than The Cowboy, a gun-slinging nutcase who wants to slaughter them both, and Hugo Troutt, who has been plotting revenge against his younger brother for over a decade.

Separately, these baddies are formidable. Together, they are unstoppable.

But Jack has even more hell to deal with. She and her former partner, private eye Harry McGlade, are in L.A. chasing an insane plastic surgeon who specializes in disfiguring his victims. And Jack's colleague Tom Mankowski has problems of his own with a snuff film auteur named Erinyes.

With four psychopaths on the prowl, Jack, Phin, Harry, and Tom will need to call on some old friends if they hope to get out of LaLa Land alive…

This thirteenth Jack Daniels novel brings together villains from Konrath's thrillers WHITE RUSSIAN, EVERYBODY DIES, and WEB-CAM, along with heroes from SHOT OF TEQUILA, THE LIST, and FLEE, for the ultimate West Coast showdown.

CHASER by J.A. Konrath

The hunt is on. But who's hunting whom?

TIMECASTER

FUNNY! SEXY! ACTION PACKED!
Chicago, 2064: Mankind Can Rewind

Talon Alalon is a timecaster—one of a select few peace officers who can operate
a TEV, the Tachyon Emission Visualizer,
which records events (most specifically,
crimes) that have already happened.

With crime at an all-time low, Talon has little to do except give
lectures to schoolkids—and obsess on his wife's profession as a
licensed sex partner.

Then one of her clients asks Talon to investigate a possible murder. When Talon uses the TEV to view the crime, the identity of
the killer is unmistakable—it's him, Talon Avalon.

Someone is taking timecasting to a whole new level and using it
to frame Talon. And the only way he can prove his innocence is
to go off the grid—which in 2064 is a very dangerous thing to do.

Time is not on his side.

Featuring all of the action, thrills, and humor of other Konrath
books, but set in an outrageous never-before-seen future, the
TIMECASTER series is ecopunk on super steroids. Add in healthy
doses of sex, some characters from Konrath's previous books
(Talon is Jack Daniels's grandson), and a lot of outrageous ideas
about technology, society, and politics, and Timecaster is a book
that will appeal to anyone who likes to be entertained, even if
they don't dig on sci-fi.

Sign up for the J.A. Konrath newsletter. A few times a year I pick random people to give free stuff to. It could be you.

http://www.jakonrath.com/mailing-list.php

I won't spam you or give your information out without your permission!

Made in the USA
Columbia, SC
01 December 2024

48072599R00185